THE MOONDAY LETTERS

PRAISE FOR *THE MOONDAY LETTERS*

"*The Moonday Letters* is a thing entirely its own, full of melancholy, a sense of wonder and hope. It takes you on a shamanistic journey to a living and breathing future, carried by a mystery that slowly unravels. Itäranta is a compelling narrator who also knows when to pause to conjure stunning images with her always confident, exquisitely polished prose."

– Hannu Rajaniemi, author of *The Quantum Thief* and *Summerland*

"*The Moonday Letters* ticks all the boxes for me. The solitary vastness of interplanetary space entwines with myths and mysteries of the ancient North; a personal tragedy interacts elegantly with the enormous ecological challenges of the future; and through the whole enchanting story echoes Itäranta's exquisite, poetic, visionary writer's voice."

– Johanna Sinisalo, author of *The Storm Flute* and *Strangers Inside*

PRAISE FOR THE AUTHOR

"[A] poetic and melancholy debut."
– The Guardian

"Itäranta's lyrical style makes this dystopian tale a beautiful exploration of environmental ethics and the power of ritual."
– The Washington Post

"Gorgeous and delicate."
– *Library Journal* (starred review)

"Itäranta's steady piling on of pressure on her protagonist grips, even as her prose soothes."
– SFX

"Where Itäranta shines is in her understated but compelling characters."
– Red Star Review, *Publishers Weekly*

"Brilliant, lyrical prose."
– Tor.com

The Moonday Letters
Print edition ISBN: 9781803360447
E-book edition ISBN: 9781803360454

Published by Titan Books
A division of Titan Publishing Group Ltd
144 Southwark Street, London SE1 0UP
www.titanbooks.com

First Titan edition: July 2022
10 9 8 7 6 5 4 3 2 1

This is a work of fiction. All of the characters, organizations, and events portrayed in this novel are either products of the author's imagination or are used fictitiously. Any resemblance to actual persons, living or dead (except for satirical purposes), is entirely coincidental.

Original edition published by Teos Publishers, 2021

English language edition published by agreement with Emmi Itäranta, HG Literary and Elina Ahlback Literary Agency, Helsinki, Finland

A CIP catalogue record for this title is available from the British Library.

Printed and bound in the United Kingdom by CPI Group Limited.

THE MOONDAY LETTERS

EMMI ITÄRANTA

TITAN BOOKS

To all those who have lost their homes

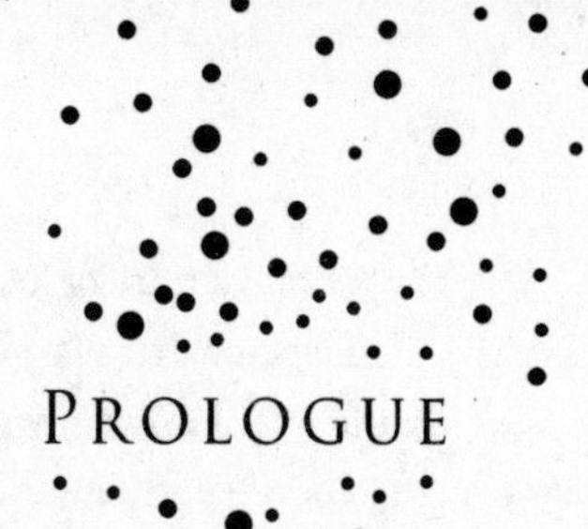

PROLOGUE

Undated

Sol,
This may be the final page, the one I write after everything has already happened. The one I will tear out at the end of the notebook and place between the cover and the blank title page. The first word on it is your name: that way you will know at once the sentences on the upcoming pages are for you as much as they are for myself.

It is the morning after everything.

From where I sit, I can see the dust-gray plain and the hills that yield to its shadows, the bare slopes of craters. The moonscape is lifeless as a sea turned to stone, unless you count the remote glow of the dome village, near invisible. The horizon runs across the desert as a black brushstroke. At the bottom edge of the sky made from night floats the rising Earth, its outlines clear and air-light. The cloud-rime on its surface looks rigid against blue and yellow and brown. It reminds me of the first frost of winter that stalls the fallen leaves on the surface of a pond.

It is as if there is more green than yesterday. It must be my imagination. It is too early yet.

In silence Earth seems to climb higher, a flawless, rounded drop of water that contains everything: each day, past and future. From this distance, not a single scar is visible on it. It seems to me that if I reached out my hand, I could stroke its surface, stroke it back to sleep. A dim glow of water and earth would remain on my fingers and linger when I'd later fall asleep in my room, a hand under my cheek. Perhaps, after waking up,

I might find a trace of it on my face, like a memory, or a dried tear.

The curve of a large continent splits the sea on the right, another on the left. I move my gaze upward, toward the North Pole.

There is nothing but the white, thick mist of clouds in the spot I'm trying to see.

I close my eyes and picture it.

It is early night, and that moment of the year when autumn has not yet descended upon the landscape, but the air no longer smells of summer. I imagine a stretch of forest where I used to walk as a child. There light grows slanted among the pines, and the trees reach their narrow fingers against the sky. The sun still coaxes scent from the needles fallen to the ground. This is the way I want to remember the place. Forged full of late-summer light, stopped in its own sphere of gold.

While filling these notebooks for you I used to think that words could bring you to me. That through them you would see what I did: the blue glow of Earth and the precise outlines space drew for it, the table at which I am sitting, my hand curled around the cup. The distances we learned to cross together.

But would you after all, Sol?

I imagine you across the table, gaze turned to me. No; you are looking out of the picture window as wide as the wall. You are looking over the desert beneath and beyond the domes glowing afar, beyond the horizon and across the darkness toward the blue drop of water. The results of your work.

I cannot see the expression on your face.

Against space, I see a reflection in the window glass, a distant and translucent figure that walks across the floor. The moment is as long as the universe.

A remark on date and time notation in the document collection entitled **The Moonday Letters**

At the time of the writing of Lumi Salo's notebook entries, space colonies still widely followed the old Earth chronology, which was frequently used in parallel with Martian chronology. Salo dated her entries solely according to the Earth calendar, presumably because she grew up on Earth and it was a way for her to maintain a connection with her home planet. For authenticity, all dates in this collection have been retained in their original format. When converting the dates from one system to another it is worth remembering that one Earth year approximates only half a Martian year. Thus the year 2168 CE[1] corresponds to Mars year 68 MC.[2]

The acronym MST, used in connection to time of day, stands for Mars Standard Time. Since a Martian day is 39 minutes and 35 seconds longer than a day on Earth, it was common to notate this by adding the plus (+) mark after midnight until a new day started from the beginning, for example: 00.00+37 p.m.

The Martian and Earth calendars diverged in the Inanna period. During this time, nearly all colonies apart from the cylinder cities in Earth orbit adopted the Martian calendar.

Since the era of new unification in the Solar System began in the Martian year 94, adopting a consistent, common-to-all chronology has been proposed a number of times. However, for the time being the proposal has failed to gain sufficient support in the Solar Council.

---

1 The acronym was used on Earth to mark chronology in cultures that had adopted the Gregorian calendar, sometimes in conjunction with other systems. From the turn of the twenty-first century, the religiously neutral CE (Common Era) and BCE (before the Common Era) replaced the acronyms AD (anno Domini) and BC (before Christ) to a degree, particularly in academic context. In everyday use it was customary to leave out the acronym and only notate the year. This practice corresponds to the current practice of Martian chronology.

2 MC = Martian chronology. The acronym was adopted in the Martian colonies in the 20s MC in order to mark the Mars calendar as separate from the old Earth chronology.

PART I

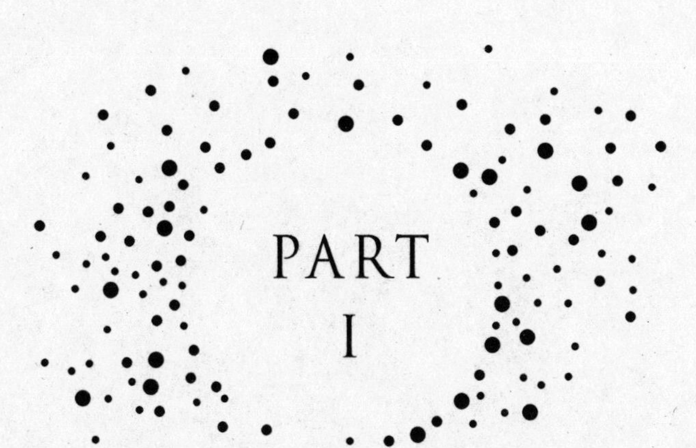

Come, call me Stardust

I'll show you worlds sky-high

Burn your rulebook, claim your new look

You know why

"Stardust Ride," Mx Mx

M. Chen & A. Al-Shamir, eds.

Shallow: An Anthology of Pop Lyrics from the 21st Century,

vol. 1. New York II: Moonage Press, 2104.

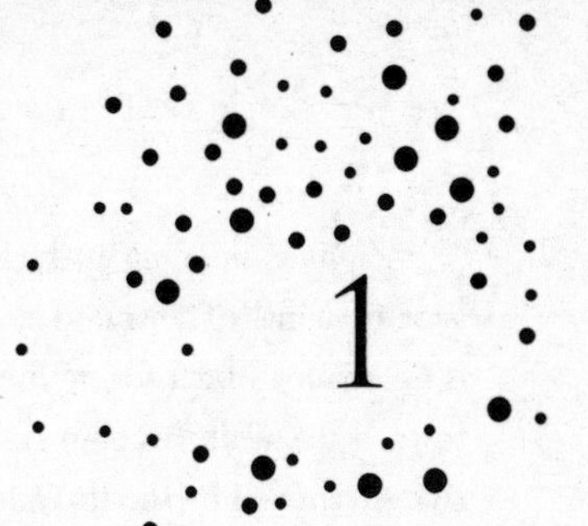

1

25.2.2168

A long-distance starship somewhere between Jupiter and Mars

Sol,

The empty space of the blank notebook opens before me as I turn the first page into view and write these words. I finished filling the previous book yesterday, the one with the green cover that you gave me for my birthday. I wrote the final sentences on the inside of the back cover. I wrapped the book in the bamboo scarf that was also a gift from you, and pushed it into my suitcase under the clothes to wait for the moment when I can press it into your hand. But there is yet more to write before we meet again.

Let me prepare everything for you, Sol: set the stage and open the curtain, so in your thoughts you may settle next to me and be with me in this moment. You said once that writing is journeying beyond infinite distances; with these words I transport you to me across time and space.

Imagine the deep blackness behind the wall.

Imagine the faint and rare bright spots sparkling in it, like scattered rain, into the heart of which the ship is journeying. Imagine the humming of the vessel's motors that are pushing it toward Mars; imagine the smothering silence of space.

Imagine the narrow bed of the cabin into which I invite you with me. Just like that: sit down next to me, place your head against my shoulder and follow the movements of my pen. The blank paper is like a white sheet, or skin wrapped in anticipation, the tale drawn on it letter by letter like the touch of the beloved.

Ziggy is sleeping at the foot of the bed, curled into a striped coil, snoring faintly. The sound is so clearly distinct from purring that there is no chance of confusing them. Ziggy's ginger-red ear triangles point toward the wall, his chin rests on his paws and occasionally the paws twitch, moved by the threads of sleep.

On the unfolded side table that is barely larger than this notebook waits my dinner, a metal bowl of soup bought in the cheapest canteen on the ship. *Delicious hot or cold*, read the digital display of the shelf. I have eaten similar bowlfuls often enough to know that neither is true (and I can hear you gagging when the smell reaches your nose).

Are you here, Sol?

Yes: I can feel the warmth emanating from your skin. Ziggy's snoring pauses for a moment when he senses your weight on the mattress. I move my leg a little, closer to you.

Now that you are sitting comfortably, I want to tell you about Europa.

· • ● • ·

On the first day six weeks ago I stood upon the surface of Europa, in a tower reaching far above the ice crust, and looked toward Earth. I couldn't see anything but the enormous orb of Jupiter and the stars glinting behind it. If I had swiped one of the telescopes along the rounded walls of the tower with my pay bracelet and looked into the ocular, I might have been able to discern a pallid blue dot in the distance, but I did not do so. The vast windows of the tower were lined with information screens that updated regularly and portrayed the starry sky in different directions, depending on the positions of the celestial bodies. Here I could see the dim rings of Saturn, that way its moons: Titan, Dione and Enceladus. Over there, the ninth planet of the Solar System, always invisible and therefore, for a long time, undiscovered.

I thought of how far away from home I was. Part of me was startled by the realization. It marked a sore spot inside me. If anything were to happen there – an accident, a technical flaw causing delays, an unexpected moonquake and ice tsunami – everything was alien, I was alone. But underneath the thought I recognized another that burned like the sun: this was how far I had made it.

I only wished you could have been there with me, Sol.

I believe you'd like Europa. The tower episode was an exception, after which I spent the rest of my time under the ice crust (surface excursions are, of course, strictly limited). Admittedly, it bothered me at first, because as you know, I'm not used to underwater cities. Yet within mere days I began to understand that for Europans the water and the ice covering it signify shelter and safety. And how the ice looks from below, seen through their glass roofs! They have created a new kind of architecture that makes no attempt to imitate any other, but utilizes the natural elements of their immediate surroundings.

A translucent, crystal-glittering network of caverns encompasses the surfaces of the oceans everywhere. One day I visited an interfaith sanctuary built in the vault of an ice cave recommended to me by my patient. The mosaics, glass figurines surrounded by flowers and the lights kindled by the tides rippled in ceaseless interaction between the edges and smooth surfaces of the ice. It was so quiet there that I could hear the breathing of the people who had stopped on their cushions and mats and benches, at times even the faint words dancing on their lips.

Apart from the ocean and ice, silence is one of the most remarkable features of Europa. My patient had mentioned it in advance, and its significance was also emphasized in the info clips repeatedly playing on the screens of my outbound flight, which briefed passengers on Europan culture and safety instructions. Even so, I was unable to imagine the reality of it beforehand. The thickness of the ice is so important to sheltering the settlements from radiation that a crack anywhere on the surface of Europa could trigger fatal consequences. The ice is sensitive to sound, so the decibels are never permitted to exceed a certain level. Europans have developed all kinds of silent ways to go about their business in these unusual circumstances, and I learned that when they first started building the settlements, almost entirely soundless new kinds of robotic machines had to be invented so the crust would not be disturbed.

My favorite place ended up being a tearoom where you could sit in peace for hours, drink Europan seaweed tea (I expect you will have your doubts about the idea, but it has a rare, sweet flavor that is not at all unpleasant), and watch the sirens swimming outside the glass wall. Have you heard of them, Sol? Of all the animals I'm familiar with they most resemble walruses, but in reality they are giant tardigrades of sorts, the discovery of which on Europa took everyone by surprise. They live in the freezing oceans, free and protected. In the early years of the settlements some businessman apparently wanted to turn them into cattle, but fortunately at least something had been learned from the mistakes made on Enceladus.

I only visited New Yonaguni because my patient lived there. They said the real gem of Europa is Teonimanu III, and I would have liked to see the library I had heard so much about. Maybe one day you and I can travel there together, Sol. Their collection includes some unique botanical works that might interest you.

Work went well this time, but after two weeks I was content to board a starship again. The pressure brushing my heart and breath loosened its grip as the ship left the spaceport behind and the distance between us began to grow narrower. On the monitor of the passenger compartment Europa looked beautiful and remote as it fell into the arms of darkness, a strange cold moon far from the sun. The ice shell of its oceans spilled with muted light. The few human-made constructs discernible on the surface shrank into shards of stone and vanished into the pale landscape. Seen from afar, red-tinted streaks crisscrossed throughout it like scratches of space, or like long-ago written messages that no one remembered how to read.

Behind, Jupiter spun slow and enormous. Its sandstone-colored storms grew and swept old ones aside. It cared little for the moons orbiting it, or for ships leaving them. It cared even less for us, children of dust and dark matter.

That was four weeks ago. I was pleased to discover on this ship an unusually large collection of printed books that passengers had left behind. Most of them are in Korean, Japanese, and Hawaiian, but there are some written in Martian English that I'm able to read. That has helped pass the long, dark days in open space. My cabin has no window – my patient was not so wealthy as to cover the cost of a first-class ticket – so I have spent as much time on the lookout deck as the radiation safety guidelines will allow.

The red-tinted light of Mars among other lights grows by the day. Today I looked into the telescope on the lookout deck and was able to discern the veins running on the surface of the planet that long ago were thought to be canals constructed by an alien civilization. I wonder what you can see from where you are, Sol, as you approach the planet from the opposite direction. Perhaps you wander around the garden deck of that other starship right now, enjoying the warmth and humidity of the air, breathing in the scent of the plants. You stop to gaze at the green leaves and their forking veins and soft stalks, considering their internal workings.

If you climb onto the lookout deck, you can see Earth from there, far behind you now, but still much closer to you than to me: a bright-blue raindrop on the tongue of space.

Everything looks more beautiful at a distance.

I should send a message to my parents.

It is late, here between all time zones, where the rhythm of waking and sleep is determined by my own body. The soup has gone cold; I have even less appetite for it now. This makes me feel slightly guilty. Perhaps I should write an obituary to it before taking it down to the zero-waste chutes near the lifts and returning the bowl to the canteen. *Here lies a mix of edible ingredients that may hold nutritional value but – alas! – so little culinary appeal.*

Soon I will place the pen and the notebook on the table, crawl under the blanket and switch off the light. I will watch the white sock of Ziggy's front paw open and close in the dusk like a flower, as he senses me next to him. Behind the thick metal wall thoughts wander and darkness reigns in all directions; one distance grows shorter while others lengthen.

You are here. You are elsewhere. In mere days I will press the notebook filled with writing into your hand.

· •●• ·

3.3.2168
Harmonia, Mars

Sol,
On Mars light never looks quite the same as on Earth. On the surface it falls wan and muted, even when there are no dust storms cloaking the sun. Between the dome cities rests a darkness: that of a world long devoid of life when our kind first arrived. We dug our way deep below the surface, so we could survive in spaces never meant for our bodies and thoughts, and we built the brightest lamps we knew how. We made fields and forests in a remote resemblance of what Earth held for us once. But we all know that just outside the fragile sphere of light the dark lays its heavy fingers onto the thick

glass. It was here before us and will remain long after we are gone, hungry, untamed, uninterested in anything but itself.

And yet, in passing moments when the angle and time of day are just right, and the season favorable, it is possible to be fooled. That happened to me this morning, when the doors of the arrivals hall at the spaceport opened into the garden dome filled with Martian spring. Far above, green beanstalks climbed the walls toward the crown of the vault. Pollinators drew their paths among the feather-white petals of almond trees, and as my eyes followed the shafts of light filtering through the frosted glass and blossoming branches, a sensation passed through me that was soft and sharp at once. For a brief spell I felt like I was home.

The moment did not last. I attached Ziggy's carrier backpack on top of my suitcase and began to drag it toward the train station. I nearly stumbled when a fast-moving robotic suitcase wedged itself between me and my luggage, then continued on its way. The owner ran behind it, in too much of a rush to stop and apologize. I hope they caught their train.

On second thoughts, I hope they did not.

The train ascended briefly to the surface between the spaceport and the settlements. Even after all this time the landscape of Mars still surprises me: the low silhouettes of the cities against the yellowed sky, the constructs buried underground for shelter, only glass and concrete peaks poking out, like parts of strange ships drowned in a sea of red sand.

Unfortunately Ziggy's appreciation for such intricacies was short-lived. He traveled the entire month from Europa to Mars like a pro, but as soon as his paws hit the Martian ground, his patience came to an end. The loud meowing in the carrier backpack did not cease when the train passed the monument of the First Settlers outside Harmonia, or when the train plunged underground again between the glass domes that covered the corn fields, or even when the train slowed down near the residential areas. We were both deeply relieved when we were finally standing at the door of your childhood home.

Your sister, on the other hand, was not deeply relieved.

"A cat?" she said after hugging me, and eyed the carrier backpack, behind the window of which Ziggy's pupils had grown to the size of asteroids.

"I thought Sol had mentioned it," I replied.

"Not to me," Ilsa said. She turned her gaze to me. I was suddenly aware of the dark circles under my eyes, of my creased clothes and my unwashed hair that lay limp against my scalp. As per usual, Ilsa looked like she had just come from a hair appointment, and her home rags (as she calls them) are without exception more presentable than my best outfit.

"Ziggy is completely housetrained," I said. "I just need to clean his litter box after the journey. Sol said they'd ordered some cat litter to be delivered here."

"A box was delivered yesterday. It's in Sol's bedroom." Ilsa moved aside and allowed me to step in. I pulled my suitcase behind me through the door. (One day I'm going to get a robotic one, I swear.) "Make yourself comfortable. I must work for the rest of the day, but we can have dinner together, if you like."

I placed Ziggy's carrier backpack on the floor and began to unzip it. Ilsa coughed and I saw her expression. I zipped up the carrier again right in front of Ziggy's whiskers and started toward your old room.

You could have warned one of us beforehand.

• •●• •

In your room I let Ziggy out of the carrier. He circled the honeycomb shape of the walls with his tail up, jumped onto the wide bed in the alcove and curled up to sleep. I took off my coat and placed it next to him. Ivy climbed on the living wall. Your mother or Ilsa had left a jug of water and two glasses on the foldable table – that was thoughtful of them. On a whim I looked for Harmonia on the old-style globe map standing in the corner that used to be in the living room. Apparently the city had yet to be built when the map was drawn. Do I remember correctly that the globe was your father's?

The wardrobe smelled of old wood when I opened it. I don't think I even looked in when we visited last year; I'd forgotten I'd left a couple of dresses in there. They were still hanging from the rail. I must have got them ages ago for some party or other that Ilsa stubbornly insisted we attend. There was also a pair of high-heeled shoes standing on the floor. I don't remember wearing them more than once.

I opened my suitcase and dug around until I found the notebook with the green cover. I unwrapped the bamboo scarf from around it and placed it on the table between the water jug and the globe map. I hung up a couple of cardigans, a clean boiler suit and my work cloak next to the neglected dresses. A shadow-filled mirror flashed on the inside of the wooden door. A memory surfaced: the two of us standing here, your face smoother than today, my hands softer.

I closed the wardrobe. The rose patterns cut along the grain of the dark wood were beautiful and blind under my fingers. I went looking for your mother.

· •●• ·

I found Naomi in the communal garden atop the building complex, where she sat on a bench under a tall, flowering quince. On my way to her I walked past two women who were swinging a skipping rope for their daughter on the paved playground – was her name Stella? Estelle? Has she started school already? I waved at them. Stella

(Estelle?) waved back, not missing a beat while jumping. One of her mothers – the one with tons of curly hair, I can never remember their names either – shouted, "Look who's back!" The other looked over her shoulder toward me and flashed a smile.

"Mom, you're going to mess up," Stella protested.

The dome that sheltered the city arched far above, its thousands of lamps casting daylight-imitating rays into the garden. The flowers flamed bright orange-red on the delicate branches of the tree. Naomi was staring at something on the lawn, perhaps an insect walking among the stalks of grass. A blue-winged butterfly sat on her knee. After a long moment she turned her gaze toward me and extended her hand. The butterfly flew off, a flicker of faraway sky and water in the air. A dark, gray-streaked braid fell onto Naomi's chest. Her eyes were nearly black.

"Lumi," she said and took my hand. "Sol isn't here yet."

"I know," I replied. "Good to see you, Naomi."

She was quiet. I sat down on the bench next to her. Her gaze wandered along the quince branches, where some flowers had already scattered their petals and swollen into green fruits the size of a fingertip. I closed my eyes and held her hand, listened to the stirrings in her. A slow, murky weight flowed into me like water. I sensed what I had suspected: the sickness was settling inside her again, making a home under her skin.

I opened my eyes and asked, "How have you been?"

Your mother smiled. A tree-branch drew a shadow on her face.

"There are good days," she said. "And there are others. This time of the year is always harder." She went quiet.

"Loss and grief are physical sensations," I said. "The body remembers them from one year to the next."

"And from one decade," Naomi responded. Her smile waned.

"Has the medication helped?" I asked, although I was familiar with the symptoms and knew the answer.

Naomi pulled her hand away.

"Maybe a little," she said.

We both knew it wasn't true. I could tell what she'd ask for next. I waited.

"Do you... do you think you could arrange a session?"

"Of course, Naomi."

Your mother squeezed my hand and smiled at me.

"Thank you," she said. "If you need any supplies, give Ilsa a list."

I did not mention to her I have carried all the essentials with me since Fuxi. As I left your mother in the garden and returned inside the building, I felt the slow weight I had sensed near her withdraw from my body little by little. Yet it left behind the kind of bone-deep chill it always does, like when you have been so cold for so long it takes hours to feel warm again. You know the kind, Sol: you have tried to chase it from my body often enough with your touch.

As I passed the closed door of Ilsa's rooms, I heard her talking on the phone. Soft classical music was playing in the background.

I must go and make peace with her soon.

Naomi and I have scheduled a session for tomorrow evening. It is not too soon; everything went well on Europa, and I have had weeks to recover on my way to Mars. However, it means I may not be awake when you arrive. Please come to me regardless. Remove your shoes in the faint night light, stroke Ziggy's neck as he sleeps at my feet. Let your gaze stop on the green-covered book on the table and let a smile pass your face. Settle next to me as I stir in my sleep.

Through sleep I will know you are there. In the rooms of the Moonday House I hear your footsteps approaching and extend my hand toward you.

• • ● • •

Sender: Sol Uriarte
Recipient: Lumi Salo
Date: 4.3.2168 23.50 MST
Security: Maximum encryption

Dearest Lumi,
Urgent work obstacle, I cannot make it to Harmonia after all. Can you come to Datong? The address is 105 Halley. I will tell you everything when we meet.
S

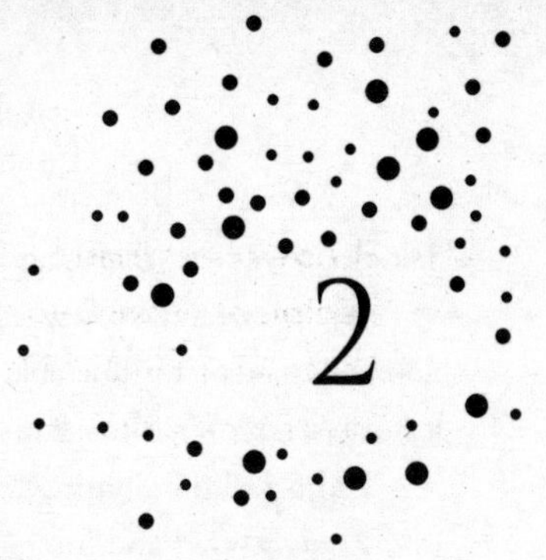

2

5.3.2168

Harmonia, Mars

Sol,

I'm happy to report that last night's session with your mother was a success. It took less time than I'd expected, and toward the end she seemed visibly better. Grief is an animal you can never quite tame: after a long silence in the shadows, it may stir again and scratch open the wounds that soul-sickness feeds on. But Naomi has always been strong. Her bond with you and Ilsa binds her more closely to life. I believe she is on her way to recovery again.

My return path from the other side seemed smooth and clear, so I was a little surprised when the after-effect lingered throughout the night. Sleep held me in the bed, and the shadows of the evening before flickered around me: the circle of candles and the scent rising from the burning herbs, coarse-golden animal fur under my fingers and the song that was born from some strange landscape, yet from me. Tall woods stood in the place of the walls. Between the dark boles I saw the door, and sharp claws scratched wood as the animal leaped onto a tree and began to climb.

But you don't need to worry, Sol. It was nothing like after we left Fuxi. This was just residue, like dream imagery that sweeps aside the meaningless rubble of daytime events, or like dust that sticks to clothes and can be brushed off. Otherworld echoes, Vivian used to call it. They have no substance of their own, and they fade before long. Every healer has encountered them.

The woods slipped away. I opened my eyes and took a deep breath.

The door was still there, and the scratching sound.

I recognized the room and sat up to find Ziggy clawing at the closed door. I swiped on my portable screen that was charging on the night table: it was just after ten o'clock in the morning. No wonder Ziggy was hungry.

I adjusted the lighting to make it brighter, poured some dry food into Ziggy's bowl and looked around the room. The other side of the bed was untouched, the smooth blanket in place. Only Ziggy's paw-dents were visible on it. The book with the green cover still lay on the desk. The only suitcase by the wall was mine. The room had empty space in your shape where your presence should have filled it, Sol.

The screen changed color from nighttime sepia to white when I picked it up and opened my messages. At the top there were two responses to my permanent advertisement on *Star Professionals of the Solar System*. After them, *Experience Europa!* requested customer feedback on my recent trip. The fourth message was from you.

Is this one of Min-soo's infamous supplemental project meetings?

Then again, I have not been to Datong in ages.

· •●• ·

I'm not sure how things went with Ilsa. I think we parted on decent terms, but I still find her hard to read.

After I'd ventured into the quiet kitchen for a quick breakfast (do you have *any* idea how much I missed fresh fruit on the flight? They grow strawberries and raspberries on the ship, but the price of one strawberry was twice that of a soup bowl), I went to check on your mother. The door of her bedroom was ajar. It was dark inside. I peered in. Her blanket rose and fell in the rhythm of her light snoring.

I walked up a second flight of stairs and stopped at Ilsa's door. It was closed, and behind it I could hear cabaret music playing on low volume. She must have started work hours earlier.

I considered going back downstairs for a shower first, but I needed to talk to her. I knocked on the door.

"Ilsa?"

No response. I knocked again, a little louder this time.

"Come in," Ilsa's voice called.

Slowly I pushed the door open. Even you don't keep your desk as impeccably organized as she keeps hers, Sol: I have never seen anything on it except her collection of screens and a pen. Today she was standing very straight before the widescreen display, and was focused on rotating a complex model of a molecular structure with her fingertips. I recognized the digital *BioBau Inc.* watermark hovering across the image. I thought you'd mentioned she wanted to get the company logo redesigned? A smaller screen propped on the desk flashed with the words *TO DO*.

The picture wall shone softly, an image of an oil painting of ballerinas putting on their shoes. The original painting must have been a lot smaller, because in the digital reproduction you could see the texture up close: the movements of the painter's wrist in the brushstrokes, the layers of color and the pores of the canvas.

Ilsa adjusted the molecular structure once again, so slightly I found it hard to tell the difference. She touched an icon at the bottom of the large screen. The image faded.

"Lumi," she said. "How's Mom?"

I thought she gave a sideways look to my outfit of cardigan and pajamas, but that could have just been my imagination. She was dressed in a sleek jumpsuit and a lightweight cashmere jumper. (Are there even cashmere goats on Mars, or is the wool imported from Earth? I've never found the nerve to ask her.) There were carefully covered shadows under her eyes. I realized she must have stayed up until Naomi and I had finished last night.

"She's sleeping," I said. "It's usually a good sign after a session."

"So you've told me."

Ilsa waited.

"I'm sorry about Ziggy," I said. "I should have checked with you beforehand. I thought Sol…"

Ilsa waved her hand.

"I was just surprised, that's all. Cats and I don't get along. As long as you keep it out of my way."

It was cold in the room. I always forget she prefers her quarters a few degrees cooler than the rest of the habitat. I pulled my cardigan tighter around me.

Qui peut dire où vont les fleurs, sang a low female voice in the loudspeakers.

"Have you heard from Sol?" I asked.

"Why?" A narrow line appeared between Ilsa's eyebrows, under her straight-cut fringe. "Were they meant to arrive today?"

"Yesterday."

I told her about your message.

"Really?" Ilsa swiped her smaller screen on and began to browse her messages. "I've only had time for work mail this morning." Her fingers moved on the screen, then stopped. "Looks like they've sent a voice message."

Sol, there was an awkward moment when neither of us moved, and eventually her mouth went tight and she touched the screen to play the message. Only when the music faded and your words drifted into the room did I realize it was terribly rude of me to expect Ilsa to listen to the message in my presence, and she was too polite to tell me so. There might be something private in it. But by then you were already talking.

"I know Mother won't be happy about this," your voice said, "but I have to cancel my trip to Harmonia. I'll call her tomorrow. If Lumi asks something—"

You went quiet for a moment. There was just white noise. Then you cleared your throat and continued, "Actually, forget about it. I'll talk to her myself."

The message ended and the music returned to the loudspeakers. Ilsa's face was slightly more restless than usual.

"Do you know what Sol meant by that?" she said.

I'd been about to ask her the same.

"No idea," I replied. "I've only had a short text from them."

Ilsa glanced at the small screen, where the letters *TO DO* had turned red. She invited a smile onto her face that she probably uses in work meetings with important clients. She is very good at that kind of thing. I don't mean this as a criticism; I admire that about Ilsa. Between the three of you, she is by far the best at putting on masks in social situations. Someone might interpret it as betrayal, but I see it differently: those masks protect her from the world, create a shield that keeps her safe. That was one of the first things I learned about her all those years ago when I arrived at your family's house. Each of you has different ways of dealing with loss.

"I'd like to talk," she said. "But I have to leave for a work meeting in half an hour. I'm going to a concert tonight with some friends. Would you care to join us? I can probably arrange an extra ticket."

"Sol asked me to go to Datong," I said. "I need to leave early tomorrow morning. I'm sorry."

Ilsa's mouth made a very slight sagging movement, but her smile recovered quickly. She nodded without looking at me. Her lips began to form a word, then allowed it to fade. The screen pinged three times to mark new messages.

"I'm sorry too," she said. "Do you need anything at all?"

I shook my head.

"You'll come here together from Datong, won't you?"

"That probably depends on Sol," I said.

Ilsa nodded again and swiped her finger across the screen, where messages began to slide past. Her polished nail tapped the side of the screen.

"Is everything okay?"

Ilsa looked up.

"Of course," she said.

When I closed the door behind me, Ilsa was writing on her portable screen with a pen. The ballerinas in the painting on her picture wall sat still, lacing their pink slippers, enclosed within their own time where the brush had caught them centuries ago.

I left Ilsa alone with them.

Quand saurons-nous un jour? sang a female voice.

I'd better start looking at train timetables.

Sender: Sol Uriarte
Recipient: Lumi Salo
Date: 5.3.2168 13.22 MST
Security: Maximum encryption

Lumi,
I need to ask for a favor. Please open the bottom drawer of the desk in my old home office, take out a small wooden box from behind the papers and bring it to Datong with you. ♥
S

5.3.2168
Harmonia, Mars
Later

Sol,
After your second message arrived, I went into your old home office on the ground floor. The door was not locked. Dust had gathered

on the desk and on the shelves. The household robot has clearly not been programmed to clean there as often as in the other rooms. The writing desk was empty, save for a photo frame that switched on simultaneously with the light as I stepped through the door.

As the light grew, a faintly glowing picture that moved every few seconds materialized from the dusk. You were in it, maybe eight years old, all spiky dark hair and high cheekbones under the baby softness of your features. Next to you stood your father, who was wearing jeans, a hoodie and a T-shirt with the logo of BioBau Inc. on it. You were both smiling at the camera, and at each other, when the photo moved and he tousled your hair, and then at the camera again, when the picture returned to the original pose. He looked younger than you are now, Sol. I didn't remember seeing the picture before. Someone had placed it on display after my last visit. You, perhaps.

I opened the bottom drawer. At the front there was a pile of reusable writing sheets that looked like they were from your student days. Among miscellaneous notes, drawings of trees and crops crossed the pages. I pushed my hand behind the sheets and felt around. My fingers met a rectangular wooden surface. I got a hold of it and produced the box.

The box was small, approximately the size of an electronic business card, and made from some vanished tree species of Earth. Spruce, perhaps; I felt a faint scent of resin in the wood. (I didn't try to lift the lid, but it seemed locked.) I wondered where you had got the box. Note to self: I must ask you when I get to Datong. I have only ever seen objects made from spruce among Vivian's tools before.

The light went out automatically behind me as I left the room. In the photo frame, your father's smile and yours faded slowly.

I have made all the necessary arrangements. The household robot is currently putting together my luggage, insisting on the high-heeled shoes despite the fact that I clearly selected "WORK" as the purpose of the trip. I suspect Ilsa has programmed it that way.

Tonight I think of Fuxi: for the first time in a long while, I could claim, but that would not be true. I still think of Fuxi often. Sometimes, when you don't see, Sol, I allow myself to travel afar and step through the gate beyond which memories live. I defy the distance that parts the past from this moment and retrieve every detail of the places I knew, bringing them back to life.

Delicate, supple branches cover the café where I often sat writing these notes for you, at the tables dappled by light and shadow. Green leaves turn in the light breeze like insects' wings. On the edges of the paved area tree roots are pushing out between tiles; sometimes also grass and moss that would soon cover the chairs if there were no people to brush them aside. Pale lichen clings to tree trunks. On the next table sits a drained coffee cup that no one has collected.

From the café I return to our apartment, walk there like a ghost.

The bamboo chairs on the balcony overlooking the park stand empty, but the balcony is full: the herbs I grew from seed spread scent from their shelves, rosemary and basil and coriander, and a flowering quince in a large terracotta pot attracts bumblebees. Their buzzing is slow and their fur shines with pollen, and I could watch them all day. We planted the quince together after arriving at Fuxi, your hand and mine brushed each other as we pushed it in the dark compost. You said you were certain it would take root; you had mixed fungi in the compost that would help it reach deeper and absorb nutrients. Still, I spoke to the shrub sometimes when you were not home. I told it I would look after it, asked it to grow strong and happy, and it did.

Above the quince a vine with an unyielding stem flowers on a frame, winding its white, bell-like flowers closed as the night falls.

The Fuxi I see when I look away from this day is not the same one that orbits Mars now. But I don't want to think about that, not too much.

We carry within us every home, including those that no longer exist, so we'd have somewhere to return to.

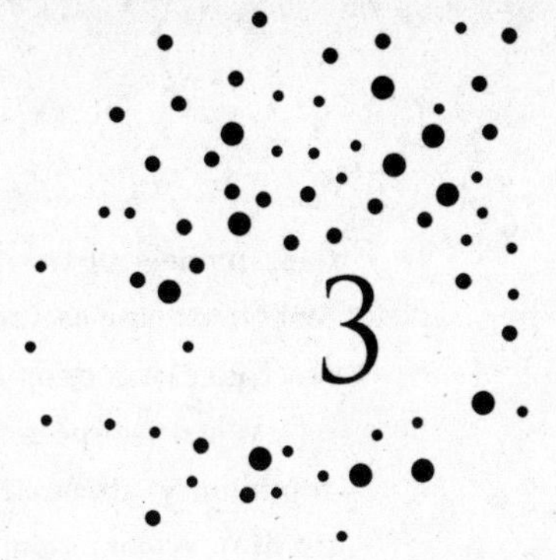

Introduction: On technological developments of space flight prior to the Inanna period

J. Kapoor. *A Short History of Space Flight.* Saraswati: Peacock Press, 127 MC.

Everyone will recognize the first crewed Mars landing as a historical landmark that, as a turning point in the colonization of our Solar System, is at least as significant as the first steps of humankind on the Moon. Today we take this for granted; however, that was not the case for the eight astronauts, cosmonauts and taikonauts who transmitted the first images from the Red Planet to Earth. The year on Earth at the time was 2040 CE (the mission originally planned for 2030 CE had been delayed for a number of reasons, which this book will explore at length below).

The foremost mission of those who first set foot on the surface of Mars was to map the possibilities of founding a potential research station – which was later expanded into a settlement – but none of them knew that a mere two years later, a technological breakthrough would enable an entirely new kind of space travel, and that a new era would be born from their pioneering work. In their eyes, a self-sufficient Mars must have seemed like a utopian dream that stood no chance of coming true within their lifetime.

When whispers began to sound from the scientific community about the potential of the DM Drive (DMD) as something that could revolutionize space travel, the early reactions were skeptical. Several tantamount experiments that had led to dead ends after a promising start were still fresh in the memory: no one wanted a new warp drive or an engine "powered" by electromagnetic thrusts that empirical tests would uncover as nothing more than a pipe dream that belonged in a science fantasy.

Yet against all probability the DMD[3] proved to be the device that made the colonization of space a reality. Since the DMD does not require weighty fuel tanks, but instead uses dark matter as its primary energy source, it shortened the duration of long-distance space flights in a groundbreaking manner. While the first crew took nine months to travel to Mars in the year 0, and a flight to Jupiter's moon Europa would have at the time required two Mars years,[4] as soon as in the year 2 flights from Earth to Mars were made within four weeks.

Replacing the old space flight technology with DMD technology was delayed by a few factors. The occurrence of anorthite required for building fully functional DMD engines was rare in the Earth's crust,

3 DMD was subsequently nicknamed "Improbability Drive" among NASA scientists.
4 Two Mars years equal approximately one Earth year.

and only once Moon mining began on a large scale, the availability of the raw materials was significantly improved.[5] The building of the settlements could begin for real – and the rest, as they say, is history.

For reasons that will be clear to the readers, the Inanna period that began in 68 MC meant an almost complete disappearance of craftmanship on Earth when it came to space technologies. During the Inanna period new kinds of space travel were developed on Mars based on theoretical technologies of Earth, which made journeying between colonies all the easier. The most significant innovation among these was the solar sail, on which Earth scientists had been working even prior to the invention of the DMD.

This book is constructed around three turning points: (1) the first successful human mission to Mars that landed in the year 1 MC and the first DMD test flights; (2) the isolationism of the Inanna period that began in the year 68 MC; and (3) the new era of unification, starting from the year 94 MC.

5 Here it is worth noting that fossil fuels required by old technology suffered from a deepening crisis from the 2030s CE onward, because Earth was running low on raw materials, and at this point nation states were strictly limiting their use due to the impacts of climate change, which had turned acute. From the 2010s CE onward the technologies were increasingly being developed by private companies in parallel with national space programs.

6.3.2168
Halley 105 Hotel
Datong, Mars

Sol,

The journey from Harmonia to Datong was dreadful. If I didn't know I will meet you here, I would scold you for asking me to endure something like that. Never mind: I'm going to scold you anyway. An eight-hour cattle transport in a crammed underground, where my knees were constantly battered by the seat in front of me, and the smell of packed lunches wafted in the air (I'm aware of the time-honored tradition of onion as an easy and durable crop, but why oh why would anyone wish to pack it for a train trip?). The worst thing, however, was my chatty next-seat neighbor, who wanted to talk throughout the journey, excluding the part where he ate three onion sandwiches and fell asleep for a quarter of an hour, during which he nearly managed to dribble on my sleeve. Only a quick last-minute move saved my coat.

I have never understood why people would rather attempt to open conversations with strangers when they could be quiet instead.

Life with you has trained my habits in a direction of which I'm not proud, Sol. My parents would be horrified if they knew of my reaction to the underground. For them it would have been an experience full of new and exciting things. Perhaps, even, a dream come true: a journey outside of Earth. When I was about ten years old, they saved from their nonexistent salary for a year and sold our best egg-laying hen so they could take me for three days to an employees' holiday village half a day's boat trip away. The place had threadbare bedsheets and the smell of urine drifted into the cottage from the outhouse, and there were so many mosquitoes that we were all still swollen from their bites a week later.

But for them it was important, and for me it is one of my dearest memories, rising above others all the more brightly the older I get. Never before had I been outside Winterland, or seen so much forest at once. Never before had I known what a fish roasted on an open fire tastes like. I had not heard the sound born from rushes bending against the side of a boat on a calm lake, where the sun burnishes the waves. And the night sky, Sol: nowhere else is it the same. I know you have seen the sky above Earth, but only tarnished by light. I hope one day I can show you the night swept clean by darkness.

But back to my onion-odored neighbor. For some reason he got it into his head early on that I resembled someone he knew, and that I might possibly be related to him. He wanted to know everything about my personal history and life, and refused to believe I had never heard of the half sister of his cousin's second cousin's brother-in-law who worked as the vice-manager of a robotic corn farm near Arcadia or something of the sort. I was curt in my responses, but made the mistake of saying that I was originally from Earth (I believed that to be sufficient proof that we were not related, he was so obviously Martian).

"Earth?" he bellowed. "But no one leaves Earth legally."

I corrected him that it was possible to leave Earth with a special visa and those were granted to professionals in fields suffering from labor shortages. He asked what my professional field was.

"Healer," I said.

Another miscalculation. I had to listen to a one-hour-and-seventeen-minutes-long (I'm not making this up, I secretly timed it) dramatically meandering case history starring the gall bladder, joints and dental roots of Mr. Onion Whiff.

I was enormously relieved when he finally fell asleep, and a little annoyed when the fast movement of my arm woke him up. At the end of the day, a dribbled-on sleeve might have been an acceptable price for peace and quiet.

Poor Ziggy had no appreciation whatsoever for the crammed train trip. As you know, he is quite the seasoned traveler and it takes a lot to upset him, but there seemed to be no end to the miaowing when we finally arrived at Datong and I was able to pick him up from the pet compartment after a long wait. On top of it all, I had to wash him, to which he also presented his sharp counter-argument.

· •●• ·

At the hotel a young receptionist looked at Ziggy from behind the desk in the lobby. He placed a smile on his face. I could imagine him practicing it in front of a mirror.

"Pet room?" he asked in Martian English.

"Yes," I said. "My spouse has probably already checked in. The booking is under their name. Sol Uriarte."

The receptionist browsed his screen and wrote something on it. He scratched his wrist.

"Your husband arrived two hours ago," he said. "The room number is 513. Your husband—"

"My spouse," I corrected.

The receptionist raised his gaze from the screen.

"Pardon?" he said.

"My spouse," I repeated. "Not my husband."

I only realized then how young the receptionist looked. This must have been his first workplace.

"My apologies," he said. I saw a growing embarrassment behind his face. "Your wife?"

Sol, how often I have wished for personal pronouns to be gender neutral in all languages, as they are in my mother's tongue.

"Not my wife," I said. "My spouse. They use gender neutral labels and the pronoun *they*."

A few drops of sweat had appeared in the receptionist's curly, dark hairline. His wrist was slightly exposed where he had scratched it. I noticed darker spots on his skin, like a map of a cratered landscape:

a telltale rash I'd seen many times, rare among the Mars-born. His accent was nearly unnoticeable, but now that I knew to listen for it, I recognized it in the way he pronounced the consonants.

"Right," he said and wiped his forehead. He read something on the screen. "Your spouse asked us to deliver a message. He… they have an urgent work matter to attend to, but they will return in a few hours at the latest."

I thanked the receptionist for the information, tapped the key code he gave me onto my screen and watched him as he informed me about the restaurants, VR gyms and other services at the hotel. His shoulders were tense and his face was twitching.

I lifted Ziggy's carrier onto my back.

"You're not from here, are you?" I asked, trying to sound kind.

The receptionist's shoulders did not relax.

"No. I grew up on Earth. Salt Lake Land."

"How long have you been on Mars?"

"I got a visa five months ago," he said.

Four months, then, including the travel time from Earth. Maybe less.

"Congratulations," I said.

"Look, I'm sorry I assumed… Where I come from, only two genders are still recognized." His face was genuinely uncomfortable.

"I grew up in Winterland," I said. "I made a lot of mistakes when I first got here. Not out of malice. Simply out of ignorance."

He stared at the points of his shoes for a moment and then raised his head. He was almost in tears.

"I will learn," he said. "I don't want to go back to Earth."

"None of us do." I paused. There was no one else in the lobby. A parlor palm grew under artificial light; a blue ocean shifted its slow waves in the pixels of the picture wall. "The hard part is not learning new things. The hard part is unlearning some of the old. The things you are so used to you don't question them, even when they are wrong."

The receptionist nodded. His posture relaxed a little.

"How long have you been here?" he asked, and added, "if I may ask, Ma'am?"

Courtesies like that always make me feel so… middle-aged. But compared to him, I guess I was. Am.

"I left Earth over twenty years ago."

He hesitated. I could see he wanted to say something else. I waited.

"Do you still get homesick a lot?"

I imagined what it must be like for him. Visas were rarely granted to whole families. He had probably left behind everything he knew, every person he could talk to or touch, every place where he did not feel like an outsider. He might never be able to go back.

"No," I lied. "Not anymore."

Ziggy gave a loud meow of disapproval in the carrier.

"One more thing," I said. "What time is the breakfast again?"

· •●• ·

You would have known better than me how to deal with the situation, Sol. But of course you had to learn it much earlier than I did, despite how progressive Harmonia is.

It was thoughtful of you to pick a hotel close to the station, although I was slightly disappointed not to find you in the room. But you are almost here already: your overcoat, your suitcase, your message that just arrived on my screen. Your work, which will hold you a little longer, but not much. I close my eyes for a moment and in my mind I walk in the rooms of the Moonday House. I warm my hands in front of the fireplace, I breathe in the scent of the flowers placed on the oak table. In the kitchen that we built together I listen to your humming from the next room. When I open my eyes, you will be here.

Sender: Sol Uriarte
Recipient: Lumi Salo
Date: 6.3.2168 17.03 MST
Security: Maximum encryption

Channel 12 at 17.15.
S

Mars Universal Media Network
Current affairs programs
Channel 12
Mars Mirror
Transcripts

Thursday 6.3.2168 CE
Interviewer: Arcturus Teng
Interviewee: Sol Uriarte, Ethnobotanist, University of Harmonia

AT: Good evening from Datong. Leading researchers from universities all around the Solar System have gathered here for an interplanetary symposium looking at food management on Mars. Ethnobotanist Sol Uriarte, who is one of the keynote speakers, is with us tonight. Dr. Uriarte, you specialized in plant grafting and disease resistance. What do you see as the most burning questions in maintaining the self-sufficiency of Mars?

SU: Now we must keep in mind that Mars achieved self-sufficiency decades ago. There is no reason whatsoever to believe that this situation is under any kind of threat. Mars is capable of producing more food than it needs, and in fact frequently does so. Due to effective zero-waste systems the surplus is utilized and recycled for other purposes, such as raw material for biofuels. Under the circumstances the question we should be asking is, how can – how do – we redirect some of the resources invested in food production on Mars.

AT: But is it not true that the flow of refugees from Earth to Mars in the past years has caused some concern over food security on the Red Planet? The issue of protecting the robotic farms from plant diseases or harmful invasive species potentially carried from Earth has also been raised. Sol Uriarte, what is your view on this?

SU: Naturally, we must ensure that we keep up the current standards, and that the quarantine regulations are regularly checked and updated. But as long as the system we have built over the past century remains functional, Mars can afford to offer refuge to those who need it. And furthermore, we can afford to double or treble our contribution to interplanetary humanitarian aid.

AT: Redirecting some of the Martian resources outside the planet is a highly controversial issue. Are you saying you are in favor of it?

SU: Yes, absolutely. In particular, I believe Mars should be providing humanitarian aid to Earth and the colonies of Enceladus.

AT: But we already are, is that not correct?

SU: Our current annual contribution is zero point thirty-nine percent of all of combined gross national product of Martian city states. In comparison, we spend two hundred times that money manufacturing weapons that are mainly exported to Earth, mostly to the worst-polluted areas where unrest and conflicts are common. These include the vast refugee camps around the major spaceports in Florida, Kazakhstan and Inner Mongolia.

AT: Some would argue that the self-sufficiency of Mars is the result of continuing efforts that required great sacrifices from the early settlers. Shouldn't Mars put its own population first?

SU: Aren't we already doing that? Mars owes everything to Earth. For the longest time, we were entirely dependent on their assets and only survived thanks to them. Martian wealth and wellbeing are based on systematic long-term exploitation of Earth's natural resources. It is time we acknowledged our role in amplifying the problems on Earth. It is vital to remember that the survival of the human species during crises, such as wars and pandemics, has been enabled first and foremost by our ability to feel compassion and offer help.

AT: There are surely those who would challenge that view. Many people on Mars feel that by opening our spaceports to migrants, we are risking our hard-gained ability to dwell on a planet that does not provide any prerequisites to support life. Many of the new arrivals are not entering via carefully defined quotas, but are instead coming through illegal routes and cannot be easily deported. Food supply is not the only concern, but housing and employment are also at risk.

SU: As I already pointed out, the food supply concerns are based on a myth that has no basis in the current reality. The wealthiest portion of Martian population has a lot more living space than they need. This is also detrimental to energy efficiency. As to the job market, there are several sectors where Mars is actually short of workers, so these so-called risks seem as asinine, pardon, artificial as the beliefs about food supply.

AT: Sol Uriarte, you were a last-minute replacement for Professor Min-soo Jung from the University of Harmonia as a keynote speaker. I understand that the choice stirred dispute in some circles. You are known as something of a rebel in the scientific community. Would you like to comment on this?

SU: I have always supported equal rights for all living things and would find it hard to live with myself if I chose to do something else. At the same time, I also think that the biocentric worldview does not go far enough. Intact landscapes have rights too, regardless of if they are capable of supporting life.

AT: We are unfortunately running out of time. Sol Uriarte, is there one last thing you would like to say to citizens who may be concerned about the situation on Mars or Earth?

[Transcriber's note: At this point Dr. Uriarte turned to look directly at the camera, an action that journalists routinely advise against.]

SU: Earth wakes and stones will speak, and darkness recedes over waters.

AT: (long pause) That... is certainly a very poetic way of expressing it. Thank you, ethnobotanist Sol Uriarte.

6.3.2168
Halley 105 Hotel
Datong, Mars
Later

Sol,
As I write this, you have yet to respond to the messages I sent you one after another. But I can see you have read them. That gives me some peace. I want to think the only thing parting us is a delayed message, and some unexpected obstacle.

After all, it has happened before.

· • ● • ·

After the news report finished, I left the screen on for a while. The strange sentence you'd spoken sounded vaguely familiar to me, especially the first part.

Earth wakes and stones will speak.

It was as if I had read it somewhere, or heard someone else use it a long time ago.

A brief section of Earth news followed. In Barrier Reef Land there had been an uprising of workers demanding better food, because a few of them had died from a poisoning caused by contaminated fish. The riots had claimed ten victims. Hollywoodland had been left unexpectedly without electricity for nearly two days, and some tourists had had to delay their return to Mars and the cylinder cities. In the largest conservation area of South America the populations of several near-extinct bird species had begun to grow. In Paris 3 the managers of the holiday isle had been mailed strange envelopes filled with tree seeds. The contents were still being studied. The police were looking into a connection with similar incidents last year in Seoul and the Vacation Archipelago of Londons.

I thought of my parents in Winterland. I wondered how much they knew about all this. Or how little.

The transmission moved via the studio to a football field where players wearing red and purple shirts were running around against green grass. I switched the screen off. Ziggy, who had been sleeping curled into a ball in an armchair, raised his head, jumped to the bed and climbed onto my lap. I stroked his orange-and-white back.

I decided I needed to get out. The conference center where the symposium was being held was not far. I could make it there before the final panel discussion ended and surprise you. Just in case, I sent you a message, left a handwritten note on the bed and notified the reception there was a cat in the room that shouldn't be allowed to escape in the event of opening the door.

High above the streets the glass domes were beginning to dim into evening-time lighting. I have always preferred Datong after dark: it is a vast improvement on the purely functional brutalism of the daytime, where every last bit of wear and tear is visible, the fact obvious that at the time of the construction of the city Mars could not yet afford luxury. Datong has none of the splendor of Harmonia, but in the dusk it looks almost beautiful.

On the way I stopped to buy green tea in my fumbling Chinese. Along the streets merchants were pitching stalls, placing various foods on display: corn bars, grasshopper wafers, hot and cold drinks. Bright-colored greetings in various languages were painted on the gray canvas walls: 歡迎! Welcome! سهلا أهلاو! Добро пожаловать! Bienvenidxs! Bienvenue! Murmurations of starlings wafted like smoke above the rooftops. Faded blossoms had fallen from a vertical garden on the side of a tall building to cover the street. Their brown petals were crushed into the surface of the pavement.

· •●• ·

The conference center was huge, but after a bit of wandering about I found a sign that announced the Food Economy Research Symposium was in progress in the East Wing. The final session of the day was finishing. I stayed in the foyer and waited. In front of the tall windows on a long bench sat a woman who had covered her hair with a dark blue, star-patterned scarf. Her pen swung from side to side as she wrote on her portable screen, looked at what she'd written and puckered her lips. A couple of guards kept watch by the doors. On the curved external wall of the auditorium, three pairs of doors remained closed. When the clock struck seven, they opened, and people began to pour out. I looked for your dark hair and angled shoulders in the crowd, Sol, the bright purple shirt you had worn in the interview.

The stream of people narrowed down and trickled away, but I did not see you. I looked around and noticed a university colleague of yours in the vicinity of the front doors. I had met her a few times. I tried to remember her name – Leyla? The woman who had been writing on the bench had got up and was chatting with your colleague. Their lips moved, but I could not hear the words. They both burst into laughter. I approached them. Leyla glanced my way and noticed me. I reached out my hand.

"Hi, Leyla," I said. "I don't know if you remember me, I'm—"

"Of course," Leyla said. "Sol's spouse. What a nice surprise to meet you again." She shook my hand, but there was something slightly strange about the way she looked at me, an undercurrent I could not quite catch. "This is my friend Enisa Karim." The woman shook my hand and a dimple appeared on her cheek. "And this is..."

Leyla trailed off. I realized she had forgotten my name.

"Lumi," I said. "Nice to meet you."

The guards were beginning to close the double doors on the wall.

"Is Sol still in the auditorium?" I asked.

Leyla's eyes shifted a little in Enisa's direction. A small crease appeared on her forehead. Enisa spoke.

"Didn't they leave after the interview?" she asked. "Over an hour ago?"

"They did," Leyla said. "That's why I was surprised to see you here." She directed these words at me.

Enisa noticed my confusion.

"Oh, sorry. I'm a journalist. I was meant to interview your spouse, but Channel 12 managed to somehow cut in and I lost my chance." Her mouth made a tight line. The dimple vanished.

"Sol and I must have crossed," I said. "If for any reason you see them, could you let them know I'm waiting at the hotel?"

"Of course," Leyla replied. "I hope you find each other."

The foyer was empty now, save for the three of us and one guard who hovered near the exit, giving us the occasional decreasingly subtle stare. The doors to the auditorium had been locked. The lights began to switch off, leaving us in a small pool of dim glow, outside which the corners could have hidden a lost shadow of any shape.

I took my leave.

• • ● • •

I returned to the hotel as quickly as possible. When I opened the door of the room with caution, Ziggy tried to slip away into the corridor. I scooped him up, held him with one arm and pulled the door closed with my other hand.

Your coat and suitcase were gone, Sol. I looked in the bathroom and wardrobe. You had not left a trace behind; it was as if you'd never been to the room at all. The only thing hanging in the wardrobe was the threadbare cardigan I'd brought from Earth. Behind it, something did not look right: the angles of light and shadow, the shape of the wall. It was as if the space had slipped out of joint, but only a little, almost unnoticeably.

The safe.

As a precaution, I had placed the locked box you'd asked me to bring in there. I had keyed in a number code on the old-fashioned keypad of the safe, and tried the door to make certain it was locked. Now the door was ajar. I pushed the cardigan on the hanger aside, reached for the safe and pulled the door wide open.

The safe was empty. The wooden box was gone.

Sol, only you know I always use your birthday as the PIN code. Then again, it is not exactly an original choice from my part and would not be hard to guess.

I left Ziggy in the room despite his protestations and rushed to the reception desk downstairs. The young dark-haired receptionist from the afternoon was alone in the lobby, and stopped scratching at his wrists when he recognized me. He quickly pulled his sleeves down to cover the dark rash.

"My room number is 513," I said. "I was supposed to meet my spouse, but they seem to have been held up by something. Have they left me a message?"

"Just a moment, please," the receptionist said. He swiped his screen and looked at it. "It was Sol Uriarte, wasn't it? They checked out a quarter of an hour ago. The room has been paid for until tomorrow."

"Did they leave a message?" I asked again.

The receptionist's expression turned apologetic.

"I'm afraid not," he said. He browsed the information on the screen. "Oh. Actually – there is one for room 513."

I waited. The receptionist read his screen behind the desk and his eyebrows drew closer together.

"I am sorry," he said. "The message is for your spouse." The word came smoothly from his mouth now, without the slightest hesitation. "It was sent in the early afternoon, immediately after they checked in."

"I can pass it on to them," I said.

The receptionist's face changed.

"We don't usually give private messages to anyone but the recipient," he said. "Not even the spouse."

I tried to think fast.

"They… asked me to pass on any messages left for them here," I said. "They were expecting an urgent work message. It must be that one."

The receptionist looked reluctant and uncomfortable.

"It is against the rules," he said.

I watched him. The sleeves of his suit were slightly too short. The crater-map lesions on his wrists were caught in the sharp shadow the sleeve-ends drew on his skin.

"That must itch," I said. "Lichen planus is a pain to live with."

The receptionist looked down, confused.

"Have you got anything for it?" I asked.

"Some cream I brought from Earth," he said. "But I haven't got a lot left. It's really expensive here."

"I have an ointment," I said. "Not identical. Better, actually. I don't have much use for it myself."

Understanding spread onto the receptionist's face. His eyes wandered. He stared at his wrists, then at me. Eventually he took a breath and said, "One moment, please." He disappeared into the back room and returned after a brief spell. "The envelope is not here. It has already been taken to the room."

"Do you know who left the message?"

"There were two of them. They wore entirely ordinary clothing."

"No uniforms?"

The receptionist shook his head.

"Jumpsuits, boots. I think one had a leather jacket and the other one a parka," he said.

"Did they speak Martian English?"

He nodded.

"Did either of them have an accent?"

The receptionist hesitated. I remembered he'd only been on Mars for a few months, and might not be able to recognize an accent.

"Never mind," I said. "Thank you."

Oh well. The ointment will improve his quality of life, and I can always make some more.

• • ● • •

I found the envelope in the drawer of the night table after a brief search. Maybe it had been there all along: when I unpacked my bag, when I watched you on my screen, when I looked for you at the symposium. It was an old-fashioned paper envelope, not a reusable permawallet. Your name was handwritten on it, Sol, and the number 513.

I hope you can forgive me. The envelope was already torn open.

I pulled out the paper note and read the words typed on it.

Earth wakes and stones will speak, and darkness recedes over waters.

The same sentence again.

I swiped my screen on and began to search.

About twenty minutes later it was clear to me that the web would not help. The only result that matched the sentence was a short story written under a pen name and published on an amateur writers' forum. The rest of the hits were coincidences of a couple of words. Nevertheless, I was certain I'd heard it somewhere before.

And now I have arrived at the moment when I began writing:

sitting on the bed, my screen next to me, all dark, not flashing or pinging with words from you. I am tired, Sol. I may lie down. Perhaps you sleep a deep and restful sleep somewhere not far from me, and when I wake up, I will understand.

6.3.2168
Halley 105 Hotel
Datong, Mars
Even later

Sol,
A knock on the door of the hotel room just woke me. It could not have been you, could it? When I went to the door and looked into the hallway, it was empty. Maybe it was a dream. It is not uncommon for me to be woken by sounds that are not from this world. On Fuxi I was often stirred from sleep by the doorbell in the mornings, and there was never anyone at the door.

I'd fallen asleep on the bed with Ziggy stretched sideways across my legs. I dreamed of a large animal walking before me, leading me through a forest with soft paws, and unfamiliar stars shone above. A tree rose on the horizon, its roots deep as the heart of the earth and branches tall enough to touch moons.

I finally recognize the sentence. Before this day, I'd only ever heard one person use it. Back then, I'd believed it was her own personal refrain, a path woven from words she used to open hidden worlds. Every healer has those, myself included.

Sol, where are you, and how did Vivian's words end up in your mouth?

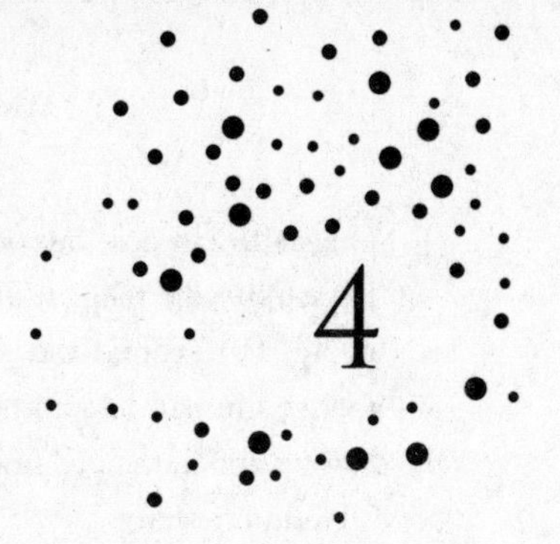

4

Sender: Sol Uriarte
Recipient: Lumi Salo
Date: 7.3.2168 00.11 MST
Security: Maximum encryption

Work emergency. It is best you return home and
wait for me there. I'll call as soon as I can. ♥
S
PS. Remember the Blue Room in the Moonday House.

7.3.2168
A train somewhere between Datong and Elysium
Isidis Planitia, Mars

Sol,
Your message pinged onto my screen after midnight. I stared at it. The air conditioning of the hotel room hummed faintly. The image imitating a window glowed on the wall, showing white silver birches with their leaves stirring in the dusk as a soft wind moved through them: a view captured somewhere far from this place and time, the trees probably long dead now. Ziggy was washing his paw at the foot of the bed, gnawing at each claw like a bird's bone.

I began to ransack the room.

I started with the safe. I lit the inside with my screen as well as I could, felt around the smooth walls and ceiling millimeter by millimeter. You had left nothing but shadows in there. I searched in the drawers and in the bed linen, on the floor and under Ziggy's water bowl. I found nothing.

The leaves made of pixels turned, their dark-stained green shone one moment, dimmed into frost-veined the next. I sat down on the bed and switched the wall off. It faded into dusk.

Remember the Blue Room in the Moonday House.

I closed my eyes and began to walk through the Moonday House toward the Blue Room. I passed several kitchens, stopped in the gallery where daylight fell through the wide window on the ceiling to the paintings hanging on the walls, I walked across the winter garden. On each step I saw the Blue Room more clearly. I hope you see it the same way, Sol: I have not forgotten that one time you claimed the Yellow Room was a bedroom, when it is definitely a library. Your memory betrays you more often than mine does me.

I opened my eyes. The hotel bathroom door was slightly ajar. Through the gap I could see a narrow stripe of my reflection.

Mirrors. The Blue Room is a hall of mirrors.

The door gave no sound when I pushed it open and stepped through into the dim lighting. I remembered another bathroom from years ago, a light filtering through a tall, frosted-glass window. Some mornings, while you still slept, I left messages you wouldn't see until later, when you'd get up and the steam from the shower concentrated on the cool surfaces of the walls.

My reflection moved, as I lifted my hand near the surface of the mirror. In the dusk it could have been you, familiar and yet out of reach, caught in a world of shadows and fading outlines. I put my face right next to the glass, taking care not to touch it. I breathed out through my mouth. The steam spread as mist on the mirror. I sighed a frost the size of my face on the glass surface and took a step back.

I sought carefully, because I knew the pattern might not be clear to see. At first, I saw nothing. Then, at the edge of the evaporating mist, I discerned an arch that might have been a part of a letter or figure. I turned the lighting up. I bent closer and breathed on the glass again. The letters grew visible, faint but comprehensible.

YSIUM, you had written on the mirror with your finger.

Elysium. It could not mean anything else.

You have been going there on work trips for years. I once asked to go with you.

If you want, you said. But there's nothing there. It's just a research station, and its botanical garden, which is closed to the general public. A few farming zones. You'd get bored.

I erased the message with a towel and soapy water.

An hour later I had made my decision.

• • ● • •

I'm writing this in the crammed sleeper cabin of a train. It is right next to the engine room, and the noise is rather like gigantic mining robots throwing boulders or cast-iron teapots at each other. You'd think they would have come up with a noiseless engine by now, but I suppose the neighbors – containers of powdered vegan milk and recycled toilet roll and corn starch, that is – don't mind. I bought a ticket for a freight train, because all passenger departures were fully booked until the day after tomorrow. I'd forgotten it is First Settlers' Day this weekend, and everyone is going home for family celebrations.

It is almost midnight. Ziggy has gone hunting. Turns out these food transfers have quite the rodent problem, and poison cannot be used for health and safety reasons. Ziggy was welcomed onboard without extra charge, when I praised his rat-catching skills. I don't know why this surprised me. Pests have hitched rides with humans to new islands and continents as long as we have known how to cross those distances; why should space be any different? We leave a trace of ourselves wherever we go: a plastic bag printed with a supermarket logo at the bottom of the deepest sea, a soft drink can half-buried in mud on a high mountain, a dump of toxic waste amid the bone-white dust of the Moon.

I expect you will know what all these words are really about, Sol. They are the wool I spin around myself and over my eyes, the better to shield worry from sight for a while. For I do worry. You sent me a message saying one thing, then left another on the mirror, near-faded by the time I knew to look for it. I might not have known to look for it at all. Why, Sol?

I would not say it in an electronic message, but I will say it on this page made of paper, only mine to read, and yours, once we meet again: I know there are things you have not told me.

There are long, idle hours ahead of me. I must fill them with something. I can stare into darkness, and think, and let memories roam. They are always present, like dense-growing trees in a far-stretching forest, and somewhere out of sight their roots intertwine. Among the roots, side by side with seeds that never sprouted and long-abandoned, half-decomposed husks, lie buried the words I seek.

Earth wakes and stones will speak, and darkness recedes over waters.

I have tried to remember when I heard the sentence for the first time. It belonged in Vivian's mouth, and when I think of it, it is as if she has stepped into the room and is standing next to me again, guiding my movements as I perform the dance and beat my drum.

Moments emerge before me: she sits cross-legged, a crochet shawl pulled around her shoulders, a thick book lifted near her face. She buys herbs from a stall in some narrow, poorly lit alley that smells of fried vegetables, incense and, underneath, cats. I hear her switch between languages until the stall keeper understands.

She scolds me so gently I don't realize until later, with delayed shame, that I've been scolded. She refuses to accept payment from a patient whose shoes are broken and room bare, and even gives him money for food, because the previous house where we healed had its own indoor garden, furniture made from extinct Earth trees and an owner who paid generously for treating his dog.

Many times I have tried to bring Vivian back to me through words. So I would not forget. So she would not be gone for good. Yet, at the same time, I admit I wished to keep her to myself. I made certain you only knew little about her, Sol. It may have been selfish. I knew I had no right to claim ownership. She had taught so many. She had the ability to see into the core of people and notice what could be schooled and strengthened. She was one of the most skilled healers I had met, but she was even better at seeing that tendency in others. She wished to nourish and train, guide like sunlight guides a vine in the right direction: not through change or violation, but through letting the student's own strength grow.

Sol, I used to think of my life before you as an open road that ran nearly parallel to yours, until one day the angle at which our routes slowly approached each other brought them together. Now I wonder if there were crossroads in the past that have remained hidden: moments when our separate paths crossed each other, unknown to either of us. At those crossroads stands Vivian, silent and white-haired, who looks both ways and knows, but does not tell.

In order to understand, I must look her way. I must tell myself of the past, and tell you, Sol: see it with new eyes through words. Stories brighten the reality and bring out something unforeseen, they make a little less broken that which bears a fracture upon it.

• • ● • •

I was sixteen when I met Vivian. I had been moved from the reindeer pen to work at the coffee shop, and it was the best thing I knew. I still had to get up at five in the morning and wash with cold water in the communal sauna, but I no longer had to spend the whole day outdoors carrying lichen and twigs, or cleaning the large corrals in the thick, fermenting-acid stench of reindeer piss. It was spring, the quiet time between seasons, and there were not many customers in Winterland.

A woman whose age I couldn't estimate walked in. Everyone over twenty-five looked like an ancient relic to me. She was wearing a loose-hanging jumper, tight jeans and ankle boots, the tips of which had worn colorless. There was no trace of makeup on her face, and the nearly white hair had been pulled into a messy ponytail at the nape of her neck. She glanced at me, smiled and walked across the coffee shop without ordering anything, straight onto the terrace despite the fact that it was chilly. She sat down at a table next to the handrail and lit a cigarette. That was unusual. Even wealthy Martian tourists rarely had cigarettes.

The day spread bright as glass around us. I watched the woman sitting on the terrace, waited for her to come in and place an order. She gazed over the handrail into the distance, blew smoke out of her mouth. It floated in the air as a gray skein. The dusty smell of tobacco smoke drifted in. I was alone at work that day, and my shift was only halfway through. I glanced at the door, then at the other tables. There were only a few people sitting at them. No one approached in the stairs, and no one seemed in a hurry to get up.

I left my place behind the counter and walked to the terrace. The table at which the woman was sitting was partially concealed behind a thick timber column. As I approached, I noticed her lips moving. At first I thought she was talking to herself, but then I saw a large white bird behind the column, sitting on the handrail right next to the woman's shoulder. The bird had a long, pliant neck, a yellow beak and a dark, mask-like pattern around its eyes.

The woman was speaking to the bird in a soft voice. Her words drowned in the air and vanished before I had time to trace their shapes.

When I stopped next to the table, the woman went quiet and turned to look at me.

A beautiful bird, I said.

There was a shift in the woman's eyes and something about her posture changed.

But it must have escaped from somewhere, I continued. I'll have to report it to the Winterland watch unit.

The woman looked at me as if I'd been standing in the dark before and now the light had caught me.

Where do you think he came from? she asked. Like most tourists, she spoke English, but I couldn't place her accent. It didn't sound like any of the Mars accents I was used to hearing.

There are birds in Lakeworld safari park, I said. Maybe it came as a stowaway on a vessel, or lost its way.

The woman turned to look at the bird. It seemed to me her lips formed a word in a language I could not recognize. The bird spread its wings and the air murmured as it took flight. Its feathers shone, a white foam against the water-blue of the sky, and then it was gone, like mist dissipated over treetops.

I lost words for a moment. I stared at the sky. Wind turned in the pine trees.

Birds don't lose their way, the woman said, but her voice was not unkind. Rather, it sounded amused. Can I place an order?

We have no table service, I said and realized I should have said it much earlier. I felt a blush rise to my face.

The woman eyed at me for a long while. I felt like I was a book she was reading, taking notes. Evaluating. A cold breeze blew past, carrying the scent of night frosts.

You can order sandwiches, hot lunch and various drinks at the counter. The tea of the day is mullein—

It tastes like hay, the woman interrupted. She stubbed out her cigarette on the handrail and swept hair off her face. You probably don't have coffee, do you?

Unfortunately not, I said. In this area it only comes included in the complete Sleigh and Fell Hike Package.

I glanced inside. The other customers had not moved from their tables.

The woman smiled a sudden smile.

I'm not here for the complete Sleigh and Fell Hike Package, she said. But I'll let you out of your misery.

She pushed her chair backward and got up. The metal legs screeched against the concrete floor.

I'd like to look at the lunch menu.

Please, I said and gave way. She walked ahead of me indoors. I returned behind the counter. She eyed the menu.

Very retro, she commented. Goes with the décor.

I did not understand at the time what she meant. I'd only ever been outside Winterland once, and the employees' holiday village had not looked too different, the shabbiness aside. There were things out on other holiday isles that we didn't have, such as beaches and cathedrals and rollercoasters: I'd seen those in pictures. And outside Earth things were significantly different. Those pictures I kept under my bed, between the pages of an old book, where my parents would not look. But I wasn't entirely certain what *retro* was, so I smiled and said nothing.

The woman ordered a soup with bread. As she was picking up the tray, she seemed to recall something. She placed the tray down and dug a portable screen out of her pocket. It fitted in her palm. A faint light was kindled on the display.

Can you tell me where to find this address? the woman asked and turned the screen toward me. I recognized it: the house surrounded by a tall fence was only a couple of kilometers from here, one of the few that were not the long, narrow, mildew-stained buildings meant for the workers of Winterland.

I told her how to find the route. She thanked me and reached out her hand.

My name is Vivian, she said.

I stared at the hand for a moment before knowing how to react. I couldn't remember any customer introducing themselves by name before.

Lumi, I said and shook Vivian's hand.

Before she walked back to the terrace, she turned toward me once more.

Are you going to report that bird?

I nodded.

They'll never find him, she said.

Her gaze held me for another moment, seeking something, and then she turned her back.

· • ● • ·

Vivian came back the following week. She ordered a soup at the counter and took it out to the terrace despite the freezing weather. She had wrapped a thick woolen shawl on top of her leather coat. I looked through the window and saw her pull it tighter around herself. There was only one other customer in the coffee shop, a middle-aged man absorbed in playing a popular game on his portable screen with headphones over his ears.

Vivian blew at her steaming soup. It wouldn't stay warm for long. I felt cold too, although it was warm indoors. I left my place behind the counter, picked up a blanket from a long bench next to the door and opened the door to the terrace. A frostbitten wind hit me in the face.

Vivian had sat down at the same table as last time. When I walked closer, I saw a glimpse of something white at her feet. The long-necked, yellow-beaked bird stood on the floor next to Vivian's chair, half-hidden under the table. I stopped by the handrail and offered the blanket to Vivian.

It's unusually cold today, I said.

Vivian took the blanket.

Thank you, she said.

I nodded toward the white bird.

Is that your pet?

Vivian was spreading the blanket on top of her legs. The movement of her hands stopped and she looked at me with a strange expression on her face.

No, she said.

I waited for an explanation of some kind, but she did not continue.

Would you like me to bring it a piece of bread? I asked. It was forbidden to feed animals in the coffee shop, but no one would know. The security cameras had been defunct for some time.

He's not hungry, Vivian said. Besides, bread is bad for swans.

I nodded. A swan. I had thought they were extinct. Vivian tilted her head and regarded me.

Are you unwell? she asked. You look a little pale.

I'm just tired, I replied. It was true. I had not slept well in the past couple of months. Restless dreams bothered me, and I woke up several times a night to strange sounds that seemed to be coming from the same room or from right behind the wall, although there was nothing there but a locked storage space. Once I had been certain there was a large animal standing next to my bed, its fur speckled and its glinting eyes watching me in silence. When I'd switched on the night light, the room was empty. My head ached, but I didn't want to tell Vivian that.

Hey there!

I had not noticed the terrace door opening. The man who had

been playing on his screen had removed the headphones and stood on the doorstep, looking annoyed.

Can I get some service here? I'd like to order another hot toddy.

The white bird stepped forward from under the table, took a few running steps on the floor and spread its wings. I didn't have time to do anything when it flew into the man's face. The white wings split the air like swirling snow. I imagined the man's bloody face, the punishment I'd be given because I had not chased the bird off the terrace before it attacked a customer. The wings beat once more, twice, and then the bird was gone.

I didn't see where it disappeared. It was as if it had melted into the gray of the land, forest and sky, plunged behind the landscape.

The ache in my head had sharpened into a shining pain behind my left eye. I stared at the man in horror. He did not have a scratch on him.

How about that toddy? he demanded.

Vivian gave me a slanted smile and nodded toward the inside. I finally got my legs to work and started in the direction of the door.

Sorry about the wait, I told the man. The bird didn't hurt you, did it?

The man looked at me like I had asked for a lift to Mars in his suitcase.

What bird? he said.

My headache uncoiled, so severe I could barely think.

Would you prefer a rum toddy or an eggnog? I managed.

The door closed behind us. I heard Vivian move her chair. I thought I heard wide wings fold.

· • ● • ·

A week later, on a clear and cold spring evening, as I was returning home from work, I saw Vivian walking along the side of the highway. The large, patterned shawl I'd seen her wearing at the coffee shop covered her shoulders, and she carried a worn leather doctor's bag in her hand. In her other hand she held a peculiar mask, on which I discerned a long, yellow bird's beak. The sky was still pale, but the first evening stars and the lights of the cylinder cities were beginning to brighten and grow visible: Saraswati, Kokyangwuti and Bastet moved along the Earth orbit, blinded by their own radiance.

Vivian walked at a brisk pace approximately twenty meters ahead of me. I found myself making my footsteps lighter so she wouldn't hear them. When she made an abrupt turn, stepped over the low metal fence that followed the road and walked directly into the forest that rose scarce, I stopped. She halted at the edge of the woods for a moment, seemed to listen. I was certain she'd see me. But she looked in the other direction, began walking again and vanished between the trees.

The ache behind my eyes was milder that day, and the glassy light of late spring made me restless. I could have continued along the road toward home. Instead, I stepped over the fence and followed Vivian to a strange path.

She had got so far ahead that for a moment I thought I'd lost her entirely. Then I saw movement farther away between the pine trunks. It had rained, and drops fell onto my face and head from the branches. My shoes slipped against the roots and sank into the mud of the forest floor. I'd have to clean them later in the evening. In the green of the damp meadow, wood anemones were closing their corollas, hundreds of dim-white stars in the dusk of the forest. I wanted to walk among them, but I did not wish to be left farther behind Vivian.

I was careful with my steps so I would not catch her attention. My movements dissolved into the whispers and rustlings of the woods. I began to realize where she was going. The path wound toward the house, the route to which she had asked me about on our first meeting at the coffee shop.

The house was built right at the edge of the forest and sheltered by a tall fence. I had walked past the gate before. It was always locked. Vivian stopped outside and rang the doorbell. There was a buzz in the loudspeaker, and the gate opened. Vivian stepped through and disappeared from sight.

I waited for the metal clang of the gate. It did not come.

When I believed I had waited long enough, I walked closer. I didn't even know why I did it. The gate must certainly have been locked after Vivian. In the worst case, I'd be ambushed by some guard and a complaint would be filed to the management of Winterland about a worker who didn't know her place.

The gate was cracked open.

I stared at it. I tried to think of a story I could tell if I crept onto the yard of the house and got caught. I was practicing juggling with my key, and it flew across the fence by mistake? I was on my way to visit a friend, and got the address wrong – as if the workers of the holiday isle socialized with people who lived in houses like this? On the way home my arm detached itself and scurried through the gate on its own, and I came looking for it?

I decided to leave some space for improvisation. The hinges made no sound when I opened the gate further and stepped into the garden.

The house was an old-time timber castle. I don't believe you have ever seen one, Sol: in my native tongue they'd been called woodlace villas once upon a time after the decorative woodcut patterns circling their eaves. It was painted a light green color. The paint surface looked so fresh it might have stained your fingers. Yet the house must have been old, because wooden houses were no longer built, unless they were part of the period look of a holiday isle.

The windows were large. I felt on display. They were covered by drawn curtains, and I saw no movement. Carefully, I stepped in my muddy shoes toward the lawn where a few shelter-giving shrubs grew. A lilac hedge enveloped the lawn, its flowers opening to early summer. I slipped behind it, and discovered that there was a narrow passage between the lilacs and the tall fence. The leaf-shaped shadows clung to my skin as I began to walk through the passage. Once or twice a branch caught on my clothes. I moved slowly, stopping every few steps, but the house and the garden remained still.

I reached the other side of the house. On the external wall a ladder ran to a terrace on the first floor. One of the windows was open, and a slow, heartbeat-like pulsation carried from inside.

A pang of pain cut through my head. I covered my eyes with my palms and took a deep breath. Slowly the pain settled into a dull ache. I had come this far. I did not want to turn back.

I crossed the lawn quickly, pressed into the shadow against the wall and waited. A wind brushed past. A cloud covered the sun. I began to climb the ladder as silently as possible.

There was a curtain-covered window on the door of the terrace. In the curtain there was a gap through which I was able to see into the house.

Vivian was moving around the room, her body swaying back and forth, and she beat a slow rhythm on a drum. I saw now that the large shawl on her shoulders was a cape with a pair of bird wings painted on it. She had placed the mask on her face. Black streaks surrounded her eyes, and the beak shone yellow against the white feathers. Vivian's low voice hummed a rolling song to the beat of the drum in a language I did not know. At the center of the room, inside the circle that Vivian drew with her footsteps and her song, lay a girl wrapped in a blanket. She was perhaps a couple of years younger than me. I recognized her. I'd seen her a few times on the yards and streets of Winterland in a dark-shining electric car, shadows under her eyes and her posture slumped, as if a great weight was crushing her.

Her thin, blond hair was spread across the pillow on which her head rested. There were marks drawn on her face in blue dye, her eyes were open and they gazed into nothingness. When I looked at her, my headache grew stronger again and cold passed through me. It was as if a piece of me had drifted away and disappeared, leaving behind a rift in which an empty darkness made a heavy nest. The feeling was the same as when I'd seen the girl in passing, but much more intense.

A slightly sweet scent of burning floated through the window. In the corner of the room the swan spread its wings like a white flame.

The drumbeats began to accelerate. I could hear whooshing of bird flight and the gallop of land-treading animals in them. Vivian's movements grew into a dance in which I discerned something akin to a chase. Her footsteps sought, stopped, and waited for the right moment. She sprung and shook and shrieked, seemed to snare something invisible. There was a slight struggle, like a breeze blowing through trees, and then silence. Whatever it was, Vivian carried it back with her, as if from afar. She placed it gently in the hands of the girl who lay on the floor and enclosed the girl's fingers around it, until she had a hold. She took a pinch of gray-white powder from a silicone pouch and rubbed it onto the girl's forehead, where it formed a shimmering pattern, like a frost-flower.

The girl's fingers stroked the air slowly for a few times. They stopped. She took a deep breath and shivered, then sat up. The absent look evaporated from her eyes. In a faint voice she asked for water. Her fingers squeezed into a tight knot, held what Vivian had returned to her. The dark weight receded, the rift under my skin closed itself, and I understood that the sensations were reflections, their origin outside of me. I felt in my own body what Vivian's patient did.

I started when Vivian looked directly at the window: briefly enough for no one in the room to pay attention, but long enough to look me in the eye.

She turned her back on me. I heard the words she addressed to someone else, perhaps the girl's parents.

You may open the curtains now, Vivian said. The session is over.

I began to climb down with a hammering heart.

· • ● • ·

I made my way to the gate in the cover of the lilac hedge as quietly as possible, the fragile scent of the flowers a mist around me. Outside the gate I began to run. The ache throbbed behind my eyes as I ran across the darkening forest, over slippery stones and roots that wriggled like snakes in the half-light. Even as I reached the highway I did not stop. I slowed down only once I was near home, around the corner from the long, low buildings, in the backyard where nothing grew but a bit of downtrodden grass and weeds. The power was down, and the whole high sky opened above, the limits of which I could not see.

That night, when my father and mother had gone to sleep, I dug out the yellowed book from under my bed and began turning the pages. Under the duvet in the fading light of a solar lamp I looked at the pictures I had torn from magazines left by tourists. My fingers brushed the tearooms glowing amid the vast, bare Moon deserts. In my mind I walked in the glass-domed underground gardens of Mars, and sat at candlelit restaurant tables before vast windows that looked into the infinity of space, with Earth a tiny watercolor speck in the upper corner.

The room we lived in had never felt so crammed.

· • ● • ·

After that night, my health deteriorated quickly. I was somehow able to get my work done, because there were so few customers, but I was scared to think of early summer, when the stream of tourists in search of the midnight sun would begin. Sometimes I had to lie down on the kitchen floor when there was no one in the coffee shop. Cold sweat streamed down my neck regardless of how many layers of wool I wore, or how airy my clothing was.

My parents noticed something was wrong. My mother felt my

forehead with a concerned look on her face and took me to the medical center for the employees, where we waited four hours. The doctor listened to my lungs and heart, gave me a packet of anti-inflammatory painkillers and sent me home. I was given one day's sick leave from work.

It's probably not contagious, he said, because your parents have no symptoms.

· •●• ·

Vivian would come to the coffee shop occasionally. A few times I spotted her watching me from the terrace through the window. When she saw I had noticed, she turned her gaze away. I'd reported the swan to the watch unit after the case of the screen man, but Vivian had been right: the guards had not found the bird.

The constant fever did not abate. The aches spread to my entire body. They came and went in waves that never disappeared entirely. Nights were the worst. I spent them mostly drifting in and out of sleep, on the outskirts of wakefulness, halfway between both worlds. Sometimes I felt like I was being slowly torn to pieces from the inside. The sounds still bothered me, and they had grown louder: a forest of whispers, too dense to discern a word – a whooshing like wind or water – footsteps that came and went. They kept me awake when the pains faded enough that I might have fallen asleep for a moment.

The turning point came on a livelier than usual day in the coffee shop. A group of twenty Martian tourists had sat down for lunch, and there were two other employees working besides me that day. The ache behind my eyes was so strong that I had to stop every few minutes to cover them with my hands. The darkness alleviated the pain a little, for a moment. I had just brought the tourists their drinks, when I saw through the window a large animal on the terrace. It stood still among the empty tables and looked directly at me. Its fur was the color of light gold, a little darker on the back side, and had black speckles. There were tufts on the tips of its ears. The look in the golden cat eyes was keen, as if it could see such stars in the sky that no other creature could perceive. The animal's tail was short, its paws wide and certain. I remembered the name of the animal, because as a child I had seen pictures of it in a book that displayed extinct species.

Lynx.

I stared at the animal. It stared back. I recited the safety rules in my head, the emergency protocol I had learned. No one had ever told me what to do when an extinct beast appeared at a coffee shop full of customers.

I went to the terrace door and locked it. When I turned around, I noticed Mira – the older coffee shop employee – watching me in a strange manner.

Is everything all right? she asked, when I returned to the counter.

I lowered my voice.

Call the guards, I whispered.

Mira's eyebrows rose.

Why? she asked. What's wrong?

There's a beast on the terrace, I said. A lynx.

Mira glanced in the direction of the terrace, looking startled.

Are you certain? she asked.

I looked to the terrace. The lynx had sat down. It was still staring at me. Its posture and face were calm. Slowly it blinked its golden eyes.

I locked the door, I said. But the customers should be warned.

Mira glanced at the terrace again, then looked at me.

Are you feeling all right? she said and felt my forehead. Her hand was damp. The sensation was unpleasant.

I've just been sleeping poorly lately, I said. The ache behind my eyes had grown into a permanent part of me. I couldn't remember the last time a whole day had passed when I had not felt it.

Your forehead is all hot, Mira said. She took my arm and walked me to the kitchen. She moved a few boxes to the floor from the top of the stool in the corner and poured me a glass of water from the tap. Sit there, she said and handed me the water glass. I'll be back in a minute.

My legs gave out under me. I sat down on the stool. Mira gave me another concerned look and disappeared around the corner. I heard her talking on the phone in a low voice. I only discerned a word here and there.

... temperature... not seem capable of working... scare the customers... her parents... all right. I'll call you back. Bye.

The floor spread into a vast, gray space before my eyes and rose upright. It drew closer, until I discerned a sticky dirt stain on it, a crack in the concrete, shaped like a tree root, and an insect crushed against the bottom edge of the worktop. Then everything was darkness and flares and ache that spread into ripples and wrenched me away.

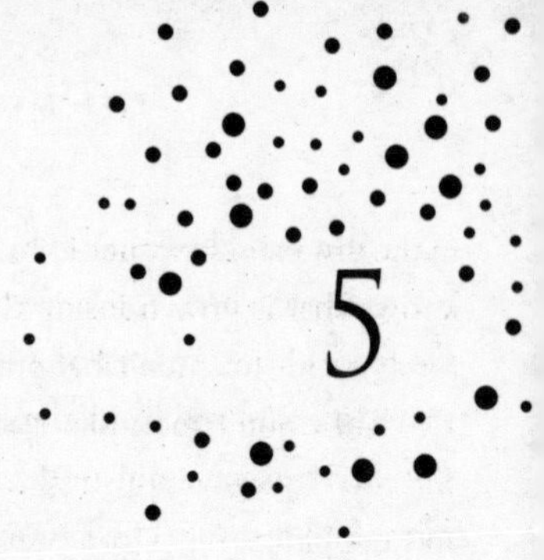

5

Sender: Sol Uriarte
Recipient: Lumi Salo
Date: 8.3.2168 09.44 MST
Security: Maximum encryption

I got your message. I'm sorry I haven't been able to pick up calls. Everything's fine.
S

8.3.2168
Still a train somewhere between
Datong and Elysium Isidis Planitia, Mars

Sol,
I'd like to believe you, but I think of the ghosts of letters in the bathroom mirror, and of other things: Vivian's words in your mouth, everything that happened after Fuxi.

If you are in Elysium, I intend to find you.

In the meantime, it is night, and the train has been running in a glass tube overground for hours by now. Long, dark moments are broken by pale globes of light that occasionally rise on the plain, like dim, white pearls scattered across the obscure landscape. They emerge in the distance, shimmer for a moment, and then it is dark again. I don't know what is grown inside the globes. Vegetarian protein, insects for food, molds for medicinal purposes? You might know.

They don't look like residential areas: the globes are too scarce and too clinically industrial for that. If ancient Earth stories were true and people had lived on Mars before we arrived, maybe this is what their cities would have looked like. For some reason I imagine them to be more plant-like than humanoid. I see one of them before my eyes: their skin is like the bark of a tall and dark tree, radiation does not gnaw it like thin human skin. They can stay still for a long time like a twig, push their long, many-forked limbs into the ground and absorb nutrition from the soil that is toxic for us.

They don't need eyes or ears, because they sense everything through their skin, and dust storms or changes in temperature do not harm them. The soil connects them with their own kind: the deep-reaching limbs keep growing longer and meeting each other under the layers of sand, until they form a network covering the entire planet and transmitting neural impulses. In these encounters they recognize the happiness and sadness and longing of their kin, recognize the small stirrings of the earth and sense the shifts in weather from hundreds of kilometers away along invisible strings. They breathe through their skin and life flows in them, ceaseless and rippling, for they are part of a larger whole. Their senses are vaster than themselves, and their home reaches far beyond the limits of their own body, and they are never alone.

But there are also moments when the never-ending experience of the emotions and sensations and moods of others grows exhausting. That is when they gather their limbs close, detach themselves from the network, move away from their spot and seal themselves in a globe, where they will only sense their own self; their mind is allowed to rest and their self return to its own outline. Only once they feel complete and whole again, they will return and take their place as part of the unending movements of the web.

I wonder what they will do when they one day sense humans in the distance, taking the first step on their land. Will they reach out for us, interested in an encounter, in opening their world to us? Or will they send a message to their own: *hide, hide, for alien life is here, and it does not care what kind of imprint it leaves in our dust.*

Sol, I was going to ask you what those dim globes in the darkness of the plain are, but I no longer need that knowledge. No answer could be as satisfactory as my own mental image of a Martian resting its senses, never mind that I know it to be imaginary. Sometimes imagination is more important than the truth. Not because it covers the truth, but because it expands it and makes its potential bigger.

Here, in the dark of the surface of a strange planet, where I cannot take your hand, I still search the nooks of the past for words that somehow found their way into you.

· • ● • ·

I remember little about the last phase of the sickness. I lay under thick blankets in my bed and sweated. I lay under thick blankets in my bed and shivered with cold. My parents had hung threadbare rag rugs and comforters on the concrete walls to keep in the warmth. Their patterns moved as I looked at them. They swirled in spirals and opened into sharp-toothed maws that did not disappear even when I closed my eyes. The noises bothered me relentlessly. Occasionally I discerned my parents' conversations among them, but it was difficult to know which ones were real.

She needs a doctor, my mother said.

How are we going to pay for it? my father said.

What if she dies?

Don't say that in her presence.

She's too sick to understand.

My mother paused and continued, There's a healer visiting Winterland. A white-haired woman. She's been going to that big house at the edge of the woods for many weeks.

We definitely can't afford her, my father said.

Real healers don't heal for money, my mother replied.

Right, I'm sure she's tending to the daughter of the manager of Winterland out of the goodness of her heart.

You don't know what you're talking about.

It's not like in your grandma's time.

I'm going to ask her anyway.

My father was quiet. His footsteps withdrew.

I remember Vivian sitting in the corner of the room. She came and felt my forehead, lifted a cup of water to my lips, and I drank. She sat in the corner again. It was light in the room even at night. It was early June. Vivian drew a figure on my forehead with a cool finger. Her fingertip was dim white with dye. She was gone again.

The same animal with speckled fur I had seen on the coffee shop terrace sat on the floor. Its slanted, golden eyes opened, closed, opened. It looked at me, into me, and saw every vein and nerve and thought. I was not afraid of it. I could discern clearly the hairs poking out of its thick, coarse fur, each pale bristle against the light spring-dusk of the room. The animal walked with large, silent paws next to my bed. The distance was short.

The lynx began to sniff me out. Its whiskers tickled my face, and a warm, tangy animal smell emanated from it. It placed a paw on my chest, ever so light. The claws remained withdrawn. As if it was stroking me.

Vivian stepped into the room. The white, long-necked bird was by her side. The lynx looked at Vivian, calm, without aggression. It lifted its paw off my chest. Its short tail twitched, and it stayed sitting down on the floor. The swan took a few curious steps toward the lynx. Vivian followed the scene from the doorway. The lynx sniffed the bird, got up to its feet and raised its tail. Its cat-face seemed to smile wider than usual.

It turned to look at me for a moment. Then it walked through the wall.

Vivian said nothing. She sat down again in the corner of the room. The swan pushed itself to her lap from the floor and settled there. My eyes fell closed. The next time I woke up, Vivian was snoozing with her head uncomfortably against the wall. Her mouth hung open. The swan was gone.

• • ● • •

Afterward, my parents said Vivian healed me. Vivian said I healed myself. She only watched as the spirits fought, and my body was close to breaking under the heavy weight of their battle. Occasionally she would bear a mug of water to me, or place a cold compress on my forehead, or burn freshening herbs in an incense bowl, so breathing would be easier. But she did not interfere with the battle, so she said, because everyone must fight their own battles, and no one else can help with that. The spirit will either endure, or give in. A spirit that gives in is not strong enough to travel along the World Tree to other places.

At the beginning of June my temperature climbed so high my mother eventually sent for the doctor who looked after the employees of Winterland. The doctor came, took my temperature, felt my forehead and reversed my eyelids and said there was nothing to be done. My mother wept. My father left the room. Vivian sat in the corner and listened in silence. Our cat Minni jumped onto the bed and curled up on top of my legs and purred, because purring is for healing the sick.

That night I had a dream that didn't feel like a dream at all. I lay in a damp swamp, my limbs wet and heavy, and I could not move. A cloud of small black birds descended from the sky, the edges of their beaks serrated, like the mauling jaws of predatory fish. They clutched my aching skin with their claws, sank their beaks in me and began to tear the flesh from my bones, piece by piece. I felt them tug out my hair and pull off my fingers one by one, shred large splinters from my legs and stomach and arms; they locked their teeth painfully around my tongue and mauled it from my mouth. I tried to scream, but the sound was sticky glue in my throat. The birds tore me apart and scattered the pieces into the swamp. The pieces drowned into the dark water, into blackness, but a shimmering thread began to interweave them again, and the pain dissipated. The water around me grew brighter and brighter, the swamp faded, and I could feel my body again. It was whole and smooth, and everything was surrounded by light.

I opened my eyes. A clear sky arched above, and the water I floated in was pure and cool. The birds were gone. There was nothing but peace. The lynx stood on the edge of a tussock under trees, looking at me. It twitched its tail, turned its back and disappeared among the trees.

I opened my eyes. Minni purred quietly, a pleasant, warm weight upon my legs. My mother took my face between her palms and cried and embraced me. I felt weak, but the fever had gone down, and for the first time in weeks I craved food.

Vivian stood up in the corner of the room and stretched. The swan was huddled next to her chair, still, the black eyes alert. At that moment I knew my mother could not see it. I knew I would always see it from that moment on.

· •●• ·

I returned to work a week after I'd woken up and my illness had receded. One evening, when I came home, my parents were there already. Vivian was sitting with them in the front part of our apartment that a curtain separated from the kitchenette and the sleeping alcove of my parents. The swan had settled under the table. Vivian had an empty teacup in front of her. On the table there was a plate with crumbs and one homemade oat biscuit on it. When I stepped into the room, all three of them went quiet mid-sentence. My mother picked up the plate from the table and offered me the last biscuit. I took it and sat down at the other end of the sofa bed.

Vivian got up.

I must go to a previous engagement, she said. Thank you for the tea, Mr. and Mrs. Salo. The cookies were delicious.

My father and mother got up to say goodbye to Vivian. I nibbled at my biscuit and wondered what they had to tell me. My mother went outside to fetch some water for dinner and my father began to darn a sock. Neither of them said anything about Vivian's visit, but I saw my mother wanted to talk to me. I decided to wait until she was ready to do it.

A few days later Vivian came to meet me at the coffee shop. My shift was just ending.

Would you walk with me, Lumi? she said. There's something I'd like to discuss with you.

I need to be home no later than an hour from now, I said.

That's more than enough.

I got my coat and said goodbye to Mira. The sun still floated above the horizon, although it was ten o'clock in the evening. It was the week before the summer solstice. Treetops were drawn green against the light sky, and a few stars were discernible in the blue. We walked in silence for a while. Vivian turned to a narrow path between pine trees. I followed her, although it was a circuitous route. I kept glancing at Vivian, but she seemed lost in thought. Eventually I broke the silence.

There wasn't really a lynx in the coffee shop, was there? When I fell ill.

Vivian turned to look at me. I discerned crow's feet in the corners of her eyes.

Depends on how you look at it, she said. What you saw was real, but visible to you alone.

Like your swan?

A smile spread on Vivian's face.

He's not mine. He has only chosen to walk with me and guide me. But yes, sort of like the swan.

What are they?

Vivian was quiet for a moment.

Inhabitants of other worlds, she said then. We call them soul-animals. Our senses give them the shape of an animal, because that is the easiest for us to comprehend. Their real form is only known to themselves.

I realized I wasn't the first one to whom she had explained this. I realized she had begun to teach me, as she must have taught many before me.

Why are you and I able to see them? Why not others?

You, me and others who have the gift of healing, Vivian said. The soul-animal chooses their human as early as the moment of birth. When the time comes, they will call upon the human to work as a healer.

I remembered the cold weight I had felt upon myself as I watched Vivian's dance in the house at the edge of the woods.

I'm not sure I understand, I said.

I spoke with your mother. She told me her grandmother used to travel and heal the sick during the Great Drought. You wouldn't be the first one in your family.

We had arrived on the crest of a hill. Before us I could see a tall, moss-covered rock and beyond, a dark-watered forest pond. I stopped and looked at Vivian.

What do you mean?

The reflection of a bird flying past or a branch bending in the wind moved in Vivian's eyes.

What plans do you have for the future, Lumi?

The question struck a hidden spot. For years, I had been saving from my small salary the remaining part that my parents allowed me to keep. I knew they would have left more for me, but they simply could not afford it. My father's diabetes medication, the heating, water and necessary food shopping required everything we had.

I've been thinking that… I could go to the coast to sort plastic for a couple of years.

That was the first time I spoke the thought out loud. Work at plastic processing plants paid better than at holiday isles, but I had seen how people were when they returned from them. Sea plastics released harmful vapors as they were collected and sorted, and the vats where bacteria disintegrated the waste were enclosed in airtight halls. The couple next door had worked in them for years before their move to Winterland. They both coughed constantly, and I had seen red stains on the handkerchief one of them used to cover his mouth.

Why? Vivian asked.

I could save money and apply for the visa lottery afterward.

Vivian turned her head and stared at the forest pond.

So you'd like to leave Earth?

I nodded. She saw it despite not looking directly at me.

Have you told your parents?

I shook my head.

Workers selected to go to colonies through visa quotas don't usually have the chance to educate themselves, Vivian said. You know that, don't you?

How do you know I'd like to study? I asked.

Vivian smiled.

I don't. Would you?

I was quiet. I followed her gaze to the forest pond, and all of a sudden there were tears in my eyes. I turned my gaze toward the ground.

I could teach you, Vivian said. Her voice was gentle.

What about my job? I asked.

Vivian turned and looked at me for a long while. She was pondering either me or her own words, or both.

You'd have to give up your job here, she said. Go with me.

I tried to understand.

To other holiday isles?

Away from Earth.

The thought surged over me incomprehensible, too big. I had to wait for it to subside a little, so I could look at it from a distance and see all that it meant. I had stood on a slope at the edge of the woods on winter nights; I had gazed at the stars and watched the paths drawn in the darkness by ships as they left Earth. I had imagined another life for myself, many lives: on Mars and the Moon, in the sky cities of Venus that were still under construction, on Europa or even Enceladus. I had known them all to be fantasies. Even if I was selected in the visa lottery, if I could leave, I could at best pick fruits on one of Mars's plantations or wash laundry in the yoga retreats of the Moon, or unload freight containers at a Venusian spaceport. Darker stories circulated of the migrant workers' conditions too.

Vivian offered something else, something closer to the fantasies I'd considered impossible. It looked like freedom to me. I didn't know much about healers' work, and I did not remember my great-grandmother who had died when I'd been under a year old. But the image of the girl in the fenced house rose to my mind again and again: detachment from the shadow she'd been carrying until then, a relief so deep I'd felt it in my own body. I realized I wished I could help people the same way.

Could I return to Earth to visit my parents?

Vivian had clearly decided to speak honestly to me. She didn't wish to embellish the truth or offer what was not possible. This made me trust her.

Only rarely, she said. Every two or three years. Interplanetary travel is still slow and expensive, and apprentice visas have rigorous restrictions.

And... Could I send them money?

I wasn't certain how my parents would fare without my income. Then again, they'd have one less person to feed and dress.

A healer's financial situation is always uncertain, and I cannot promise a steady income for you, Vivian said. Many are skeptical of the healers' profession, and even those who believe in it will often try to get you to do your job for free. But I can promise you'll always have food, clothes and a roof over your head. Anything you make on top of that, you can spend whichever way you like.

She paused for a moment, then continued:

Getting a visa for you is not certain. I believe it will work out, and I've made some initial inquiries, but it's important you brace yourself for the possibility of the application being rejected.

We began walking again, toward the pond that reflected the trees on its dark surface, and a couple of bright stars in the sky. Perhaps there might be a home among them one day, another pond, in the water of which I would see the reflection of Earth.

Do you want me to speak to your parents? Consider this carefully.

But the answer was already in me, had been for a long time.

Yes, I said.

Vivian nodded.

It's important you also talk to them yourself, she said.

I will.

I squatted at the water's edge. A few small fish had stopped in the shallows of the shore. They were visible as streaks between the stones and vibrated into movement when I touched the surface of the water.

What will happen if I don't go? I asked.

Then you will have given that future away, Vivian said. That doesn't mean you are not left with others to choose from.

I lifted my hand from the water. The drops trickled down my fingers and fell onto the ground.

Yet there is one thing you need to know before you make your decision, Vivian continued. The kind of sickness you had is a summons, the way of those from other worlds to show you the way. If you remain here, you will not be serving with your full capacity, not as well as if you leave and learn the healer's skill. There are many ways to respond to the call, but rejecting it has consequences.

The reflection of Vivian's face was angular in the brownish-bright water.

Have you had the same sickness? I asked.

Twice, Vivian replied. A long time ago.

I knew then she had rejected the summons once, but not for a second time.

When I raised my gaze, I saw movement between trees on the opposite shore of the pond. A large animal with speckled fur inspected me from behind the tree trunks, waiting to see which path I would choose.

• • ● • •

When I think about my final weeks in Winterland, I feel as if I betrayed my parents somehow, because I remember little about that time. They must have tried to organize something memorable: a meal, a day trip, a modest celebration on one of the few days off.

On the day I left I attempted to memorize things, but there was a burn behind my eyes and a tightness in my chest, and it seemed easier to let words, gestures and expressions slide past than cling to them. We lifted two bags, neither particularly heavy, onto the cart behind the bicycle. At the door of our apartment I scooped

Minni into my arms, but she bit my thumb, wriggled herself free and vanished behind the building. My father walked the bicycle and the suitcases to the ship pier a few kilometers away. My mother and I walked behind him. From the ship I would switch to a train, which would take me to the spaceport. My father and mother stood on the pier and waved, as the ship turned and headed toward other islands. Vivian stood next to me onboard.

Most clearly I remember the departure from the spaceport, the gravity that crushed me into my seat and blurred my vision, as if Earth had clung to me and squeezed me tightly into its arms: *don't go, don't go*. And eventually a floating lightness, when the crushing weight let go. It intermingled with sadness, akin to physical pain, when I first looked at Earth glowing in space through the window of the vessel. Yet at once I was light and bubbling, all roads open unlike ever before, the future a shimmering, branching path of gold.

• • ● • •

My strongest memory of the early days with Vivian is the night I saw the Voynich Lights for the first time from outside Earth. I had seen the lights before: we all have. They have been in the sky too long, too persistent and too inexplicable for us not to. Like the sun and the Moon for me, like Phobos and Deimos for you. They are part of our sky, the landscape where we belong, if we belong anywhere at all.

On Earth, the Voynich Lights were so dim that most of the time they were impossible to discern. In Winterland the electricity available to workers was rationed, but the artificial lights put up for tourists shone bright. My parents would often cook dinner in the red-tinted glow of the neon signs. The sky was so light in summer that even stars grew pale against it, and in winter it was a black ceiling covered in orange light-dust. During power cuts it got pitch dark. The stars would come out then, like coins in the sand of the shore revealed by low tide, glittering and distant. And the lights.

They flashed in a rhythm in which I could not perceive any regularity, a pattern as shapeless as a constellation: you could only see something recognizable in it by imagining. My father had been a teenager when the lights first appeared. From him I'd heard about the great fear and excitement they had revoked, how they had been studied, how their sender and their intentions toward humanity had been guessed at, how there had been rearmament against a possible attack, what kind of preparations had been made for a potential visitation. But you and I know this decades later, Sol: when the unexplained, the fear-inducing, the exciting continues unchanged long enough, it merges into the landscape, becomes a part of life. The human mind molds itself into the new shape of things, until it ceases to be new.

Since I'd grown up on Earth, I had no idea what the lights might look like from another celestial body. When I became Vivian's apprentice, we first traveled to the Moon, to a small village that had once been a mining community, but at that time functioned mostly as a spot for moon-hikers. The village was located on the edge of the bare plain of Lacus Somniorum, near Mare Serenitatis. The lodgings of former mine employees had been converted into simple accommodation globes where the hikers could eat and sleep for a small fee. On the edge of the village, up the slope of the crater, rose a tall tower from which you could view the plain. The place reminded me a little of the Extreme Package of Winterland, but in Winterland there had always also been luxury accommodations available to tourists. Those did not exist here.

Lake of Dreams by the Sea of Serenity, Vivian said. And water only where you imagine it. This is a good place to begin.

· • ● • ·

That first evening we took a slow funicular up the slope of a crater to a simple lookout spot with a view over the Sea of Serenity. Vivian walked me to the handrail, and I heard her voice through the rustling communications equipment in my helmet.

Look, she said, and tell me what you see.

I saw a colorless Moon desert below, a few dimly lit accommodation globes near the crater and far across the Lake of Dreams a glow I knew to be a city. HYPATIA – LUTHER, the text on the side of the underground had read, when we had boarded it that morning at the central station of the city. The sky was entirely black, more so than ever on Earth, and the bright crystals of stars flared cold. The blue and white half-globe of Earth had sunk into shadow for the night. In the direction of Montes Taurus, where the plain turned into a desert broken by craters, burned garish lights. I saw how the joints of large machines bent, picked, lifted and moved in their slow columns.

I see an unfamiliar landscape, I said, and human marks on it. What's that over there?

I remember how light and yet stiff my arm moved inside the space suit as I lifted it to point at the machines in the distance. Vivian had rented thick, old-fashioned protective suits for us, because they were cheaper than thin biosuits.

A mine, she said. Probably for mining anorthite. Or perhaps ilmenite.

I'd never heard of either.

I thought mining activity was limited to the dark side of the Moon these days.

The loudspeakers inside my helmet rustled. It may have been Vivian sighing.

It used to be, she replied. Until the Hou Yi City environmental treaty was terminated last year. Many corporations want to expand their mining activity to the Sea of Serenity.

I looked at the Sea of Serenity, its colorless, untouched landscape, across which petrified lava ran in dead veins and which small, infrequent craters mottled. Nothing had ever been built there. I knew you could see it all the way from Earth. I tried to imagine what the Moon would look like, if human-made machines began to hollow out its vast protected areas. On Earth, my parents would stand on a hill on the edge of Winterland and look into the night sky, and as years passed, bruises would appear around the eyes of the Moon that would spread and slowly stain its shining face into another. And it would never be the same again.

Can no one stop it? I asked.

Some are trying, Vivian said. She was quiet for a moment. What else do you see? She asked then.

I was slightly cold inside my suit. Cautiously I stepped closer to the handrail. The boots were heavy, but I nearly tripped and fell regardless, because the Moon gravity was strange to me and I was still looking for a balance.

I see a dark sky.

Just dark? Vivian asked.

I gazed at the horizon and at the sky. Some stars were so dim you could only get an impression of them by looking slightly aside. Others formed patterns in which I could see something familiar. They arranged themselves unlike on Earth, but I saw the three bright stars of Orion's Belt and the W of Cassiopeia: something to anchor me in this loose, homeless state.

And then, the Voynich Lights.

The first flicker was barely discernible. It was followed by others in quick succession. Back on Earth I had tried to find a recognizable rhythm to them, although I knew well that the series were too long for a human mind to remember. Now I focused on the flashes that were kindled and extinguished in the sky like sparks flying into the night from a fire, or like remote thoughts. Bright, dusk, bright: a path drawn in the darkness that summoned you to walk and vanished amid strange mists. I breathed the vision in, wished to enclose it behind my eyes, so I could invite it back again whenever I wanted.

I've never seen the lights so clearly, I said.

I know.

What do you believe they are?

What do *you* believe they are?

I was taught at school that they are probably a message from some distant civilization.

To whom?

To whoever might see it. The same way the Voyager probe that was sent from Earth long before the time of colonization. *Greetings, you are not alone in the universe*. Something along those lines.

Do you think it's true?

It's the most probable explanation.

Vivian was quiet. After a while I understood she expected me to continue. Or maybe she didn't, but allowed me the chance to continue if I wished.

But I have wondered sometimes... What if it isn't a message? What if it's... a memorial?

What do you mean?

Maybe those who built the sources of light have not been alive for a long time now. They knew their civilization would disappear one day. Maybe they just wanted to leave something behind. Like pharaohs had pyramids built, or the emperors of China made large terracotta armies to be buried with them. So death would seem a little smaller and easier to understand. Maybe the lights tell a story we just don't know how to read. *This is who we were, this is what we cared about, this is how our world vanished, this is what we wished to leave behind*.

An interesting idea. Why would they have gone into such trouble?

Maybe it was no trouble to them. Or maybe that's part of the memorial, of the story. *This is what we could do. And even so we faded into nothingness*.

Vivian nodded inside her helmet and I saw a smile on her face behind the glass.

The lights in the sky flickered in a long and quick rhythm.

Vivian said: There is a story I like. I once met a healer who told me that his people regarded stars as the eyes of those who have journeyed into the Sea of Souls, watching the world. Guarding, protecting. Judging, too. He would have thought the flickering was souls blinking.

What is the Sea of Souls?

Vivian's face fell serious.

The place where healers believe souls journey when they have left this world. It is also called the Underworld.

She went quiet for a moment.

Now, close your eyes and imagine the landscape opening ahead. What do you see?

I did as she told me. I was able to imagine the view with fair precision. The dim lights of the accommodation globes were still ghosts on my retinas, and the details of the desert of the Sea of Serenity were not hard to remember.

The same landscape, I said.

Nothing else?

I continued to stare at the landscape in my mind.

No, I said eventually.

Open your eyes, Vivian said.

When I opened my eyes and turned to look at her, the long-necked white bird stood on the handrail. It was impossible, of course. No bird could have survived in the Moon desert without atmosphere, and no protective dome covered us. The swan looked directly at me with his bright eyes and then flew away, sinking into the darkness of the sky like in the water of a black river.

At the same time I felt a soft touch against my leg. It reminded me of Minni walking past and hugging me with her tail. I sensed it clearly, as if I was not wearing a thick space suit at all. I looked down. The lynx with the speckled fur butted its head against my leg, looked at me. Waited.

Cautiously I reached out my hand and stroked its head. Its sides began to tremble with purrs. It licked my gloved hand and nibbled at my little finger lightly. Then it tensed its body for a jump and leaped over the handrail into the blackness, dissolving into the air as a shadow, like it was flying.

If you call her, she will come back, Vivian said.

What name should I call her by?

She will tell you when the time comes, Vivian said. Let's go. Aren't you hungry yet?

She turned and started walking toward the funicular in long, floating strides.

9.3.2168
As ever, Isidis Planitia and
that same damn train

Sol,

Somewhere in the middle of the endless plain my screen connected to the server and all my messages were updated. I had hoped you'd been in touch. You had not. Instead, I scrolled through the news. There had been a toxic leak on the corn plantations behind Datong, which had fortunately been contained. Yet another vessel left on the orbit by human smugglers had been brought down, this one no larger than a capsule and bursting at the seams with people running from Earth's famine. No survivors. In the Pacific, the riots had spread from Barrier Reef Land to the neighboring Whale World. Both holiday isles had been closed to tourists for the time being.

You remain silent, Sol. I know you wouldn't do that without a good reason. I trust you. What I don't understand is simply something I don't know yet. When we meet face to face, all will be clear again.

Won't it, Sol?

I will arrive at Elysium tomorrow morning. While I wait, I close my eyes, step into the Moonday House in my mind and build a new room there.

Today I choose an entrance hall with a tall ceiling and wide windows. Birch trees and Japanese maples grow behind them; light draws shadows of branches on the plain hardwood floor. In the middle of the room rises a narrow spiral staircase along which I climb to the upper floor, into the room we both love the most. It was one of the first Moonday House rooms we built together.

Here, too, the floor is light wood, and the tall walls are covered everywhere by bookshelves. You have always said you wished to build a secret room behind the shelves, but we have never done it.

I let my finger run across the spines of the books; I see the titles engraved on their worn leather. I stop my hand at the one I'm looking for. I grab the book and pull it toward me.

Soundlessly the bookshelf begins to move, opening like a door.

An empty space is revealed behind the shelf, filled with white light.

I begin to work.

With a few waves of my fingers I set the floor planks in place and cover them with a soft, handwoven rug. I make the walls white and wood-paneled: you like wooden surfaces. I only hang one picture on them, a painting of stars glowing in the night. The ceiling of the room I make into an arching skylight that always shows us the skies exactly as we want them.

In the middle of the room, I mount a sofa upholstered in gray velvet, the right size for the two of us to sit on. Next to it, on a small table, I place a steaming pot of jasmine tea, two cups, an untouched notebook and a fountain pen.

This is a good place for you to come.

I sit down on the sofa to listen to the sounds in the house. A blue-winged butterfly flutters into the room. It must have lost its way and come in from the garden, through a window left open in the library. It lands on the edge of a teacup and folds its wings.

I listen to your footsteps and don't know if they are drawing nearer, or moving farther away.

6

The principle of inviolability
I. Valli (2309). "Glossary of Eco-activism,"
***Encyclopedia Ecologica* on the**
interplanetary web. Retrieved 12.7.2312.

The principle of inviolability usually refers to the idea stemming from *biocentric* environmental philosophy, according to which the value of or need for protection of the environment is not defined by the occurrence of life forms, but the untouched natural landscape is of inherent value in itself.

The principle of inviolability was first formulated by environmental philosopher Mirai Parata, who wrote about it in the following manner in 2032:

The idea that the world and universe exist for humans alone, and that the perusal of the natural resources of the Solar System is the exclusive right of our species, is both hopelessly outdated and staggeringly self-centered. We have nearly burned out one planet. Repairing the damage will take hundreds, if not thousands of years. Our only hope to survive as a species is to honor the untouchability of other celestial bodies, to only claim the very minimum of space that is absolutely necessary.

One might ask, where is the sense in protecting a dead landscape that is hostile to humans? Surely there is nothing to protect there? Yet this question reveals a blind spot: the intrinsic value is not born of the presence of life. The intrinsic value is the landscape that humans have not altered through their actions, that which falls outside the scope of the anthropocenic – and such spaces now only exist outside of Earth. What gives us the right to destroy them wherever our influence extends, to consume the already limited resources and produce environmental toxins on moons and planets that human impact had not even begun to scrape upon as recently as two hundred years ago?

I propose that from now on we follow the principle of inviolability: to leave landscapes as they are, wherever we go. For too long, the human species has compulsively striven to place its banner everywhere. It is a greater display of strength to show that we can leave a place alone. For the former, the only thing necessary is money and influence. For the latter, an understanding is also required that not all things of value are embodied in those.[6]

Many environmental organizations adopted the principle of inviolability as their directive from the 2030s onward, when mining activity on the Moon and the construction of Martian colonies began. After the events of the 2160s, and

6 Mirai Parata. *Landscapes of Loss: Beyond the Anthropocene*. New Delhi: Cosmic Canon Books, 2032, p. 14.

in particular as a consequence of the Inanna incident of 2168, Parata's writings fell out of favor because they came to be associated with eco-terrorism. Recent re-evaluation has, however, argued that Parata's core philosophy was always one of nonviolent resistance, and she would likely have rejected any attempt to interpret her writings to justify acts of terrorism or any other kind of aggression.

The neo-animistic, non-life-form-inclusive school of thought in particular has made vast efforts to reintroduce Parata's remarkable contribution to twenty-first-century environmental philosophy into the twenty-fourth-century context.

10.3.2168
Hotel Picard
Elysium, Mars

Sol,
I sit in one of the two hotels of Elysium with Ziggy, and I write, because if my pen stops moving, I will have to face what waits outside the words. If formerly these sentences were at least in part for you, for the future you to whom I will hand this notebook, now there is no doubt that they are for myself first and foremost.

If I write about it all as if it is a made-up story, or as if it is happening to somebody else, perhaps it will be easier to bear.

· •●• ·

This morning upon my arrival at Elysium I headed for the research station on the outskirts of the city. It was easy to recognize despite the fact that I had never been there before: on the empty plain of dust rose a gray, industrial-looking building with a glass wing, inside which grew a glowing botanical garden. If I'd known how impressive it was, I'd have demanded to accompany you on one of your work trips, Sol! The domes far above shone with the morning light of Mars, and under it the green of the trees looked deep enough to be unreal, as if some impossible imagination had painted their leaves in the middle of the lifeless landscape.

I saw from afar that something out of the ordinary had happened. Temporary barriers had been erected around the research center to prevent access, and there were guards standing at the entrances. A few people dressed in civilian clothing were taking photos of the building and writing on their screens.

I will admit my plan was not very thoroughly considered. I knew I probably wouldn't be allowed in without an access pass, but if you were there, I could say in the foyer that I was coming to see you. When I approached the main entrance, a guard wearing a dark red uniform stepped forward and stopped me.

"The research station is closed," he said in a voice that was not kind or unkind.

"I have an appointment with one of the employees," I said.

As soon as I had spoken the words, I saw a change on his face. I had seen it often enough to be able to interpret it. The guard had recognized my accent. I know my Earth-born pronunciation is almost imperceptible nowadays: on Earth I often get mistaken for a Martian. Yet I also know I'll never entirely shed my accent. On Mars, I don't fool anyone despite the fact that over the years I have without realizing begun to imitate your pronunciation and word choices, Sol.

The shift in the guard's expression also trickled into his voice, in which I now heard a cold undercurrent.

"There are no employees here," the guard replied. "Have a good day."

A stone rolled into my belly, but I had not come this far to give up so easily.

"Do you know where they can be reached?"

The guard sniffed.

"No," he said. "I would advise you to leave. The area is closed to the public."

"Can you give me any further information at all?" I asked. I changed the tone of my voice a little. "My spouse works here. I was meant to meet them."

The guard's eyes moved on me. He let out the kind of breath that made it difficult to tell if it was a sigh or scoff. His face petrified again.

"I can't help you," he said.

"Can I come back tomorrow? If I have not managed to reach them by then?"

"You can if you want to," the guard said. A ping sounded from his pocket. He pulled out a small portable screen, swiped the display and spoke the last words without looking at me. "But you will find the exact same things as today."

I decided to pull a card I hadn't known I held.

"I appreciate that you're clearly busy," I said. "But I am here as a guest of the Embassy of Nüwa on Mars. If you don't at the very least advise me on who to talk to, I will call my contact at the embassy. You can have a conversation with them, if you will not have one with me."

The guard turned his eyes to me, gave me a look of evaluation. I planted my boots more firmly on the ground and stared at him in the eye. This time I recognized the sound he made as a fed-up sigh. Yet a new kind of tenseness had appeared in his posture.

I pulled my screen out of my bag and switched the display on.

"Shall I make that call?"

If he accepted the offer, I'd have to improvise something. I hoped I'd be able to.

The guard twisted his mouth and said, "Do you see that woman over there?"

He tilted his head toward the garden wing. In front of the building a uniformed woman stood talking to two people who were writing on their screens, pens whizzing. I realized they were probably not police, as I had first assumed, but journalists.

"She may be able to help you. But don't get your hopes up."

I thanked the guard. Before I turned my back, I couldn't stop myself from adding, "My contact at the embassy will appreciate your help."

His face looked like a bad smell had wafted into his nose from somewhere.

Only once I approached the garden wing, I noticed that the glass wall protecting the plants had cracks in it. Where the wing connected with the gray concrete of the research station, a tall bamboo thicket had fallen. Dark soot stains were visible on the broken stalks and the large-leaved plants surrounding them, and part of the garden had burned into gray ashes. One of the journalists, a woman dressed in blue, had walked to the other end of the wing and squatted close to the ground to take a photo of the glass wall. I saw one of the guards stride toward her. The woman started and stood up.

The guard said something to her. I could not make out the words. The woman lifted her screen to take another picture of the building. The guard raised his hand. The woman lowered the screen. I only noticed then that there was something written on the glass wall in red spray-paint letters. The text was neat, shaped with a stencil. I tried to make out the words, but the text was too far. The guard raised his voice. The woman's fingers split the air in sharp movements as she explained something to the guard. He listened and shook his head. He reached for the woman's screen. The woman did not give it up.

The guard tore the device from her and browsed the display. The woman spread her hands in bewilderment. Apparently the guard found what he was looking for and began to swipe the display in swift, repeated movements. I realized he was deleting the photos the woman had taken. The guard's fingers stopped. He examined the screen for a little longer before handing it to the woman. She spoke. The guard stood without budging. The woman stared at him, then pushed the device into her bag, turned her back on the guard and began to walk toward me. As she came closer, I realized I'd seen her before. She did not as much as glance at me. The hem of her tunic flitted and the bag beat against her side as she strode past me.

I walked after her. A little farther down she slowed her pace, straightened the blue scarf covering her head and stopped.

When I caught up with her, I saw she had closed her eyes and was taking deep breaths. Her mouth was pursed into a tight line. She gave a loud huff, opened her eyes and noticed me.

"Excuse me," I said. "Could I talk to you for a moment? We met last week in Datong."

The woman – Enisa, I remembered – frowned and looked at me like people look at a half-strange landscape through mist. I saw the memory grow clearer in her thoughts.

"That's right," she said. "Lumi – I do apologize, I don't remember your last name. Sol Uriarte's spouse, was it? Leyla Ali introduced us."

"Lumi Salo," I said. I found my electronic business card in my pocket and handed it to her.

A sudden smile surfaced on the corners of her lips. She dug out her screen and swiped the card across it. My contact information appeared on the display. She saved it and handed the card back to me.

"I'm sorry if I seemed rude," Enisa said. "I'm here to write a report, but these guards..." She paused and swung her hand in an arc.

"I noticed the same," I said. I glanced in the direction of shattered glass and soot-black, torn plants: the broken bruise on the garden that must have taken decades to grow. The guard who had removed the photos from Enisa's screen had planted himself on the route that led toward the text painted on the glass wall. He made a gesture of rejection with his hand at a journalist who tried to get past.

Enisa eyed me.

"I don't mean to steal your scoop, but did you manage to get anything at all out of them?" she asked. She must have noticed the tightness I felt on my face because she added, "You don't need to tell me, of course. But maybe we could help each other out."

"I don't even know what happened here," I said. "I only just arrived."

"What did the guards tell you?"

"Nothing."

Enisa swiped her screen and found her handwritten notes on it.

"I don't know much either," she said. "There'll be a press conference later today at Elysium Police Station. All I got is that there's been an accident of some kind at the research station. A fire, maybe an explosion, in which potentially hazardous biomatter spread outside enclosed spaces. They've isolated the station until further investigation has been carried out."

Fear gripped me like the dark, icy void of space.

"Was anyone injured?" I asked.

"The employees found at the station have been quarantined," Enisa said. "And the leak is under control. But some employees are missing."

The chill stalled in me.

"Do you know their names?" I asked. My voice was weak and narrow.

"No," Enisa said. "But I'm sure they'll inform the media soon enough, if we wait."

Meteorites enclosed in ice spun inside me, approached as a sharp flock in the dark. I didn't wish to be left alone with them. I had to tell someone.

"Sol was at the station," I said. At the same moment as the words left my mouth I realized I did not even know that for certain.

The dark chill brushed Enisa's face too.

"As far as I know, no one died or was in lethal danger," she said. She paused and looked at me with a new weight in her eyes. "You're not a journalist, are you?"

"No," I said. "I'm a healer. I was only here to meet Sol."

"I'm so sorry. I thought..." Enisa's voice trailed off. "I have a contact. I can ask them right away if Sol Uriarte is among those placed under quarantine."

She waited for my consent. I nodded. She raised the screen to her face, dictated a short message into it and sent it.

"Now we wait," she said. "My contact is usually quick."

"Thank you," I said. I closed my eyes and tried to get the trembling inside me to stop.

"Let's go and sit over there for a while," I heard Enisa's voice say. I opened my eyes. She was pointing at a bench by a footpath a little way away. Her expression was concerned.

I let Enisa walk me to the bench. Behind it rose a thin bamboo grove. The hiss of the irrigation systems slithered among the stalks, its whispers coming and going.

"I have tea in a thermos," Enisa said. "Would you like some?"

"Thank you." I dug out the metal mug from my bag and screwed the lid open.

The tea was strong and spicy, sugared sweet. It burned my tongue, but warmed my belly and made me feel slightly better.

"May I ask something?" Enisa said.

"Yes." I managed a smile. My tongue and lips felt sore, as if words were sharp-edged, clawed things.

"How was Fuxi?"

That was not the question I'd expected.

"I'm sorry, I didn't mean to be intrusive." Enisa placed her thermos on the bench next to her. "It's just that I never had the chance to visit."

"How do you know we lived on Fuxi?"

Enisa lifted her hands onto her forehead as if suddenly realizing something important. Her mouth fell open.

"Oh crap, you must think I'm some crazy stalker!" She placed her palms together and pressed her forefingers against her lips. She stared at me for a moment, then dropped her hands into her lap. "I looked into your spouse's work for that interview I was meant to do in Datong. I know they worked on Fuxi for a few years. So I figured you probably lived there too. Also, until you told me, I had no idea your spouse worked at this research station. I live in Elysium, and I was sent here on a tip that something had happened."

"A quiet place for a journalist," I said.

Enisa shrugged.

"I like quiet. Besides, the schools are great here. I've got two kids."

"Sol only comes here every couple of months. On Fuxi they worked on something called Project Earth. They've been trying to get it started again ever since. I think their visits to Elysium were connected with that."

"I've heard it said Fuxi was the most beautiful of the cylinder cities," Enisa said. She offered me more tea. I pushed my mug closer.

"I've only ever been to Fuxi and Nüwa," I said. "I don't know how it compared to the others. But yes, it was beautiful." I blew into my tea. "We lived next to a green park. Tall sycamores and jacaranda trees. I grew herbs on the balcony, and the building had a roof garden. I used to sit there and watch the bees in the lavender plants. Until the moonrust."

The thermos cup Enisa was lifting to her lips stopped mid-air as the movement of her hand halted.

"You were there until the end?"

"We were among the last to leave," I said.

Enisa was looking directly at me. She placed the cup on the bench and brushed her face.

"I'm so sorry," she said, her voice soft. "I didn't realize. I thought you'd moved away earlier."

"No," I said.

I remembered watching from the ship as they switched everything off. I remembered imagining how the trees looked, and the birds and the clouds, after they stopped being trees and birds and clouds. I swallowed down the memory.

"And Project Earth was shelved because of what happened. Sol didn't take it well. They'd been working on it close to a decade."

"May I ask what it was about? I understand if you can't talk about it," Enisa hurried to add.

"You probably know as much as I do," I said truthfully. You never told me a lot of details, Sol. "One of the main research areas of Project Earth was possible water purification using microbes like fungi and algae. Sol has studied lichens and their utilization on Mars extensively."

"I gathered those things from my journalistic homework," Enisa said. She looked contemplative.

"I still miss Fuxi," I said. "It was the first place that felt like home since I left Earth as a teenager."

Enisa gazed at me, nearly placed her hand on my arm, then seemed to think better of it.

"I don't claim to know what it's like," she said. "But I do have a secondhand impression, handed down through generations. Like dark hair, I guess, or a spine structure that means you're likely to develop scoliosis. Something you don't tend to think about, until you realize not every family has it." She paused for a moment. "My family left Earth a few generations ago. One of those stories everyone has heard: drought, famine, a war that ground everything to dust. My great-grandparents wished to be able to return sometime." She looked somewhere far away. "When I was a child, my great-grandmother didn't talk about it very much, but I could tell she missed Earth. She would say that there was always two of her: the one who left, and the one who stayed."

I knew exactly what Enisa meant. I imagined her great-grandmother, a dark-haired young woman, continuing her life in a landscape already lost, in a city where the trees had been bombed to carcasses and the buildings crushed into the ground: a shadow that always walked by the woman who left. I imagined my own other, left-behind self in the landscape of Winterland, a specter that no longer belonged in my world, but could not disappear either, because she had nowhere else to go.

"I'm sorry," I said. "Did they ever return?"

Enisa was quiet.

"There was nowhere to return to," she said eventually. She drained her tea from the mug.

"We live on Nüwa now," I said. "It's almost like Fuxi."

I drained my tea too. The word "almost" floated between us, turned heavy and fell to the ground.

I glanced toward the research station. The group of journalists had begun to scatter and move in the direction of the underground, which was a short walk away. The plants of the garden wing shone green where the soot had not turned them black. I remembered the spray-painted letters.

"What was written on the glass wall of the station?"

Enisa huffed.

"It looked like a biograffiti. Effing guard deleted the photos, said photographing that part of the building was not permitted," she said. "But I memorized the words."

"What did it say?"

"Wait..." She closed her eyes and read the sentence she had learned by heart. "*Earth wakes and stones will speak, and darkness recedes over waters*."

Breath turned into gravel in my lungs. Water hissed in the invisible pipes. The stalks of the bamboos bent in the artificial wind.

"What's wrong?" Enisa asked. She had opened her eyes and was staring at me.

"Are you certain?" I asked. "About the words on the wall?"

"Completely. Do they mean something to you?"

"Do *you* know what the words mean?"

"I've never heard them before."

"I have," I said slowly. "A couple of decades ago I knew someone who used those words often. But recently I've come across the sentence in other places."

Enisa was about to say something, but then her screen pinged. She swiped it on.

"That's my contact," she said. She glanced around: the guards were still standing and walking around the walls of the research station, but most journalists had left. There was no one at a hearing distance.

Enisa lifted the screen to her ear and listened to the message. Her face betrayed its contents even before she switched the loudspeaker on and began replaying the message from the beginning.

"Here's everything I've found out so far: in addition to three employees, also one six-person surface rover and some of the cultures kept in the labs went missing from the research station. The names of the disappeared are listed in a press release that will go public in less than an hour," a low voice said. "Sol Uriarte is among them."

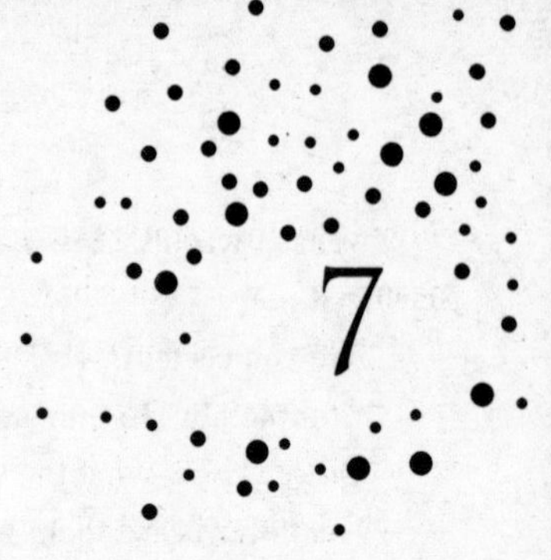

7

11.3.2168
Hotel Picard
Elysium, Mars

Sol,
I cannot see you, so I must imagine you.

You sit in a rover that is moving under a bare sky along a smooth, wide road across the desert. You are wearing a biosuit, and you hold a helmet in your lap. Your fingers trace its scratched surface absently. The helmet is a necessary precaution: if you stepped out of the vehicle without protection, the thin atmosphere and the gnawing temperature would enclose your skin immediately, they'd poison your lungs and thicken the blood in your veins. You wipe your forehead and look through the window at the mountains rising on the edges of the landscape; in passing, you think of something superfluous, such as the color of your socks, or when you last got a haircut.

There are two other people traveling in the vehicle, your workmates from the research station and the university. Your screen does not pick up a signal, because here, in the middle of a rust-colored plain, it does not exist. The nearest city is still hours away. When you get there, you will pick up your screen and tell me that everything is fine, everything is a big misunderstanding.

There was a fire in the lab. You had no choice but to pack the cultures of the water-purifying algae your research group had been working on, and to leave in order to take them to safety. Since there is no other place in Elysium that would provide the right conditions, you are transporting them to the nearest similar laboratory hundreds of kilometers away. You had to leave in a rush; losing these cultures would mean years' worth of labor lost.

You are probably on your way to Arcadia. You will arrive there today, no later than tomorrow. You are growing weary of sitting in the vehicle. The landscape does not offer much variation: dust, mountains and an orange-glow sky, like gilded with Earth autumn colors. You scratch your scalp, you'd like to have a proper wash already. You are tired of your travel companions, they of each other and you. Early in the journey words were flung back and forth in the air; now you take turns every few hours to drive, and for the rest of the time you stare at the horizon or at your own hands in silence. Each one of you would rather be somewhere else.

You look at your screen, which you have switched off in order to save power. You wish you could tell me.

Today, no later than tomorrow.

This is what I want to see.

But this is what I really see:

I see someone you have worked with for a long time switch off the surveillance cameras at the research station. I see someone you trust pack the algae cultures and all-important research data in a rover. I see someone you consider a friend close behind you, and I see a needle piercing your skin, a finger pressing the plunger of the syringe down. I see you turning around and understanding too late, when your legs are already giving out. I see someone you know start a fire in the lab.

I see you waking up on the backseat of a rover, your throat dry, nausea spreading sticky tentacles throughout your body and a cold sweat running down your back.

So many things that happened on Fuxi and after look different through this lens, clearer. I can finally see their actual shape, distinct, sharp as a shard of ice in Earth sunlight. And it stuns me I did not see it before.

• •●• •

After the message sent by Enisa's contact had finished, I spoke to the female guard I had been directed to by the first one who hated my Earth-born accent. She advised me to go to the police station in the center of Elysium. Enisa helped me find it. Before she left me in the waiting room, she insisted on giving me her card.

"Call me if you need anything," she said.

"I don't want to bother you with this."

"How many people do you know in Elysium?"

"None, but—"

"Exactly." She put the card back in her bag. *Contact information saved*, my screen flashed.

"Thank you."

I hoped I said it with enough emphasis. The dimple appeared on her face again, then smoothed away. She turned and went back to her life.

At the police station I spoke to a detective dressed in a red and white jumpsuit. I don't think I said a lot of things that made sense. To be honest, I don't remember much of it. She listened, then told me the case was for now investigated as a property crime, because the University of Harmonia had not had an agreement with the employees about moving equipment and lab cultures. Because the Arcadia Highway was the only direction in which the missing rover could have gone after passing to the surface of the planet through an airlock, troops had been sent along the road to look for it. It was only a matter of time before the vehicle and the personnel would be found. It was best for me to stay calm. The policewoman gave me her card and the contact information of a crisis worker.

"If you hear from your spouse," she said, "or if there's anything at all that comes to your mind you think might be important, give me a call."

I said I would. All morning I have been filling out electronic forms they sent me. Information on the person reported missing, surname: Uriarte. First names: Sol Haru. Date of birth: 03.02.2131. Sex? I suppose the form was last updated sometime in the 2090s. In some Earth regions and in the more conservative cylinder cities one might expect such a question, but on Mars? At least there were several options.

Ziggy is bored. He comes occasionally to scratch at my screen.

I know this silence may not be your own choice, Sol. At its center it's as though I'm in the eye of a storm. Somewhere ahead, a wall of destruction approaches; eventually it will move upon me and shred everything into something else. Before it happens, I must think, receive what silence has to offer. Once again it opens paths ahead of me that run from the past toward this moment. They fork and fade into dusk. Among them I seek that which I want to see in its entirety: the one Vivian drew with her words between us, and beyond.

Earth wakes and stones will speak, and darkness recedes over waters.

I remember seeing the sentence written in the margin of one of the books that Vivian gave me to read. There were a lot of books, and she was in the habit of scribbling in the margins, so I might not have paid any attention to it, if I had not heard her use the sentence too. I have tried to remember the situations in which she did that.

I recall the first time she took me with her to a healing session, near the beginning of my apprenticeship on the Moon. We had been there for about six weeks, and I was getting used to the fact that once a week Vivian left me alone for a day or two. She said she was going to visit patients, and she would always return with water and groceries.

One morning after breakfast Vivian said: You must change into different clothes.

She went to her suitcase, in which I had seen her carry a drum, a notebook and a mask. She produced a roll of fabric tied with ribbons and offered it to me.

Open it, she prompted.

I pulled the bows open and the fabric unfolded into a loose, wide-sleeved cape. Patterns reminiscent of speckles on an animal's fur coat were painted on it, and a narrow tree that settled at the center of the spine.

You will assist me today, Vivian said.

What do I need to do?

You'll see.

She would not tell me more, even when I asked. *You'll see* was her response every time I requested more information. She saw my nervousness, because eventually she said, You cannot prepare yourself for it, because every time is different. You must simply accept what is coming.

What if I don't know how? I asked.

That's what I'm there for, Vivian said. Oh, and you'll probably want to go to the toilet just before we leave. It might be a while before you can get out of the suit. Would you like a diaper, just in case?

· •●• ·

We walked in our thick suits, helmets and boots a short distance along the surface of the Moon to the elevator at the tiny Luther station. Vivian had zipped a protective cover over her doctor's bag and carried the whole thing slung across her shoulder. Moving in the suit was never comfortable, but I was still enchanted with being able to take leaps in the lifeless landscape as lightly as in water. Vivian had, however, warned me about the effects of low gravity. Therefore I constantly wore shoes and jumpsuits equipped with weights when I stayed in the accommodation globe. She had also demanded I exercise for a minimum of an hour every day on the bouncing track of the dome village, where travelers jumped along the surface of the Moon in order to keep their muscles and bones intact.

If your own body is not healthy, you'll have no strength to heal others, she said.

It did not seem laborious. I enjoyed the stolen moments when I felt like stardust in cosmic wind, an illusion of breaking free from the restraints I'd known on the surface of Earth.

We stepped into the elevator, which took us underground. The doors opened into an airlock, then closed behind us. We followed the instructions on a display on the wall. The red light switched to amber and green, as the air flowed in. *You may now remove your helmets*, the display announced, flashing from one language to the next. The announcement also came through the rustling radio inside the helmet. We exited the elevator along a ramp. Vivian took off her helmet. I did the same.

The train had a lot of room. There were a couple of tourists who looked like moon-hikers with their backpacks, a woman who wore official-looking work clothes and no space suit, and a family of three. The journey to Hypatia took just under an hour of Earth time, but Vivian nodded at me when the train began to slow down half an hour in.

We're getting off here, she said.

The station looked old and poorly maintained. Concentrated humidity dappled the walls, the paint was flaking and one of the lights embedded in the ceiling flashed. We were the only passengers to get off there. The elevator stank of dirt.

It did not take us all the way to the surface, so there was no airlock. It stopped on a level where it was surrounded by a few streets. Buildings rose on both sides; above I saw a stretch of a lit-up ceiling. The streets seemed even more crammed than in Hypatia. People walked past pushing carts loaded with metal junk and groceries. I discovered later that it was a residential area mainly for Earth-born migrant workers.

Vivian led me to a place a few streets away and through a dusky doorway, behind which an unclean corridor opened. Something was written on the wall in Chinese. I recognized the characters: I had seen some of them on signs in Winterland before. Yet the words were unfamiliar to me.

We walked up two flights of stairs and turned a corner to a door on which Vivian knocked. Footsteps sounded from within.

A teenaged girl opened the door. Her eyes were narrow in an even narrower face, her black hair tied back against her head.

My name is Vivian, Vivian said. I'm the healer your family called. Where's the patient?

The girl said nothing. She glanced behind her back and then opened the door wider. Behind her stood another girl, a couple of years older, whose facial features resembled hers closely.

Dad is in the living room, the older girl said in English. I'm Nara. That's Neel.

She gestured toward the younger girl.

Don't step off the rug.

The floor under it was made from smooth-polished stone slabs, in complete contrast with the cracked walls, worn-out set of drawers and battered door.

Beautiful floor, I said.

Dad made it, Nara replied. When he was well.

Rugs woven from rags were spread along the floor, held in place by hooks and weights in the Moon gravity. Nara walked ahead of us on top of them. I took great care not to step on the stainless stone slabs with my boots. An older woman with silver strands in her dark hair peeked out from the kitchen. I noticed Vivian giving her a light nod. The woman nodded back before her head withdrew back into the kitchen.

We came into the living room. A middle-aged man lay on a sofa bed bolted to the floor, covered with a weighted blanket that showed threadbare fabric under it. There were deep creases on his forehead, and the long, sand-colored hair was woven into a messy braid. The thick, striped bathrobe hung half-open. On the floor next to the sofa there were many unwashed cups and plates. The man did not look at us when we walked into the room. He stared with murky eyes at a news transmission running on a small screen.

Vivian stopped in front of the man and spoke to him.

Hello.

The man was silent.

You must be Lee. My name is Vivian. I'm here because your daughters and mother invited me.

The man turned his head a little and nodded, but said nothing.

How long have you been feeling unwell?

The man closed his eyes and did not respond. He seemed to deflate. I felt a heavy coldness reach to me from him and trickle slowly inside me. It was like space-dark smoke that floats everywhere and then sinks heavy toward the ground, fills your limbs and thoughts and heart until it can barely beat. I had experienced the feeling before: it was like the sensation that had flowed into me when I'd watched secretly through the window into the room where Vivian sang and drummed for the daughter of the manager of Winterland.

He began to be late for work almost a year ago, Nara said. Five months ago he stopped going altogether, and now they won't take him back. He hasn't left home for over a month.

I tried to estimate the girl's age. I had recently turned seventeen. She seemed younger than me.

Do you have enough food and water? Vivian asked.

The neighbors help, Nara said. Granny knows some people who help too. And I quit school to take a job as a waitress.

I wondered what had happened to their mother. I knew on the Moon people did not live as long as on Earth or Mars.

Vivian watched the man lying on the sofa. She placed her worn leather doctor's bag on the floor.

I need half an hour for the preparations, then we will be ready to begin, she said. Do you want to stay and watch? It's not always pretty.

Nara hesitated, but the younger girl said, I want to stay.

Nara was about to say something, but remained silent and nodded.

Carry the table aside, so there is enough empty space in the middle, Vivian said.

I took hold of the end of the table, and Nara and Neel grasped the other end. We moved the table next to the wall. There was no other furniture in the room.

And clean those dishes away, Vivian said and gestured at the cups and plates. Can we remove our space suits somewhere?

The man paid no attention to us as we made preparations. Nara switched off the news transmission and folded the screen closed. The man muttered something and turned his back. Vivian opened her doctor's bag and ordered me to sweep the edges of the room with a bundle of branches in which I recognized at least balsam fir, rowan and rosemary. In the meantime she placed the drum in the middle of the floor and set a bundle of dried herbs alight. She dropped it in a small bowl. A sweet smell wafted from it.

When everything was ready, Vivian said, Dim the lights.

Nara and Neel turned the lighting down from the wall switch and sat down near the doorway. The man still lay on the sofa, facing the back. A few lanterns imitating candlelight burned in the dim room. The dark-cold weight inside me did not let go.

Vivian stepped to the center of the room. She wore a cloak that resembled a white plumage. A mask with glistening eyes and a long, yellow beak made her human features wither. She held a drum and a drumstick in her hand.

The first sound that rose from her throat was low and slow. It was like the sighing and screeching of stones turning against each other within the earth, stretched across many moments.

The swan landed in the corner of the room, its wide wings

murmuring against the air. I felt a nose poke at the back of my hand. The lynx was by my side. As she touched me, a faintly vibrating warm current jolted through my body, and I sensed the cold weight emanating from the sick man shift. I felt a little lighter. The lynx licked her lips. Without anyone telling me, I knew what she had done. I looked at her in surprise. Her golden eyes closed slowly and opened again.

Vivian began to drum.

· •●• ·

Afterward, when all the lanterns had been switched off, we left the man lying on the living-room sofa. A symbol glittered on his forehead that Vivian had drawn with the same dim-white powder I had seen her use in the house of the manager of Winterland. His eyes were closed, but his breathing ran freer, as if a strange weight was no longer holding him. The cold shadow had also withdrawn from me. The feeling was not as sudden and loaded with relief as it had been in Winterland while I watched Vivian's healing work; it was slower and more gradual, but still recognizable. The man's daughters stood in the corner, holding hands. There were dark shadows under Vivian's eyes and she moved slowly. I had seen the symptoms before: she looked the same as when returning to the accommodation globe from her day-long absences.

When we stepped into the kitchen, the elderly woman stood up at the table. The daughters followed us there.

Well? The woman said.

I retrieved what he had lost, Vivian said. He should start feeling better in the next few days.

And if it doesn't happen? The older woman asked.

Call me again, Vivian said.

There was something else you wanted to discuss with me, the woman said.

Vivian nodded and glanced at me.

Lumi, she said. Would you go and pick up all the equipment from the living room? Nara and Neel can help you.

Neel seemed delighted at the idea. I had noticed how curiously she was looking at the bundle of herbs, the drum and Vivian's cloak painted with bird wings. I let the girls through the door ahead of me and left the kitchen.

Close the door behind you, Vivian said.

As I was pressing the door closed, I heard the words she spoke to the woman.

Earth wakes and stones will speak, she said.

A brief pause.

And darkness recedes over waters, the elderly woman's voice said.

The door closed, and I did not hear more.

· • ● • ·

I believe that was the first time I heard Vivian speak those words. When I think of it, I remember that she always uttered them in the presence of someone else, most often in the context of a healing session. Therefore I had presumed them to be her personal way of focusing, like a mantra that helped her direct her attention toward the healing work and the patient, to close out distractions. But it could have been something else too: a way to catch the attention of someone who was familiar with the words, a way to announce they were on the same side, initiated to a matter that most knew nothing about. A password – but for what?

On the way back to Luther an exhaustion hovered about Vivian, like a mist that stopped me from seeing her clearly. Yet I noticed her observing me through it, as we sat on the shaky underground.

From amid the long silence she spoke.

What did you feel during the healing session?

I was not able to respond right away. I was uncertain what she meant. I thought about it.

I felt a weight, I said then. When we stepped into the room where the patient was.

Vivian's expression encouraged me to say more. I described the space-dark, heavy chill that had flowed into me.

Have you experienced a similar sensation before? She asked.

A few times. On Earth, when I was… close to a sick person.

My face felt hot. I wasn't ready to tell her that I had secretly followed her to the large villa in Winterland. I was not certain if she'd seen me then.

Vivian nodded.

So I thought.

I told her how the feeling had abated when the session was over.

Not all healers have the ability to sense the disease physically in their own body, Vivian said. For those who do, it is important they learn to protect themselves from it. Otherwise they will not last long.

I thought of the lynx's nose at the back of my hand, of her coarse fur against my leg and the smooth skin under it.

I felt the weight shift, I said. Lighten. When the lynx touched me. She did something.

Vivian looked surprised.

Yes, she said. Your soul-animal will carry part of the burden. She will guard you when you learn to summon her.

What else can the soul-animal do?

Vivian leaned back on her seat and closed her eyes, but I knew she was listening.

She knows the path to the other side and back, she said. She will lend you her senses and strength. One day, she might teach you something I cannot tell you about, because everyone must discover it by themselves.

Her voice trailed off. I waited, but she did not continue.

Is there only one path to the other side?

Vivian's eyes remained closed, but she smiled. Lines appeared above her cheekbones.

There are many paths, she said. But only some of them are safe. The other worlds will take the shape the mind gives them. If you wish to cross a river, you must imagine a crossing. If you wish to open a path, you must think of it as open. Your soul-animal will show you which routes to walk and which to avoid. There are places we cannot go.

She paused and took a deep breath.

And those we can, but never must.

How do I know them?

You will, she said. In time.

What happens if we stray from the path?

The smile withered from Vivian's face.

The way back may look clear, she said. But the paths are marks drawn in the landscape by countless generations of healers, they are signposts between worlds. Outside of them the view is unpredictable, susceptible to delusion. A healer who strays from the path may lose it on the first footstep.

Is it forbidden?

Vivian opened her eyes. Their gray was thunder-dark in the dim artificial light of the underground.

Nothing is forbidden, she said. But everything has consequences. If a healer chooses to stray from the path, they must be willing to face them.

What are they?

Vivian was silent. The train came to a curve and shook.

Wounds, she said after a long while. There are things in other worlds that may injure the healer or their soul-animal. Sometimes invisibly, so the healer doesn't even notice the wounds, because they are disguised as something else. But they are wounds nevertheless.

They can be fatal. A healer can only continue to heal others if they are able to heal themselves.

She went quiet and did not say more.

When we got back to the dome village, a couple of guards met us at the station.

The village has been evacuated, one of them said. There's been an accident at the mine a few kilometers away. We suspect the water pipes of the village have been contaminated. We must ask you to leave. Emergency accommodations have been arranged in Hypatia.

We boarded the underground again. I wished I'd said yes to the diaper. Vivian did not say many words on the whole journey. Her head tipped against the window and I heard her breathing weave into a faint snore. The swan curled up in her lap, placed his head on her arm, his white neck curving. I would have liked to ask him how well he was able to protect her, but he would not have responded, not to me.

11.3.2168
Hotel Picard
Elysium, Mars
Evening

Sol,

Approximately an hour ago I received a phone call on the hotel room number. I had only given it to you and the police.

I pushed Ziggy out of my lap to the floor, strode three steps to the phone and picked up the receiver.

It wasn't you.

"Police Detective Jenny Owoeye from Elysium region police force, good evening. Could I speak with Lumi Salo, please?"

"Speaking."

"We met yesterday when you visited the station. Have you heard anything from your spouse?"

"No."

"We have new information," the detective said.

"Have you found them?"

Owoeye was quiet for a moment.

"We have found the vehicle that disappeared from the Harmonia-Elysium Bioprocesses Research Station. It has been tracked to near Elysium Montes mountain. Apparently it had deviated from the road and continued toward desert areas that have no settlements whatsoever."

"What about..." Sol, I almost said, but modified the sentence "... the people in the vehicle?"

Owoeye's words came clear and considered, without tangles or stumbling, like they would only from someone who has had years of practice in conveying such messages to next of kin.

"The vehicle had been abandoned in the middle of difficult terrain. We only found a rover without food or water supplies. The trunk was empty. Apparently the solar panels had stopped working. We believe the staff of the research station had strayed from the road in order to try to reach a remote weather station in Propontis, probably in order to replenish their provisions. Yet they were not found anywhere between the vehicle and the weather station. There might be a dust storm forming in the area. If you have any idea at all where your spouse might be headed, that would help us."

Memories shifted and sought shape in my mind, restless figures beyond a gate.

"I think it's best if I come and see you at the police station again," I said.

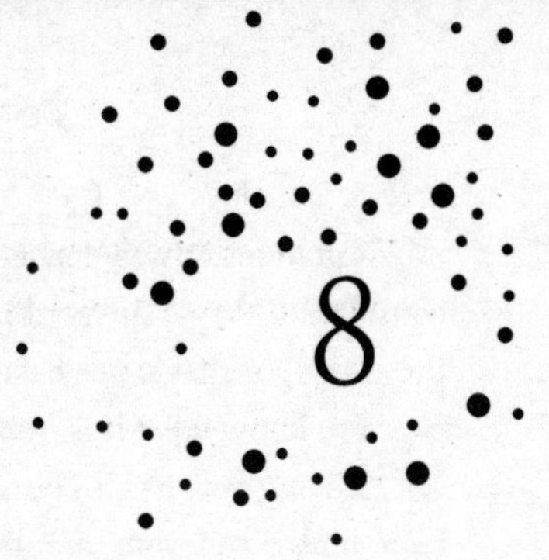

13.3.2168
Hotel Picard
Elysium, Mars

If you have any idea at all where your spouse might be headed.

You stand in a brick-red desert, Sol, among boulders and sand. You are wearing a skintight biosuit and a helmet; nothing but their thin material separates you from the lung-rending cold of the atmosphere outside. A wide ravine opens before you, a crack between worlds. A yellow and gray sky arches in the background. Your legs feel entirely made of bone: heavy, dead and impossible to bend.

When the rover broke down, your workmates argued. You lay on the backseat, pretending to sleep, although the drug they'd been giving you merely left you drifting in a half-haze. You had no intention of letting them know this.

We should go to Propontis, one of them said. The weather station is at a walking distance, just about.

The terrain is too difficult, the other responded. Only underground routes are safe, and they're being watched. We can make it to Arcadia, if we ration food and water carefully. Air, too.

Arcadia? On foot? You're out of your mind.

Night began to fall fast, as it does here, and they could not reach an agreement. There was nothing to do but sleep in the rover, for now, and continue at dawn. They took turns keeping watch.

Just before dawn – you could tell by the color of the sky – you woke with a full bladder.

They were both asleep.

You knew it was dangerous. You'd be safer with them, all things considered: they'd do anything to keep you alive. You have something they need, or they'd not have taken you with them.

You know what it is. You can't let them have it.

Moving was hard. The sedative was a soft and heavy chain upon your limbs, and your mouth and eyes felt full of sand. There was a surface-safe water canteen they'd left for you in the backseat. You picked it up. It was half-empty. That would have to do.

Sometime later, you stand outside the rover with shaky legs, the helmet sealed in place and the canteen strapped across your body. They have not woken up yet. In the morning dusk you look to the horizon, check the direction using the compass on your wrist. You mark the change in the color of the sky. Is that dark stain a dust storm approaching from the direction of the plain of Utopia Planitia?

Everything buzzes with aches: your shoulders, the muscles of your thighs, the landscape as it pierces your eyes. You cannot stay where you are. You begin to walk where you know the road lies. The journey is long by foot, but you believe you will make it. You have enough air for six hours. There are a few resting places along the way, complete with airlocks and water stations. Police vehicles will be moving on the road, looking for the three of you. You have a good chance of coming across them, of being caught on their radar.

I see you move one slow foot, then the other. You are headed toward me.

This I could have told the police. But it is only an image I've conjured, and a ridiculous one at that: a far-fetched fantasy, nigh impossible. Not knowledge.

To gain the knowledge I will need other paths, and even those may not lead to you, Sol.

I started my fast two days ago.

· •●• ·

I went to the police station again. Jenny Owoeye gestured at me to sit down on a chair. She was robust, and her short-shaven, curly hair coiled against her head. There was no gray visible in it yet. Her nails were polished orange and much better groomed than my own. A file lay on the desk.

"Would you like something to drink? Tea, water?" she asked. "I might even have biscuits."

Hunger writhed within me, but I said I'd only have a glass of water. Owoeye walked out of the room and left the door open. I looked around. It was surprisingly bright in the room. One of the walls was full of lightweight bamboo shelves installed with plant lights that lit an entire herb garden. Water gargled in hydroponic pipes. I spotted chives, coriander, marjoram and mint.

Owoeye stepped back into the room, carrying a water jug in one hand and a steaming mug of tea in the other. I twisted my metal mug open.

"I'm not much of a gardener," Owoeye said, as she placed the jug and the tea mug on the desk and nodded toward the plant wall. "But I do enjoy growing herbs. That's the shared spice shelf of the workplace." She sat down behind the desk.

I poured water into my mug and breathed in the scent of coriander. On Owoeye's desk I noticed a framed photo that dissolved occasionally into a different one. In both Owoeye was standing on the shore of a clear-watered lake between a man and a woman. She had curled her arms around their waists. In front of them, two children posed in light summer clothes. In the first photo they all stared at the camera with exaggerated seriousness. In the second, a joyful chaos prevailed.

"Is that your family?" I asked and pointed at the photo.

A wide smile spread on Owoeye's face. I could see that looking at the picture made her happy.

"Well spotted," she said. "That there is my husband," she pointed at the man on the right side of Photograph Owoeye, "and that is my wife." She pointed at the woman to the left. "Those are our kids. We went to Octavia last year."

"I've always wanted to go there," I said. "I hear they have the most gorgeous lakes in all of the cylinder cities."

Owoeye opened the file before her. On the first page I discerned your name, Sol, and below it some notes.

"Any lakes on Nüwa?" she asked.

"Just one," I said. "There's lots of parks and forest there."

"Does your spouse enjoy them?"

"Sol loves trees," I said. "They wanted an apartment next to a park."

"You were lucky," Owoeye said. "The waiting lists for the population quotas of cylinder cities are years long."

"I know," I said. "Sol was able to get a special visa because of their work."

"They are," Owoeye glanced at her notes, "an ethnobotanist, is that correct?"

I nodded.

"What does an ethnobotanist do?"

"Sol is specialized in practical applications of traditional Earth plants in Mars conditions."

"You said on the phone that something occurred to you that you wanted to tell me." Owoeye's smile had not faded for a moment, but I realized she was observing me, weighing my words and taking notice of them. "I hope it's all right with you if I record our conversation? I prefer that to taking notes. Dyslexic."

"Of course."

Owoeye touched a flat recorder lying on the desk. A red light switched on. I realized I had curled my fingers tightly in the folds of my coat. I straightened them and said, "I think Sol was taken from the research station against their will."

Owoeye's gaze was sharp. She opened a desk drawer and produced a plate with corn biscuits on it. She placed it on the desk.

"Biscuit?" she said.

I shook my head. Owoeye picked a biscuit from the plate.

"Do you mean your spouse was kidnapped?"

"Yes."

"That's a strong accusation," Owoeye said. "Why do you think someone might have wanted to kidnap them?"

I tried to organize the memories surfacing in my mind.

"I believe it had to do with their work," I said. "The research project they worked on on Fuxi was known as Project Earth. I got the impression it was partially secret. The funding came from people who didn't want to make their connection with the project public."

"Hmm." Owoeye snapped the biscuit in half and took a bite.

"The project was shelved after Fuxi was shut down. Sol led me to understand the research group was on the verge of some groundbreaking discovery at the time."

"What exactly was the focus of this Project Earth?"

"I don't know, because Sol didn't talk about it very much," I said. Spoken aloud, my reasoning sounded fragile. "But it had something to do with cleansing the oceans of Earth through using symbiotic processes."

"No mean feat." Owoeye's eyebrows lifted. "So you think your spouse had some new scientific knowledge that was groundbreaking enough that someone might have kidnapped them in order to squeeze the information from them for their own purposes?"

"Yes." I took a sip from my mug. I swallowed more loudly than I'd intended. "Perhaps the box that was taken from the hotel room in Datong had something in it that was connected with the project."

"I'm not ruling out any possibility at this point," Owoeye said. "But I have a few questions. Firstly, if this is about information connected with Project Earth, why was your spouse only kidnapped now? Why not earlier?"

"Perhaps the big breakthrough was not made on Fuxi. Sol has been trying to restart Project Earth since then. Maybe the breakthrough only came now, and the same people who followed their work on Fuxi are pressuring them to give up the information."

Owoeye's eyes shifted toward the ceiling and she nodded slowly, as if considering the credibility of my speculation.

"Very well. Question number two: Who could want such information? About ocean cleansing?"

I had wondered about it myself.

"Some commercial body, perhaps," I said. "If some interplanetary corporation managed to patent the method for cleansing the oceans, we could be talking about large profits."

Owoeye tilted her head, raised one corner of her mouth and squinted her eyes, as if to see the possibility more clearly.

"Right. Question number three: Has something in particular happened that gives you reason to believe that someone has tried to pressure your spouse into giving up information? Have they been threatened, bribed or blackmailed? Have they seemed fearful, or behaved strangely otherwise?"

I took a breath and told her, Sol.

I told her about things that happened on Fuxi, and after. Things you may not know I know about. I told her about the snippets of conversations I'd heard, when you'd talked on the phone and had not yet realized I'd come home. I told her about the strange notes on your desk, the messages that arrived in the middle of the night onto your screen. About heated exchanges of words that you had at the door of our home with invisible visitors. About strangers who would come to our home, and that I'd sometimes see by chance about town, talking to you in a tone that frightened me.

I mentioned the week after we'd left Fuxi when I thought I'd lost you.

As I spoke, I heard the hollowness of my own words; I heard how many other ways the events could be interpreted. And yet: each image filled in a new way, connected with others, gained meanings I'd previously sought without success.

Owoeye listened and stayed silent.

Eventually she said, "How certain are you about these memories?"

"I have an exceptionally good memory."

"Hmm." Owoeye's nails tapped the edge of the biscuit plate. "Just out of curiosity, do you use some memory technique? Memory Palace, linking or similar?"

"Something like that."

My hands shook a little. My body felt heavy, as if I'd walked a long way over difficult terrain: quagmire, pathless forest, where I'd squeezed between snow-white tree trunks time and again. The gratings on the ceiling of the room began to hum and blow cool air. Owoeye turned a page in her folder.

"It's good that you came," she said. "I'd have asked you to come in anyway, because I wanted to show you something." She swiped the screen on the corner of the desk to switch it on, picked it up and found something on the display. She placed the screen before me. "Have you ever met this person?"

The face in the photo looked about thirty years old. It was framed by ginger, slightly curly hair and thick-rimmed spectacles that highlighted the paleness of the skin.

"They don't look familiar."

Owoeye swiped the display.

"What about this one?"

The person in the next picture had dark eyes and a lean face. Their brown hair was shorn short. There was a large mole on their lower lip. I estimated their age to be between forty and fifty years old.

"I don't remember seeing them before."

Owoeye placed her finger on the display again and swiped a new picture into the frame.

"What about this person?"

I recognized the man right away. His hair was bleached, his skin reddish and his eyes gray. He was maybe fifty years old. Heavy silver rings hanged from his ears.

"I remember him."

I told Owoeye about the man. I knew I'd seen him on Fuxi talking to you more than once, Sol. I didn't know his name. You'd never introduced us.

Owoeye scratched her hairline, switched off the display and moved the screen back to her side of the desk.

"That's very useful," she said. "Do you know if your spouse is or has ever been part of the activities of any radical environmental organization?"

The question took me by surprise.

"Not that I know of. Maybe as a student, they've mentioned collecting names for petitions and such in the past."

"I mean something far more aggressive. Sabotage of mining equipment, arson of plant grafting facilities, attacks on the offices of big corporations."

I tried to imagine you taking part in something like that, Sol. I could not.

"Sol's work is partly connected with plant grafting," I told Owoeye. "I find it extremely hard to believe they'd ever do something like that."

"I'm asking," Owoeye said, "because we have reason to believe that some of their past and present co-workers are active in an environmentalist organization that is under surveillance and suspected of terrorism. Have you ever heard the name the Stoneturners?"

I sought the word in my memory. If it was there, it was buried so deep I could not grasp it.

"No."

Owoeye pouted her lips and nodded.

"Thank you for your help," she said. "That's everything for now. I'll be in touch immediately if I have new information on your spouse." Her face softened. "You must be very worried. You have the contact details for the crisis hotline, don't you?"

"Yes."

"You probably have nothing against it if we send someone to search your home on Nüwa? In case it helps us find your spouse."

Of course I gave my permission. I tried not to think about our home where books would be lifted off the shelves and the drawers of your desk emptied, where there would be nothing but dust-drawn outlines in the places of paper-filled folders, and the tomatoes in the kitchen would have died from thirst, because we were meant to return to water them weeks ago. I tried not to think about the balcony where no one sits in the evenings.

Owoeye got up from behind the desk and reached out her hand. I got up and shook it. I was already on my way to the door, when she spoke.

"One more thing. Why didn't you say anything about your suspicions two days ago, when you first came to the station?"

I stopped with my back turned to her.

"Because," I said and turned to look at Owoeye, "I had to call some things to my mind. I didn't want to tell you something I wasn't sure about."

"And now you're sure?"

"Yes."

I felt Owoeye's gaze on my back as I walked out. But it could have been my own imagination. She may as well have been looking at her herb garden, or at the photo of her family, or at her nails, the color of which was perfect and unchipped.

· • ● • ·

14.3.2168
Hotel Picard
Elysium, Mars

Sol,

Today I have walked in the Moonday House, sought you in its rooms and hallways. The kitchen is full of fresh, scented flowers and fruits piled in bowls. That is how you like it best. And light that reminds me of early autumn on Earth, when the days are still bright. I follow you from one room to the next, and you have always just stepped out. I can hear your faint humming, your footsteps drawing away, sometimes almost your breathing behind the corner. The surface of the water in a glass on the table still ripples, because you just placed the glass there a brief moment ago.

Eventually I reach you. A balcony has grown out of the Moonday House, from which a view opens into the park at home on Nüwa. There reality has not slipped out of joint; everything is as it should be. Darkness is falling. You sit on the balcony in the still-warm outside air, at the small bamboo table on which we place our teacups in the morning. On the table a bonsai tree is opening a few pink blossoms on its branches. I sit down on a foldable chair across the table. We drink ice-cold quince wine from glasses we only take out rarely, and the scent of elder and jasmine drifts in the dusk.

Do you remember that time you went missing? I ask.

Don't remind me, you say. It is distant as a dream, of which you can only recall the atmosphere and a few fading images.

We clink our glasses together. The wine is sweet and tart on the tongue, the touch of your fingers light and heavy at once.

· • ● • ·

I called your mother. At the other end of the line, there was a rustle, then a hitched breath: a sob, Naomi trying to pull herself together. I gazed at my own reflection on the dark screen. She didn't want to switch the camera on.

"How are you, Naomi?"

"Hanging in there." She paused. "How are you, Lumi?"

"Hanging in there." I paused. "Sorry I didn't call earlier."

Your mother blew her nose. We listened to each other's silence for a long time. I knew what she was thinking of: another vehicle abandoned at the edge of a gorge almost thirty years ago, footprints swept away by the dust and gales that dragged the landscape.

Your father was never found.

"They'll find Sol," I said.

"That's not your promise to make."

I heard the sad smile on Naomi's face even though I did not see it.

"You're right," I said. "It's not. How's Ilsa?"

"Throwing herself into work," Naomi said. "I don't think she sleeps much."

"Do you want me to come to Harmonia?"

Naomi sighed. I could imagine her face: how she closed her eyes exactly the same way you do, Sol, breathed in silence and gathered her thoughts.

"If you can," she said.

"The train trip will take about four days."

"That long?"

"I'll have to go through Datong. There's no direct train between Elysium and Harmonia."

Silence stepped between us again like a ghost. Eventually Naomi spoke.

"I think Sol was taken against their will."

"That's what I think too."

"Sol knows what it's like to live with specters," she continued. "What it is to believe that vanished traces mean hope, not the end of it. They would not leave us behind like that, not unless they were forced to."

Sol, I remember you telling me about a fantasy you used to have as a child. When your father disappeared, you thought he'd be back for your birthday. You turned nine that year. All day you waited. When by the evening he had not come home, you went and buried something under the flowering quince in the rooftop garden: that first year it was a crumb of cake. You continued to do it for several years. Every birthday you would save something – a spoonful of honey, a biscuit, an almond – and bury it under the tree.

It was a magic trick, you told me. If you gave something to the tree, it would send a message to all other trees on Mars, and eventually your father was bound to hear it, and then, by your next birthday, he'd return home.

You don't believe in magic, I reminded you.

Well, you said, and the corners of your mouth quirked. It never worked, did it?

How old were you the last time you buried something?

I don't remember. Probably in my twenties.

Surely you didn't believe it by then?

Of course not. You shrugged. But old habits die hard.

It reminds me of something, I said. In my country it used to be tralatitious to leave food out for the guardian spirits: of the house, of the forest, of the cattle. It was important to keep them happy, or bad fortune would befall your home.

Tralatitious? That's a complex word.

I'm fond of complex words. I didn't have a lot of them as a kid. I've been trying to make up for the lost time ever since. Besides, living with you—

You were saying, about the traditional customs of your country?

Oh, people haven't done it in a long time now. I only know because I read about it somewhere.

Of course you did.

But basically, you were making an annual offering to that tree.

It was just a child's magical thinking. A way of surviving.

Naomi's voice brought me back to the present.

"Do you think Sol is alive?"

It was a question I had not wanted to think about, and one I would not have asked your mother.

"Yes," I said immediately. "I know this may sound odd, but if Sol was... not alive," I had to stop there and take a few breaths, "I think I'd know it."

Sol, I've never told this to you, or anyone. I can hardly bring myself to write it down now – although all circumstances considered, it feels like a lesser thing to lose.

I believe that if your heart stopped beating, I'd feel it. Something inside me would break loose and shatter, and in its place it would leave an empty, dark place that scar tissue would eventually grow to cover. Around it, my body and mind would continue their lives, and somehow, on the surface, I'd look recognizable, but within I'd be forever altered. For how could a universe without you in it still be the same? How could I not sense such an all-altering shift?

You'd probably be the first to tell me this is just another offering under another tree.

Naomi's voice was soft, gentle. It was the voice I could imagine her using when she was putting you and Ilsa to bed, when you were small.

"I used to think that too," she said. "That I'd feel it. That I'd know. But the truth is, I don't. Maybe Oskar is still alive. Maybe he departed and left us behind. Maybe he gets up every morning and walks in an empty apartment and on crowded streets somewhere far away. Maybe he goes to sleep next to someone else. Or maybe his bones lay at the bottom of a canyon covered by dust. Maybe those too are gone now. Wherever he is, I do not feel it. We, those left behind, have nothing but emptiness and whatever we choose to fill it with."

Grief is an animal you can never quite tame.

I remained silent.

"Lumi."

I may have let out a sob. Naomi's face appeared on the screen. She had switched the camera on. The lines on her skin looked deeper than usual, and the normally neat dark braid was messy, as if she had slept several nights without braiding it again.

"Lumi, there's nothing you can do right now. Come here. We'll hug. We'll talk."

I have always said your mother is stronger than she seems.

"There's something I need to do first," I said. "But I'll come as soon as I can. I'll let you know when. Call me anytime."

"You too."

"Love you."

"Love you too."

The screen went dark and pinged to mark the end of the call.

Do you remember that time you went missing, Sol?

18.3.2168
Hotel Picard
Elysium, Mars

Sol,

Two days ago I woke up to a strong-pawed, tuft-eared animal brushing my face with her whiskers; she sat down in the corner of the room to watch me. Ziggy, who slept at the foot of the bed, jumped, arched his back and hissed. His tail woke up into a feather boa. He stared at the lynx.

The lynx blinked, unhurried. Ziggy's back straightened. Slowly he sat down on the bed and licked his lips. The lynx paid no attention to him.

It was the sixth day of my fast.

You have not asked me often how I travel to other places, those that are invisible to you. And I have not spoken of it much. We both know the reason. Your world is built from science, from what can be proven and measured. My world looks toward that which can be sensed but not shown to others.

Now, however, I will tell you. Of how I went looking for knowledge, looking for you, lost to me: from places and in ways that you would call figments of imagination.

I opened my suitcase and took out the cloak Vivian had given me, the tuft-eared headpiece and the collapsible drum. I attached the cloak over my shoulders, placed the headpiece on my head and unfolded the drum. It opened into an oval, a light metal frame covered with a thin, light film. I considered shutting Ziggy in the bathroom but decided he would be less of a distraction roaming around free, rather than meowing behind the bathroom door. I checked that his litterbox was clean, set up the automatic feeder and made sure there was enough food and water for a minimum of three days.

I knew the path. I had learned it under Vivian's guidance until I could no longer lose my way. I knew the routes to places I could not go, and the gates to those I could, but must never. I knew the map of the patterns on the drum, yet even so I traced them with my eyes and touch, like I always did before beginning a soul-journey. I dimmed the lights. In the corner of the room, the animal with speckled fur waited.

I began to drum.

I started the journey with a faint chant summoning the route to meet my feet, the landscape to surround me: I sang to make visible the tall spruces of the ancient forest and the breezes shaking their branches, the green twigs under the trees and the faint-flowing waters. I sang the life that ran through each root and leaf-vein, the shifts of light and shadow on the forest floor, the stones that water wore down. I sang the scent rising from rain and ice and spring, and from the sun on the skin of pine needles. The path grew longer before me, its outlines grew sharper against the landscape, and above rose the sky, an endless web of stars. I drummed the rhythm that was the rhythm of my breath and heart and blood in my veins. The sky darkened above and the stars shone brighter. The holes in the space widened, the pathways to other places, the shimmering wormholes that dilated into vast tunnels.

The lynx stepped in front of me from among the trees. She was larger, or I was smaller, for her back was at the level of my chest. I whispered her name, which I cannot tell you, Sol, for it only belongs to the lynx, and to me. The entire landscape rippled and throbbed in the rhythm of the drumming. The lynx crouched before me. I mounted her. I placed the drum down, for I no longer needed it. Its rhythm was in me and in the landscape, was in the ground and trees and skies. I held tight onto the skin of the lynx's neck and pressed myself against her coarse fur. Among the speckles, I felt the narrow scars that had grown on her skin in the course of our shared journeys.

The lynx got to her feet and began to trot at a deliberate pace along the path. I felt the movements of her muscles under me, the warmth emanating from her, as she picked up pace. The trees whispered and rustled. We swept past them. The path ahead began to glow, as the lynx's wide paws hit it. The forest turned into a tunnel of green and light and dark.

And the glowing path rose up, the sky folded toward us, and we were no longer in the woods. The road surged among the stars, taking me and the lynx with it. Space shone around us. Suns and moons floated as bright and dim dots in blackness, and occasionally planets, red and purple dust. I knew where the lynx was taking me. I had been there before.

We crossed a narrow, black crevice, a crack in space that twisted like a dark current. A flock of meteors settled around us like a group of gray, sharp-beaked birds, but the lynx dodged each one of them. Eventually I saw it: in the distance, where the horizon might have been drawn if there had been horizons in space, rose something that shone a faint light. At first it was so far that it seemed no bigger than a fragile, uprooted twig. As we approached, it began to show its outline against the darkness: a tall tree with a strong trunk and branches reaching in all directions. The path ran to its foot.

The lynx did not stop, did not even slow down. When we arrived under the tree, she leaped directly up the trunk, sank her claws into the bark and began to climb among the branches with agile movements. We rose up toward the treetop. At the peak of the tallest branch a star shone like a flower, and under it opened a hole, a doorway into the trunk.

We reached the top. My fingers squeezed into the fur of the lynx as she jumped into the hole without a moment's hesitation.

We fell. We flew.

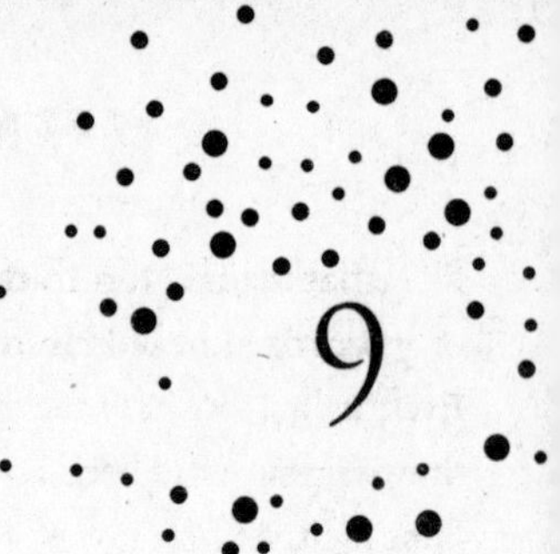

9

Sender: Anonymous
Recipient: Lumi Salo
Date: 18.3.2168 17.03 MST
Security: Maximum encryption

Lumi, my love,
My current circumstances prevent me from describing the characteristics of my surroundings or telling you the coordinates of my location. Due to reasons independent of myself, my communications are limited. I have spent the past days contemplating how to contact you and what to recount. I have concluded that there are two things you need to know.

The first one is this: I am not in immediate danger. You must not worry about me. The project I have been working on for nearly ten years is now at a critical phase. It has been met with unexpected difficulty, but I intend to see it through. If I gave up at such a moment, I would regret it forever.

The second thing is this: you must stop looking for me. I know how hard it is for you. I can guess that until now you will have left no stone unturned. However: trust me, Lumi. I will contact you and return to you as soon as possible.

I really did mean to come to Harmonia, as we had agreed. When I moved our rendezvous to Datong, I sincerely imagined it would actualize. But something happened that forced me to make acute decisions. I am sorry for the worry I know I have caused you.

Thank you for bringing the wooden box I asked for.

If I were you, I'd consider returning home to Nüwa the most rational course of action. I'd plant some more tomato seedlings, organize old papers. I'd read a good book. There are several volumes of interest on the shelf of my home office. I'd write more entries in the notebook you are filling at the moment, so I can read it when we are together again. Ziggy must be missing his absolute favorite place in my work chair.

In my thoughts we are sitting together in one of our forever-changing rooms in the Moonday House. In this variation, the sofa under us is worn leather: hefty and stabile, safe. A cast-iron teapot stands on the table. The Japanese-style ceramic teacups are steaming with freshly poured tea. Leaf-shaped cakes have been placed next to them on a cake stand. On the other side of the table a fire burns in the fireplace. The scent of burning wood floats in the air. On the mantelpiece stretches the bronze statuette of a lynx that you placed there when we first built this room.

I seize your hand across the distance.

Outside the windows, in the blue dusk, light snow falls. Beyond, the green of the garden withdraws into shadows.

Bury something under the flowering quince for me, Lumi.

Holocene
Encyclopedia of Geology.
Harmonia:
Harmonia University Press,
125 MC.

The *Holocene* refers to the geological epoch that began after the Weichselian glacial period, approximately in the year 9600 BCE, when the climate warmed. After the deglaciation, the land revealed from under the ice was first populated by tundra flora, such as grasses and shrubs, and later by trees, such as birch and pine. The Holocene is considered to have come to an end with the first nuclear test in 1945 CE, which the International Commission on Stratigraphy officially approved as the starting point of a new geological epoch, the *Anthropocene*, in 2040 CE.

Despite relative stability, there were some variations in the climate during the Holocene, most notably toward the end of the epoch. Approximately a thousand years ago farming was possible in several regions of Europe that later cooled down to an Arctic climate. After the Holocene these locations, Greenland and Iceland among them, warmed again. The cool period (approximately 1400 CE–1900 CE) is called the *Little Ice Age*.

The Holocene is strongly characterized by the rapid development of the culture of modern humans (*Homo sapiens*), which can be roughly divided into hunting and gathering, farming the land, and the birth of cities, or urbanization. The last-mentioned is also connected with the creation of written language, which is usually timed at approximately 3000 BCE.

The name Holocene is derived from ancient Greek: *holos* (whole, complete, entirely) and *kainos* (new), and it means "very recent."

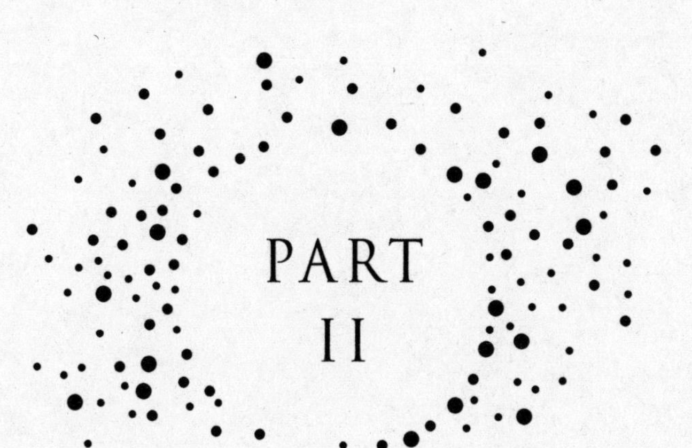

PART II

Five billion years

And then we can go

A million lightyears

How far – I don't know

To walk on the moon

There's nothing to explain

And if you open your eyes

We'll force you to close them again

"Dark Earth (Kill One, Get One Free),"The Workshop Sound

M. Chen & K. Montez, eds. *Born To Die: An Anthology of Pop Lyrics from the 21st Century*, vol. 3. New York II: Moonage Press, 2099.

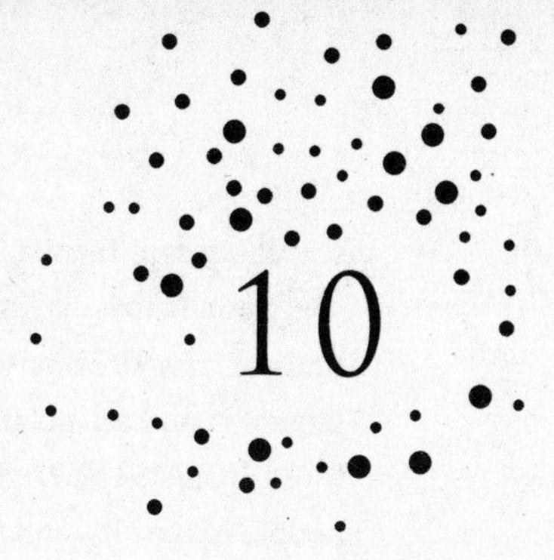

10

Inanna and the Raven
Myth retelling based on ancient Sumerian texts. Author unknown.

Inanna was a goddess: she was the queen of heavens and daughter of stars, and where she walked, meadows grew with scented flowers, and battlefields grew with bloodstained spears. When she was young, she traveled between worlds, gathering knowledge and learning about her own powers.

After wandering for a long time, Inanna arrived at a city in the middle of a desert, and in the city there grew a garden surrounded by a wall. A Raven worked in the garden. It was no ordinary bird, but one descended from the heavens, its beak sharp as a celestial sword and its wings wide as night. Inanna followed its work: The Raven dug a careful hollow into the ground and placed a delicate sapling in it, covering its roots from sight. The bird carried water to the sapling and used its kohl-dark beak to pull weeds around it. It brought wriggling worms near the sapling, so the tree could grow in soft soil.

The tree grew tall and narrow, and its wide leaves sheltered the other plants in the garden from the scorching sun. Inanna lay down to sleep in the shadow; she slept many cycles of the moon, many cycles of the sun. Her dreams wrapped every stalk and leaf and blossom, and all plants grew large and lush, for they loved Inanna. The tree bore mellow fruit that fed the people of the city, and the garden flourished. The Raven considered its work done, and placed a man named Shukaletuda to tend to the garden and protect it.

Shukaletuda looked upon Inanna, above whom the fruits of the tree hung sweet and heavy. Their smooth skin glowed in the afternoon light, and their scent was intoxicating.

One day after a long sleep Inanna woke up. Shukaletuda was lying on top of her and had exposed himself and spread Inanna's legs. Inanna fought back, but the violation had already happened. The plants of the garden lay dry and dead in the sun, and many of them had been uprooted. Before Inanna could gather her wits and move, Shukaletuda got up and ran away.

A rage rose in Inanna. She swore to catch Shukaletuda and bring him to justice. She summoned three plagues upon earth: she filled the wells and streams with blood, and she bent punishing winds and an all-swallowing flood to sweep the city, and she severed every path and road that people could have used to escape. But still she could not find Shukaletuda.

Far beyond the stars, the Raven heard the commotion and descended back to Earth. It flew to Inanna and asked, What has happened to my garden and to the plants I grew?

Inanna said, You placed Shukaletuda to tend to your

garden, but he did not water the plants, and he uprooted them, and in the shadow of the tree he took me by force. You chose wrong, and now you must help me find Shukaletuda, so he can be punished as he deserves.

The Raven hung its head before Inanna and regretted its mistake. Come, it said. I will carry you to the ends of the earth and not cease my flight until we have found him.

Inanna mounted the Raven, and together they flew past the wrecked world below: the once-green garden that had turned to dust, the bloodstained fields, the storm-lashed cities and bruised roads. For a long time they flew and searched every corner of the earth. They searched in forests and on fields, and in deserts and on ocean islands, and leaves and seeds and grains of sand and drops of water caught in the Raven's plumage. But Shukaletuda was nowhere to be found.

After Inanna had gone around the heavens, after she had gone around the earth, she eventually said to the Raven, There is only one place Shukaletuda could have escaped to, and there I must go alone.

Inanna dressed in her power. She put on the necklace and the skirts, the mask and the beard, the cloak and the headpiece, and in her hand she carried the drum that would open the Seven Gates of the Underworld. She told the Raven: If I do not return, come for me. Then she bade farewell.

Each gate opened for her, but each gate demanded a sacrifice. At the first one she lost her necklace; at the second, her skirts. The mask, the beard, the cloak and the headpiece were stripped from her each in turn. The last gate claimed her drum. When she arrived in the Underworld, she was naked, and she had no means of opening the gates again to go back.

Inanna's sister Ereshkigal, who reigned over the Underworld, stood up from her throne.

I have come for Shukaletuda, Inanna said.

Ereshkigal said, Shukaletuda is here, but he belongs to me. You cannot have him.

Why would you want him? Inanna asked. Do you not know what he has done?

He has only done what is in his nature, Ereshkigal said. You cannot judge him for that. He was made that way.

No, Inanna said. He was given free will. It was his choice. And he must answer for the consequences.

Oh, little sister, Ereshkigal said. You still have much to learn.

If you do not give him to me, I will claim him by force, Inanna said.

She stepped forward and pushed Ereshkigal to the side and took to her throne. But Ereshkigal had her servants seize Inanna, and their gaze was made of death. As they looked at her, life faded from her body. Inanna collapsed. Darkness shrouded her, and she was hung from a hook above the dark stream that separates the living from the dead.

Meanwhile, the Raven grew restless. Three days and three nights passed. All plants on earth began to wither and die, because they missed Inanna. Three weeks passed, then three months. On the first morning of the fourth month the earth was bare and dead. That was when the Raven cloaked itself in leaves that had caught on its feathers and passed through the Seven Gates unnoticed. It arrived at the dark stream, and saw Inanna's lifeless corpse hanging from the hook.

The Raven found Ereshkigal sleeping in her bedroom. It pulled out a few feathers on which seeds had caught from the fields where they had sought Shukaletuda. The Raven scattered the seeds over Ereshkigal and watched her breathe them in.

When Ereshkigal woke, she was in terrible agony, like hundreds of scorpions were squirming inside her. The Raven was sitting at the foot of her bed.

What do you want? Ereshkigal asked.

Give me Inanna, the Raven said, and give me Shukaletuda, and I will help you heal.

Anything, Ereshkigal said. I will not stop you, as long as you take this pain away.

The Raven shook loose a single feather on which grains of sand had caught from deserts.

These grains will counteract the poison, it said. When you swallow them, your agony will disappear.

So the Raven went and gathered the lifeless body of Inanna, and it went and gathered Shukaletuda, who was hiding and cowering among the dead. The Raven sprinkled Inanna's body with the drops of water that had caught in its plumage from the oceans of the world, and they were made of life: Inanna drew a breath. Her heart began to beat again. She opened her eyes. Her gaze fell on the Raven, and her gaze fell on Shukaletuda, whom the Raven was holding tight in its claws.

What will you do to me now that you have found me? Shukaletuda asked.

I wish to ask you a question, Inanna said. Why did you destroy the garden and violate me?

Because I wanted to, Shukaletuda said, and because I could.

Inanna said, Death is not punishment enough for you. I will strike you blind, and I will place you up in the sky in the heart of a star where you will burn until the end of days. And I will place your name in songs that people sing, so your crime can never be forgotten, and it will never be repeated.

The Raven flew Inanna and Shukaletuda through the Seven Gates of the Underworld into the realm of the living. There winter had come, and all flowers and trees had withered. Inanna struck Shukaletuda blind and placed him in the sky and placed his name in songs.

As Inanna walked the earth again, plants came alive in her footprints and trees grew new leaves and meadows flowered with a thousand blooms. People saw it and said, Earth wakes and stones will speak, and darkness recedes over waters.

18.3.2168
Hotel Picard
Elysium, Mars

Sol,

Do you still remember how we began to build the Moonday House?

When I think of our beginning, I think of other things: How you almost touched me, how you watched the expressions on my face. How I was wary and wanting.

I remember our first meeting. I had arrived at your childhood home a few weeks earlier. It was late night. Your mother was asleep, I remained exhausted from the session of the day before, and your sister was out somewhere partying. She still used to go out back then.

I stepped into your family's living room, larger than my parents' home on Earth. A tapestry portraying a starry sky covered one wall, and the chairs were heavy wood. Electric lanterns with shivering lights that imitated live fire burned in the corners.

You must be the new healer, a voice said from the dusky corner of the room.

I turned around. You sat in a tall-backed, upholstered chair, the sort I had rarely seen. Your face remained in the shadow.

I'm sorry, I said. I didn't realize there was someone in here. Ilsa said I could borrow books from the shelf.

Be my guest, you said, and half bowed while seated. Anyone who enjoys reading is welcome to my living room. Don't let me disturb.

My living room: of course. I remembered on the first day Ilsa had mentioned a sibling who was away on a work trip and would return soon.

I turned back to face the bookshelf, but the words on the spines of the books seemed to scatter and fade. I could not grasp them, because I felt your gaze on my back.

The light shifted. You had switched a lamp on in the corner where you sat.

Randomly I picked a paperback volume from the shelf in order to be able to leave the room. *Geological Particularities of the Southern Hemisphere of Mars*, the cover read. Without a doubt the book was packed with compelling plot twists.

I turned toward you to nod a goodbye. I saw you watch me intently, and I kept looking back. Your dark hair was tied at the nape of your neck, and presumably it fell down your back. You wore a pine-green collared shirt, a well-fitted waistcoat and jeans. Someone else might have found your features too angular. I wished to reach my hand toward them at once.

You can stay here and read, you said. If you like. I can't sleep. My internal clock is messed up from traveling. But I promise I won't disturb you.

My tiredness receded. I responded something of consent.

Handsome chairs, I said.

My grandparents brought them from Earth, you replied.

I thought bringing furniture from Earth was forbidden to the settlers.

You looked at me and smiled. The light reflected in your eyes.

It was, you replied. That doesn't mean it never happened.

I nodded. I opened the book and stared at the introduction. The words crossed the pages in meaningless ribbons. You got up, walked to the wall and opened a sliding door that revealed a fitted cupboard. I sensed a current of cold air on my skin.

From the cupboard you picked up a decanter that held dark amber liquid. You found a glass on the lower shelf that you placed on the small table between the chairs. It looked illicitly fragile to me, because I was used to the durable aluminum mugs of the zero-waste systems on Mars and other colonies. I had only seen glasses in an expensive restaurant where a wealthy patient had insisted on taking Vivian and me.

You poured some liquid into the glass. I noticed a red tinge in it, like a deep Earth sunset blended with a drop of blood.

What's that? I asked.

You raised your gaze.

Smell it, you said.

You picked the glass up and brought it before my face. I took a deep breath. The scent brought colors to my mind, even deeper than those I could see.

What is it made of?

Quince wine. Would you like a glass? Or would you prefer something else, nonalcoholic perhaps?

The golden apple Paris gave Aphrodite, I said. I'd like a sip.

You know Greek mythology.

You found another glass in the cupboard and poured some wine at the bottom. I took it from your hand. The liquid was frost-cold through the glass.

My teacher was very particular about botanical knowledge, whether it was myths or facts, I said. Some scriptures claim that the forbidden fruit Eve gave Adam was a quince. If you're familiar with Christian tradition. Although I find that implausible, because quinces are too sour to eat raw. In Renaissance-era England they were used as an aphrodisiac. The pips and syrup boiled from them are good for stomach ailments.

Impressive, you said. Your voice and your face were sincere; I sensed no sarcasm in them.

I wasn't trying to impress, I replied. Immediately I felt embarrassed, and a sudden sorrow flicked through me. For a moment Vivian had been alive again, I'd been sitting with her at a table where she showed me pictures of different medicinal plants and examined my knowledge of their uses.

You watched me in silence, a contemplative expression on your face.

I thought quince became extinct long ago, I continued, in order to shatter the silence.

It did, in most places, you said. My family brought a sapling of a flowering quince from Earth over a century ago, and miraculously it survived.

It's the last one in the known universe, then?

No, you said. My grandparents' biotechnology company worked for a long time in order to graft a new variety optimized for Mars cultivation zone conditions. Nowadays there is an entire orchard.

Only one, though. There's no mass market demand, because preparing the fruit to eat is so laborious. But many connoisseurs regard it highly.

What about the original tree?

Grows in the communal garden accessible from the top floor. I can show it to you if you like.

I lifted the glass to my lips and took a sip. The wine was sweet and tart. It reminded me of apples and pears and citruses, and of unknown flowers.

It's delicious.

I'll give you a bottle to take with you when you go.

You sat in a chair and regarded me. I was aware of my worn clothes, my appearance that I knew to be weary. I had never strived to make my sessions an attractive show of theatrics, like some healers did. Any external thing was a distraction to me, making the journey harder and the chances of succeeding weaker. But I didn't see disapproval or judgment from your part. Nor boredom. I only saw genuine interest.

I've been terribly rude, you said. I haven't asked your name.

I'm Lumi.

Lumi, you repeated, and it seemed to me that you held the word in your mouth, getting used to its strange shape, feeling its taste. Trying to decide if you enjoyed it. What an unusual name. It feels like light tied in a knot on the tongue.

I only told you much later what a ridiculous pickup line I thought it was.

It means snow in my native tongue, I said.

Snow, you said.

You know. The white flakes that fall from the sky on Mars now and then. And even on Earth, once in a blue moon.

I saw thoughts move behind your eyes and knew you must have understood where I came from. Perhaps I had confirmed your suspicions. But you said nothing about that. Instead:

Pleasure to meet you, Lumi. You raised your glass. I'm Sol.

I should keep my distance, then, I said and was surprised at my own words. Flirting had always been alien to me, something that made me feel like I belonged to a different species altogether.

Why?

Surely you're aware of what sunlight does to snow?

Are you worried you might melt if you come too close?

Are you?

When two different worlds meet, the end result may be unpredictable, you said and clinked our glasses together.

It was a response, but not to my question.

• • ● • •

The Moonday House didn't come until later. That first time I stayed in your childhood home for eight months. Your mother was used to having a healer in close proximity; you said once you couldn't remember a time when that was not the case. The Moonday House came after the quince wine, after dozens of exhausting sessions, after you first came to my door in the middle of the night. But it came before Fuxi. When we began to spend our days and nights together, for the first six months I avoided traveling so I could wake up next to you. I know you did the same. Yet we could not avoid it forever. You had to leave again for your conferences and seminars and research symposiums. I had to keep traveling to see patients. Distance was always a part of us, from the beginning.

This is how I remember it happening, as clear as if it were here and now:

I lie in a capsule hotel somewhere on Earth with the lightness brought by fasting inside me, preparing for the next day's healing session. I think of my parents: how sharp my mother's bones had felt as I embraced her for the first time in two years, how my father tried to hide his tears when I left again. But they'd both looked happy while I was there, and I knew their new, warm winter boots must have been bought with the money I'd sent them. My screen pings. I pick it up.

When I go to bed alone, I imagine us in a house where two full moons always shine into the garden from a blue sky, you write. *I go to sleep there next to you.*

Here on Earth it is Monday, the day of the Moon, I reply. *I pull web-thin curtains to cover the window, but I see the pale coins of the full moons through them. In the Moonday House I am always with you, at home.*

And so we had a shared home, in our thoughts.

Weeks later we lie next to each other in your room on Mars, in the narrow light of the night lamp. The living wall has switched off, its plants dark silhouettes. It is past midnight, but neither of us can sleep.

The kitchen is wide and faintly lit, like in an old English country mansion, you say. There are copper pans hanging on the walls, reflecting the lights of candles and oil lamps. Herbs have been hung to dry from the thick ceiling beams. The scent of rosemary, thyme and lavender drifts in the air. The windows are small, behind them the gray twilight of the morning is slowly beginning to turn into daylight. A crackling fire burns in the fireplace, and the stone floor by it is warm, although it's cool elsewhere.

I don't want a faintly lit kitchen, I say. My kitchen is full of light. The windows cover an entire wall and the sun shines in through them. A hydroponic indoor garden grows on the internal walls, vine tomatoes and bean stalks wind their ways across them, and courgettes and strawberries and lettuce leaves. Each surface is smooth and unbroken, and the floor is always warm, even under bare feet.

You place your hands on my face and trace your finger along my cheek.

The Moonday House can have two kitchens, you say. Or twenty. Two thousand, if we want.

I know.

There's frost lichen growing on the external walls of the house,

I continue. And sometimes on the internal walls too. It has a faint shimmer to it that you can only catch in certain light.

What's frost lichen? You ask.

The Seal of the Spirit, I respond. An old remedial plant from the region of Scandinavia and Siberia. It survives in the most austere conditions. It forms patterns on rock and tree trunks, and the concrete walls of houses.

What does it look like?

This, I say and draw patterns on your bare skin with my finger.

I think, *It doesn't matter what every detail looks like, or how many rooms there are in the house. What matters is that through all the windows we see the same garden, the same moonlight in daylight that no one besides us can see.* But I don't say it aloud. It seems obvious.

All this I remember.

Do you, Sol? And if you do, do you remember it the way I do?

19.3.2168
Hotel Picard
Elysium, Mars

Yesterday I was barely capable of anything. The soul-journey had drained me. When I woke up, I had no idea what time of day, or even what day, it was. Clothes had glued themselves to my skin, and Ziggy slept next to me, a warm roll curled up against the back of my knees. The only source of light in the room was a narrow strip under the door.

I switched on the light and sat up in the bed. I switched on my screen. It showed the date: 18.3. The time was 4.28 a.m. I estimated I had slept around thirty-five hours. It is difficult to judge the length of soul-journeys on your own. Sol, you have seen me disappear to the other side for minutes, for hours, sometimes for days, even, although that is not safe without an assistant, because time has a different flow there. The lynx was gone. The tuft-eared headpiece lay neatly placed on the side table and the drum was folded next to it. I didn't remember putting them there. I was still wearing the speckled cloak. It had become tangled with the blankets. I detached the brooches from my shoulders and wriggled out of the fabric.

Memories of the journey drifted into my mind. The strong muscles of the lynx under me and the sparks of the wide paws, the tree rising ahead and on top of it the wormhole diving into the trunk. We had traveled a long time, the lynx and I, and she had known which of the long and winding paths to choose even when I was uncertain of the direction. The landscape had been stony and strange, bright and dark-brushed at once. We had met familiar creatures and unfamiliar. Some I asked for advice and others I didn't, and from some I hid altogether. They walked past with sharp teeth and eyes that glinted cold, their bones like glass under the translucent skin. Entire worlds fit in their opening and closing maws. The lynx and I hid in rocks and ravines, and we passed a black forest, and a snow-white gate, and a red lake. Once we dove into a river, breathed the water like fish and allowed the stream to carry us.

Across it all I held an image of you on the surface of my mind, Sol. I wished to reach a trace, a sign, a thread I could seize and follow, even if it was to the heart of a labyrinth. Once I believed that the lynx saw something. Her keen eyes opened wider, she stopped to sniff the air and turned her head. But no paths led in that direction. A mist rose from the ground to surround us, the wings of moths moved on tree branches and star-filled chasms opened in the sky.

Somehow the lynx carried me back, although I could not remember it. If you were there, you remained hidden from me.

I fed Ziggy, drank water, ate a handful of almonds and fell asleep again.

I woke up to a message arriving onto my screen. It had been sent anonymously from an unknown address, a private location that was not traceable.

Lumi, my love, my current circumstances prevent me, it began.

I tried to reply to it directly, but the response function had been disabled.

I have read through the message dozens of times. It must be from you. No one else knows about the lynx statuette on the mantelpiece, about the Moonday House. It belongs to the two of us alone.

You are alive, Sol.

There was little I could do. I thought of my time with you, Sol. I wrote about it.

You walk into shadows, look at me over your shoulder. You turn your face away and continue to walk until all I see is a stretch of black, and I don't know if it is part of you or a piece of darkness that will dissolve if I try to touch it.

Sender: Lumi Salo
Recipient: Enisa Karim
Date: 19.3.2168 18.12 MST
Security: Maximum encryption

Hello Enisa,

Sorry to bother you, but I wanted to ask you something – as an environmental journalist you might know more about this than I do. Have you ever heard of an organization called the Stoneturners?

I'd love to buy you a cup of tea before I leave Elysium. If you cannot make it, let's do it another time.

Lumi

21.3.2168
Hotel Picard
Elysium, Mars

I think of you, Sol: cleaning your spectacles and placing them back on your nose, pushing your hair back from your face with your fingers. Reading in a dark room as I wake up in the middle of the night, roll over and see you not sleeping.

I think of you here, next to me on the edge of the bed.

What is this place? I ask.

We're on Europa, you say. Don't you remember?

I shake my head.

You came here to treat a patient. Your healing session put too much of a strain on you. You were burned out. You've slept for nearly a week.

I don't remember, I say.

We were supposed to meet on Mars, but I was worried. I came to bring you home, you say and take my hand. I wanted to see Europa. You wrote such intriguing things about it.

In my thoughts it is true. In my thoughts you can be anywhere, even in the most impossible places. Here.

· ••• ·

This morning I received a message from Enisa. *When are you free to meet?* She wrote. I sent a response: *I'm free anytime*. Shortly the screen pinged and a coffee shop marked on the map appeared on it, with a virtual note attached: *14.00?* The place was fairly far from the hotel, but the underground would take me close enough. I sent Enisa a *Yes*.

The coffee shop turned out to be a shabby Irish-style pub with several letters missing from the neon sign, which caused a delay in me finding it. The inside stank of malt, and the seat covers were threadbare.

I didn't see Enisa anywhere. I ordered a tea at the bar and took a seat in a corner from which I could see the door. The waiter brought a battered metal pot and a cup that had been stainless once upon a time.

I was beginning to suspect I'd come to the wrong place, when Enisa appeared in the pub and waved at me. She too ordered a tea, placed her bag on the bench attached to the wall and sat down.

"Sorry I'm late," she said. "A delay on the underground. Have you heard anything from your spouse?"

I'd already decided I wasn't going to tell her about your message, Sol. "I haven't heard anything."

Enisa's expression shifted like a shadow on a wall.

"I'm sorry," she said. "Are you all right? If you need company, you can come for dinner. My spouse makes the best *zereshk polo morgh* in the entire Solar System. It is—"

"I love *zereshk polo morgh*," I said. "We used to make it sometimes on Fuxi. Without chicken, though, despite the fact that lab meat was easily available there."

"I thought you couldn't import barberries there because of the quarantine regulations?"

"That's true. We always left them out," I confessed.

Sol, we have violated the unwritten laws of traditional Persian cookery: Enisa's face was appalled.

"The rice gets its flavor from the barberries! You must try the one my spouse makes."

"Thank you," I said, and meant it sincerely. "But I have to depart for Harmonia tonight. To see Sol's mother and sister."

Enisa nodded.

"I understand." She smiled. "I'll write the recipe down for you. I'm on a work trip in Harmonia at the end of next week. Let me know if you'd like to meet up then."

"Deal."

Enisa lifted the lid of the teapot, sniffed the yellow-brownish liquid and scrunched her nose. "I only have slightly over an hour so I'll get right to the point. You asked about the Stoneturners."

"Do you know something about them?"

"Nobody seems to know much." Enisa poured a cup of tea for herself. The steam rising from the metal spout of the pot smelled remotely of star anise. "My curiosity has been piqued enough that I'm planning an article on them."

"What have you found out?"

"The name seems to refer to some kind of environmental organization," Enisa said. "The sources contradict each other. I made a list." Enisa sought her screen in her bag, and a piece of paper she handed to me. Titles and publishing information of books, journals and electronic articles were handwritten on it. There was only a handful of them. "The oldest mention I found was from about a hundred years ago. It portrays the Stoneturners as a secret society with esoteric beliefs and practices, a mix of soft occultism, neopaganism, tree worship and such. In the past fifty years the Stoneturners are usually referred to as an environmental organization, a harmless grassroot-level body – meetings where they drink herbal tea, peaceful demonstrations, nonviolent resistance. Planting trees in surprising places, seed bombing cities."

She sipped her tea, grimaced and added hot water and sugar to it.

"Are the Stoneturners active on Mars?" I asked.

"So it seems," Enisa said. Her spoon clinked in the cup as she stirred her tea. "They kept a low profile for a long time, but about five years ago there was a clear shift. Their campaigns became more visible. Together with several other environmental organizations they objected to the expansion of mining in southern polar regions of Mars."

"I remember the campaign," I said. "They demanded that the Mars landscape should be preserved on the same basis that some Moon regions were protected. The principle of inviolability."

"You're familiar with it?"

"Yes, for a long time. I first heard about it from my teacher who trained me to be a healer. She considered it one of her guiding ethical principles."

Enisa placed the spoon on the plate. She adjusted the edge of the scarf framing her face and glanced at her watch.

"Why are you interested in the Stoneturners?" she asked.

I couldn't think of any reason not to tell her, so I described my visit to the police station.

"They believe several of Sol's workmates are members of a radical environmental organization. The Stoneturners doesn't sound very radical," I added.

Enisa's eyes turned to the steaming tea. I could practically see words shifting in her mind before she raised her gaze back to me.

"I haven't told you everything yet," she said. "In the past twenty years or so there have been dozens of anonymous strikes that are suspected to have been committed by environmental organizations. No one has died in them, but there have been many near misses. Sabotage of mining equipment, railway construction sites, luxury hotels and new residential areas on the Moon and Mars. A few journalists have speculated that the Stoneturners might be behind the strikes." Enisa switched on the display of her screen that was lying on the table, then scrolled down until she found what she was looking for. "I thought this in particular might interest you." She handed the screen to me. On it was an article captured from a news site I was unfamiliar with, dated two years ago.

Sol, I only remember the headline of the article, but that is enough. *Was the Fuxi fungal disease sabotage? Mysterious environmental organization the Stoneturners under the magnifier*, the page read.

The news site didn't look like one of the more reliable ones. In the sidebar of the screen capture such headings were visible as *Learn to astral travel to Earth* and *Was there life on Mars before us? Secret evidence REVEALED!*

"I know," Enisa said. "Not the kind of source I'd quote myself. But this is not the only speculation of the Stoneturners' activities expanding into more aggressive strikes."

"Do you have other sources?"

Enisa was quiet for a moment.

"There's a paper report," she said. "I can't get it for you, but I've seen it. The police have been watching the Stoneturners for more than ten years. They speak of them as a terrorist organization."

The word sank into my consciousness like a sharp stone that breaks the surface of water.

Terrorist organization.

I found it difficult to breathe. News footage of burning buildings, people lying on the streets and grainy images of hostages flooded my mind. My throat closed around my voice, when I tried to speak.

"Have they ever..."

I tried to pour more tea into my cup, but the pot was empty. Its metal lid clanged, as I placed it back on the table. My hand shook.

"They're not known to have ever taken hostages before," Enisa said in a calming voice. "Or to have hurt people on purpose. There's no reason to believe they plan to do so now."

Another mental image that had returned often to haunt me: someone you trusted forcing you to the backseat of the vehicle in Elysium.

"Why do the police think Sol's workmates belonged to the Stoneturners, specifically? Couldn't they have been active in some other organization?"

Enisa took a breath. Her fingers settled on the dark screen.

"There's a good reason," she said. "It took a while to come across this information, because I hadn't thought of the language barrier. The Stoneturners was founded in United Korea, and from there it spread to China, Vietnam and Japan. In its early days the organization only used Southeast Asian languages. They've had a slogan from the beginning, but the translation into Martian English only seems to have been established in the past twenty years or so, when the organization has gained a stronger foothold here." Enisa observed my face. "Do you remember the biograffiti on the wall of the research station?"

I understood.

Your sentence, Sol. *Earth wakes and stones will speak.*

And Vivian's. *And darkness recedes over waters.*

I stared at Enisa. In my mind the pieces moved, but none of them found their right place.

Sol, what do the Stoneturners want from you?

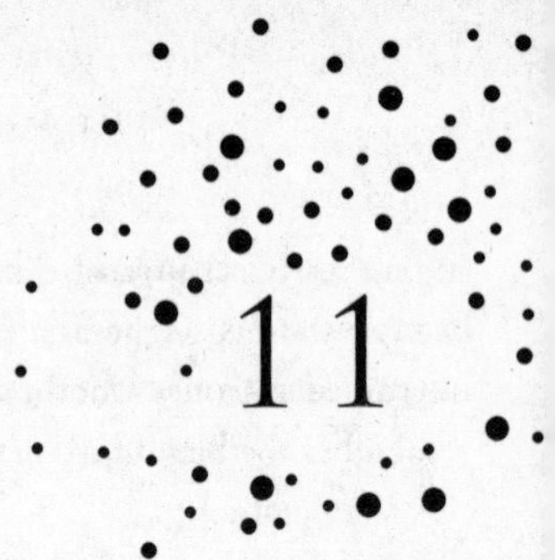

11

Incident at Bradbury Food Refinery
Copernicus local news 15.6.2151

A minor incident took place in the crater town of Copernicus at Bradbury Food Refinery late on Thursday night that caused all operations at the refinery to cease temporarily. Shortly before midnight, the surveillance equipment registered a malfunction in the machines of the refinery hall that are usually left on overnight. The operations of the machines slowed down considerably and even came to a halt in some parts of the hall. The night watch alerted law enforcement. An investigation revealed a thick growth of algae in the machinery that hindered the operations of the conveyor belts, crushers and the vat mixer rods.

According to the officials, the accident poses no danger to the inhabitants of Copernicus. The algae is nontoxic. However, cleansing the equipment may take several months. It is unclear when the refinery will be able to continue its operations again.

Bradbury Food Refinery was the target of heavy criticism last year when environmental organizations slammed the manufacturing and marketing of artificial meat grown in laboratories from animal stem cells on the Moon. According to the organizations, the energy needed for producing artificial meat and processed food items made from it requires large resources that could be utilized in other ways in the harsh Moon conditions. Furthermore, environmentalists have repeatedly questioned the ethics of lab-grown meat on the basis that the practice is still rooted in the idea of eating animals, instead of attempting to offer true alternatives to it.

The CEO of Bradbury Food Refinery could not be reached for comment.

22.3.2168
A train somewhere between Elysium and Datong Isidis Planitia, Mars

I can guess that until now you will have left no stone unturned. That's what you wrote, Sol.

In these parts of the plain the train runs mostly underground. Darkness shrouds the windows, hiding the world away, except in spark-like moments when some lit maintenance tunnel or station that is no longer in use flickers past. I have time to see a closed metal gate or a dusky opening that leads to strange places, letters faded on the wall in a language I cannot read. Dim lights mark the direction of tunnels, like stars in distant orbits.

From those fleeting shards of light my mind puts together an image that probably resembles the network of rail tunnels as much as the first draft of a blueprint does a finished building: if you have seen the building, you will recognize its outline in the drawing, but if you have only seen the drawing and never the building, your imagined visualization of it can only be wrong. Likewise, among your sentences I see carefully chosen words and clusters of words, fragments that my mind wishes to make into something hidden but whole. A shadow whose shape only I might see, because others would not know to seek it. A message you wanted only me to be able to read.

You will have left no stone unturned.

Did you know that sooner or later I would come across the name the Stoneturners?

If you did, Sol, what did you want me to do with it, what did you want me to understand? I only see the blueprint, not the building.

You did not write, *Don't tell anyone about this message.*

You wrote, *Thank you for bringing the wooden box I asked for.* You wrote, *Bury something under the flowering quince for me.*

They took you against your will, in order to get something they needed from you. It is my job to find out what it is.

Before I boarded the train I called Owoeye and told her I'd heard from you.

This train is better than the freight trains. (Ziggy's behavior, however, indicates the rodent situation may not be entirely under control here, either.) The cars have a wireless connection. Ilsa and Naomi know to expect me; I let them know when I'd arrive. The sleeper cabin has trees painted on the wall for decoration, or so I gather. It's possible that the twisting, forking lines are meant to portray the cardiovascular system. Yet that seems an unlikely wall decoration. Perhaps the pattern is abstract.

I propped my screen up on the tiny table next to the bed. The loudspeaker played the ringtone for a long time. Eventually I heard a rustle, and the circle vibrating in the middle of the screen was replaced by Ilsa's forehead. The image swayed as she corrected the posture of her screen, and her entire face came to view.

"Just a moment," Ilsa said and reached beyond the edge of the image. The lighting grew brighter. Ilsa returned to the screen. Shadows settled on her face, between the eyebrows, under the eyes.

"Ilsa," I said.

We stared at each other. She looked somewhere past me, then at me again. She didn't respond.

"How are you?" I asked eventually.

Ilsa's expression was hard to read.

"Functioning," she said. "It's more than you can say about Mom." Ilsa went quiet. She sniffed and drank amber-colored liquid from a wide glass.

"You haven't heard from Sol, have you?" I asked.

"No. Have you?"

"No," I replied without pause. The lie took shape with surprising ease. Ilsa didn't seem to notice it. "I'll be there in a few days."

"Great."

I heard a clank as she placed the glass back on the table. It sounded the same as the tone of her voice. You were an invisible wall between us, Sol, muffling and distorting everything.

"Why are you calling me?" Ilsa asked.

"What do you mean?"

Her shoulders rose and fell. The sigh rustled in the loudspeakers.

"Lumi," she said. "We both know we're not in the habit of calling each other just because. And that's fine," she added. "I don't like you any less for it. Or more."

A crack appeared in the wall. It wasn't much, but I reached toward it.

"At least you're being honest about it," I said. "Better that way."

Ilsa's expression stilled, then stirred. It wasn't quite a smile, but close enough.

"I wanted to ask something," I said.

Ilsa was quiet. Then, "What?"

Before the call I had spent a long time thinking about what would be the best place to start. I decided to go straight into the heart of the matter.

"Has Sol ever mentioned an organization called the Stoneturners?"

The shadow between Ilsa's eyebrows deepened.

"Why do you ask?"

"Have you heard about them? From Sol, or somewhere else?"

Ilsa's mouth stretched into a line and relaxed again, but not all tension disappeared.

"As a student Sol was part of all kinds of scenes," she said. "Haven't they told you?"

I tried to ignore a pinch in my gut.

"They've only talked about that time in very broad terms."

"Sol attended protests against Moon mining, collected names for petitions and organized open discussions about whose responsibility it was to clean up space junk," Ilsa said. "All very proper, clean-cut, suited-to-the-supper-club rebellion. Nothing to permanently tarnish their reputation for the future."

I remembered you telling me about those things, Sol. I'd had no reason to pay much attention to any of them, not until now.

"They used to go to some meetings," Ilsa continued. "I asked to join them a couple of times, but Sol said it was a closed group, members only."

Thoughts writhed inside me, restless animals in the dark.

"Did Sol mention the name of the group?"

Ilsa did not respond immediately.

"I guess it's possible. It was a long time ago," she said eventually. "What are you getting at?"

"Just trying to make sense of some things." It was not a lie.

Ilsa drained her glass and placed it down. There was a noise in the background. Through the loudspeakers it sounded like a door slamming. Ilsa glanced somewhere outside the scope of the camera, then turned back to the screen.

"Sol did get arrested once," Ilsa said. She rubbed her eyes. Dark kohl spread into stains that made her look like a 1920s movie star. "They took part in occupying a water purification plant, but only got a fine. Mom threw a fit though."

"Sol has mentioned that."

You had shrugged it off as a stupid weekend prank of a hard-partying student group. Your sister's version sounded different. If Naomi had thrown a fit, I would have liked to see what Ilsa's reaction had been.

"I also wanted to ask about a sentence," I said. I had wondered if I should bring it up at all, but if Ilsa knew something, it might help. "Sol used it in a TV interview before they disappeared."

Something happened in Ilsa's gaze. She was wary.

"What sentence was that?"

The words flowed out easily; I'd repeated them in my mind so many times.

"Earth wakes and stones will speak, and darkness recedes over waters."

Ilsa was quiet.

"It's not the first time I've heard the sentence," I said. "My teacher Vivian used it often. I was surprised to hear it from Sol's mouth."

Ilsa's face had petrified. Even the slightest trace of a smile had vanished. The hollows under her cheekbones looked deeper; the circles under her eyes were black holes despite the makeup covering them.

"Lumi," she said in a worn voice. "I must hang up now. Mom needs something."

"Can't you at least tell me—"

"We'll talk more when you get here," Ilsa said and hung up.

I tried to call back, but she didn't pick up.

I switched off the screen. Ziggy scratched the cabin door and turned restlessly. He has started washing himself constantly. I hope he is all right. Clearly, none of the rest of us are.

23.3.2168

A train between Datong and Harmonia

Isidis Planitia, Mars

Sol,

I turn stones in my mind. I walk on the paths of the past, moving memories around. I try to look at them from all sides, find others underneath. On some paths I meet you; on others I encounter Vivian and the often-repeated stories my memory tells me about you and her. But you are both silent, if I ask something, or is it my own imagination that speaks with your mouth? You turn away or just look: unreachable, closed, unforgiving reflections.

We'd been together for two years when you asked if I wanted to move to Fuxi. Your mother was going through a better phase, and I'd been traveling, seeing other patients for the past six months. We were lying in bed in your childhood home, in the light-sphere of a dim lamp that span a cocoon around us and sealed everything else outside. A moth had found its way into the room and its shadow whirled on the walls.

Isn't it terribly difficult to get a visa for the cylinder cities? I asked.

I've been offered a job there. The university will take care of the visa. Yours, too, if you want.

I thought they didn't take Earth-borns.

They do. Spouses.

Is this a proposal?

Do you want it to be?

You know how I feel about marriage.

I do.

How badly do you want this job?

You were quiet for a long time, Sol. I ran my fingers through your dark hair.

It would help me reach a new level in what I have been working on for years, you said eventually.

Do you want to tell me about it?

I've been asked to participate in a project that is mapping the possibilities of helping Earth with new biotechnology. The project is being developed on Fuxi. They have the best resources.

What would that project mean in practice?

It's early days, you said. But sometime in the future, perhaps? Living coral reefs. Freely breathing forests. Lakes where it's safe to swim. Seas not suffocated by plastic.

A world where the Earth-born get to choose their future freely? Educate their children, live longer?

Maybe.

Could I continue my work?

You were quiet just long enough for me to expect words of doubt, to remember what an ill fit my profession was for your worldview framed by science.

But instead you said, Absolutely. There's a lot of demand for healers on Fuxi. And it's easy to get to Mars from there.

I do.

You lifted yourself up to lean on one arm. The shadow of the moth floated across your face, drew a new light into your eyes.

You do what?

Want to move to Fuxi with you.

For a moment your smile was bright and without shadow. You kissed me for a long time. Then you turned serious.

It'll be years, you said. Decades. The project may not produce results within our lifetime, if ever.

That doesn't matter.

No?

I intertwined my fingers with yours, wove our bodies together. In the fragile cocoon of light in the middle of all-consuming space we were one creature and yet two, far away from home yet home.

There is no magical quick way to fix Earth, I said.

I know, you said. You raised your voice a little. But don't you sometimes wish—

What matters is that we are willing to do slow and tedious and frustrating work in order to improve things bit by bit. Even when we know we'll never see the results. Even when others question if it makes sense. That defines who we are.

You were quiet. The moth landed on the wall over your head, like a thought. You pulled me closer.

What's the project called?

Project Earth, you replied.

• • ● • •

The next day, when you'd left for another work trip, I put on my biosuit and took the train to the observatory on the outskirts of Harmonia. I had discovered it when I first came to Mars with Vivian. Although I never told her, she must have known I was homesick, because one day she took me there. It was old-fashioned even then, all white spaces and wide, energy-consuming HD touchscreens. The train was faster now, the route slightly changed, but the observatory remained a time capsule, reminiscent of the first settlers' era over a century earlier.

I took the elevator to the surface of the planet, where the thick glass globe of the observatory looked away from the buried city, and I waited for the dark. That time of the year the Earth and Moon were bright in the evening sky: a blue-pale star, like the living heart of a flame, and in its vicinity, a smaller, bone-white speck. I sought an available telescope, brushed it with my pay bracelet, looked into the ocular and focused the image.

Northern Europe was turned toward Mars, with sunlight still just brushing it, but a feather-like swirl of white clouds covered most of it: it would almost certainly be raining in Winterland. I imagined plunging through the clouds in my biosuit, their humidity clinging to its surface, and landing, miraculously unaffected by gravity, at my parents' door. The drizzle would fall on my hair as I removed my helmet: real Earth rain, toward which I would raise my face to let my skin drink its fill. My parents would invite me in, and I'd help them make quick oatmeal cookies, and just that evening we'd have enough electricity for the oven to work. The flat would feel warm for once, and we'd all sit on the sofa and talk late into the night, and they'd tuck me into bed like they used to do when I was little.

When I'd watched Earth sufficiently, I turned the view to the slow-flashing speckles of the cylinder cities that circled Mars. Twelve of them were scattered along the orbit, and another ten orbited Earth. I knew their names, but had never been to any. Fuxi and its twin Nüwa were the oldest, largest and wealthiest. They were the closest to Mars, and they'd been founded soon after the first colonies on the planet. Against the black sky they looked like glimmering mechanical insects stretching their wings in the night.

I watched Fuxi through the telescope, in my mind building a life for us there like a spell, a castle on a dragonfly's back. *Carry me across the void so I can never fall.*

· •●• ·

Sol, it is terribly late. I search my screen for new messages from you. There are none. Ziggy was so restless in the cabin that I put a harness on him and took him for a late-night walk along the train corridors. We stalled at the end of the car, between the sleeping compartment and the restaurant car that was closed for the night. A middle-aged lady dressed in a boiler suit, lace-up boots and a loose green coat was wiping the windows with a rag, occasionally dipping it in a bucket. When she spotted us, she stopped and watched for a while as Ziggy twisted and turned, scratched his ear, pit, ear, neck and ear.

"Is your cat all right?" she asked.

"I hope so," I said. "I don't know what's the matter with him."

The woman dropped the rag into her bucket and picked the bucket up. She pulled a rolled cigarette out from the chest pocket of the coat.

"Have you considered fleas?" she said, and placed the cigarette into the corner of her mouth.

Damn it.

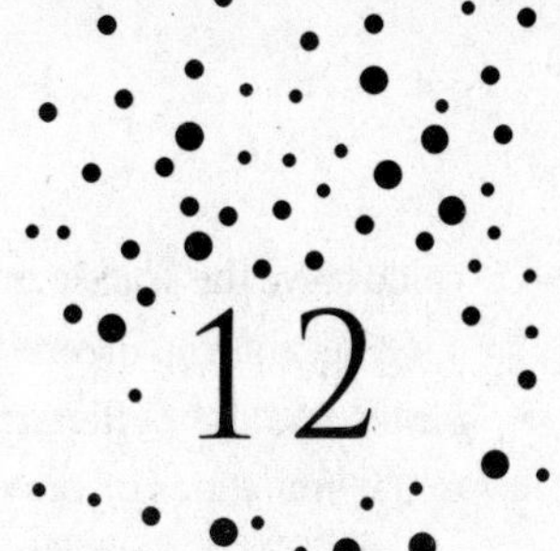

12

High hopes at Earth Conference on Fuxi
University of Harmonia on Fuxi e-newsletter
2.5.2164 Lea Kaplan

Does the brighter future of Earth begin here? Absolutely, if you ask the group of researchers that gathered on the cylinder city of Fuxi this week to discuss the applications of the newest biotechnology in environmental protection projects. The interplanetary Earth Conference brought together the best and brightest of the Solar System from various fields including biology, botany, physics, chemistry, climate-change science and environmental research, and the hopes were high.

"I have rarely seen optimism on this scale," enthuses Yang Tingting, professor of physics at the University of Harmonia on Fuxi. "The faith of the scientific establishment in the future of Earth is the highest it has been in over a century. The field of biotechnology aimed at cleansing oceans in particular is making significant leaps as we speak."

The team leader of the much-publicized Project Earth, ethnobotanist Sol Uriarte, speaks along similar lines.

"I can't wait to be able to tell the world about the results of the project," Uriarte comments. "There are two years left to go with the five-year research project, but I can already say that the results regarding the potential of seagrasses that increase the oceanic uptake of carbon dioxide on Earth look extremely promising. We are also studying their possible applications in neutralizing ocean acidification."

On Earth, where the struggle with ecological challenges is ongoing, one of the long-sought Holy Grails of science is biotechnology that could solve the double problem of both the ocean carbon sink that has a significant impact on global temperatures and the acidification that places a strain on ecosystems. Yet Uriarte urges caution when it comes to the limitations of biotechnology:

"While we are all hopeful, we must remember science is not magic. If something sounds too good to be true, it probably is. Everything has consequences, so solving one problem usually creates several others. Our job as scientists is to find knowledge based on objectivity and facts, and to apply it, but we are not capable of miracles."

Uriarte's words are worth heeding. Nevertheless, the idea of solving ecological problems with one stroke of a magic wand is enticing. May we believe in it, even if just for a while, until the reality hits again?

24.3.2168
Train
Isidis Planitia, Mars

One has not traveled on Mars with a cat until one has traveled on Mars with a flea-ridden cat.

25.3.2168
Train, etc. etc., an endless lifeless landscape on a hostile piece of rock floating in space where no human should ever have set foot, but the hubris of our species knows no bounds.

Sol,
Of all the places where I have lived, I remember Fuxi most clearly. I can tell you exactly how many steps I needed to take to walk from the kitchen into the bedroom, or on which part of the living-room floor the light fell at three o'clock in the afternoon in mid-April. I know

the order in which the basil and thyme and rosemary and mint I had planted on the balcony grew. Even now, I can see the shapes of the branches of the jacaranda trees that rose at the edge of the park nearest to us. I can hear how many minutes passed between the underground trains going to the spaceport as they drove past our building.

I have walked in those memories so often that they are brighter to me than Earth or Mars, sometimes brighter than our present-day home on Nüwa. In some moments they are closer than the jolting train carriage in which I write these words. Each time I summon Fuxi before me again, it is as if I fade a little more in the face of its brightness.

To you it was not new. You had visited cylinder cities often and you knew Fuxi. I, on the other hand, memorized every detail. I couldn't get enough of the fact that on Fuxi I could imagine I was on Earth, but like Earth had once been, before the time of the great disasters. I knew that the horizon's arc was too steep, and that the sky was a mere concave, artificial shell that separated us from space. I knew that the corn and bean orchards on the roofs and external walls of tall buildings were supported by machines, and that at my favorite café the living sycamore walls bent into arches with metal supports were only able to grow because of light-adjusting panels and hidden irrigation systems. But the air was fragrant and fresh, and the lighting and temperatures imitated day and night so precisely that the sky-shell was blue as a smooth egg in a robin's nest, the landscape of a new life. It was easy to step into it and bury the thought that the city was only a shard of metal floating in space, its machine heart an apparatus assembled by humans, without which everything would stop.

On our first evening on Fuxi you sought among the moving boxes one that was marked with a green cross and lifted the lid aside. It revealed a large terracotta pot and a milky, oblong silicone bag. A label was attached to the side of the bag that showed the words PLANT PASSPORT and several rows of different number codes. You lifted the bag out of the box and handed it to me.

Open it, you said.

I slid the mouth of the bag open. The humidity gathered inside clung to my fingers as I looked in.

Is this from your home? I asked.

Yes, from the same Earth-born individual. Would you plant it with me?

I pulled the quince sapling out carefully, so its pointy, dark green leaves wouldn't be caught on the mouth of the bag and break off. The sapling was approximately the length of my arm, and its roots sank deep into a fist-sized, damp lump of synthetic peat.

Is it permissible to bring shrubs to Fuxi? I asked.

All paperwork is in order, you said. I began to sort it out as soon as we decided to move here. I thought it could grow on the balcony.

You stripped the plastics off the terracotta pot and carried it to the balcony. You placed the pot in the corner, which I did not yet know was the spot for the morning sun, and poured compost into it. You dug a hole in the soil with your hands and sprinkled gray powder into it from a small glass jar.

What's that? I asked.

The spores of a fungus. It forms a symbiosis with the tree roots and helps it grow.

We can expect a fruit crop large enough to start a wine business for Fuxi gourmands later this year, then?

And a jam factory to boot.

You nodded toward the sapling and pointed at the pot. I held the delicate but hardy stem and seized the root lump with my other hand. The soil packed around the roots felt as damp and porous as a sponge. You placed your hand on top of mine, and together we lowered the root lump into the compost. You pressed it carefully into the hole, and we patted the soil to cover the roots, until the sapling stood steadily in the pot.

Do you think it will survive? I asked.

The conditions on Fuxi are very similar to Harmonia, but it is still far away from home, you said. Trees and shrubs do better the closer to their origin they grow. The soil is imported from Mars, just in case. We can acclimatize it to Fuxi soil little by little.

Our fingers intertwined at the base of the sapling. On the edge of the park jacaranda trees shed blue petals like rain, and on a gently arching branch a pearl-eyed row of sparrows and turtle doves murmured.

Some soil had scattered on the balcony floor. I went to get a dishcloth from a box marked KITCHEN and wiped the soil off. As I got up, the dishcloth slipped from my hand and fell a little aside from where I'd expected it to hit the floor. The yelp was out of my mouth before I realized.

It's because of the rotation of the cylinder, you said. Didn't you know?

I've never been to a cylinder city before.

You didn't mock my ignorance, Sol. You never have. You were genuinely surprised.

Nevertheless, my inexperience embarrassed me. I picked the dishcloth up. The next day, when you'd gone grocery shopping, I took the dishcloth in my hand again and dropped it, just to see it fall aside. Soon I'd begin to take it for granted; I wanted to feel the thrill as long as it was new.

Three months later the quince began to flower on the balcony. When you noticed, you called for me to come and see.

It believes it's come home, I said.

25.3.2168
Train
Isidis Planitia, Mars
Later

My hand is cramping from all the writing, but there's nothing to do on this bloody train but scratch flea bites, gaze into the darkness and write. In the middle of last night I sought out the train cleaner again. She stubbed out her cigarette without hurry and dropped the butt in her bucket when she saw me approaching. I eyed her cleaning cart. Just as I had thought, on the side of one of the bottles there was a label that said *Vinegar*.

"How's your cat?" the cleaner asked.

"Flea-ridden," I replied. I pointed at the vinegar bottle. "I've come to trade."

The cleaner pulled a rubber glove off her hand with a snap.

"Valid currencies at Gertrude's Cart are coffee, tobacco products, cannabis, alcohol, drugs that relieve radiation sickness, chocolate – except if it's made on Europa, that's sub-standard – and sheep skins."

"I don't have any of those," I replied. "How about this?"

I handed her a small silicone sachet. She took it, gave me a suspicious look, opened the mouth of the sachet and sniffed the contents.

"Mushrooms?" she said.

"The best and safest psilocybin this side of the Moon," I said. "When used correctly, a guaranteed trip to cosmic spheres, no harmful side effects."

"I don't trade in illegal substances," Gertrude said.

"Maiden's cloak is not illegal in professional use."

Gertrude twisted her face.

"Very well," she said. "But only one bottle."

She pushed the canvas sachet into her pocket and handed me the vinegar bottle. I tilted the bottle in order to see the amount of the vinegar.

"It's not full."

"How regrettable," Gertrude said. "The resources of our store are limited. Take it or leave it."

I sighed and took the bottle. It wasn't the best flea repellent in existence, but it was the best I could do for now.

"It's been a pleasure doing business with you," Gertrude said.

I nodded at her and turned. Then I remembered something that had been bothering me.

"Sheep skins?"

"My lower back can't stand drafts," Gertrude replied.

26.3.2168

A train that is finally approaching Harmonia, thank heavens – Mars

Ziggy has not left his carrier since I washed him with vinegar. He has turned his back toward the window on the backpack and refuses to acknowledge my existence: the orange and white stripes are squashed against the transparent plastic. The scratching, however, seems to have mitigated a little. Fuxi orbits Mars far above, will not come closer, or draw farther away. Darkness strokes the window, dissipates for a moment, reveals holes in itself and puckers together again. Like a memory.

On Fuxi we used to pack water and food, lace comfortable shoes on our feet and take the train to the forest that grew at the other end of the city. It was artificial, of course, like everything on Fuxi, human-made. But it had been grown to resemble Earth forests as closely as possible. Sycamores and bamboos rose over paths edged by moss and small white flowers, ferns spiraled as airy, green fans and a narrow brook rippled over stones. In the eternal warmth of Fuxi, pine trees emitted a scent that spread within me as light-like peace when I inhaled it. Beyond the pines flowed a waterfall, not very tall, but bright and wrapped in the color of the sky. On top of it, the only birch trees of the forest grew in a circle.

Sol, I don't know if you remember a day during our second year on Fuxi when we sat at a viewpoint spot by the waterfall and drank wine. You had ordered it specially from Mars, and we were celebrating your birthday. I packed plates grainy from cake crumbs into my rucksack as you poured the last drop from the bottle, dividing it evenly between our glasses. You'd been asking me about a healer's work and worldview, and I'd tried to explain, although I knew well you would never look at it from the same perspective as I did. A blue-winged butterfly landed on the edge of your glass.

So the helper spirit usually takes the form of an animal? You asked.

Often, I replied, but not always. Human mind gives it the form that is easiest to understand.

And the form the helper takes somehow reflects the healer's own personality?

So they say. That makes it easier to work together. For instance, a healer who likes a close-knit group and enjoys a clear hierarchy may see their helper as a wolf. The helper of a healer who moves a lot and enjoys traveling may take the shape of a migratory bird, such as a swan. My teacher had one of those. My helper, my soul-animal, is a lynx. They like being on their own.

And are keen-sighted.

You took my hand. Your fingers were warm and dry.

What kind of shape would my helper take? You asked.

I thought about it.

It would be a raven, I said eventually.

You lifted an eyebrow.

An ill omen? Scavenger, bringer of death?

That's superstition. Except for the scavenging part. Ravens are intelligent and curious problem-solvers. In some myths they have a part in the creation of the world. In old Sumerian writings a raven helps grow the world's first date palm while the goddess Inanna watches. In Northern Asia and Europe the raven has been one of the most common soul-animals of healers for thousands of years.

Interesting, you said and smiled. Don't lynx hunt ravens?

Just like the sun melts the snow, I replied.

Your thumb moved along the lines of my palm.

I know you consider it unscientific nonsense, I continued. But in many ancient cultures you'd have been regarded as someone with a gift for healing.

How so?

Presenting gender outside the binary was sometimes seen as a sign of power and hidden abilities. Healers combined androgynous elements in their costumes, like a beard with a dress. They were believed to have greater insight into the world because they were not bound by one gender.

My hand settled into yours, like coming home.

Shouldn't I be able to see my raven, in that case? You asked.

Perhaps they just haven't shown themself to you yet.

Would your lynx be able to see my raven, if I had one?

Maybe. I cannot say. She saw my teacher's swan, but Vivian was an experienced healer, and her connection with the spirit world was strong.

The blue butterfly drifted into the air from the edge of the glass and fluttered into the ferns like a flame. We were quiet. The humidity of the waterfall fell in drops onto my skin. The sun that wasn't the sun drew prisms in the mist floating above the water.

How much do you miss Earth? you asked after a long silence.

It's always there, I replied. The longing. Like breathing. Most of the time I don't pay attention to it, but sometimes it clogs and hitches and tightens into a knot. Why do you ask?

If you could, would you go back?

I had never even suggested we move to Earth, Sol. It wouldn't have been possible for your work. Neither for mine. I liked the freedom of being able to work and travel freely without the visa restrictions of Earth.

Earth is largely uninhabitable, I said.

If it could be fixed?

Haven't you heard? They are trying to fix it. The cleansing of the oceans has been going on for over a century. Flooded nuclear power plants are being dismantled, near-extinct species are being revived in the conservation areas. But all of that takes time.

Mars could help, you said. Project Earth is the first of its kind. If it opens doors for others—

Mars doesn't care, I replied.

Don't you think that's wrong?

Something stung my ankle. I reached to brush a mosquito away. The bite was already starting to turn red and swollen.

I grew up on Earth, I said. You've only spent short periods of time there. You've never slept in accommodations worse than a luxury hotel. You've never visited my childhood home, or even the region where I lived the first sixteen years of my life. You haven't cooked on a gas stove in the glow of the neon signs of a holiday isle, wearing a coat full of holes donated by tourists and four layers of wool because electricity is being rationed and the heating doesn't work. You have not queued at the medical center for a day and a night with a high fever. You have not looked at the future where your only choices are to stay and clean the toilets of the holiday isle, go breathe the toxic fumes at a plastic-sorting plant or work under radiation hazard at a nuclear power plant dismantling site. Or hope that the raffle will pick you as a migrant worker on Mars, where you will forever be treated as a second-class citizen. How can you even ask if I don't think it's wrong, the way Mars treats Earth?

You stared at me, allowed my outburst to linger between us in the bright water-mist.

I'm sorry, you said. It was a stupid question.

You took my arm. I pulled it away.

You went quiet.

Did you know that even people who have never been to Earth miss it? I asked after a while.

I've heard of the phenomenon, you said. In medicine it is known as the birth-home syndrome.

I've seen it in my patients. People who were born and grew up on Mars long for Earth. For the horizon, the open sea, the sky and the sun. Science believes it is because evolution has not caught up with the changes. As a species, we evolved in Earth conditions and for them, not for underground artificial light. A longing like that can lock itself under the skin and eat a person from within. Healers believe it is one of the reasons for soul-sickness. The soul will try to wander toward the home from which it has been ripped away and tears itself apart. The healer's job is to retrieve the lost part and make the soul whole again. But once the soul has been torn, the loose part will rarely settle back for the rest of a person's life. Even in the best case, a scar will grow where the soul was broken. In the worst case, part of the soul will wander away and get lost time after time.

My mother, you said.

I nodded.

If you could fix Earth, you said. What would be the highest price you'd pay for it?

You noticed my expression.

I'm not talking about money, you added.

I know.

Every single day Earth inhabitants die from epidemic diseases and hunger, from environmental toxins, in the vessels of human traffickers in the darkness of space, you continued. If you could change that, but the condition would be you'd have to make a big sacrifice in order to achieve that outcome, what would you be ready for?

On a personal level? Would I give up my life, my home? You? Is that the sort of thing you mean?

Or on a wider scale.

You smiled, but behind the smile you were serious.

What exactly would be the result I'd achieve with my sacrifice?

An independent Earth, you said. That cannot be economically exploited by Mars. But first and foremost, a planet where the ecosystems begin to repair themselves and recover, until most of it is healthy again.

Hmmm.

I picked up a small stone from the ground and placed it on the table.

I'd sacrifice this stone.

I picked up my wineglass, drank from it and put the rest next to the stone.

I'd sacrifice this sip of wine.

I found a pine cone in my pocket that I had previously collected from the path.

I'd sacrifice this pine cone sticky with resin, and all my thoughts from last night.

You gave a laugh and looked at my installation on the table. You added a small branch you found under the bench.

I could bring my helper, I said. And you could bring yours.

My helper?

The raven. Together you could make everything right, fly around the world and do what ravens do.

Scavenge?

Solve problems. Build tools. Repeat "nevermore."

The day was warm and the wine languid in my limbs. Words were light on my tongue. You got up from across the table and sat down next to me on the bench. You wrapped your arms around me from behind. I closed my eyes. We were quiet, and I heard the waterfall. Time and gravity moved drops away from us.

I never asked what you'd be willing to sacrifice, Sol.

• • ● • •

When I look at the years we spent on Fuxi, I face an obstacle. I want so badly to see the Stoneturners in the past, to have something give a comprehensible shape to what I don't comprehend. The trouble is, if I see them, it is because I want to. I lack the ability to evaluate the reality of what I see. It's not that I don't remember. It's that I don't know how to interpret those memories.

I still packed my drum, cloak and headpiece often, but now I had a place to return to. I traveled to Mars, Nüwa, the Moon, even to Earth once or twice a year. Every time I visited Winterland my parents walked a little slower than before, and the time I spent with them seemed shorter, my chest full of weight as I said my goodbyes. When I came back to Fuxi, my body felt less heavy and the ground carried me unlike anywhere else.

And you, Sol: you seemed so happy. Your project was going well; so you said. Work took a lot of your time, but it was the same with me. Around the hours spent at work, we still had our cocoon of light.

In my mind I step into our past living room on Fuxi. I look at us, you and me, and neither of us know there is a specter in the room with us, nor that we are specters ourselves. You are almost a decade younger than now, and so am I, but I see you more clearly. The lines on your forehead are thinner than hair, barely visible, and when the corners of your eyes crease, the creases will smooth from your skin without leaving a trace. I sit in the corner of the sofa, reading. You have just returned from a seminar on Nüwa. You are still wearing your overcoat when you place a chirping carrier box on the floor. You go to close the balcony door and open the door of the carrier.

A small, tar-colored kitten totters out. Its eyes are still blue, its fur feather-soft and its paws the size of the tip of my thumb. I get up from the sofa and squat next to the box. The cat says *meep*, climbs into my arms and pushes its head inside my cardigan.

I love it at once.

It's ours, you say. Do you want to name it?

We've been talking about getting a cat for a long time. I've made a list of possible names. David Bowie is playing in the loudspeakers just then. I don't need to think about it.

Major Tom, I say.

The doorbell rings. Major Tom starts and his face appears.

I'll get it, you say.

You disappear to the entrance. I hear you speak with someone, but I cannot discern the words. The door closes, and you step back into the living room with a large, brown envelope in your hand. You walk straight into your office. I only catch a glimpse of your face. Is your expression restless, frightened? Do you hide it from me on purpose, Sol?

Wasn't mail delivered earlier already? I ask when you return with empty hands.

Yes, you reply. A colleague came to drop off an urgent work thing.

I don't think about it anymore at the time. Later – a day, a week, a month later – I go to your office to return a book I had borrowed from you, *Terraforming Earth*. On the edge of your desk I see the same brown envelope, opened, and under it, half-hidden, a tightly sealed, flat glass dish with thinner-than-thin greenish web growing in it.

When I bend over to look at it more closely, it stirs and grows denser, as if reaching away from me. Or perhaps toward me.

I flinch away.

I ask you about the web that same evening. You say a petri dish of yours got moldy.

The following morning, when you have left for work, I go into your office. The brown envelope is gone, as are the glass dish and the web. Major Tom climbs up my trouser leg with his pinprick claws and I pick him up. I stroke the small, warm body that shifts constantly, like a beating heart.

Sol, when we moved to Fuxi, I thought it would become a permanent home. But so few things are permanent. Deaths, births. And little else.

13

Zereshk polo "ba morgh"*

4 large vegan cutlets
2 medium onions
½ tsp saffron
2 tbsp sugar
650g rice
a handful of barberries
salt
pepper
2 tsp turmeric
butter
2 tbs vegetable oil
2 tbs tomato purée
2 tbs lemon juice
pistachio flakes

(* While the traditional recipe uses chicken – ba morgh – oat cutlets, other vegetarian protein or lab meat will work well. METHOD ON THE REVERSE Best, Enisa 😌 →)

Sender: Ilsa Uriarte
Recipient: Lumi Salo
Date: 27.3.2168 05.30 MST
Security: Maximum encryption

Lumi,
I'm on a work trip until the day after tomorrow. Mom is visiting a friend and won't return until then either. Take Ziggy straight into the downstairs bathroom. You will find cat food, flea medicine (dosage instructions on the side of the bottle) and pest spray in there. The medicine should take effect within 48 hours.

Ziggy is not welcome elsewhere in the house until four days have passed. Wash every single piece of your clothing twice in a minimum of 60 degrees and spray all of your items. The robot is programmed to clean the floors several times a day.
Ilsa

27.3.2168
Harmonia, Mars

Sol,
It is quiet today in the Moonday House, and not even the lamps, lanterns, candles and fires burning in every room can banish the dusk that weaves persistent webs around them. Behind the windows a stone-heavy grayness encloses the house, reminding me of November in Winterland, or late autumn in the northern hemisphere of Mars. I sit in the living room, one wall of which we built entirely from glass

so we could watch the green of the garden through it. The scratched leather cushions of the sofa are soft under me, and the fire burning in the fireplace warms my cheek. Colors are almost entirely gone from the garden: thin frost has gathered on the bare branches of birch trees and Japanese maples, wrapping them into bright white bundles, like the fingers of a ghost whose touch lingers, although it is already gone. The lawn is covered by fallen, brown-faded leaves. The sky is not night-dark, but metal-colored clouds have grown a thick cover for it, like an armor behind which I cannot see the blue.

Only one tree still carries green on its branches. The quince at the center of the lawn reaches in all directions, its leaves rolling as dark green flames, and among them coral-red buds push their way from the branches, bright drops in the landscape stripped of color.

I listen to the house, its stirrings against your movements, something to suggest you are here.

It is silent. But the house is vast, and not all sounds carry through it.

• • ● • •

I arrived in Harmonia early this morning. There is no one home save for the household robot, but luckily Ilsa had not erased my face from the memory of the electric lock. Ziggy does not appreciate the quarantine measures. However, I agree with your sister that they are necessary. My ankles are swollen with flea bites, and Gertrude was not up for further vinegar trade talks despite the fact that I offered my last hallucinogens.

When I'd made myself at home, I had a telephone conversation with Enisa that you might want to hear about. (Look at me, chatting away in an ordinary manner, as if I knew you will read this tale in the corner of the sofa home on Nüwa, as if there is no empty space where you should be.) I will scribe it the way I remember it: what is forgotten does not matter. You know, Sol, how accurate my memory is, when I want it to be.

"How are you?" Enisa's voice asked from the dark screen. I too had covered the camera of my screen at her request.

I told her how things were.

"Have you heard from Sol?"

"No." I was still not ready to tell her about the message you'd sent after you went missing.

"I'd like to say something encouraging, but I don't know what."

"That already helps." I wasn't sure if it was true.

"I've done more background research on the Stoneturners for my article," Enisa continued. "It's turning out to be bigger than I'd anticipated. I came across something I believe will interest you."

The timer-based plant lights of the living wall switched on. The ivy, spider plants and snake plants bathed in brightness. It hit the globe map standing in the corner, drew shadows on the surface of Mars.

"I'm all ears."

"I found out what was stolen from the Elysium laboratory. Just a moment." I heard papers rustle. "The missing employees took everything connected to one particular research project. The project is known by the name Inanna. Does that ring any bells?"

Inanna: the Mesopotamian goddess of love, fertility and war, who traveled to the Underworld and came back from the dead. I'd read about her in some thick old book, the kind Vivian used to buy for me and sell or donate onward later in order to make space for new ones.

"Not immediately."

"The materials also include the lab cultures that were taken," Enisa said. "I don't know their function, but they all seem to have something to do with the properties of different lichen species."

"Do you know the names of the species?"

"Give me a minute..." The papers rustled again. "They're only in Latin. *Letharia vulpina, Xanthoria elegans, Physconia glacialis, Arthonia leucopellaea*—"

"Did you say *Physconia glacialis*?" I interrupted.

"That's the name mentioned in this information. Do you know something about it?"

"Healers use powder made from it for medicinal purposes."

"You sound surprised."

"I didn't know Sol was studying it."

"I'll send you a list of the names of the lichens," Enisa said. "The second thing I wanted to talk about concerns the background of the Stoneturners. I haven't found much new information about their origins, but their modus operandi has evolved through the decades. For the past fifteen years or so it has been dictated by certain internal rules. It has recurring, recognizable features."

"Such as?"

I heard a few taps and swipes, as Enisa's screen-pen moved on her display.

"As I already mentioned last time, the Stoneturners don't use direct violence," Enisa said. "Yet they've had no problem with sabotage, at least within the past decade."

"Do you have examples?"

"Do you remember the construction of the Hellas Planitia reservoir?"

"Remotely. Weren't there all kinds of delays? Some freak accident?"

"The completion of the reservoir was delayed by nearly two years," Enisa said. "It was never public information that the 'freak accident' was a sabotage attack, and those responsible were never found."

"What happened?"

"A fungal growth appeared overnight in the equipment hall where the machines were kept sheltered from dust storms and destroyed all the equipment. Most of the machines were robots, but when the supervisors came to work in the morning, everything was covered by dark red, web-like fungi. It had spread everywhere: the controls, the motors, the fuel tanks. The web was tough as a spider's and took months to remove. Some machines were permanently rendered useless. Parts of others had to replaced."

I'd never heard of a fungus that could create such damage.

"Did the fungus spread anywhere else?"

Enisa was quiet. I heard the pen on her screen, as she browsed the pages.

"I can't find any mention of that sort of thing."

I pondered what she had said.

"If those responsible for the Hellas Planitia attack were not found," I said, "why do you think the Stoneturners were connected to it?"

"Because of this." Enisa's pen tapped the screen again hundreds of kilometers away on the other side of darkness. A small icon appeared on my screen, paired with a question: *EkoJourn-al wants to send you an image. Accept?* I brushed the *Yes* option.

A blurry picture taken from a distance opened on the screen, with an excavator robot covered in thin, red-tinted web in the foreground. The web looked like blood-colored mist against its metal surface.

"Enlarge the picture," Enisa's voice prompted.

I did as she told me.

"What am I looking for?"

"In the upper-right corner, behind the tractor robots," Enisa said. "Do you see?"

I moved the picture in order to bring the upper corner to the middle of the screen. Behind the robots on the wall I could discern letters, words and parts of words: *rth wakes and stones will spe.*

"I do," I said. I swallowed. It felt like air packed itself into a dry knot in my throat.

"It's not a usual graffiti," Enisa said. "They used the same technique at Elysium. Do you know how biograffiti are made?"

"No."

"They are created with a special stencil and with the help of growing organisms. They need hours in order to appear."

"You said they have a clear modus operandi," I said. "So are there other similar cases?"

Enisa sighed. Her breath rustled on the microphone.

"A couple of dozen, at least," she said. "A handful of them have been confirmed. Fungi, algae, vines, weeds... Another rule they seem to have is that they never use plants that could permanently damage the local farming areas and thereby put the food supply of the colonies in danger. And a third is that they tend to send a warning beforehand."

"What kind of warning?"

"Usually it's seeds of some harmless plant in an envelope," Enisa said. "Nothing dangerous to humans, or anything that breaches quarantine regulations." I heard a click, and another image file appeared on my screen for acceptance. "This is one of the earliest sabotage cases I've been able to find," Enisa continued. "There was an anorthite mine on the Moon that used to discharge emissions in secret too close to the dome villages. The manager of the mine received an envelope in the mail with dried seaweed inside. A few months later a persistent layer of algae grew inside the airtight, crewed mining equipment and made working with the machines impossible. The robot devices continued to function, but the sabotage case drew attention to the mine's practices and it was revealed that the wastewater had been contaminating the drinking water supplies of the nearest dome village for years. As a result, the mine was closed down."

The image opened on my screen. I felt like I had inhaled the knot stuck in my throat. There was a tall tower in the picture I recognized immediately. I had watched it from the accommodation globe by Luther crater when I had first arrived on the Moon with Vivian at sixteen.

"When was this?" I asked.

"A little over twenty years ago."

I did a quick calculation in my mind. Twenty-one years ago I'd just left

Earth. Vivian and I stayed on the Moon for seven months before continuing on to Mars. The attack had probably taken place right after our departure.

"How did the Stoneturners know about the illegal practices of the mine?"

"Maybe they didn't," Enisa said. "The attack may have been directed at mining in general. Perhaps it was a coincidence that the mining corporation was guilty of criminal activity."

A thought had begun to form in me. It was not pleasant. It whimpered like a mosquito that will not leave you alone and that you cannot catch.

"Do you know the exact date of the attack?"

Enisa was quiet for a moment. Papers rustled again.

"April 15, 2147," she said then. "The location was Luther on the Moon."

I wrote the date down in the margin of the notebook.

"I recognized the place," I said. "Could you send me a list of the dates and locations of the suspected Stoneturner attacks?"

"Can do," Enisa said. "Do you also want photos of the places? I couldn't find visual material of all, but some I've got. I haven't looked through quite all the photos."

"Send those too." The things Enisa had told me revolved around each other in my mind like moons of a planet locked in orbit. The connections between them looked inevitable as gravity, but unfamiliar: I could not get hold of them. "You should go to the police with this information," I said.

Enisa was quiet again for a moment. Then, "Lumi, most of this information comes from the police."

"Oh." It took a while for the meaning of the sentence to sink in. "Your contact?"

"Correctly deduced." The silence stretched. "I wanted to ask you something."

"Go ahead."

"When was Project Earth shelved?"

"A few months after Fuxi was evacuated. Around four years ago. Why?"

"It was surprisingly difficult to find precise information," Enisa replied. "I wanted to check with you, because it coincides with an almost year-long pause in the Stoneturners' activities. For them, it's a long silence."

"Does it matter?"

"It may be just a coincidence."

I heard a door clanging and noise in the background of Enisa's voice.

"I need to go now," she said. "My children need help with homework. Thanks for making time for a chat."

"Thank you." I was trying to process everything she had just told me. "Why are you helping me?"

"I'm a journalist. Some of us still believe in the ethics of this profession," Enisa said. "Besides, I like you."

"Can I do anything to return the favor?"

Enisa laughed in a low voice.

"You can cook me a meal when we next meet. Now I'm going to send you a whole lot of documents. Ideally, I'd give you the paper copies, but since that's not possible right now, I'll transfer them as multi-encrypted files. Do you still have the recipe I wrote on a piece of paper?"

"Yes."

"Good. You'll need it."

We hung up. I was left wondering what she meant by her last comment.

27.3.2168
Harmonia, Mars
Later

After lunch, I began to go through the files Enisa had sent. There were fourteen in total. Enisa had numbered them. I tried to open the first one. *Insert password*, the screen announced. I tried a different file. *Insert password*, the display demanded again.

I nearly sent Enisa a message to ask for the password, but then I remembered what she had said about the recipe. I sought it in my suitcase. There were fourteen rows on the ingredients list.

4largevegancutlets, I wrote in the password box of the first file.

The screen thought for a moment, turned a slow virtual cog in the middle of the display. Then an animated letter after another appeared. The green letters grew onto the dark background like moss, forming a text: *BIOGRAFFITI. Tutorial*.

The text vanished.

I swept the biograffiti file out of the way. It would have to wait. The others interested me more.

I typed in the password *2mediumonions* and swiped the next file open. It contained a page-long catalog of the dates and locations of the sabotage attacks. I browsed the files until I found the one in which Enisa had listed the names of the lichens used in the lab cultures of Elysium. Halfway through the list I saw what I was looking for.

Physconia glacialis. Known in the healers' vernacular as frost lichen.

• • ● • •

Sol, when I walk among my memories, I am on Fuxi again. I return home from a work trip after traveling for nearly twenty-four hours. I open the door with care so I wouldn't wake you up, but as it moves, I see the living-room lights are on. I've been away for three weeks.

You sit on the living-room floor in a bathrobe, cross-legged. Objects are scattered around you: a bowl with white liquid and a paintbrush in it, a transparent spray bottle, dark green jelly in an aluminum jar, dishcloths.

Before you there are flat stones brushed with liquid and a globe-shaped glass terrarium in which you are placing a palm-sized stone. A cracked, dark gray scab covers the surface of the stone. By the wall between the living room and the balcony there are more terrariums, with something growing in each one. Above them, you have fixed several plant lights.

Hey, I say.

You start and turn around.

Hey, you say. I thought you'd only arrive in the small hours.

It's nearly four in the morning.

Not possible.

The message sound of your screen pings.

You get to your feet, pull me into your arms. You smell of shampoo and coffee and faintly of sweat.

I only meant to take a quick look at my garden before going to bed, you say. I brought work home. I hope you don't mind.

Are there lichens in all of those?

Sort of. You pull away from me, pick up the terrarium from the floor and carry it to the row by the wall. Come and see.

I recognize most of them: they are common on Fuxi and in the gardens of Mars, pioneer species that were among the first to be planted when the building of the colonies and biospheres began. Yet there is unfamiliar-looking green pilling, powder-like brown patches and blue-gray webs growing on the stones of a few terrariums; they remind me of dew-covered cobwebs in the forests of Winterland.

It's an experiment, you say. It's been known for a long time that the algae symbiont of lichen can live independently and survives well without the fungal one. But the fungal symbiont dies if it's separated from the lichen. At the lab, we've been trying to create a fungal symbiont that could live as separate from the algae.

I have rarely seen you so excited. I take your hand.

Well?

You point at the brown patches on top of the stone in one terrarium.

That's a fungus separated from the lichen, you say. It has lived in the laboratory for six weeks already. I wanted to put it in different conditions to see if it would survive outside the lab.

I squeeze your hand gently. You notice my expression and add, It's entirely safe. That lichen lives everywhere on Fuxi, and there's no damage it could do if it spread.

The message sound of your screen pings again, twice.

You walk to the table. I hear Major Tom jump to the floor in the other room, probably from the bed. He pads into the living room and twists around my legs, purring. What passes through your face, Sol, when you read the message with your back turned to me?

It's just Mom, you say and switch the screen off.

It's great your work is going well, I say. But what would you say to sleeping? I'll pass out on my feet soon.

You kiss me; a smile folds the corners of your eyes. I take your hand and begin to walk you into the bedroom. Major Tom follows.

I look at the row of glass globes over my shoulder. I don't see the white crystal shapes of frost lichen glimmering in the faint light. But this is not your laboratory. This is only home.

• • ● • •

I must sleep for a moment now, even at the risk that it will further confuse my daily patterns. I'll leave the rest of the files until later. I've been up for nearly twenty-four hours, and I want to be able to think clearly when Naomi and Ilsa come back.

27.3.2168
Harmonia, Mars
Even later

Sol,
Do you remember when I told you about the frost lichen?

Or had you already heard about it by then?

The past is a map I imagined was fully drawn, but I have begun to see blank spaces in it that I'm trying to fill. Right now I'm studying the landscape here, where the paths are drawing closer to each other, toward an inevitable crossing:

Vivian never allowed me to drink tap water on the Moon.

No, that is not true. She never let me drink tap water in the first place where we stopped, the crater village of Luther. She used to bring freshwater from her day-long trips. At the time I didn't consider this strange in any way. I thought everyone did that on the Moon.

After the evacuation of the mining village, we returned to pick up our few belongings, and after that we traveled to other cities and villages. One evening shortly before we left the Moon we sat in a dusky room in the town where Vivian was looking after patients just then. The lamps burned dim, and the window-imitating digiwall rested black as the surface of a night pond. Vivian did not like the artificial landscape images of the walls.

Vivian's medicine bag lay open on the floor. She had arranged the dried herbs, mushrooms and lichens in rows. She'd given me a wooden mortar and sat down cross-legged before another. She picked two dried plants at a time from the rows, handed one to me and we both began to grind them into a powder. To finish with, we moved the powders into airtight silicone sachets. My arm ached. We'd been sitting like this for at least two hours.

Vivian picked up a small, resin-scented box, opened it and took out a pale lichen shaped like a deer antler. She dropped it into the mortar. Her arm began to twirl the pestle and grind the lichen into a dim-white powder. Its shade was like snow on a cloudy day.

I watched her work. I thought I recognized the powder as the same one I'd seen her rub onto the sick girl's forehead on Earth, when I had followed her in secret to Winterland's manager's house. I still had no courage to tell her what I had done then.

What's that? I asked.

The movement of Vivian's arm did not stop. The pestle scratched the mortar.

The Seal of the Spirit, she responded. Frost lichen. It binds the soul to its bearer more tightly, especially if a piece of the soul has already lost its way once. But you must be careful when carrying it. It's illegal in many settlements.

On the Moon?

The shadows on Vivian's face moved when she smiled.

Everywhere on Mars. On the Moon it's legal. For now.

Why is it forbidden? I asked.

Vivian was quiet.

Its working mechanism is not understood, she said then. It has been studied, but it cannot be explained.

Vivian's hand stopped. She picked up the mortar, opened the mouth of the sachet and began to pour the powder into it.

White dust fell, fell like snow that had never touched the surface of the Moon.

Sol, I have gone through the rest of the files Enisa sent me.

• • ● • •

The preview organized the pictures into thumbnails. There seemed to be dozens and dozens of them, maybe a couple of hundred. The first ones were clear color photos from a demonstration. I placed my finger on the screen and searched for the additional information on each picture in order to see if anything had been saved there. *Protest for Earth environmental rights, Harmonia, 24.4.2150*, it said.

A crowd of people holding posters, hand-painted banners and placards marched along the largest boulevard of Harmonia. *Enceladus Nevermore*, read the text in red letters on the wide banner. Protesters wearing green shirts held its edges. A weeping Moon carved hollow; an Earth wrapped in bandages; a Mars drowning in space junk – the placards walked past as I browsed the pictures. I looked for your face, for your familiar posture, for a garment I could remember seeing in your closet.

Then there you were, Sol: on my screen, a student of about twenty, your short dark hair swept back, wearing a T-shirt with the picture of Earth, your gaze turned to look past the camera. You held a half-lowered sign in your hand with the text *Justice for Ear* showing. The final letters of the word disappeared behind the head and back of a woman wearing dreadlocks and a bright green dress shirt next to you. Behind you spread a dense group of protesters. There was no doubt it was you in the photo. You were also visible in the next one, this time somewhere behind the people, side profile against the greenness of the park.

I continued to browse the photos. The setting changed. It was another protest, but on the surface of Mars. The group of people was clearly smaller, and everyone was wearing a biosuit. Light fractured on the arching glass visors of the helmets, large letters were drawn on the yellow-red sand. MY MARS IS NOT (A) MINE, they announced. It was impossible to discern any facial features in the picture, because the helmets hid them. *Earthlight demonstration, Surface near Datong, 15.1.2153*.

Pictures from various protests, different cities. Most from Mars, a few from the Moon, none from Earth. But then I came across a photo that did not look like a protest. It was dark and blurry, like pictures taken by security cameras in poorly lit halls tend to be. The place seemed like a factory of some kind. I left my finger on top of the picture until the information attached to it appeared. *Bradbury Food Refinery, Copernicus, the Moon, 14.6.2151*. I swiped the information away.

Conveyor belts and tall vats were visible in the background. A group of five people stood in the foreground. On the left a curly-haired figure in a hoodie, next to them someone short and dark wearing spectacles, and on the far right a person with a long braid and checkered shirt who I thought looked male. Their faces were strange to me.

You stood next to the checkered shirt, Sol, your face turned toward the person at the center of the group who was talking to you. Your expression was focused, alert, and your hand rested on her arm. Your heads were bent close to each other: the leader and the follower, the master and the apprentice. Her words had vanished into space long ago, but in that moment stopped beyond time you were listening to them.

Her blond hair was tied back at the nape of her neck, and the worn leather coat hung over a loose jumper. I would have recognized her face in any world.

Vivian.

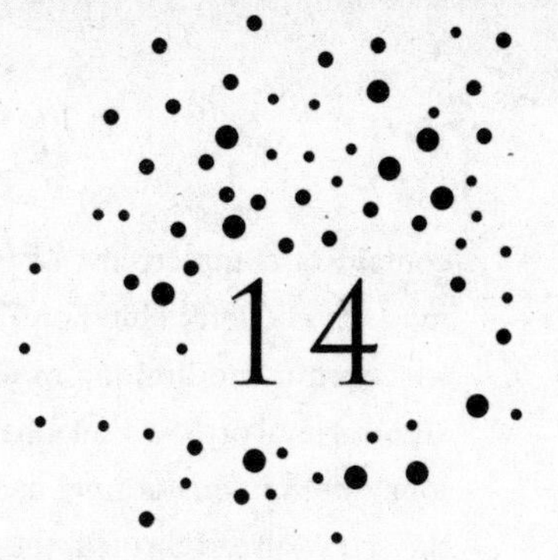

14

Evacuation order:
the cylinder city of Fuxi
9.5.2164 08.00 MST

A mandatory evacuation order has been given this morning regarding all inhabitants of the cylinder city of Fuxi. The evacuation will take place in phases on vessels that will take the inhabitants of Fuxi to Mars. The inhabitants will be informed in the next 48 hours about their evacuation group. If you have not been allocated an evacuation group by 11 May 12.00 MST, please contact the nearest registration office.

The reason for the evacuation order is the quick spread of an unknown fungal disease on Fuxi. The disease does not infect humans, but turns all crops unsuitable for human consumption. The stockpiles of food, water and medicines on Fuxi will last for over two months. The evacuation will be completed within the next five weeks. During this time, it may be necessary to ration some groceries, as the fungal disease will have an impact on the availability of fresh fruits and vegetables in particular. However, the local government of Fuxi is able to guarantee that a sufficient amount of food, water and medicines will be available to the inhabitants in the meantime. If you require regular medication or have other special needs (for instance, you are a wheelchair user), please get in touch with officials responsible for the evacuation as soon as possible. A list of contact information is attached.

Everyone has the right to take 30 kg of personal belongings with them. Groceries and plants are not permitted (the attached document contains a complete list of forbidden and restricted items). All pets must also be left behind on Fuxi. While you wait for your evacuation, we recommend limiting moving around the city to a bare minimum. Upon arrival on Mars, all inhabitants of Fuxi must be prepared to spend four weeks in quarantine, because the spores of the fungus destroying the crops spread through the air and may be transported in garments, hair, on skin or within possessions. It is of extreme importance that the fungal disease does not spread outside Fuxi.

After the quarantine, inhabitants of Fuxi may apply for a residence in the colonies of Mars or in the quotas of other cylinder cities using the newly created fast track system.

28.3.2168
Harmonia, Mars

Sol,
When I close my eyes, the Moonday House grows around me.

The surface of the sofa cushions is cool under me, and a chill rises from between the floorboards. The fire in the fireplace has gone out, leaving a drift of white ashes behind. The lynx statuette on the mantelpiece is crouching low in order to attack, its ears flat against the head, its sharp fangs bared, its hind limbs tensed for a leap. A spark-narrow flame burns in a sole lantern.

Behind the window that fills the wall, the garden stands still. Faded leaves have been squashed into the lawn. Frost has melted off the bare leaves of the birches and Japanese maples and the quince. Something else has grown in its place.

As I push the door, it opens with a slow creak, and I step onto the grass. The damp leaves slide under my feet. The footsteps make marks on the grass that does not rise up again where I have pressed it to the ground.

I stop at the base of a thin birch tree. A dark gray web runs along its bark, covering everything, each tip and bole and base, like smoke, like a heavy thought. A similar web has grown over each tree and bush to blur their shape: the mourning veil of the garden. I reach out my hand and touch the web. Viscous dark residue sticks to my fingers.

The ground shifts beneath me.

My feet slip on the damp mat of decomposing leaves, as I try to gain balance. The quake slithers into my body through the soles of my feet and flows into each limb, cuts my heart in half and sends stabs of pain behind my eyes. I turn toward the house and run across the lawn, through the door into the living room. I slam the door shut behind me. The bang makes the glass walls shudder, and I no longer know where the movement originates, in me or somewhere else.

Outside the window a narrow crack grows into the grass, spilling blackness, widening like a predator's maw. A low growl sounds from its depths, growing louder little by little. It nips at the birches and Japanese maples, scratches the ground broken at the very base of the quince, reaches toward the house.

A crack appears at my feet and the walls tremble.

I seek your voice amid the noise of the earthquake, Sol, your shadow where shadows gather.

• • ● • •

Of all mornings on Fuxi, one is the most sharp-edged in my mind. I brewed a pot of fragrant jasmine tea, filled my thermos mug and climbed on top of the building where we lived. The sky that was not sky coiled as a blue sphere above the concave horizon. I walked across the tall-growing sweetcorn and rows of beans, across the cool shadows to near the edge of the roof, where the lavenders planted for pollinators flowered. I breathed in their scent and watched the bees purring in the blue-purple flowers while their hives bathed in light on the roof of the building next door.

I stopped at the edge of the roof terrace and placed my tea mug on the wide handrail. From above, the trees in the park and by the streets looked like large, green animals curled to sleep against each other. The chill of the night was still in the air. You had left for work early, Sol. You said you wanted to take care of your backlog of correspondence. The week before, a group of your colleagues had gathered on Fuxi to an expansive Earth conference, which had taken all your time.

I tasted the tea. The hot liquid burned my tongue numb. A distant radio sounded from a balcony somewhere, the theme of a news broadcast and a chain of words in which I could not discern shapes. Down on the street, invisible beyond the cool curtain of leaves, the sound of an emergency vehicle passed and made a long slash in the air. A small spider walked across my instep.

On the roofs, in the courtyards, on the arching walls of the world, rice and potato stalks and opening sunflowers swayed in the draft, still green as Earth forests that once were.

The news began to arrive throughout the day, but I only heard it in the evening. I had decided to clean my healer's regalia, to do some maintenance on my drum and oil its metal joints, and the work had absorbed me so I barely noticed when dusk began to fall. I was brought back by the clang of the door. You strode into the living room, Sol, and switched on the TV screen on the wall.

What is it? I asked.

You gestured at the screen with your hand.

A camera drone showed footage of rice plantations. It approached the field, flew lower, until it slid in close vicinity of the stalks. The stalks were stained by a black rash that was surrounded by large yellow spots.

– the spread of an extremely destructive fungal disease that has already been found on most food plantations in the city, said the voice of the news reader. *The Cylinder Cities Community and Mars have placed quarantine orders on all traffic from Fuxi. The Community emergency summit that has been scheduled for tomorrow will discuss possible evacuation measures…*

Does that mean us? I nearly asked, but when I looked at you, I knew.

You took my hand. Or I took your hand.

How long do we have?

Weeks, at most, you replied.

This is bad, then?

You nodded.

Your fingers pressed around mine. The light of the screen hovered on our faces, turned us into ghosts in our own home.

The evacuation flights began two days later. We'd been allocated to the last vessel. I didn't know if I should have been thankful for that, or not. It gave me a few weeks to let go and say goodbye, but it also gave me time to watch the spreading destruction. Climbing onto the roof was no longer permitted. I imagined the yellow-dark stains in the green of the plantations I'd be able to see from there. I imagined the rows of corn between which I had walked with my teacup. I saw in my mind how they blackened and rotted and turned into dark sludge.

A week before leaving I could not sleep. You had not come to bed at all. I got up, pulled on a thick jumper and walked to the balcony. You were sitting there in the dark and gazing into the park, where dim night lights still burned between the trees. All the other balconies were deserted. No one moved on the streets. I sat down in the other chair. The coolness of the metal seat poured onto my skin through the thin pajama trousers. Your face was a crossroads of shadows.

We lost all plantations and cultures at the laboratory, you said. Years of work.

I'm sorry, I said.

The processes were recorded, of course, you continued. The knowledge will remain. But many things need to be started from scratch. We were just on the verge of finding what we were looking for.

What will happen to Project Earth?

I don't know.

I reached for you across the table. Our fingertips brushed.

Where do you think it came from?

You looked at me as if you didn't understand the question.

The fungal disease, I clarified.

What do you mean?

Quarantine measures on Fuxi are even stricter than they are on Mars. All medicinal plants, mushrooms and lichen that I need for my work were either grown here or not available. Nothing like this has happened in the cylinder cities for decades. Where did the disease spread from to get into the plantations of Fuxi?

You were quiet. The wind that wasn't wind stirred the leaves. A row of birds slept on the branch, their outline visible in the late-night light.

The quarantine systems are not entirely reliable, you said eventually. I heard a suspicious strand in your voice.

Maybe we'll still be able to come back, I suggested.

Several environmental organizations had demanded that life-support systems on Fuxi should be left on. The fungal disease only affected the crops harvested for human consumption, they said. Other plants and animals brought to Fuxi had the right to continue their lives in the city, even if humans left. Part of the artificial ecosystem might survive. And if a pesticide could be developed for the fungal disease, Fuxi might be habitable again one day. It could function as a living laboratory; the research information gathered from there used and applied in other colonies.

No, you said. It will never happen. The cost is too high, and there is no guarantee whatsoever that a pesticide will ever be found. This is a new, far more adaptable variant of a rust fungus that has never been eradicated from Earth. If the disease were to spread to Mars, that would be the end of the colonies. The most certain way to wipe out the fungus is to remove the conditions in which it can live. That means—

The death of Fuxi.

Exactly.

The morning glory climbing onto the walls from the terracotta pots had twisted its white flowers closed. The scent of jasmine drifted from somewhere. The trees were green and the air fresh. It could have been any night on Fuxi.

Today I wanted to break everything, I said.

Why does this have to happen to us? I said.

It's unfair, I said.

You said nothing.

I'm going to bed, I said.

When I left the balcony, you said to my back, We still have a home.

But I didn't, not anymore.

Three days before our departure we took Major Tom to the vet. We had not been able to get an appointment earlier. Most vets had left by then, and those who remained had their hands full. Pets were popular on Fuxi.

I stroked Major Tom's paws while his eyes closed slowly on the operating table and his side stopped rising and falling.

The body was cremated. We were given a biodegradable urn to take with us. We walked into the forest and buried the ashes under a white silver birch. There was no need to mark the place.

• •●• •

Five weeks after we had stood in the living room staring at the images of darkening fields on the TV screen, we boarded a gray vessel with four suitcases. They held my cloak, headpiece and drum, the notebooks I had filled for you, a few books of yours, all research connected with Project Earth on memory chips, and some clothes and shoes.

I watched on the monitor of the ship how we left Fuxi behind, until I saw it no longer.

These memories are yours too, Sol. But each of us remembers differently.

28.3.2168
Harmonia, Mars
Later

Sol,
Where did you go then, after Fuxi?

When the quarantine was finally over, we lived temporarily in Harmonia, in this very room where I am now writing. I felt as if we'd stepped into a mirror maze, the old-fashioned kind that Winterland had, dimly lit and decorated with fiberglass elves. Every time I reached for you, my touch met a cold, smooth surface: I only saw my own reflection where you should have been. I knew you grieved, like I did, but in a different, hidden way that eluded my understanding. You slept next to me and spoke to me, but you were not there, not the way you'd been before.

Then came the morning I woke up in an empty bed, and you were gone. You'd only taken a small rucksack with you. You had not left a message, and you didn't respond to our attempts to contact you. Not your mother's, not Ilsa's, and not mine.

I went to the university and spoke with your colleagues. Emergency accommodations had been organized in the student rooms of the campus for those evacuated from Fuxi, because it was not term time, and everyone had other things to think about besides you. I wandered around the coffee shops and parks and libraries that I knew you'd frequented before we'd moved to Fuxi. No one had seen you. On the third day I went to the police station, only to learn that there was nothing they could do. You were an adult, and you'd only been gone a few days.

Sol, I thought of your father's bones at the bottom of some Martian ravine, deeper than an Earth ocean, never to be found. I wondered how much of their weight you still carried, and if it was enough to make you fall and not get up again.

You returned a week later, dark circles under your eyes, your hair unwashed, clothes stained and smelling faintly of some strange chemical.

Lumi, you said, as if you hadn't expected to see me again. You pulled me into your arms and did not let go for a long time.

What happened? I asked. Where have you been?

I'm sorry, you said. I shouldn't have disappeared like that.

No, I said, and tears ran down my face. You shouldn't.

Has anyone come here? Anyone you didn't know?

I don't think so, I replied. I don't remember.

It's important.

No. No one's been here. A plumber the other day. They said they were checking the heating system of the buildings.

What did they look like?

Blond hair, reddish skin. Why does it matter?

You closed your eyes and took a deep breath.

I'll never disappear again, you said, and wiped a tear away from my cheek. I promise you. Your fingertip felt coarse against my skin.

You slept for two days. I crept into the bed alcove next to you, wrapped my arms around you from behind and pressed myself against your back. The hair at the nape of your neck tickled my face.

Where did you go? I asked, when you finally woke.

Your face was a desert stripped bare by a dust storm. Your hand squeezed mine.

I'll tell you about it sometime, you said.

You scrunched your nose.

I need a shower very badly.

You never told me, Sol.

• •●• •

But there were two of us in that maze, chasing each other's reflection. Your voice in the dark: *Lumi, Lumi*.

The otherworld landscape clung to me, tried to pull me back in like a quagmire, and my eyes saw a barren plain and a winding path and a gate made from living trees. Silver birches, they were, their intertwined trunks snow white and their leaves the only green thing in sight. The lynx sat next to me, inert. Her ears were pressed low against her head, and a narrow ridge of fur trailed her spine. My fingers met scars the lynx's skin did not bear when she first came to me. She growled.

Lumi?

I seized your voice like a rope that would pull me to safety.

I've been trying to wake you since this morning, you said.

I held on to your words. I took a step in the quagmire. It gave way under my weight. I took another step.

Yes, you said. That's it. Come back. Please.

Slowly, slowly you guided me to this world. I opened my eyes, and I was here, in this room, all those years ago.

My throat was made of dry leaves and sand as I spoke.

How long was I in a trance?

Nearly fifty hours, you said. Again.

You handed me water in a metal cup.

It's not safe, you said. Your body can go into a shutdown. Your kidneys might stop working.

I'm fine, I said. Healers have been known to stay in a trance for seventy-two hours without any complications. It's not like sleep. It's more like…

Coma? Death?

Deep meditation.

You never used to do this, you said. On Fuxi. And before.

I was quiet. You used to do this less frequently would have been a more truthful statement, but you did not know that.

I'm sorry.

You pulled me close. I hugged you and breathed in the scent of your skin.

How many times has it been this month? you asked. Three, four times a week? Or more?

I don't know, I said. I haven't kept count.

You withdrew, looked me in the eye. Your words were pressed thin and dry.

Why don't you want to be with me anymore? you asked.

The sharp tip of an icicle moved along the flesh of my heart, looking for the softest place to pierce it. I swallowed.

But I do, I said. I squeezed my eyes closed. That's exactly what I want.

Then why… you started. Your voice trailed away. You shook your head slowly.

I'm right here, you continued. Where do you go, Lumi? When you disappear from me?

I had no words for you, Sol. Not the ones you needed, not then. So I spoke some others.

We could go to the Moon. Have a holiday. See a healer. I could, you know. Seek help.

You ran your hands slowly down my arms and up again.

I think that sounds like a very good idea, you said.

And maybe… you too. Could see a healer. If you wanted.

The movement of your hands stopped. You pulled away. You sat on the side of the bed, turned your eyes to the living wall. The lights were reflected in your eyes. If I'd looked closer, I'd have seen the shapes of the leaves on the dark surfaces of your irises: a garden of ivy and snake plants.

When would you like to go? you asked.

· • ● • ·

I found the healer on the Moon through a colleague I'd known since my apprentice days with Vivian. As soon as we stepped into the healer's treatment room, I trusted them. There were no flashy crystal decorations, no colorful symbols painted on the walls, no headache-inducing scent of incense or ethereal music floating from hidden loudspeakers. The room was a simple hexagon with nothing but a small table with a few items on it, and a thin, rather uncomfortable-looking mattress in the middle of the floor. The healer wore a long dress and a long beard, and as soon as they saw me, they said, You carry some wounds that have given you soul-sickness.

That was when I was certain they knew what they were doing.

It took three visits. After the third, I felt fragile, but whole again. The healer had brought back the part of me that had lost its way and couldn't find the path home.

After, I watched you lying on the mattress, Sol, and I hoped they'd be able to do the same for you.

· • ● • ·

I'm going to tell you something I've never told you or anyone before. Or maybe I will still change my mind: cross over the lines so many times that they'll be impossible to decipher, or tear the pages out.

This you know:

When we traveled to the Moon to see the healer, I would have liked to stay in Luther in order to revisit the places where I'd spent time with Vivian after leaving Earth. Enough time had passed since her death that the thought of returning no longer felt painful. Rather, it was a distant ache that would never vanish entirely and through which life looked a little different, maybe more important to live than before. The dome village where I had stayed with Vivian was no longer operational. The area had been contaminated after the mining accident. We settled in a different village, not far away, and rented an accommodation globe.

This you don't know:

One day, when you had a headache, I decided to go out alone, so you could rest and recover in peace. I didn't particularly plan my route. There was a viewpoint on the edge of a nearby crater. I thought it might be the same one where I had watched the Voynich Lights with Vivian years earlier. I decided to go there.

The funicular was ancient, and rocked and twitched as it climbed the rails. There were only a couple of other passengers on it. When it stopped at the edge of the crater and the gate opened, I realized the place was not the same. I had never been there before. The viewpoint was not the narrow balcony on which Vivian and I had stood, but a level terrace that circled the entire crater. Narrow stairs ran uphill in one place toward a bubble-shaped structure I imagined to be some kind of a café. I began to climb the stairs, enjoying the floating feeling because I knew I could not spend a long time in the thin gravity of the Moon. At the top of the stairs I stopped before a worn metal door and searched for a button until I saw one on the wall. I pressed it, and the door slid aside. As soon as I had stepped in, the door closed behind me and a red sign was lit on the wall with the text in several languages saying *Do not remove your helmet! Please wait for the airlock to be filled*. I waited until the sign turned green before detaching the helmet from my shoulders.

Another door opened in front of me. I expected to see a bar and a few tables behind it. Instead, the door revealed a circular room with a narrow bench rounding the walls. In the middle of the room there was an old-fashioned, glass-walled phone booth. One of those had been used as a decoration in Winterland. A black-haired person stood in the phone booth with their back turned to me and talked into a heavy, clumsy Bakelite receiver. The glass walls blurred the words so I couldn't make them out. I sat down on the bench. I saw the shoulders of the person twitch in the phone booth as they spoke.

After a while they placed the receiver back on the holder, wiped their face with a hand from which they'd removed the glove and turned around. They started when they saw me. Their eyes were red.

I'm sorry, I said. I didn't mean to disturb you.

They nodded at me and said something in a language I didn't know. I thought it might be Europan Korean. They made a gesture in order to indicate that the phone booth was available to me. I stepped into the booth.

The booth looked like authentic antique. The push buttons of the phone machine were worn down with dents and the digit two had faded away altogether. There were traces left on the glass walls from stickers once glued to them, on which Liliana in a red lace corset was serving steaming hot coffee every afternoon. Someone had even gone into enough trouble to place a genuine-looking phone catalog on the shelf under the telephone machine. It seemed to be from Germany and the year 1996. I was astonished that no one had stolen it.

I didn't understand the function of the booth right away. There were no instructions anywhere. The machine had a slot for coins, but no one used coins anymore. And who would call from the Moon; where to? Experimentally I lifted the receiver and pressed it to my ear. Silence, then a click. A recording in Chinese began to roll. I recognized some words, but had to wait for the next voice in English until I was able to understand the whole message.

Welcome, friend, it said. *You have arrived at the Afterlife Phone. After the great radiation tsunami of the year 2130, Moon-based artist Misty Sakamoto installed an antique phone booth at this viewpoint as a memorial to its victims. Soon people who had lost loved ones in the tsunami began to visit the booth. On this phone, they had conversations with those who had passed, telling them things that had been left unsaid. The phone has remained in place for over twenty years and visitors still keep coming. If you have arrived to speak to someone you have lost, they are listening. Dial the asterisk in order to begin the conversation. On your departure you can make a donation on the pay machine by the door. All donations go to the families of the victims. This art therapy project has been sponsored by Moon Retreats Limited.*

The recording finished and was replaced by a quiet white noise. I hesitated. I pressed the asterisk.

I listened. The white noise continued. I opened my mouth. No sound came out. Unexpectedly, there were tears in my eyes.

Vivian? I said.

The noise did not respond.

Did you leave the gate open for me on purpose? I asked. All that time ago in Winterland?

I wanted to tell Vivian I was lost. I wanted to ask her for advice. I could hear many things in the hum when I let my mind wander: ripe grains through which wind moved in the field, treetops bending in a breeze, water rippling in waves. Your breathing in the dark, Sol. I could not hear Vivian in it. Or perhaps she was now all those things, and more.

• • ● • •

At the foot of the crater I boarded a train. I had my passport with me, and there was enough money on my bracelet. Everything else I could obtain elsewhere. I traveled to the nearest spaceport. I sat there watching ships that arrived and departed. I tried to choose my destination.

Two hours later I boarded a train and returned to the accommodation globe. You did not wake until I settled next to you in bed.

How long did I sleep? you asked.

Hours, I said.

You pulled me closer. I kissed you.

Behind me the reality forked into paths. On one of them, I had not returned to the accommodation globe. I had not looked behind, but walked through the security and boarded a ship that took me to Earth or Europa, and I never saw you again.

• •●• •

When we returned to Mars, I traveled to the observatory. There I looked through the telescope at the ring of the cylinder cities around the planet. Where Fuxi should have been, there was only darkness.

I imagined a roof garden, lavenders frozen in place and bees fallen next to them, limbs covered in thin white rime. I imagined the frost on the green leaves of the trees and in the grooves of the bark; I imagined the balcony on which no one sat anymore. I imagined the circle of white birches in the forest.

Fuxi had closed its wings. It drifted in space as an empty, unmoving husk of an insect, a ghost ship that the lights of living vessels averted from. It had carried us for a moment. Then we had fallen apart.

The healer on the Moon had brought back the missing piece of me. But once the soul has been torn, the loose part will rarely settle back for the rest of a person's life.

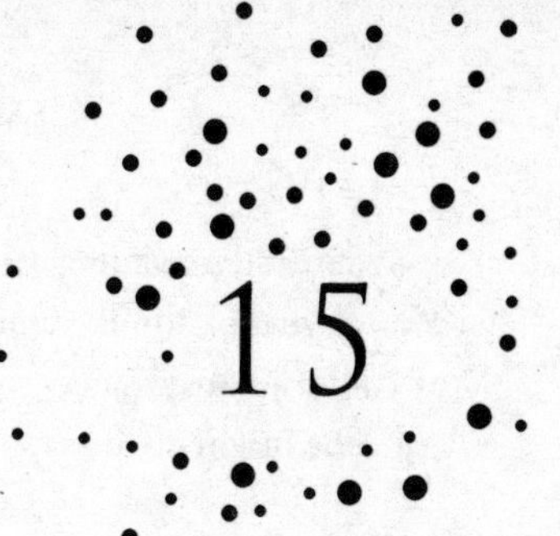

15

Discovery of strange sapling perplexes scientists in Victorian London
Reuters Earth
9.10.2153 / 17.02

A strange tree sapling found on the holiday isle of Victorian London last week has been identified as a young Norway spruce. Norway spruce *(Picea abies)* is an evergreen conifer that was very common in Europe, Asia and many parts of North America as recently as a hundred years ago. The discovery of the sapling has perplexed scientists, because the tree species was believed to have become extinct. The information was first reported by Reuters news agency.

"It is unlikely that the sapling could have been transported to Victorian London by natural means," comments Professor of Biology Hanna Pärn from the University of Sorbonne. "Furthermore, the sapling could not have reached its current size without surviving several winters. This suggests either a mutation or a variety that has been genetically manipulated through biotechnology. We have no knowledge as to why anyone would plant a spruce sapling in the middle of the factory landscape of the holiday isle, but the discovery is welcome."

The extinction of the Norway spruce was caused by global warming. The species requires sub-zero temperatures in order to winter successfully. The discovery of the sapling has created excited optimism among researchers. Beside the cleansing of the oceans, reviving and rewilding species from the verge of extinction is a central goal of the Reykjavik environmental treaty to which dozens of countries are signed.

The origin of the sapling is being investigated.

Sender: Lumi Salo
Recipient: Enisa Karim
Date: 28.3.2168 23.58 MST
Security: Maximum encryption

Enisa, have you come across the name Vivian Berg in connection with the Stoneturners (or anything else)?
Can you find out anything about her?
A thousand times thank you, as always.
L

29.3.2168
Harmonia, Mars

Sol,
Today I finally spoke to your sister. I am not entirely sure about everything we said. We may have said other things too.

I don't know when I will speak to her again.

It was already evening when I heard her footsteps in the stairs. The robot suitcase had parked itself in front of her door. I found Ilsa in the dusky living room. She was wearing a dark suit and had taken off her shoes. An expensive-looking handbag was sprawled open on the sofa next to her. She had poured a glass of wine for herself.

When I stepped into the room, she raised her gaze, but did not get up to hug me. I stopped in the doorway. For a long time neither of us said anything. Ilsa had switched on the spotlight over the sofa. I stood outside its sphere, on the edge of darkness.

"Hi," I said. "How are you?"

Ilsa did not reply.

"Thanks for getting the flea medication," I continued.

Ilsa looked at the ceiling, then at the floor. She rolled the wine in her glass and took a sip. She placed the glass on the table.

"Mom has not come home yet, has she?" she asked.

I shook my head.

"Do you have siblings?" Ilsa asked. The light fell steep onto her face, drew visible the lines on her forehead.

"No."

The corners of Ilsa's mouth turned up slightly. She nodded slowly. Her eyes were fixed on the wineglass.

"Of course not," she said. "I forgot."

She'd not forgotten, Sol: no one forgets about Earth's one-child policy that was introduced as an emergency measure as the climate catastrophe progressed.

"You have no one who shares your memories," Ilsa continued. She finally turned her gaze to me. "Who has known you since you were a child. Who was a child with you. Who looks at your parents the way you do, yet differently. You couldn't possibly know what it's like when that is taken away."

I had not expected that of her, Sol: that she'd try to weaponize my Earth background against me, undermine my place in your life to gain firmer footing for herself. As you know, Ilsa and I have had our differences, but I thought we'd put them aside.

"I've experienced other losses," I said.

Something passed Ilsa's face, regret perhaps, but it vanished before I had a chance to seize it. It was replaced by a harshness I had rarely seen in her. A cool draft blew onto my skin from the temperature control machinery in the room.

"You don't talk about it very much," Ilsa said. "Fuxi. Or Earth."

"There's not much to say about Earth."

Or not the sort of things I believe will interest you, I thought. Ilsa lifted her spectacles and rubbed the bridge of her nose. The spectacles had left marks on it.

"On the whole it's strange to realize how little I know about you," she said. "You've been a part of Sol's life, our family's life, for over ten years. But what have you told us about yourself?"

I had no response to that.

"You don't want to see my friends, or spend time with me," Ilsa continued.

Maybe I should have known the cocktail dresses abandoned in the wardrobe and high-heeled shoes and society invitations I had rejected would come back to haunt me. Yet I didn't understand why Ilsa brought them up now. She moved her wineglass. It made a cold sound against the surface of the table.

"Sol changed," she said quietly.

"In what way?" I asked. "When?"

Ilsa watched the dark wine at the bottom of the glass, tilted the glass slowly back and forth, then raised her gaze to me.

"If you have dragged Sol into anything—"

I only realized then where her words were carrying the conversation. I tried not to show how deep they cut.

"Do you think I have something to do with Sol's disappearance?" I said.

Ilsa stared at me. Her fingers moved like the limbs of a mechanical toy as they wind down. Her nails clinked faintly onto the convex surface of the glass.

"How should I know? You never talk about your past. I don't

know you at all."

Sharp and venomous sentences tried to get out, but I forced myself to hold them back for now.

"I haven't seen Sol in weeks," I said. "I don't even know if they're alive. If I knew of their whereabouts, why in the world would I keep it from you and Naomi?"

But I thought of your message, Sol, which I had kept from them.

The corners of Ilsa's mouth twitched. A nighttime Moon surface lay behind her eyes, dark and deserted.

"Sol began to hide things. Around the time you arrived."

I wanted to walk out of the room. Instead, I drew breath and let the words come.

"Was it around the same time Vivian died?"

Ilsa's fingers froze against the glass. Ice glinted on the Moon surface.

"What do you mean?" Ilsa said in a voice that was no louder than a whisper.

"Vivian Berg," I replied. "You knew her, didn't you?"

Ilsa did not look at me. She took a sip from her glass.

"And Sol knew her too," I continued.

Ilsa placed the glass on the table and closed her eyes.

"How long?" I asked.

Ilsa took a deep breath and sighed.

"Vivian was Mom's healer. Your predecessor. She came to us when I was ten and Sol was seven."

All the times I had sat in your family's house, or at home with you, Sol, and talked about Vivian to Ilsa or Naomi or you, flooded my mind. I'd never seen anything on the face of any of you to suggest that you knew her.

"She was with your family for about twenty years?" I asked.

Weariness weighed on Ilsa's nod.

"Why didn't you tell me?"

Your favorite chair at the end of the room was shrouded by shadows, Sol, and among them your specter from another time sat watching us. Ilsa's face was bare. It was the first time I'd seen her that way.

"Vivian made us swear we wouldn't tell you."

"Why?"

"I have wondered about the same," she said. "I didn't understand back then why it was so important to her, and I don't understand it now."

When I'd started my job with your family, Sol, I'd tried to gain an understanding from your mother about what kind of techniques her former healer had used. I thought it would give me a better chance at helping her. Yet Naomi only told me little and avoided details.

"What happened in autumn 2152?"

Ilsa held her breath for a moment. She does that when she is particularly stressed.

"My mother's condition got worse," she said. "But Vivian didn't abandon you because of that. That was when she realized she herself was ill."

I still remembered the shock when Vivian had suddenly pushed me away, ordered me to continue alone. I remembered the empty years after, traveling and healing, but never staying anywhere for long.

"She sought a cure for a couple of years without success. Eventually she came back to stay with us. Until she was too unwell to continue."

"Where did she…?" I was unable to finish the sentence.

"There's a palliative care home on the outskirts of Harmonia," Ilsa said. "You can see trees from every window there."

We were quiet. *I'd have wanted to know, Vivian*, I thought. *I understand why you didn't want me to know. That was your right. But I am selfish, and I'd have liked to choose the final words I spoke to you.*

"Vivian and Sol worked together," Ilsa said. "When she was still well." She saw my expression. "Looks like you didn't know that."

"No."

I didn't feel like mentioning the photo of you and Vivian together to Ilsa. Your specter in the armchair adjusted its posture, Sol. Cold emanated from it.

"Vivian helped Sol acquire botanical samples and conveyed oral lore about the uses of native Earth plants. I think it was Vivian who got Sol interested in ethnobotany."

I nodded. My neck was ice-stiff. It all made sense: Vivian had always been very precise about botanical knowledge and asked me a lot of questions about medicinal plants used in Winterland. I remembered her somewhere along a plain on Mars, in the crammed sleeper cabin of the underground, taking notes of what I told her in the blue-tinted night light. Sol, if Vivian conveyed information to you about Earth plants, which other information did she convey, and to whom?

"Did Vivian ever talk about the Stoneturners?"

Ilsa looked like she had not slept for three weeks. Maybe she hadn't.

"I don't remember," she said. "It was too long ago. What does it matter?"

It may be the only thing that matters, I wanted to say.

"You could have told me," I said. "About Vivian."

"Lumi—"

"I know you don't understand why Sol chose me," I continued. "You think they could have had anyone. You can't comprehend why they'd pick a strange Earth-born whose profession is suspect to say the least, and who doesn't understand about style or society."

"Is that what you think?" Ilsa said.

She got up from the sofa and walked to me, to the edge of light. I remained standing in the dark. Ilsa looked at the floor, then at me.

"Sol is like a different person with you. Happier. That's the only thing I wish for them."

Her eyes glistened. She reached out her hand. I hesitated for a moment before I took it.

"Vivian was ill," Ilsa said. "Promises given to the dying have a special weight to them. Who'd break such a promise?"

"Some would," I said quietly. "Because they'd think of the living."

Ilsa let my hand go.

The lights dimmed into automatic night mode just then. The sounds of the nocturnal forest programmed for the room began to drizzle quietly from the hidden loudspeakers. The hum of wind walked past. Light rain susurrated onto invisible leaves that had gone yellow and fallen and turned into earth in some distant place many lives ago.

"Do you think Sol will come back?" Ilsa asked. Her voice caught in the invisible branches; rain halved it.

Yes, I wanted to say. Instead I said, "I don't know."

A tremble crossed Ilsa's face. She turned, went and picked up her bag from the sofa and walked past me without looking at me. The light went out. Only the dim night lamps over the wall hanging portraying constellations were left on. I stared at the empty doorway; on the other side, in the stairs, a light switched on. Ilsa's footsteps grew distant.

Sol, you are standing in the nocturnal forest that no longer is. Rain runs in rivulets down your skin, it gathers your hair into bundles and glues the clothes onto your arms and back and legs. You are looking intently at something looming behind the trees, your face sharp with focus. I want to turn my eyes in the same direction and look at it too, but I don't know which I am more frightened of: what I will see there, or that I will see nothing.

29.3.2168
Harmonia, Mars
Later

Sol,

I have sought a moment in the memory that I could have seized in order to turn everything around. But even if I saw it, the past is a road we have made in the landscape. You can draw the map anew, but you cannot make a mountain into a sea, or a sea into a desert. You cannot remove human traces from where they have once been left.

Six years after I'd departed from Earth with Vivian, she told me what I'd been afraid to hear.

We had stayed in Datong for two months. For over a year she'd allowed me to see patients on my own, but still attended the healing sessions with me from time to time. We took turns between the roles of healer and assistant. Often, the assistant was not strictly necessary, but having someone else look after the practical matters like carrying the tools, preparing the healing room and collecting the utensils afterward eased the strain of the soul-journey.

It was late night. I had made a soul-journey on my own the day before, and I had only woken up a couple of hours earlier. I sat eating a simple rice and pea broth for supper, when Vivian returned to the accommodations we shared. The lynx cowered in the corner of the kitchen, ceaselessly washing her ear. I heard the door. The swan entered the kitchen first. He moved slowly, his long, white neck bent and hanging his head low. He sat down on the floor at the end of the table and began to groom his feathers. There was something painful about his lethargic movements.

Vivian stepped into the room. I placed my spoon on the table.

Hi, I said. How did it go?

Vivian said nothing. She glanced at the swan, pulled a chair for herself from under the table and collapsed onto it. She lowered her head into her hands. Her eyes fell closed, as if keeping them open required great effort.

Would you like some food? I asked. There's broth on the hob. It's probably still warm.

Vivian nodded, and I got up to ladle food into a bowl. The steam warmed my face as I carried the broth to the table, but the metal surface of the dish was cool against my hands. Vivian looked up as I placed the bowl and a spoon before her.

I watched her eat in silence. Her white hair was pulled into a ponytail at the nape of her neck, as usual. The dim light of the kitchen softened the lines on her face and made her look younger. She lifted the bowl to her lips and drank the remains of the broth from the bottom.

Thank you, Vivian said. Will you help me do the washing up?

We washed up in silence. When we had set the bowls to dry, Vivian dried her hands on the tea towel and said without build-up or explanation, Lumi, you are ready now.

What do you mean?

I cannot teach you anything more. When I leave Datong in a few weeks' time, you won't be coming with me.

Coldness spread through my entire body, as if I'd been pushed into space without warning.

I don't know everything yet, I said.

Vivian smiled.

I'm glad you say that, she said. If you believed you know everything, then you definitely wouldn't be ready.

There was a burning behind my eyes. Vivian stepped closer and hugged me.

You know enough, she said. You'll learn the rest on your own. That's what everyone must do.

I closed my eyes and tried to memorize the way Vivian felt. She was not small in stature, but just then she seemed fragile, as if she could crumble to dust any moment.

There was a faint screech close to us. I opened my eyes. Vivian stepped backward and turned to look. The kitchen was not big, and the lynx curled up in the corner had got to her feet. Her back hair stood on end. The swan stood before her, frozen in place. The bird's neck was extended toward the lynx, the beak in the near vicinity of the ear of the spot-furred animal.

Vivian stared at the swan and the lynx. She took a few quick steps and squatted down before them. She lifted her hand toward the lynx, who started and hissed.

What is it? I asked.

You tell me, Vivian said.

I'm not sure I understand.

Your soul-animal is injured. Vivian gestured at the lynx. What happened to her ear?

It was true: the lynx's ear was slightly torn, and dried blood was visible on it.

It was yesterday's journey, I said. My voice shook a little. We encountered something angry along the path. We weren't able to get out of the way in time.

Vivian and the swan leaned carefully closer to the lynx. The lynx growled in the corner, tried to snap at the swan, but did not leap away. Vivian and the swan examined the lynx's coat, her sides and her back, tried to look at her paws. I felt uncomfortable, as if I were naked, each hair and mole and scar on display.

It wasn't the first time, was it? Vivian said eventually and turned her gaze to me.

I felt like I had in Winterland, when I'd first met her: as if she could read my mind. Her face was closed, as it was wont to do when she was unhappy with something.

They're just scratches, I said.

They're wounds nevertheless, Vivian said. Your soul-animal is here to protect you, but it goes both ways. It's also your responsibility to protect her.

She touched my shoulders lightly. Her eyes were dark in the dim light, and their gaze saw deeper than I would have liked. It was not angry, simply filled with worry.

Lumi, Vivian said. Nothing is forbidden, but everything has consequences.

She took a breath.

If we had more time, she continued, and then she said nothing more.

She stroked my hair, like my mother used to do when I was a child. She had never done it before.

I must go to sleep, she said.

As Vivian walked into her tiny alcove, her shoulders were hunched. The chill that had slotted into me when she'd said she was going to leave Datong without me began to withdraw slowly. I should have recognized it for what it was. I should have known those were the last days I'd ever spend with her.

30.3.2168

Harmonia, Mars

Sol,

When I got up this morning, Ilsa had left. Naomi had come home so late I was already in bed. Ziggy was meowing miserably in the bathroom. He tried to rush out through the gap when I opened the door to bring him food. I picked him up in my arms. The last dead fleas had dropped to the floor from his coat.

"No more vinegar," I promised Ziggy. He put his head on my shoulder and purred. When his weight began to strain my arms, I put him to the floor.

I closed the door behind me and heard his paws begin to scratch the surface of the door. I went to throw my clothes into the washing machine.

I found Naomi in the garden, sitting under the flowering quince. She gazed at the treetop, the synthetic sky above and the light that imitated Earth daytime. A strong déjà vu flooded over me. The last time I'd seen her, she'd been sitting in the same place. For a moment I was certain that I had never left, that distance had never flung us apart, Sol, that no time had passed, that I had returned from Europa with Ziggy only yesterday. That the blue-winged butterfly sitting on Naomi's knee was the same that had landed there seconds ago, when I'd come to say hello to her after Europa.

"Naomi," I said.

She turned to look at me. The butterfly took to the air and danced toward the dome arching above. Naomi got up from the bamboo bench, took a few steps and pulled me into an embrace.

"How are you?" I asked.

Naomi sighed and stepped back. Weariness weighed her face, but the long braid was smooth and she was dressed.

"Dreams," she said. "They come and smooth all edges away. And then you have to wake up." But her face did not crack. She was calmer than I remembered her being in a long time.

"I know," I said.

"How are you?"

"I need to talk to you about something," I said.

I searched for my screen in the healer's bag I'd slung across my shoulder. I swiped it on. The image I had brought to the display beforehand emerged. I handed the screen to Naomi.

Naomi's face changed. Something large and shapeless surfaced on it, a shock that tensed her features. She stared at the photo and drew a breath. She looked at me.

"Where did you get this?" she asked.

"Why didn't you tell me?"

Naomi's face fell. She closed her eyes and took a deep breath. The screen hung in her hands like a dead animal.

"Vivian demanded it," she said. "It was easiest to say yes. I thought that whoever this new healer was, she'd probably not stay long. I thought that keeping the secret for a few months would be all the same." Naomi opened her eyes, and her gaze was full of sorrow. "But then you and Sol... none of us expected that."

"Eleven years," I said. "I came to your house for the first time eleven years ago."

"The longer you carry a secret," Naomi said quietly, "the harder it becomes to talk about it."

She pushed the screen back to me. On the display Vivian faded into dark pixels, and you too, Sol.

"I first fell ill when Sol was born," Naomi continued. "I was unable to look after them when they were small. Ilsa was only a few years old, and Oskar was constantly on work trips. Healers came and went."

I felt as if I was beginning to see a bit more clearly, like some light pierced the dusk.

"Vivian?" I asked.

Naomi nodded.

"She was the first to stay longer. In my better times Vivian journeyed elsewhere to heal. She might be gone months, even years, and then come back. As you know, she'd take apprentices and would only visit rarely then."

I thought of the time I'd spent with Vivian on Mars, her repeated absences, especially toward the end of my apprenticeship.

"When Vivian was too ill to continue working, she recommended another healer."

Naomi looked directly at me. I understood.

"She said she'd guarantee you personally," Naomi said. "She had taught you everything she knew."

Another piece of the past cleared, or perhaps darkened into a different shape. *Many things happen by coincidence*, I heard Vivian's voice in my mind. *Yet fewer than we might think*.

"What do you know about the Stoneturners?" I asked.

"I don't know what you're talking about." Naomi's expression was blank. I tried to discern if it was the same kind of blankness I'd seen many times when I had spoken of Vivian in her presence.

"An environmental organization," I said. "Sol may have been a member since their student days."

"I don't remember ever hearing that name," Naomi said.

"Sol never spoke of them?"

"I was not well at the time," Naomi said. "I wasn't even home for Sol's first couple of years at the university."

I remembered then what you had told me: Naomi had spent nearly three years in a place she'd called a sanatorium. Eventually her healer – Vivian, I knew now – had helped her leave the place.

"I think they have something to do with Sol's disappearance," I said. "You really don't know anything about them?"

Naomi's head turned slowly.

"I'm sorry."

Grief and anger squeezed my throat. I closed my eyes. I felt a tear escape to my cheek. Naomi stepped closer.

"Lumi," she said. "When Oskar disappeared, I wanted to know everything about him. Every private dream, each childhood memory he'd never told me, every thought in the middle of the night. I turned his home office upside down. I believed there'd be a key somewhere into what had happened."

I wiped my cheek.

"I know what you're going through right now," Naomi continued. "And it will never be over. If Sol does not return..." Her voice crumbled and she paused for a moment. "If Sol does not return, you will be searching for the rest of your life."

"I'm going to find Sol," I said.

Naomi took my hand.

"Bring them back," she said. "If you can. And yourself too."

I squeezed Naomi's hand.

"Vivian would have been proud of you," she said. "I'm sorry I didn't tell you so."

"Do you know why it was so important to her for me not to know about her connection with your family?"

Naomi shook her head.

"If anyone knows," she said, "it is Sol."

"I'll ask them when I find them."

Naomi smiled.

"It's a relief to be able to finally say her name," she said.

"Vivian's?"

"Vivian's." She paused. "Do you know where you're going next?"

"Yes."

How to make a biograffito
Handbook of Ecosabotage.
Datong: Moonstone Press, 2140.

You will need:
A stencil (for stencil-making instructions, see page 36)
Bio dye and activation liquid
A spray bottle equipped with a dosage nozzle for spraying the dye
Gloves
A respiratory mask

Place the stencil firmly on the surface where you wish to paint a text or pattern. The surface does not need to be smooth. Most bio dyes take well to metals, glass, plastics, stone, wood, paper and fabrics.

Holding the stencil in place, spray the bio dye in its holes. Use a respiratory mask and gloves.

Remove the stencil from the surface. At this point, practically nothing will be visible, because bio dyes consist mainly of the spores or seeds of the base organism and are colorless before activation.

Spray activation liquid on the surface.

Within 24 to 48 hours (depending on the bio dye used and the conditions) the pattern will begin to grow visible. See photos on the following spread for some finished biograffiti. Clockwise from top left: (1) "Treehuggers rock" – moss-based biograffiti on stone, (2) "Let's save the face of the Man on the Moon" – lichen-based biograffiti on metal, (3) "Mars for microbes" – fungi-based biograffiti on the glass wall of a conservatory, (4) "Tardigrades were on Europa first" – algae-based biograffiti on underwater glass, (5) "Mars is red, Earth is blue, Moon mining sucks and so do you" – lichen-based biograffiti on bamboo.

Tips for achieving better results:

Speed and dosage are crucial. With a good-quality nozzle and carefully shaped stencil the entire process should take no longer than 30–60 seconds.

We recommend a lichen- or fungus-based bio dye for ease of usage and non-toxicity.

We do not recommend cleansing the surface before painting on it. Strong cleansing liquids will kill the microbe base that is necessary for allowing the dye to grow.

Depending on the conditions, it may take from a couple of days up to several weeks for the bio dye to grow to its full size.

The durability and longevity of the bio dye and the visibility of the graffiti will depend on conditions and the composition of the bio dye used. It is advisable to choose the dye according to the purpose. For instance, if the idea is to paint a bioluminescent pattern on the wall of a dark space, the best results will be achieved with a fungus-based bio dye that does not need light in order to grow. Dyes that require photosynthesis, such as most algae- and moss-based ones, are not suitable for this purpose. ATTENTION! While the spores of many bio dyes will survive even in harsh circumstances, such as a vacuum or considerably low temperatures, they will need a carbon dioxide-containing atmosphere in order to grow.

Do not give up if your first attempts produce a clumsy-looking result. Anyone can become a skilled biograffiti activist or artist. Practice makes perfect!

Sender: J. N. Owoeye
Recipient: Lumi Salo
Cc: T. F. Liang
Date: 1.4.2168 07.51 MST
Security: Maximum encryption

Dear Lumi Salo,
You asked if there is any news on the case of your spouse's disappearance. We are following several investigation routes. Unfortunately I am not at liberty to tell you more at this stage. Crisis support is still available to you at all times, and I am copying in my colleague, Detective Constable Liang, who works on Nüwa. Please feel free to make an appointment with him if anything new emerges that might be of help in investigating the whereabouts of your spouse.
Best,
Jenny Owoeye

PS. Apparently the tomatoes in your kitchen looked a bit the worse for wear, so I gave the detectives who searched your apartment permission to switch the irrigation system back on.

3.4.2168

A starship between Mars and Nüwa

Sol,
What do you think of when you think of home?
Do you think of the Moonday House?

Do you think of the low landscape of Mars, of cities buried in the shelter of the soil? Do you think of the kaleidoscope horizon of Fuxi, where clouds and light and the green of the fields turn, forming ever new shapes, not yet aware that they must soon stop?

Or do you think of the view that opens from the lookout deck when the spaceliner approaches Nüwa?

I have a steady bar stool under me, in front of me a steaming pot of white tea that you would not find on Earth these days. The conditions for cultivation are better in the cylinder cities. Behind the huge window the space expands like a thought, its darkness holding scant but invincible lights. The large, smooth metal circle of Nüwa grows water and lushness: I see the stripes of trees and fields, I see the pointed, blue ribbons of lakes, like the glinting sides of fish. Behind the city I discern the cylinders of Ursula and Octavia in the Mars orbit, their shapes glimmering with faint light like jewelry hanging in space. There are only a few hours left of the journey. We land tonight.

Steam rises from the spout of the teapot, draws a narrow mist to blur the view that is not exactly the one I remember.

• • ● • •

Tell me about your teacher, you said once.

That took me by surprise.

You've never asked before, I said. Why now?

Because, you said and shrugged. You keep mentioning her occasionally. You talk about the places she took you. If I knew more about her, I'd know more about you.

It was early days between us, and we were lying in bed, lightheaded from the closeness of each other's skin and the many ways our bodies fit together. I felt the brush of your breath on my neck. Your hand rested on my hip.

She was kind, I said. But uncompromising. She would heal for free wherever she could, only asking for accommodation and travel expenses in exchange. But if a wealthy patient tried to squeeze services out of her for nothing, she told them off.

You shifted behind me, traced the knots of my spine with your fingers. What else?

She didn't try to change who I was. She allowed me to make mistakes because she knew I'd learn from them.

You pressed yourself against my back. Your skin was warm, and your hand moved to my chest.

Where was she from? you asked.

She never told me. And I never asked. I used to think she was from Earth, same as me, but I now think maybe she was from Mars. Or Europa.

Europa?

She knew so much about it.

Sounds like she knew a lot about everything.

True.

I turned around to kiss you, S ol. It was the kind of kiss that people share when they are still learning each other, urgent and slow at once.

Truth is, I don't know very much about her at all, now that I think about it, I said.

What was her name again?

Vivian. Vivian Berg.

Your eyes were turned to me, Sol. I remember what I saw in them, but each memory is just a story of the previous remembrance, and an interpretation of the original moment. When you were a child, did you play the game where you would stand in a circle and the person chosen as the first player would whisper a word into the ear of the person next to them? They'd whisper it forward, and the next one forward again, and eventually the word had made a round in the circle and reached the ear of the last player.

Sometimes the word stayed the same. But most often it was transformed into something else. Occasionally it would lose shape altogether. And yet everyone had passed on the exact whisper they believed they'd heard.

When I look at this memory, I hear a whisper, but I don't know if it describes what I saw, or if it has, in being spoken time and again, taken a different shape.

4.4.2168

The cylinder city of Nüwa

Sol,

I'm home. Ziggy – who, thanks to the medicine, is now a walking death sentence to fleas and therefore mercifully pest-free, at last – toured the apartment with his tail up and purred loudly enough to make the walls tremble. Then he jumped into an armchair and fell asleep, paws extended over the edge of the seat.

I picked up envelopes that had piled on the doormat. There were surprisingly few of them. I was confused when I walked into the living room and saw another pile that lay unopened on the table. Then I remembered Police Detective Owoeye had sent someone to search the apartment. On the whole it is a lot neater than I'd expected: as far as I can tell, nothing has been taken. Surely Owoeye would have let me know if they'd confiscated something?

And the tomatoes in the kitchen had survived! The bottom leaves show that they got dry at some point, but the stems had been revived and grown to touch the ceiling while we were away. I can see green tomatoes on at least two of them. I'll have to send a special thanks to Owoeye for this. I threw away the apple tree branch you'd left in a vase on the table, which had scattered its browned petals onto the kitchen worktop. A new ecosystem was clearly brewing at the bottom of the vase.

It is night on Nüwa. The cool air carries the scent of elderflowers in through the open door of the balcony. I have been sitting on the floor of your office for hours. I have the document sent by Enisa in front of me, with all suspected strikes by the Stoneturners listed from the past thirty years. I also have several notebooks in front of me that I have filled with writing during our years together, Sol.

You gave me the first notebook nearly ten years ago. Do you remember? We were sitting in the living room of our Fuxi apartment that was a near-perfect copy of our current one. Nüwa and Fuxi were built to be twins, to reflect each other in a number of ways. You had spread the valerian you'd grown on the balcony all over the table and were tying it into bundles in order to hang them in the bedroom. It was the darkest place in the apartment.

I was typing a packing list onto my screen. I was departing for Enceladus early the following morning. You had to stay at the university on Fuxi. I would not return until eight weeks later. We hadn't been separated for such a long time since we'd first met. We knew we could not talk the entire time. The communications delay was too long. We'd be able to send voice messages and emails, but conversation in real time would be impossible.

I wish I could go with you, you said. I've never been to Enceladus.

Do you have a blank notebook? I asked. I got the idea just then. It was so simple I wondered why I had not thought of it before.

Probably, in my office. Why?

I'll take it with me and write in it about the journey. When I come back, you can read about what it was like. I'll tell you about the wondrous sky of Enceladus and the strange foods. I'll also tell you about the people, their sorrows and diseases and how they find the will to live out there, far, far away from the sun. You will see it as if you were there with me.

It's not the same thing, you could have said. But you didn't.

Instead you said, I'll get the notebook right away.

You got up from the table. I heard you moving piles of paper in the other room, and you returned a moment later. You handed me a simple notebook with black covers and lined pages.

Since then I have carried you everywhere with me, Sol, built the landscape in which I walked from words, so it would be within your reach too. I can speak to you even when you don't hear, without having to fear the words will vanish into space, where no one will pick them up.

Or so I used to think.

For I admit fear has settled in me, unnoticed, like invisible radiation that crawls under the skin in secret and slowly begins to burn the tissues of the body from within. As I have been filling these pages, I have thought – not for the first time, but for longer and with more weight than ever before – that you may never read these sentences. I may not see you again, may not hand you this book I have carried with me from one planet or moon to the next. You drift farther, and there is empty space between us. I try to form words and gesture at you, but I cannot see if you are looking my way, or away. I am alone on this journey, and although I hope you will walk in the same direction along a route that will eventually cross mine, I do not know if it is so.

When we moved to Nüwa after the evacuation of Fuxi, it was important to you to have your mahogany bookcase shipped here from your childhood home, no matter the cost. I was surprised you managed to get a permission for that. Everyone knows it has never been possible to grow mahogany on Mars, and it is one of the hardwoods forbidden for sustainability reasons. But antique is, of course, granted more flexibility. It is better to keep what has already been made than to make new things.

The key of the bookcase was in the lock of the glass door. I felt strangely guilty about opening it, even though it has never been a secret where you keep the notebooks, and even though I myself wrote every word on their pages. I felt like I was offending something private to you, Sol. Perhaps also to my past self. As if I had intruded a life that was no longer mine, and of which I therefore had no right to be the voyeur.

You must have guessed by now why I'm studying those old notes.

I need to know.

If I were you, I'd consider returning home to Nüwa the most rational course of action, you wrote. *I'd organize old papers. There are several volumes of interest on the shelf of my home office. I'd write more entries in the notebook.*

Was that your way of saying there is something in the notebooks to provide a clue to your whereabouts? That you wanted me to look for a trace of you on their pages?

And whether that is the case or not: I must know.

I must know where you were when the Stoneturners conducted their strikes. Were you there, Sol? And was Vivian?

I have been sitting, and reading, and comparing the places and dates with the list Enisa sent me.

Eight strikes where you might have been present. Seventeen, where you were not even close, because you were somewhere else with me. And over twenty I have no way of knowing about.

Vivian's statistics are equally unclear. In only three cases I can be certain that she was not even on the same celestial body. In five, I know she was close enough to maybe have been present. But of the remaining forty I have no data. Vivian may have been three moons farther from the sun than the place where the strike happened. Or she may have been there, in the tractor hall brushing algae on the metal skins of the robots, sowing the seeds of persistent vines where the interplanetary corporation intended to build a uranium-enriching plant under an expensive dome. At a location where a rice field could have been planted, or a new residential area for migrants equipped with services and transportation connections planned.

What am I supposed to deduce from this, Sol?

I sought on the screen a saved photo of the blood-red fungal growth covering the construction machines and of the background where part of the motto of the Stoneturners was visible. The growth was enormous, like a forest of thick webs in which the machines had got lost. According to Enisa, the fungus had covered the entire contents of the machinery hall in one night, and yet had not spread anywhere else.

It did not seem possible. Unless the fungus had been modified. Unless its growth had been boosted and some kind of built-in kill switch inserted that would halt the growth after a period of time. Along similar lines to how biograffiti was controlled through an activation liquid that triggered the growth of lichen or moss. Only this was a much more sophisticated and precise modification.

Biotechnology. The kind biologists, botanists, chemists and physicians could use in their work. Like your research group in Elysium, Sol.

There is a world in which you lay in my arms when the fungus implanted by the Stoneturners destroyed all equipment that was building a new road in the direction of Chryse Planitia, and you had nothing to do with it. In that world each received letter, each meeting in a coffee shop, each empty doorbell ring is just a coincidence, related to your work. Your connection with the Stoneturners ended over fifteen years ago.

In that world you talked to Vivian as a teenager about the use of plants in traditional medicine. You wanted to know more about the lichen *Letharia vulpina* and its uses among Native American peoples, and you were interested in how lingonberry lowers blood pressure. When you went to the university, you could always get in touch with her and ask things no one in the academic world could tell you. Vivian never mentioned you to me, because why would she have done that, or me to you, until she recommended me to Naomi. You were members of the same environmental organization, but never took part in anything more serious than peaceful demonstrations.

And there is another world in which you and Vivian worked together as members of the Stoneturners. You packed seeds in envelopes, grew algae in tanks, crept in the darkness of the night into locked halls and painted biograffiti on the walls, and I knew nothing about it all.

Between those two worlds there is space for many others.

Perhaps there is a tower in the Moonday House from where you observe all this: my movements, my footsteps as I look for traces of you. Perhaps you try to cry out, but the walls have enclosed you, the door has sealed itself and the windows are swollen shut. You can do nothing but watch, voiceless, as I wander about and do not see you. The house grows and stretches between us to separate where it once connected, pushing us ever farther from each other, until you can no longer catch even a glimpse of me.

Sender: Enisa Karim
Recipient: Lumi Salo
Date: 5.4.2168 06.50 MST
Security: Maximum encryption

Salaam Lumi,
Vivian Berg has turned out to be a tough nut to crack. Either she lived an incredibly low-profile life, or she was exceptionally good at erasing all traces of unusual activity. In other words: I barely found anything.

She traveled a lot – but I think you knew that already. I presume she was your teacher? When she was younger, she had something of a position at the University of Europa, but she gave it up in order to work mainly as a traveling healer. She was one of the authors of a few academic articles on medicinal plants nearly two decades ago. In two of them, your spouse was also listed as an author. You hadn't mentioned they knew each other.

Vivian Berg was born in 2098 and she passed in 2156. This, too, you presumably knew. I have not been able to find out her place of birth. Mars seems the most likely. She appears to have had networks in practically every colony, even on Purity, Mercy and Glory, despite the fact that the immigration policy is extremely conservative in the cylinder Bible Belt and newcomers are rarely welcomed.

I found a few documents, but they hardly have anything new to offer you. I'm attaching them nevertheless.

I also dug up a bit more info on the Stoneturners. It seems that previously the activism was of intrinsic value to them, and media attention mattered little until they began to claim the strikes around five years ago. I don't know the reason for the altered line, but my guess is some kind of new division of power took place within the organization. Law enforcement has wanted to keep their influence limited by giving their actions as little publicity as possible.

I may not be able to write for a while. Intense times at work and home are coinciding with the worst of the flu season right now, and you can guess the result. If I find anything else, I'll be in touch.

Take care,
Enisa

6.4.2168
The cylinder city of Nüwa
Night

Sol,
In the evening before going to bed I whispered a summons for a long while. I repeated a name that I cannot tell you until I fell asleep.

I drifted in a lucid dream where I flew over the dead landscape of Fuxi, when I heard a clang, as if a door had closed somewhere. The sound broke into the dream at a close distance, pulled me from under the surface into wakefulness. I thought I felt Ziggy's warm weight on top of my legs, but as I moved, I understood it was only an extra blanket. I switched the light on and listened. I was half certain that the clang had not originated in this world, but was instead one of the noises that my ears often catch in light sleep before waking.

The clang was not repeated, but I heard something else: Ziggy was scratching the balcony door in the living room.

I got up, took the portable alarm from the nightstand drawer just in case and went into the living room holding it. Ziggy's soft paws drummed the glass door like rain. His back hair had risen into a narrow ridge and a slow, low meowing rose from his throat. The curtains were closed. I only saw my own reflection in the glass door: light-colored pajamas and a shapeless face. No raindrops were visible on the glass.

I opened the balcony door and switched on the outdoor light. Ziggy slipped onto the balcony, leaped onto a chair and meowed. Something about the view seemed strange, out of joint, but I couldn't place it immediately. My gaze circled the space confined by the balcony: kitchen herbs grew on the shelf by the wall – their irrigation system had remained active the whole time I was away – and the blue pot of the bonsai tree stood in the middle of a delicate bamboo table. Red-tinted buds swelled on the dark brown branches.

There was a rustle under my slipper. When I shifted my foot, I saw a branch had broken off from the bonsai tree. Its buds were trampled into a red-tinted mush on the sole of my slipper, and a few green leaves the size of my pinkie nail had fallen off. I didn't know what could have thrown the branch to the floor. The night was entirely calm.

Ziggy leaped to the handrail of the balcony and a low, stretched mewling rose from his throat. The hair on his back had risen up; his tail was startled bushy. I followed the direction of his gaze.

A speckle-coated lynx sat in one of the trees of the park, her paws soundly in the fork of the tree and her claws sunken into the bark. She was staying at a distance, as if she didn't want to come closer, but stared directly at me. She tilted her head. Light flashed in her golden eyes.

I understood.

I scooped Ziggy up into my arms and closed the balcony door behind me.

Sol, I have hoped to find an explanation to everything that would free you from responsibility. I have tried to interpret the evidence to your advantage, and I have tried to see your part in all of this as innocent. But the image that has taken shape before my eyes is not the one I wished to see.

I must find you, Sol. And I must stop you.

I have but one means left to discover your location. I would rather not resort to it, but all other paths are blocked or lost in the dense thicket of the landscape.

You asked me once how a session with a patient differs from a journey I make on my own. I responded to you with a question: How does a lecture in front of an audience differ from delving deep into your own research? Revelations often grow secretly in silence; they need their own time in order to become visible. But in solitude come the realizations that shift the boundaries of our world, show new directions and grow something in us that was not there before.

You listened with great attention, Sol, and you thought, and then you said, I understand.

I believed you really did. Not everything, because not all of it can be understood if you have not journeyed to other worlds, but enough.

I omitted to tell you something then, not for the first time.

When I travel alone, I see the most. The landscapes I cross are at their clearest. I encounter creatures that would otherwise remain hidden from me. I journey farther and deeper than at other times, and I bring back knowledge I could not find and carry if I were watched.

But traveling alone is also the most dangerous. If I have no need to bring back a message but for myself, no obligation to retrieve the lost part of a soul, it is easier to stray, to take my gaze off the road and landscape altogether. I might barely realize I have strayed from the path, as I walk deeper, always toward the next stone or tree or miraculously glowing creature, until the way back has disappeared from sight.

And straying from the path is the most dangerous part of traveling alone. There are places we must not go; the maps drawn of them are full of holes. If I do not return soon enough, my spirit will be left wandering around other worlds, bound to their snares or spells, until my material body in this world fades and dissipates. The life of the body can be upheld, but without spirit it is merely a hollow husk. And if the spirit ever finds its way back but has no body left into which to return, it will turn into a hungry stray in the borderland between worlds, without a home on either side.

Some say it becomes a ghost who is jealous of the peace of the dead and the warmth of the living, and therefore it moans and throws things and chills the air around it.

Vivian never forbade anything: it was not her way. But she did warn me about straying from the path.

I have prepared with care. I'll have water and food in reach when I wake up. I have moved everything out of the room, except for my cloak, my headpiece, my drum and a few cushions on which I can sit and lie down. I took Ziggy to my neighbor's care. They probably think that I believe I'm a werewolf (full moon, such as it is here, happens to be today). I gave them instructions: They should come to the apartment and lock the bedroom door from outside at eight o'clock sharp tonight. They will come again and unlock the door at eight o'clock sharp tomorrow morning. If it looks like I am not well, they will take me to the hospital immediately. Twelve hours is a long time if something happens to go wrong, but a shorter time will probably not be enough for what I must do.

In a moment I will place down the pen and the notebook. I will put a spool of thread in my pocket. I will focus on the flame of the candle, and when it begins to die down, I will close my eyes. When I open them again, the flame will have gone out and I will pick up the drum.

The animal with speckled fur waits, keeping her distance. But she has intertwined her life with mine, and she must come, when I whisper her name again and again. Finally, one step at a time, she begins to approach me: my words, my summons, the path drawn with song and the reach of my hand. Her paws know the way when I do not, and they make cracks in the dark when stars are beyond the reach of my eyes and the night is without light. She sees where others do not, into hidden spaces with her lynx eyes.

This is the first time I have felt afraid to climb onto her back.

• • ● • •

MAIL DELIVERY SUBSYSTEM

There was a temporary problem delivering your message to Lumi Salo. Our service will retry for the next 48 hours. Reason for incomplete delivery: the recipient server could not be found. You will be notified if the delivery

fails permanently.
MESSAGE QUOTED BELOW:
Sender: Enisa Karim
Recipient: Lumi Salo
Date: 6.4.2168 09.13 MST
Security: Maximum encryption
Notes: Marked by sender as OF HIGH IMPORTANCE

Lumi,
I just spoke to my contact. They have new information on Sol's case. There is reason to believe Sol has left Mars and is traveling under a false identity, possibly several. Unfortunately my contact doesn't know where they might have gone. I wish I could tell you more. Call me?
Enisa

17

Undated

long table
chair
fridge
petri dishes
tweezers
microscope
no windows
branch in vase – which tree?

Sender: J. N. Owoeye
Recipient: T. F. Liang
Date: 9.4.2168 09.12 MST
Security: Maximum encryption
Notes: Marked by sender as OF IMPORTANCE

Dear Constable Liang,
I hope you have had a good week and the weather on Nüwa is as pleasant as always. On Mars it is as… well, always.

I have been trying to get hold of you since yesterday. Could you respond to my voice message in the first possible instance, please, and give me the information

I requested? It concerns the case of Sol Uriarte: their whereabouts, to be more specific.

I would also be grateful if you could confirm that all is in order with Lumi Salo. She is not responding to my attempts at contacting her. She is still at her home on Nüwa, isn't she?

Best,
Jenny Owoeye

PS. Thank you for the apt screen show recommendation – my kids are completely hooked on The Fantastic Adventures of Ghost Warrior Liu, and my spouses enjoy watching it too.

10.4.2168
Chang'e Hospital
The cylinder city of Nüwa

Sol,
I'm writing this in the blue-tinted glow of the night light in the hospital room where I have been lying for nearly two days and nights. The sheets are some heavenly material that always feels dry and fresh against the skin. A light scent of disinfectant and tea trickles from behind the door. There are no others in the room. It is still dark outside; the morning of Nüwa does not begin until over an hour from now. Then the light will open the sky toward the day with soft fingers. At seven o'clock the nurse will wheel in breakfast, which consists of different porridge-like sources of nutrition. He will take my pulse, ask how I'm feeling and

see to it that I obediently eat all the porridges, the pale gray and the green and the pink. I have been promised that once I have done so, I will be allowed to go home today.

Breathing deeply hurts, and my left wrist aches under the cast. The wrist is fractured, and I have a bruised rib. The neighbor found me unconscious on the floor and brought me here. I told them that I lost consciousness while rehearsing a physically demanding dance routine and fell to the floor, my left hand first. They repeated the story to the doctor. It was not exactly a lie, and they didn't seem to doubt it. I was so badly dehydrated that I was put on a drip immediately. I knew they would not find traces of intoxicating substances in my blood.

The fracture will heal and the pain will fade in time. However, I have received another wound, Sol, the kind that does not show on the surface and that may not be possible to heal. The ache behind my eyes has returned for the first time in years.

But let me start from the beginning.

More than two days and nights ago I was sitting at home with the last light of the candle-flame on my eyelids; the scent of smoke drifted into my nostrils. After the candle went out, the room was left in near-complete darkness. I waited until my eyes began to discern a few outlines. I put a smooth-worn stone into my pocket. I placed my hand on the drum, laid it on my lap and began to beat a faint rhythm. I allowed it to seek animal sounds: claws scratching against tree bark, hooves hitting the forest floor, web-thin wings swishing against air currents. In my own language I hummed a song of a road and a journey ahead, of the guidance and protection I requested. The forest grew before me, and at its heart the path, and above treetops the wind and the star-filled sky.

One by one the spirits arrived.

I saw them as bright shadows that gathered quietly around me. The speckle-coated lynx arrived first, but on this journey I needed to invite others too: she was followed by a reindeer with delicate antlers and two butterflies with wings that bore the colors of water and sky. I knew all their names, and they knew mine. The lynx alone had the power to bring me back from where I was going. Yet the others offered their strength for my protection, and I accepted.

The lynx settled before me like an Egyptian statue. I mounted her. Her skin was warm, and I felt the sinewy shifts of her muscles, the even beating of her heart. The animal grew and I shrank. I sank my fingers into her thick fur, as she got up to her feet and stepped onto the path. The reindeer stepped to the lynx's left side. The butterflies fluttered in the vicinity of her right ear tuft.

The path sparkled under the lynx's paws, the sky folded toward us. We crossed the plain of space and the black crevice that twisted like a dark current. When we reached the star-top tree, its trunk offered a road for all of us, and together we dove into the hole through which I had passed many times.

I knew the path.

We crossed the plain of the other world and the dark current splitting it, and beyond the stream a star-top tree rose again on the horizon. Its trunk offered a road for all of us, and together we dove into the hole through which I had passed before.

I knew the path.

We crossed the plain of the strange world and the deep current splitting it, and beyond the stream a star-top tree rose again on the horizon. Its trunk offered a road for all of us, and together we dove into the hole through which I had never passed.

I no longer knew the path.

Here the lynx stopped. She sniffed the air, pricked her ears and turned her head. The reindeer stopped by her side, and the water-winged butterflies landed on the antlers of the reindeer. The reindeer scratched the ground with her hoof and then stood still. My helpers had been here before, but I had not, and they knew it. From here I'd find my way back: the current and the plain and the tree, and the current and the plain and the tree. From here onward, the terrain was unfamiliar to me.

What I was looking for was somewhere behind the plain.

I had prepared by inviting in my mind an image of something that I could use to mark the route. I had ended up with the strongest and most easily maintained of all images. It may have been banal, but it had also been etched into my spine since I had as a child found a book about Greek mythology in an abandoned house. The image surfaced before me stronger than any other, and I had chosen it because of that.

There, on the cliff edge of a strange world, I dismounted the lynx and pulled a spool of red thread from my pocket. It glowed with faint light. It felt heavy enough in my fingers that it would not be torn away by wind, and long enough that it would not run out, and strong enough that nothing would break it. I tied the end of the thread around the trunk of a tree standing on the cliff and pushed the spool back into my pocket. A plain opened below the cliff, vaster than those before. I remounted the lynx.

The reindeer scratched the ground again and shook her head. She took a step closer to the cliff edge and then backed down. I realized the path that had offered her a solid base to walk on ended here. The fall was too much for her.

I turned to the butterflies and spoke to them.

"Are you able to help?" I asked.

I did not see the butterfly grow or the reindeer shrink, but when the blue wings opened again, one of the butterflies was large enough for the reindeer to climb onto its back without trouble. The smaller of the butterflies fluttered in front of me, landed between the lynx's ears and folded its wings, lifting their gray bark-sides up.

"Thank you," I said. "Will you now take me where I will be able to see beyond distances?"

The lynx made a run-up and leaped off the cliff, and we went flying over the strange, pathless plain. The butterfly followed behind us, carrying the reindeer on its back. The spool of thread began to unravel behind me. It left behind a narrow, red-glowing strand that floated in the air and showed the way back to the tree.

Tall tree trunks rose here and there on the plain, and we flew past structures that from a distance resembled the human dwellings of our world. As we passed the trees nearby, I saw that no life flowed through their veins: their branches reached toward us as bare as the surface of the Moon. No insects climbed their bark, and birds did not build their nests in the forks of the branches. Here, there was no sun toward which the trees could have grown.

The structures revealed their shapes as high piles of boulders rising from the ground, shaped by strange winds and the whims of the sky, earth and spirits. They were not dwellings, or not the abodes of anything human, at least. My human eyes had simply wished to see something recognizable where it did not exist.

In silence my helpers transported me above the landscape. The terrain began to change. We approached a dark, wide body of water. Under the surface I sensed maws and teeth and sharp, sharp claws. A web of lethal fire and electric current sparkled from the heavy clouds in the sky. The lynx wound her way through the meshes so it would not catch us like fish swimming to a net that bites into their slippery scales. I turned my head to check that the thread still glowed behind us, marking the route back.

Beyond the water opened a realm the like of which I had never seen in any world. The undulating outlines of the giant sand dunes seemed to reach to the edge of the universe and beyond. I saw a barren slope where narrow figures like shadows elongated by evening climbed in groups of four or five. At first I took them to be human-sized, but as we flew farther, I began to see I'd been wrong. They were not human-sized at all.

Against the dark, which I had already concluded must be the

perpetual state of this sand-world, the desert birthed into being enormous creatures in the shapes of humans and animals. Their heads pushed from the sand below me, and their bodies were larger than anything built by human hands. The creatures were taking shape everywhere I looked, and as they clambered to their feet, they began a slow march toward something, perhaps our world. I saw enormous faces in crude human likeness, as if someone had taken an axe to wood or stone and carved the roughest possible semblance that was still recognizable. Among them were also shapes of rhinoceroses and parrots and monkeys, and dragonflies and ants. Ceaselessly the sand squeezed them from its depths, and they walked blind, without hatred or compassion, stepping where their heavy feet would land, indifferent to what might be left underneath.

The red thread hovered in the air, fragile, yet unbreaking.

After the plain was finally behind us and we were far enough from the horrific sand creatures, the lynx dropped to the ground with soft paws from her infinite leap. The blue-winged butterfly and the reindeer landed next to us. As soon as they touched the ground, they were back to their former size. The butterfly settled in the reindeer's antler crown and folded its wings. The other fluttered next to it.

Short grass, blue-tinted with dew, covered the ground. Around us rose tree-like plants that reminded me of white birch trees of Earth. Yet their branches twisted and forked like nerves, or blood vessels. Their trunks shone with a faint white light.

I knew we had arrived.

At the center of the circle of shine-trees rested a hole, like a bottomless pond where no light landed. It was deep and dense, as black as the shadows of all worlds had gathered into a tight knot in its embrace. In slow steps I walked between the shine-trees near the hole, like the edge of an abyss. My helpers followed. They knew what to do: they settled behind me and by my side, watching. Guarding.

It was silent. I stared into the dark tear in time and space, into its eye that gazed at me and waited. In my own language I spoke the words I had prepared for this moment.

A ripple ran through the hole like on the surface of water.

There was a rustle among the shine-trees. Whispers walked on their branches. I saw no one and nothing, but my guardians grew alert. The reindeer turned her head. The wings of the butterflies stirred. The body of the lynx tensed.

I repeated the words. The surface of the blackness began to rise. The smooth darkness tilted toward me, until it hung vertically in the air like a large, oval mirror. I saw nothing in it. It was as if it absorbed all light, crushing worlds within into dark dust, into the heart of which it alone could see.

Whispers brushed the trees again. The lynx pulled back and gave a faint growl.

I pulled from my pocket the object I had brought for this. It was a rounded, light-colored stone that you had picked for me on the beach of the Martian underground artificial lakes, Sol. I'd been carrying it with me ever since. I threw it into the vertical blackness. The stone sank into it. New and ever new rings spread from it, and little by little they swept darkness out of their way. The light leaked and trickled, brightened the image, until the view was as clear as if I had looked at it through a window.

Sol, you sat leaning over a long, white desk, and there were several petri dishes in front of you. You wore a white coat with sleeves rolled up to the elbows, and your hands were protected by white, skin-tight gloves. You moved the prepared slide to a glass disc under a microscope. The room was bare: the desk, a chair and a fridge aside, I saw nothing else in there. A shelf hung on the wall; a vase stood on it. Apart from the microscope I saw no other light sources, yet the room was bright.

I took a step closer to the hole in order to see more clearly. The twigs on the edge of the pond rustled under my feet. In the dark mirror, worlds away from me, you raised your gaze, straightened your back and turned to look directly at me.

In the forest of the shine-trees, a breeze that sprang from emptiness bent the branches and narrow boles. A wave of whispers followed that grew into sizzles and hisses. The reindeer twitched as if a stone hurled from among the trees hit her. She thrashed the air with her antlers. The butterflies took to the air, their wings a restless fog. The lynx revealed her teeth.

"Sol," I said.

You stared at me. Your lips formed my name and the expression on your face folded into a question, but I could not hear your voice. You rose from the desk and stepped toward me. It was obvious you could see me somehow, but I didn't know what I was in your eyes: a physical figure that had unexpectedly materialized in the room, a reflection as bright as a mirror image, a translucent specter?

"Where are you?" I asked.

You didn't understand the question. I glanced at my helpers. They growled at empty air, butted it with their heads and reached for it with hooves and paws, they beat their wings and ducked to avoid invisible attacks. A bruise had appeared on the speckled coat of the lynx, and I saw a bleeding cut on her nose. A bare wound pierced the reindeer's shoulder blade, as if made by the sharp beak of a bird of prey. The butterflies fluttered in distress, and I saw blue dust come off the scales of their wings.

There was not much time.

"Where are you?" I asked again.

It seemed to me you understood this time. You opened your mouth and closed it again. Then your eyes darkened. You looked at me. You shook your head.

I felt a strong blow on my side. I fell backward. A piercing pain surged through me and my breath caught. At the same time I saw the lynx fall and squirm in agony. Blood began to trickle from a long cut on her side. Her left front paw had twisted unnaturally. Something large and invisible had attacked the lynx. The reindeer rushed toward the attacker antlers first. The wings of the butterflies beat ever faster, and they began to divide and multiply: two butterflies became four, four became eight, eight became sixteen, and so on. Everything happened so quickly that when the reindeer's antlers hit the invisible enemy, the air was thick with the blue mist of the butterflies that gathered around the attackers in all directions.

The pain was so intense that tears forced their way out of my eyes. I held on to my side, trying to catch my breath. The lynx lay still on the ground and tried to get up. A long strip of skin had been torn off her side, and the raw flesh showed bare and red with blood. Her leg did not carry her weight. She had been wounded more seriously than the others. She was also the only one who would be able to take me back.

"Sol," I said. I raised my hand and reached for you, for the crack in time and space, for the window that would take you away once it closed. The expression on your face was confused, shocked.

You too reached your hand toward me.

Our fingers approached each other. I dragged myself closer to the hole despite the pain that radiated into my entire body. Your hand was very close, as close as if you were next to me, and I prepared to receive your touch...

When our fingertips met, I only sensed a cool, liquid surface, like water. Rings began to spread in all directions again. I tried to grasp your hand, but it eluded me. Light grew weary, gave way to darkness, and blackness trickled back. The image blurred, the room grew murky. You vanished, Sol.

The lynx pushed herself up from the ground. Her limbs shook, and her tongue hung long from her open maw. She panted like a dog.

Butterflies flickered as a shivering column of fog, but I saw shreds of wings and hair-thin black limbs falling to the ground from the column. More stab wounds had appeared in the neck and back of the reindeer, and she had begun to withdraw. I climbed onto the lynx's back. I felt a jab in my side, and sensed the animal sagging under my weight. I stroked her neck gently and whispered healing words into her ear.

"Spirits," I cried, "carry me home!"

The lightless hole splintered to the green ground, its darkness flared in tall drops, splashed over me and my helpers. The cloud of butterflies lifted the reindeer into the air. The lynx pushed herself into an endless leap, but I could feel her strength running out. We flew again, but now none of us was whole.

The red thread undulated through the air ahead of me. Its glow grew brighter against the colorless landscape, discerned clear and sinewy. I glanced behind me and was confused for a moment. I pushed a hand into my pocket while still holding on to the skin of the lynx's neck with the other. The spool was there, but another red thread floated behind us. The lynx twitched under me, and I understood.

A glowing-red trail of blood trickled ceaselessly from the lynx's side. It fell in drops along the realm of the horrific sand creatures; it dyed the dark, sharp-toothed water and the lifeless plain, as we flew past.

Eventually the cliff and the tree standing on it onto which I had tied the other end of the thread came into view. I leaned down and pressed my hand to the wound on the lynx's side, but the blood trickled from between my fingers, and the pain on my own side grew so unbearable I had to sit up.

We were almost at the root of the tree when I understood the leap of the lynx would not carry far enough.

The cloud of butterflies and the reindeer landed on the cliff before us. I began to hum the strongest healing spell I knew into the lynx's ear, the "Blood-stopping," and for a moment it seemed to me that the edges of the wound puckered slightly. But it was too late. The lynx struggled in order to make it to the cliff, but she did not have enough strength. Her front paws caught the rock, but the rear end of her body did not reach solid ground and was left hanging in the air. I yanked the spool of thread out of my pocket and twisted it around my wrist as many times as I could manage. The lynx attempted to cling to the cliff's edge, her claws screeching against the stone as she slid backward. I let go of her and allowed myself to hang from the thread, so she wouldn't need to carry my weight too. I felt a crunch in my wrist. A twitch stabbed at my side as if I'd been clubbed. The pain dazed me like too-bright light.

When I was able to see again, the lynx hung from the cliff's edge for a moment, staring at me with her cat eyes. I reached my hand out to her, tried to get a hold.

The lynx's claws slid over the cliff's edge. With a screech she fell into the lifeless landscape, amid the tangle of dead tree trunks, and vanished under the branches. I did not see her anymore.

Tears blurred my eyes and pain pulled me into darkness. The last thing I remember from the journey was a tug of the thread, as if someone had begun to pull me up to the cliff.

• • ● • •

Sol, it is hard for me to explain this loss to you. You think that this was an imaginary animal. Lynxes went extinct decades ago. This lynx only lives in my mind, and therefore I can bring her back.

But this is not how healers see the cosmos. My helper does not live in the material reality you know and study, but she is no less real because of that. This lynx has been with me since I was sixteen; according to Vivian, she may have been with me always, since I was born. She said soul-animals choose the healer at the moment of their birth, and they remain with their human until their death. They take the healer where they must go in order to help others, and they guard the journey so that nothing can harm the healer.

A soul-animal should never die before their human.

I should not have strayed from the path, should never have asked her to carry me to the places in the maps that are full of holes.

The rib will heal in a couple of months. Yet without my lynx, I cannot gain my healing skills back. I have nothing else; it is the only thing I know how to do.

The stone I put in my pocket before the journey is gone. My lynx is gone. My skill is gone.

And I still don't know where you are, Sol.

13.4.2168
The cylinder city of Nüwa

Sol,
I'm home. Ziggy has been purring in my lap almost without a break since I was released from the hospital three days ago. Maybe he knows what I need right now; I remember reading once that the purring of cats has a favorable effect on strengthening bones. Not that the pain has alleviated much yet.

Since I returned from my journey, I have been calling the lynx by her secret name day and night. I have kindled fires for her, and I have sung songs for her. I have hoped she would still come to me, but in her place is an emptiness, an ache that will not vanish.

Last night when I couldn't sleep I began to go through the list I wrote after waking up groggy from medication in the hospital after my journey. I tried to include as many things as possible about the room in which I saw you, Sol. I believe it was a real room, not simply a construct of my mind. I have long known of healers who can not only see others from distances away, but also send an image of themselves.

You saw me too, Sol, didn't you?

Remembering the details of the room was unexpectedly difficult. The memory wishes to mold the reality into a story and convert what it has seen as soon as it preserves. The smooth walls, the desk, the petri dishes – had there been any material that was used only on one celestial body, or a brand that was only known in certain areas? I could not recall seeing such a thing. Apart from the microscope, I had not set eyes on other devices. There had not been a screen with a display providing hints of the location. There had not been any food on the smooth surfaces, not even a half-drunk cup of tea.

What had you been wearing, Sol? Under the white coat, ordinary clothes – a T-shirt, collared shirt, jeans and flat shoes. You were not dressed for space, and there were no clasps, weighted boots or other equipment designed for zero gravity. You were not on a starship, then, or on the Moon, but somewhere the permanence of gravity could be relied on. Could the even light have been that of a cylinder city coming through a skylight?

Some detail hovered on the edge of my mind. I could not catch it, but I knew there was something I'd forgotten to think about. I closed my eyes and tried to see the room.

The desk, empty save for the petri dishes, glass slides and tweezers. Your bare arms, one circled by a delicate tattoo, and your gloved hands. A white coat made from a smart material that was used everywhere in the Solar System. Walls.

The walls. Were they blank?

I opened my eyes and glanced at the list again.

branch in vase – which tree?

I remembered.

A narrow shelf had hung on one of the walls, on it a glass vase. A single branch was placed in the vase. You had the habit of doing that anywhere you lived, Sol: in your childhood home you were used to breaking off a branch from the flowering quince, on Fuxi it had most often been a sycamore branch from the park next door.

The branch on the lab wall had looked like it had only been there for a moment. The leaves were still green, and they had not begun to curl around the edges. The branch had been broken off from a nearby tree a couple of days earlier at most. The leaves were oval-shaped, and their edges undulated in a symmetrical pattern.

Such leaves only grow in one place in the entire Solar System.

Sol, I know where you are.

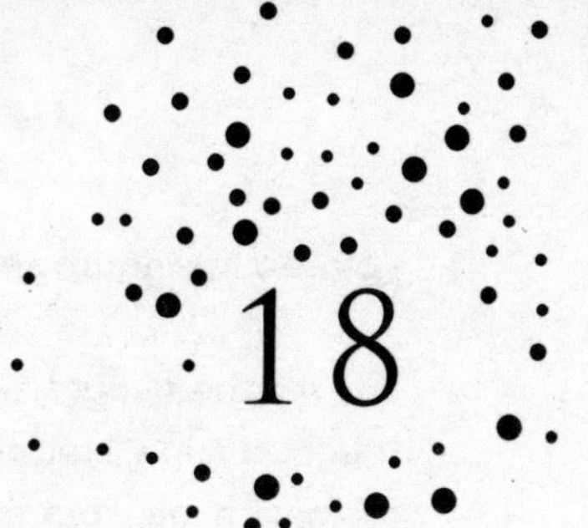

18

Sender: Anonymous
Recipient: Lumi Salo
Date: 18.4.2168 19.12 MST
Security: Special encryption (password required)

My dear Lumi,
I have no rational explanation to what happened this morning. I was working in my lab (which, due to circumstances, is a rather minimalistic model focusing on the essential), when I saw you.

I heard a crackling sound. It reminded me of a breaking branch. I turned to look, and there you were, but not entirely material. There was something fragmentary, something imprecise about you. You resembled a reflection in a dusty mirror, or a figure behind a rain-stained glass. You stood in the corner of the room and your lips moved. I could not hear your voice. You repeated your attempt to vocalize multiple times. Eventually I understood it to be a question: *Where are you?* I nearly told you, so surprised was I. The situation seemed too absurd to be real.

I remembered your stories about the abilities of healers. I remembered my own skeptical stance toward them. Yet I also remembered what I had seen of your work. If it really was you, I would have to keep silent.

I closed my mouth and shook my head.

You reached your hand toward me. When your fingers touched mine, I felt them, as physical as if you were in the room with me. Your eyes fell closed and you collapsed to the floor, holding on to your side. An intense pain showed on your face. You lay there, and your limbs twitched, like they do sometimes when you are asleep.

You began to fragment to a greater extent before my eyes. I was alarmed. You slid ever farther. Some visual element was discernible against your garments: a thin red thread that seemed to unravel from your pocket. I curled my fingers around it. At first they slipped through the thread, but when I focused my mind and imagined it staying between them, it did.

I centered my attention on the thread. Slowly and carefully I began to haul you closer. The thread wavered, it grew looser and tenser, but did not break. Pulled by it, you floated toward me, your eyes closed, in some dark and distant place I could not access. Eventually you were before me again: in this world, but not with me. You opened your eyes. I knew you could no longer see me. The thread snaked into your pocket and disappeared within. Then you were gone.

I am inclined to explain this through the overexertion I have been experiencing lately. I have stayed awake. I have worked. After a few scattered hours of sleep I have got up to work again. My thoughts melt into abstractions, among which my mind constructs many unreal creatures. It is only logical you would be among them.

I have never kept from you the fact that my worldview is different from yours. I do not mean I don't believe your healer's experiences to be true in some way, from your subjective point of view. When you say you travel into other worlds, for you it is accurate. When you tell me you bring back the parts of your patients' souls that have lost their way, for you it is true.

But I explain it all by the placebo effect. The human mind is capable of nearly unlimited acrobatics. You believe you are a healer. You believe you journey to retrieve your patients' souls. From your point of view this is true. And from theirs, too: they will feel better when they believe some lost part of their selves has been returned to them. If the feeling does not last, it is simply because that part has wandered away again, and must be brought back again. Furthermore, when it comes to the medicinal plants you use in your work: all of them have proven effects on human physiology. Their influence on your patients and on yourself is undeniable; mathematically, neurologically and biologically measurable. To this I can subscribe.

This is all I have ever believed. Now some part of me demands more.

If you were with me this morning, I brought you back from some metaphysical dimension from which you might not have otherwise been able to return.

I have avoided communications and reading screen messages on my usual accounts for security reasons.

A few days ago I strayed from this principle because – I cannot lie – I wished to hear from you. I saw your message in which you asked about Vivian.

I can tell you now. Earlier it was important you did not know. It no longer matters.

Vivian worked as my mother's personal healer for years. She recommended you to us when she found that she had fallen terminally ill. She was absolute in her demand that you must not be told about her previous position with us. I am the only one to whom she told the reason. Ilsa and my mother were telling the truth, if they said they did not know.

You may have guessed the reason by now.

Think of Vivian's job. As a healer she was able to travel on practically all celestial bodies, in all colonies. She met people from all classes of society, learned local customs and culture and languages, collected medicinal plants and information on their use. Among her patients there were marginalized and underprivileged people who had reason to rebel, as well as high-ranking, influential politicians, businesspeople and military officers. Many of her patients shared very personal matters with her. She had the chance to hear all manner of things.

The Stoneturners had a use for someone like that.

I know what you are thinking. Vivian was bound by confidentiality. You consider it sacred, because she educated you to honor its inviolability.

Vivian did not want you to know about her work with my family. She was afraid that might lead you to discover her work as a spy of the Stoneturners. She believed you would lose respect for her. Do not judge her too harshly, Lumi, my love. I asked you once what you would do, what you would sacrifice for the greater good. Vivian, too, asked herself that question. She believed the ends outweighed the means. She also knew she was dying. She wished for you to stay the same to her as you had been before. She wished to stay the same to you as she had been before.

There was yet another reason. There are tendencies within the Stoneturners that I can't say more about. Vivian did not wish to put you in danger. The less you knew, the safer for you.

For the same reason, you must give up trying to find me. I must finish something I started a long time ago. I promise I will do everything in my power to return home to you as soon as possible.

Come to the Moonday House whenever you wish to see me. Wherever I am, part of me is always there, with you.

Anthropocene
***Encyclopedia of Geology*. Harmonia:**
Harmonia University Press, 125 MC.

The *Anthropocene* refers to the current geological epoch, which follows the *Holocene*. The term was first proposed in the 1980s, but it was not fully adopted in the scientific context until 2040 CE, when the International Commission on Stratigraphy approved it officially. The Anthropocene is considered to have begun with the first nuclear test in the New Mexico desert in the year 1945 CE, because the radioactive fallout from this and later large-scale nuclear tests were still visible in the late 2000s in ice core samples from the Greenland glaciers, among other things.[7]

The most notable characteristic of the Anthropocene is the strong impact of human activity on Earth ecosystems and geology. The traces of human activity were already perceivable during the Holocene, but during the Anthropocene their scale increased dramatically. The industrial revolution started this climate change, as a consequence of which the carbon dioxide concentrations in the atmosphere were increased, the average temperatures rose and the living conditions on Earth turned less favorable to humans, as well as many animal and plant species that had no opportunity to adapt to the swift changes. The Anthropocene is, then, apart from climate

7 Paleoclimatology has moved to alternative methods from ice core sampling after the last glaciers melted in the early 2100s.

change, characterized by a sixth wave of mass extinction. This is considered to have been caused by human activity, and has accelerated significantly during this epoch. Parallel to the wave of extinction, the diminishing of the living space for wildlife is considered to have increased the opportunities for mutating viruses to jump from animals to humans and the probability of worldwide pandemics.

Some experts also count changes caused by human activity outside Earth as belonging to the Anthropocene, such as Moon mining and the landscape-modifying impact of Mars colonies. Others oppose this view on the basis that no ecosystems have been discovered on most celestial bodies known to humans, so human activity cannot have had an impact on them. Europa, one of Jupiter's moons, is regarded as an exception, as original life born outside Earth has been found in its oceans.

PART III

O my Earth whom I ill-treated

Earth who in your turn ill-treated

me, won't you at last forgive me?

You watch, you watch, you never move.

"The Sun's Farewell," Eino Leino

Niemeläinen, Hertta, ed. *Sleep Shrouded You: An Annotated Selection of 20th Century Finnish Poetry*. Helsinki: Ursa Minor, 2107.

19

Welcome to the Vacation Archipelago of Londons!
Excerpt from the brochure of Earth Excursions Ltd. Advertising agency Uranus, February 2168.

A visit to the Vacation Archipelago of Londons is a comprehensive experience that begins the moment you board the landing vessel on Earth orbit. As the vessel approaches the spaceport of Atlantis, you can admire the shapes of the continent of Europe from the air, as well as the shards of the British Archipelago glimmering on the side of the continent. East of the green mosaic of Ireland, south of the gray Scottish peaks, you begin to catch flashes of Londons and anticipate the adventure ahead of you. Little by little a view opens before you of the Ferris wheels whose bottommost cabin dives underwater as the topmost one shows an immeasurable cityscape. Sailing boats have gathered at the foot of skyscrapers, and in all directions they are surrounded by museums, theaters, cathedrals and royal palaces.

Londons offer more alternative versions of the city than any other holiday isle in the world. You can start your day in Victorian London, walking in the footsteps of Jack the Ripper and Sherlock Holmes, and solve the mystery of the Queen's stolen necklace. You can take the cable car that will transport you for a luxurious lunch in the largest floating shopping center in Europe and continue from there to the British Museum, Victoria & Albert Museum, Natural History Museum, Brexit Museum, Tate Modern or take your pick among dozens of other museums – Londons have something to offer to everyone. You can experience the atmosphere of the Live Aid concert in a virtual rock circus, acquaint yourself with the underground tunnels on a guided tour in a mini submarine, enjoy afternoon tea in the magical ambience of the School of Sorcery and move along a bridge or an underwater tunnel to Theatre Island to spend your evening in the company of Shakespeare or the most recent top hit musical.

Book your trip today! Ten percent discount applies to journeys from Mars spaceports departing between 1 April and 30 April.*

* Offer valid until 28 February. This offer cannot be combined with other offers.

Sender: Lumi Salo
Recipient: Sol Uriarte
Date: 10.5.2168 00.00+12 MST
Security: Maximum encryption
Notes: Marked by sender as OF HIGH IMPORTANCE

Sol,
I hope you get this message.

I have not stopped thinking about the last time I saw you. I can still feel your touch, which carefully pulled me closer and brought me back from where I had lost myself.

I am on my way to Earth. Tomorrow I will arrive at the Vacation Archipelago of Londons, where I intend to stay for approximately ten days. I'm sure you remember the glamrock club we went to together six years ago? I was thinking about going there again, although it will of course not be the same without you. Perhaps, when I sit down in the corner with a glass of something, your figure will watch me from the shadows. Perhaps, when I reach my hand toward them, it will momentarily meet you.

From Rock London I will take a ship to Winterland. I would very much like you to accompany me on that trip too. My parents were asking again when they could meet you.

The journey from Nüwa has taken four weeks (such a strange thought that a journey on board a ship from Londons to Winterland will take half the time it took me to get here from Nüwa, when the distances are on a completely different scale!). On the plus side, I was able to get the cast removed today – my wrist is still slightly stiff, and the physiotherapist on the starship said it may never be quite the same. But I can write again without trouble, and that is good enough for me. Ziggy is well cared for by our neighbor; I had no heart to expose him to another long trip so soon.

My cabin is chilly and small, so I have spent as much time as possible on the lookout deck of the vessel, where I can write without my hands being constantly stiff from the cold. Earth is bigger every day. Today I can already see the outlines of the continents where the clouds do not cover them. But I only need to shift my gaze a little in order to see how much bigger the space is: in the dark, stars float by at a distance, other vessels, people's lives.

When I close my eyes, I'm in the Moonday House. There

the rooms open silent, and the garden waits. For you; for me. For us, whose thoughts are its only home, just like it is the only home for our shared thoughts.
L

11.5.2168
Hotel Mercury
Rock London, Earth

A memory:
Vivian and I sit in a portacabin-like apartment she has rented for us on Venus. The planet is a large construction site, and we have spent four months in the unfinished float-city of Porta Collina I, healing the robot operators and construction workers, few of whom last longer than a year before returning to Earth. The circumstances are harsher than they have ever been on Mars. Vivian has taken me with her to every healing session. Four times she has allowed me to make the entire journey in her stead. I'm beginning to know the path, and I'm beginning to know my helpers.

I'm sitting on a hard cushion on the floor. Vivian is sitting opposite me on another, cross-legged. In her hands she is holding a screen on which she selects a photo of a tree, and next to it, an enlarged picture of a branch where the shape of the green leaves is clearly visible. Vivian turns the screen toward me. I look at the leaf, which is like a many-forked flame. Autumn gold has begun to blend in with its greenness.

Maple, I say. Tea brewed from the bark treats kidney infection and relieves the symptoms of the common cold. The sap is used as a foodstuff. Speeds up traveling and learning. Was previously very common in the northern hemisphere of Earth. Nowadays is found in the protected areas of Asia and North America, and a few holiday isles in Europe. Outside of Earth occurs in the colonies of Mars and most cylinder cities.

Vivian nods and chooses another image on the screen.

Spruce, I say. A symbol of resilience and immortality. Has antibacterial properties. A concoction made from young shoots was used to relieve respiratory symptoms. Was at one time extremely widespread in Eurasia and Northern America, but went extinct in the 2120s due to a warming climate. Objects made from spruce wood are nowadays much valued.

Good, Vivian says. What about this one?

Her fingers place another tree on the screen, which she shows me.

Oak, I say. The bark contains tannins, and can be used to make remedies for diarrhea, symptoms of cold, fever, cough and improving digestion. One of the most powerful trees when it comes to magical properties, particularly esteemed by druids. Protector. In many mythologies the World Tree, the trunk of which connects the different planes of reality. Was robust and widespread in Europe before climate zones shifted, but was destroyed by a fungal disease almost everywhere. Only grows in one place in the entire Solar System, in the Vacation Archipelago of London on Earth.

Vivian smiles, turns the screen and switches it off.

Very good, she says. You have made enormous progress in botanical knowledge.

Is it really necessary for me to know so much about trees that went extinct ages ago?

Knowledge is never futile, Vivian replies.

Sender: Lumi Salo
Recipient: Naomi Uriarte
Date: 12.5.2168 00.00+02 MST
Security: Maximum encryption

Dear Naomi,
The money arrived on my bracelet. I cannot thank you enough. I will pay back as soon as I can. I intend to find new patients once I have left Earth, and when Sol comes home, my situation will become easier.

I would appreciate it if you didn't mention the loan to Ilsa (or Sol, when they have returned). You know well I have never asked you for such a thing before. I wouldn't do it now if I had any other way of scraping the money for the trip together quickly.

Stay well and safe, and thank you, thank you, a thousand times thank you,
Lumi

12.5.2168
Hotel Mercury
Rock London, Earth

Sol,
The cheap hotels of Londons are exactly as I remembered. The duvet and the sheets have probably been washed sometime, but more frequently they have been sprayed with a "freshening" textile fragrance, the stench of which will not come off my clothing for weeks. It is best not to think about where the stains on the bathroom carpet came from. The walls are painted with the same dull shade of beige that has been used here from at least the twentieth century, once probably to cover the stains left by cigarette smoke. Luckily it is not winter, because there is only one small electric heater in the room.

The breakfast consists presumably of two slices of toast and a cup of something caffeinated that you can with good imagination interpret as a distant second cousin of tea.

The only thing visible from my hotel room is a strip of the wall facing the window and the ventilation pipes that fill the courtyard, so I climbed to the upstairs bar of the building next door to see the view. I'd expected the archipelago to have changed more after the last time I was here, but so far I have only seen a few new billboards and amusement rides swirling on the horizon. One of the many Carnaby Streets starts around the corner, and on the digital boards as tall as buildings long-dead rock stars advertise virtual concerts. In the distance the treetops spread like mist that will dissipate if you stare at it long enough.

On the way back I popped out to buy a blue wig, large sunglasses and a silver sequin jumpsuit, the material of which was made from CDs collected from the oceans.

If words could stop or turn time, weave its crevices closed, now is their time to do so. Somewhere in the future you are reading these sentences, Sol, and you are smiling as you remember how I looked in my ridiculous outfit. You are smiling, because you were there too: here, at the birthplace of these words.

Tonight is the first night.

13.5.2168
Hotel Mercury
Rock London, Earth

Sol,

I arrived at the glamrock club early yesterday evening, before eight. There was no queue outside the large pavilion, and only a handful of people were sitting at the tables inside. I saw my fragmentary reflection in the supporting column covered with mirror mosaic: the dark eyeshadow mostly resembled bruises, and the red spotlight gave an odd tinge to my face, as if I'd burned my skin in the sun.

I walked to the bar to order a virtual cocktail and sat down at a table for two from which I could see both entrances of the pavilion. Just in case, I'd downloaded a few recent books onto my screen so I'd be left to sit in peace (surely you too must have noticed that almost everywhere in the Solar System reading is interpreted as passing time while waiting to meet someone).

The stage at the center of the pavilion was empty. The background screen ran a trailer of a hit musical of Theatre London, in which two vampire rock stars engaged in bloody rivalry sang a grandiose final duet about their epic love-hate relationship.

I looked around.

There was no one sitting at the tables that could be you, even in disguise. Each time I saw movement near the entrances I turned to look. Once a dark-haired customer wearing a wide-brimmed hat and long coat stepped in, and their body shape was similar to yours, Sol. But when they removed the hat, I saw their face was unfamiliar.

People came and went, but the club remained spacious. Eventually the performers started. They were skilled, but not memorable: a woman in a leotard spinning a double bass, a man in wide-legged coveralls and enormous spectacles decorated with jewels.

I walked the few blocks back to the hotel around midnight, my feet aching in the high-heeled shoes. I thought about sending you another message. I did not do it.

Tonight is a new night.

14.5.2168
Hotel Mercury
Rock London, Earth

The second evening progressed like the first.
The ache behind my eyes remained all night.

15.5.2168
Hotel Mercury
Rock London, Earth

The third night: see yesterday and the day before. The only variation on the theme was that today a couple tried to pick me up. They were very young and very pretty, and they didn't mind when I told them I was not interested. We spent an interesting couple of hours talking about the status of minorities on Enceladus and everything that should have been done differently there. Before I left, I saw them on the dance floor with a woman slightly older than myself.

I slept restlessly and called to my soul-animal between the dreams. Just before the dawn I woke to a sound that was like claws scratching at the door of my hotel room. When I got up to see, no one and nothing was behind the door.

16.5.2168
Hotel Mercury
Rock London, Earth

The fourth night: nothing new to report.

17.5.2168
Hotel Mercury
Rock London, Earth

The fifth night. A thought rose, not for the first time, but its outlines clearer than before: what if you have walked past me at the club, Sol? Maybe every night, but I no longer recognize you, because instead of your actual shape I have begun to look toward the image of you that my mind has built?

What if you stood next to me at the bar, or watched me from a half-dark corner? What if I turned my gaze directly at you, but didn't see, because I have drifted too far, and the space hides you from my eyes, will not refract light far enough?

18.5.2168
Hotel Mercury
Rock London, Earth

The sixth night was different. But you may know that already, Sol.

I arrived a little later than on the other evenings, under the illusion that the club was always quiet outside the peak season. However, I saw from far away that a queue had formed outside the pavilion. A hologram poster above the doorway flashed a shimmering advertisement: *Tonight: TWD – the best tribute show this side of the Moon!* The tickets cost more than usual.

After a long wait in the queue I stepped into the packed club. There were no empty tables, and I would in any case have to walk around in the crowd if I wanted to have any chance of knowing if you were there, Sol. I went to buy a virtual gin and tonic ("ZERO CALORIES AND A CLEAN LIVER!" a neon billboard advertised on the wall) and began to walk in the pavilion. The noise level had multiplied from the previous evenings. I tried my best to block my ears from the noise and focused on looking for a familiar body shape, facial features, a scent, anything that might belong to you. I saw a back dressed in a purple shirt and short dark hair with glitter sprayed on it. I approached the purple-shirt cautiously; they had your gestures, Sol. I touched their shoulder. They turned around.

"I'm sorry," I said. "I mistook you for someone else."

A group wearing half masks and velvet was sitting at a corner table. Two of them resembled you in terms of age and body shape, but would you have arrived with a group to see me, Sol? To be certain I walked past the table. Neither of the two mask-wearers reacted to me in any way, and one of them was showing pictures of their children, also dressed in black velvet, on a screen to the rest of the group at the table.

Mirror-shards glittered on the columns of the pavilion and people were gathered at tables with colorful drinks. The stage was not big, but it shone with a pearl-white brightness, so electric it could have been a hologram show. I followed the edge of the pavilion to be close to the stage, attempting to let my gaze gather everyone in the pavilion in turn: I sought a familiar posture or movement of a head, outline of a face or footsteps the rhythm of which I could feel in my own muscles. I only saw strange hands holding up glasses, eyes that did not catch my gaze, thoughts turning away, indifferent to me.

The lights dimmed and a drum resounded, unexpected like the heartbeat of someone risen from the dead. Another followed. I withdrew farther to the back, next to the wall, and allowed my gaze to scan the faces of the crowd once more, before it got too dark in the auditorium. The heartbeats continued, and the whiteness of the stage grew sharper, making the murky corners and folds of the pavilion bleed darkness. There were places I could not see: from which you perhaps could see me, or perhaps couldn't. A breathing grew next to the heartbeats. Air swelled in the lungs of shadows and blood surged through their veins, bringing a ghost back to life as we waited. A door at the back wall of the stage opened, and a figure stood in the doorway that everyone in the audience recognized, even I. The large holoscreens on the walls of the pavilion switched on, opened into a close-up: paper-white skin, eyes surrounded by blue shadow, red hair.

When the piano riff began out of sight, a scream rose from the audience.

The voice was the same. I knew it wasn't; instead, the result of years of practice, an impression honed to perfection, but I could not hear the difference. Since I had found my parents' old digital recordings and listened to them through the rustling speakers of the computer, I had tried to imagine what the concerts had been like. I'd also seen the videos, later: not all of them, of course, because there were so many, but enough to construct an image of the artist. I'd heard of the tribute shows in Londons, but had always thought they couldn't impress me, that the specter of the original would always be mightier in its heart-bursting glitter, distanced by time.

Yet now I forgot you, forgot myself, forgot my search and the shadows waiting silently in the corners. I stared at the performer, and my lips followed the lyrics of the song, stars entwining into a pattern or drops that grew into a stream. His gestures and expressions were learned, but did not look it. Each shift of the body, each blink of an eye, each glance downward or at the audience – I saw before my eyes how the performer journeyed into the Underworld and brought back a soul he clad in his own flesh. The person brought back from the dead breathed in front of us, cast a glow on ever new people who longed for it.

The refrain climbed toward its peak for the last time, and then the rhythm slowed down. The performer stopped, strayed from the original, lengthened a note, paused.

"Is there..."

He went silent and closed his eyes. The lights blazed white, his suit shone a pale turquoise and his hair a bright red. A scream grew from the audience. The performer's lips cracked open, turned into a grin. Even the teeth were slightly crooked in precisely the right way. He looked at the audience and asked in a voice that was the living voice of someone who had turned to dust a long time ago, "Do you want it?"

"Yes!" sounded from the audience.

"Do you want it?" he asked again.

"Yes!" the crowd shouted, louder.

"I can't hear you!"

"Yes!" the audience bellowed.

The piano riff climbed toward the heights. The performer took a breath and sang again.

"Is there..."

He paused. The crowd held its breath.

The singer laughed into the microphone and sang the last three words. The final note sounded high and long, and before it began to descend, an enormous scream rose from the audience, like a storm had struck through the entrance of the pavilion, tearing the walls and roof scaffolding, fluttering in the canvases and shattering the dark for a spell.

The performer bent his head backward, closed his eyes, and at that moment each one of us wanted to touch him.

The song ended in massive applause. I turned to get another drink from the bar. I had only walked a few steps when something in my field of vision began to bother me. It was like a rock left under streaming water that breaks the surface and alters the stream, or one leaf that does not shift among leaves turning in wind. I stopped and let my gaze move in the pavilion. Eventually I grasped it: on the opposite side of the tent a figure wearing a dark half mask decorated with feathers was looking at me, when all other eyes were turned toward the stage. Only the mouth and the arc of the jawline were visible, and the mask bore more resemblance to a ritual mask of a healer than to the decorative carnival masks sold on the street stalls. It was simpler and more primitive, like pictures drawn on rock or ancient drumheads. The figure turned its head a little. I saw the beak was straight and sharp, the garments black, they too decorated with feathers. Like a raven.

The crowd sat packed between us. The idea of trying to pass through the rows of chairs was impossible, so I began to walk along the wall of the pavilion toward the figure wearing the raven mask. Moving forward was slow, because the tent was so full. I left my glass at the bar as I walked past. If you had come to see me, why did you not start moving toward me? Or had you not seen me after all?

The figure in the raven mask began to walk away from me, toward the back entrance of the pavilion. I hastened my footsteps. I bumped into a woman standing next to a wall, whose drink spilled onto the floor. I made a rushed apology. The figure had turned away from me. I only saw dark hair pushing out from under the mask and a back that was not wide or narrow. I reached the figure right at the entrance. I grasped their shoulder. Sol, was it your shoulder?

The raven figure turned toward me. The eyes were hidden behind the mask, and in that dusky corner they might have been any color. The mouth looked like yours, and the body looked like your body, if you had lost a little weight over the past few months.

"Sol?" I said.

The raven figure breathed in, as if to say something. Yet the words did not come out. They stared at me and brought their face near mine. A gloved hand brushed my arm. Then they took a step back, turned around and disappeared through the doorway of the pavilion.

I ran after them. The road wound toward an oak grove that was barely lit at all, although the night had already turned dark. The tree trunks rose tall and wide enough to hide a person with enough patience to stand between them without moving, until the searcher would give up.

"Sol!" I cried out. "Sol!"

I thought I saw something shift between the trees. I took a step toward the movement. Something flashed by ahead of me, climbed up the trunk of an oak tree in the dim circle of the streetlight and disappeared into the branches. I looked up. The movement stopped. I breathed, and somewhere above me an animal breathed in the same rhythm, observing. I had a feeling it could see me, although I could not see it: not the color of its coat, not a flash of its eyes.

I walked among the trees for a long while, but found no one.

Eventually I returned to the pavilion. *Ashes to ashes*, sang the performer in the turquoise trouser suit.

· • ● • ·

As I walked back to the hotel, I tried to see the stars, but the lights of Londons wove a web across the sky that concealed them almost entirely. I saw flashing lights of landing vehicles, the twin glimmer of the cylinders of Saraswati and Kokyangwuti, and the swelling half-moon. From here one might have imagined that this was all there was. And yet on Europa people walked in their silent under-ice cities, on Enceladus the inhabitants somehow continued their lives despite everything that had happened there, Fuxi circled Mars as a silent specter. On Mars trees grew and waters flowed and humans were born and loved and wanted and hated and died. It meant nothing to the universe where you walked, or I.

The night was warm, and the oak leaves dark and whispering.

When I returned to the hotel, a notification began to flash on the screen.

Two new messages. Priority level: important.

I swept the first message open. The sender was unknown.

Check your pay bracelet. Immediately.

I stared at the message, then at my bracelet. A faint blue light burned on it, signaling it was functional. I'd charged it less than twelve hours ago and paid with it at the club only an hour earlier.

I removed the bracelet and plugged one end to the port in the screen. *Bracelet recognized*, the screen announced. Then a flashing text framed with red opened on the screen: *No credit*.

I tried to log in to my bank account. *Fingerprint recognition and account number do not match*, the bank announced. After the fifth attempt: *Maximum number of login attempts exceeded. If you continue to have problems logging in, please contact our phone customer service during the opening hours.* It was 00.36 Greenwich Mean Time. The opening hours of the phone customer service were from 7 a.m. until 7 p.m.

The screen pinged.

Reminder:You have one unread message.

I opened the second message.

You must leave Earth immediately, it said. Nothing else. There was a document attached. I scanned it for viruses before opening it.

It was a ticket for a flight to the Moon, scheduled to depart in ten hours' time.

20

Fog (noun)

Also: 8K72, *Avalon, Ectoplasm*

S. Cholewa & M. Sundholm.

***The Encyclopedia of Intoxicating Substances.* New Delhi: Soma, 2165.**

Synthetic cannabinoid 8K72, colloquially known as *Fog*, Avalon or Ectoplasm, is a new-generation cannabinoid that was developed on Mars in 2089. Like the older generation synthetic cannabinoids, the substance is usually sprayed in liquid form on plant matter and sold as a herbal mixture for smoking. It can also be taken internally as a liquid.

The effects of Fog imitate those of marijuana, but its psychoactive ingredients are approximately a thousand times stronger. Synthetic cannabinoids have been on the market since the early twenty-first century, and they were initially sold legally under such names as K2 and Spice, until their high potential for addiction was noticed and they were classified as illegal in most countries.

Among the first generations of the colonies, life in Martian gravity was a common cause for severe muscle pains. Therefore the pharmaceutical industry began to develop new kinds of painkillers. The new generation synthetic cannabinoids were intended to function as drugs that would be available to people from all socioeconomic backgrounds and would not cause intense physical dependence.

The early research into Fog seemed to show positive results. However, only a few years after it was patented, it became clear that the substance causes not only a very strong physical dependence, but also an almost complete psychological dependence. The effects are dozens of times stronger than those of Spice products, for instance, but of shorter duration. Users have described their experiences with Fog as intense euphoria, a sense of omnipotence, inability to feel pain and deep relaxation.

Manufacturing Fog is relatively easy and its price has remained low for a long time. In the twenty-second century its use has spread to many colonies. Fog is most widely used on Enceladus, where nearly 70 percent of the population suffers from various pain-causing long-term illnesses and birth defects due to illegal genetic experimentation.

There are big impurities in Fog, and its side effects are life-threatening. Fog has been described as causing an almost coma-like state in users, which makes them indifferent and incapable of reacting to external stimuli. Toxic shock resulting from the impurities in Fog, such as pesticides, is a common cause of death in users. The user may also die from malnutrition, because Fog virtually removes all sensation of hunger.

Sender: Lumi Salo
Recipient: Erna ja Eero Salo
Date: 21.5.2168 04.27 MST
Security: Maximum encryption

Hi Mum and Dad,
Unfortunately I have to cancel my trip to Winterland this time. Sol's work trip continues to stretch on unexpectedly, and they are still unable to return because of reasons beyond their control. As to myself, I have to go see a patient on the Moon. I am so terribly sorry – I would have loved to see you, it's been so long.

I promise I'll come and visit home as soon as I can, hopefully no later than a few weeks from now. Luckily, the Moon is not far, so I'll arrange to come before I head back to Mars. I miss the light of Winterland and the warm evenings of late summer. And both of you, of course.

In the meantime, look after yourselves and each other. I hug you from afar, and if all goes according to plan, soon enough from near vicinity.

Think of me when you watch the Moon.
Hugs + ♥ from
Lumi

22.5.2168
Hotel Tsukuyomi
Sinus Medii, the Moon

Sol,
I saw no other option but to board the Moon vessel.

My pay bracelet had stopped working. The bank did not recognize me, so I couldn't recharge it. When the customer service finally reopened, I tried to find out what had happened.

"One or more of the account holders has temporarily frozen all rights to operate the account," the customer service person said.

There was a stab of pain behind my eyes. I should never have consented to a shared account, Sol.

"How can one account holder close the operation rights of everyone else?"

"If all holders have authorized it when the account was opened," the customer service person explained in a voice that told me they considered me slightly slow-witted, "it is entirely possible."

Also on the list of things I should never have done: let you do banking for me. I had a vague memory of putting electronic signatures and ID information on various agreements years ago. An ache climbed up the left side of the back of my head, behind my ear, and carved a route from there toward the center of my head.

"Can I reopen my access to the account?"

"Not without the consent of the second account holder."

I wrangled with the clerk about the matter a little longer, but the end result was inevitable: I could not use the account or the bracelet.

I'd paid for the hotel in advance and taken some cash with me, but it wouldn't take me far. I walked to the reception desk and told the receptionist I'd have to leave three days earlier than expected. I asked if there was any chance I could get my money back for the canceled nights.

"Not part of our usual policies," the receptionist said. She had a tall hairdo and, for a member of staff at a half-star hotel, a suit that fitted surprisingly well.

"I understand," I said. "But this is an emergency. My aunt, who lives on the Moon, is fatally ill and I must go see her immediately."

"I cannot be of help, I'm afraid," the receptionist said, stone-faced.

I had not known I'd be able to improvise such a story at a moment of distress. Teary-eyed, I told her about the trips I'd made with my aunt as a teenager, and how I had her alone to thank for my career as a travel writer. Without a doubt I'd mention this place in favorable light in my next audio series, if I could trust to get good customer service.

I suspect the receptionist didn't believe a word, but decided eventually to show mercy at my performance and agreed to refund the price of one hotel night.

The ache behind my eyes gets worse by the day. I recognize it: it is the same pain that intruded my dreams when the soul-animal began to summon me to walk the path of a healer a long time ago. But this time I cannot follow the summons. I can only turn about in pain and hope that it will leave me alone one day, for my lynx is gone, and that is my own fault.

As I was reading my messages on the Moon ship, a new reservation had appeared among them: Hotel Tsukuyomi along the hiking route by Sinus Medii plain, a double room booked for a week. I recognized the name. Sol, did you pick the place because you and I stayed here a few years ago? Despite the circumstances, I cannot fault you for the choice. A scenic window opens toward Earth on the top floor tearoom from which the view to the plain is magnificent. I don't know if you ever visited it, but I used to sit there in early mornings, while you still slept.

I'll admit I'd hoped I'd find you waiting for me at the hotel, Sol. I'll admit I was disappointed.

There is also a practical matter: there is no way I have enough money left for a week, if I want to eat. I supposed it didn't occur to you to book a full board? If I scrape together all my cash, I may be able to buy a ticket to the nearest abandoned mining village. Earth, Mars or Nüwa aren't even a distant dream.

I don't know what I am meant to do here. Wait? And wait for what, or whom, precisely – you, Sol? Or something else?

But my most acute concern is money. On the flight I browsed through the responses I'd received to my permanent advertisement and looked for the crucial words: Cash payment possible. There were only a couple of suitable ones. Neither of the addresses were near the hotel. I picked the one that was closer, and sent a message from the vessel in which I said I was interested. The reply arrived an hour ago.

Come as soon as you can. D. Quinn.

Sol, I have not healed anyone after I lost my soul-animal. Now I must try, although there is no one to bear the weight of the task with me, although the ache of loss is making a home in my body and in my mind, and I have no means to drive it to a distance.

I told the patient I'd come tomorrow.

23.5.2168
Hotel Tsukuyomi
Sinus Medii, the Moon

Sol,

I will try to give a comprehensible form to what happened today, although much of it is beyond words and belongs in worlds I cannot access, not now or ever. There are places where healers cannot go, and those they can but from which they must stay away.

But I'll start from the beginning.

I came down with fever last night. This morning I shivered, as I put on an old-fashioned space suit I had rented at the hotel, and boarded the underground. My patient lived nearly four hours away. The lunar train brought me to an abandoned-looking station, from where I ascended up the slope of the crater on a shaky funicular to a place near its edge, like the patient had instructed me. A couple of narrow footpaths started at the top of the funicular station. I found a sign that read *Space Junk Museum III*. A red line had been painted across the words by hand. The weatherworn sign pointing in the other direction showed the name *Sputnik Park*. I headed for the crossed-out Space Junk Museum.

The edges of the path began to resemble a junkyard more and more the farther I walked. Things had been left lying around: pieces of age-old Moon modules and metal rubble that seemed to originate from ancient satellites, vehicles removed from operation ages ago, mining equipment, first-generation habitat structures and countless gadgets I didn't recognize at all. I wondered why the metal had not been reused and recycled like on most other celestial bodies. The loopholes in waste management presumably originated from the mining-village era, before the Moon had been transformed into a retreat for health enthusiasts and people looking for spiritual growth.

The door of the habitat was so small and unnoticeable that I'd have walked past, if the path had not narrowed down into a passage between rubble mountains where you could not mistake the direction. I stopped in front of the battered metal door and after a moment's search I found a button worn into a dent that I thought might be a ringing bell. I pressed it. After a while the door slid aside. I glanced around. There must be an electronic spyhole somewhere.

I stepped into the airlock. It was equipped with a standard signal light similar to those in most Moon airlocks. I waited until the light turned green to signal it was safe for me to remove my helmet. The inner door of the airlock opened before me. I began to detach my helmet and stepped through the entrance.

I sensed the weight of the illness right away. It gathered around me like mist or toxic smoke, piercing my lungs, enveloping my skin and pulling me down like a large animal that had jumped onto my back. Everything went black and cold waves moved through me. I had to stop for a moment and take deep breaths.

When I opened my eyes again, I was standing in some kind of a low entrance hall lit by a few hard-white LED lights. The floor was unpainted concrete, as well as the walls. Old movie posters had been attached to them with Blu Tack: *2001: A Space Odyssey*, *Planet of the*

Apes, *Solaris*, *Godzilla*, *Galaxy Quest*. (The inventor of Blu Tack would without a doubt be thrilled about the conquest of space and longevity of their brainchild if they knew.) It was quiet. No, not after all: from somewhere far away, as if deep underground, music sounded. Slow, perhaps jazz. My ear, unfamiliar with classical, placed it intuitively somewhere in the early decades of the twentieth century.

"Mr. Quinn?" I cried. "I'm Lumi Salo. The healer. We'd agreed on a home visit."

Nobody answered.

With the helmet under my arm I began to walk toward the end of the hall where I could see two doorways. My magnetic boots clanked against the concrete floor. A sharp pain cut through my head on each footstep. I felt the dampness of the cold sweat, as it clung to the skintight undergarment inside the space suit. The doorway to the left led to a corridor, at the end of which shone a dim light. I turned to the corridor. The music seemed to stream from a little closer. I followed its path to the end of the corridor.

When I stepped into the room, I saw my patient. His withered body sat straight and upright in a chair that looked like it had been welded together from different pieces of junk metal. A safety belt held him in place in the low gravity. He was neatly dressed, which I had noticed to be unusual among lonely patients who had little human contact. The man's gray hair rose from his head in a tall swirl, like a column of smoke ceaselessly fed by the thoughts smoldering in the mind under it.

The room had a narrow bed alcove, and next to the wall stood an old-fashioned gramophone. It looked like an Earth antique, but must have been of a special make, or it wouldn't have worked on the Moon. A jet-black disc turned on the plate. Music filled the air. Next to the bed alcove a table had been made from rubber tires piled on each other. A soldering iron, a stained metal mug and an opened packet of Fog lay on the table, all in clamps.

The man's eyes rested closed and the expression on his face was calm. I wondered how to make my presence known. If he'd taken Fog recently, he might not notice me for a long while.

"Come in," the man said then without opening his eyes. "I was just finishing."

"I'm sorry," I said. *Finishing what?* "I didn't mean to interrupt."

The man opened his eyes and smiled at me.

"There's nothing to apologize for," he said. "I invited you. You're welcome."

"Lumi Salo, at your service." I reached out my hand. He squeezed it.

His breathing flowed thin, as if there were dense obstacles in its way. Yet I did not see in him the slowness brought by Fog, only a cautiousness of movements and shifts of pain that crept to his face occasionally. The influence of the previous dose had worn off, then.

"You'll forgive me if I don't get up to greet you, I hope," the man said. "My legs have not quite carried me lately." He looked at me head to toe. "Although you seem a little worse for wear yourself."

The weight of the illness was heaviest here. The room was dense with it, in the corners light vanished entirely into its thicket. The healers' sickness that burned in my body was blended with the cold breath emanating from the man and made me nauseous. I missed the fur of the lynx under my fingers, her warm nose and long whiskers that tickled the back of my hand, her strong back that would carry part of the weight for me.

"Is there somewhere I can change from my space suit into the healer's outfit?"

"There is a kitchen along the corridor that has enough space," Quinn said.

• • ● • •

I dimmed the lights, asked Mr. Quinn to lie down and placed a weighted blanket on top of him.

I began to ask about his symptoms. He'd been ill for a long time. There were few healthy spots left in his body; I sensed that even without the clarity brought by the soul-journey. But I had to try. That's what he was paying me for. And I had to know what I could do without the lynx.

Quinn closed his eyes.

I allowed myself to hope.

I began to hum the summoning song and beat the drum at a slow pace. The pain smoldered as glowing embers behind my eyes, the chill on my skin slithered like ice-born snakes. I attempted to push them away with my voice, make a sheltering wall of song between them and myself. The notes bled out of me, collected into pools on the floor and in the air and in the corners. The words wove a call, drew the path for large paws to walk upon.

The path remained empty, the woods around it distant. The lynx did not arrive. The star-topped tree shimmered somewhere far away, in the middle of darkness, but I had no strength to find my way to it alone.

I had two options. I could continue and build the session into a performance, a surge of song, dance and gesture that an untrained eye would have trouble telling apart from a real healer's soul-journey. I'd seen people who called themselves healers do so. I didn't have their props, no skintight clothing that had been decorated with glitter, or flashy headpieces, every last strand of hair arranged to look messy or musical instruments of delicate design. Yet I'd made the journey so many times I'd be able to imitate my own movements with enough precision to convince the sick man whose focus had curled itself around the pain. And whose money I desperately needed.

Or I could be honest.

I had just enough cash for two days. Maybe four, if I only ate one meal a day.

I stopped beating the drum and went silent. I let my arms fall to my sides. My head was heavy as glass and full of cracks.

"Mr. Quinn," I said. "I'm sorry. I cannot help you."

The man's breathing rustled. He shifted on the bed and stirred with pain.

"What the hell are you talking about?"

This was the last moment to back down. I could still choose differently. But I already knew the words I'd hear from my own mouth as I opened it.

"I shouldn't have accepted your job offer," I said. "I'm no longer a healer. I was careless and I lost my ability."

Quinn was quiet. Some machine started in the guts of the building. A distant hum carried into the room.

"And there's nothing you can do?"

"I'm sorry," I said again. "I can give you medicines that will ease your pain, if you like. Or others that will carry you out of this world. But to be honest, Fog is stronger than anything I have. Unless you have developed a high tolerance for it."

The bed creaked as Quinn sat up. He used his elbows to lever himself higher under the weighted blanket.

"Get the hell out of here," he said in a voice worn coarse.

"Would you like me to help you up onto the chair or…?"

"Get out."

I folded the drum, nodded and started walking toward the kitchen so I could put on my space suit.

I'd only taken a few steps in the corridor, when I sensed movement somewhere behind me. For a moment I thought Quinn had got up and come after me. When I turned around, there was no one to be seen. That was when I heard a swish above me, and a figure landed before me from the ceiling that I'd not seen in a long, long time.

A white, supple-necked bird whose face was adorned by a dark, mask-like pattern folded his wings and stared at me with black eyes.

Vivian had never told me the name of her soul-animal, so I couldn't call out to him. Yet I recognized him at once. If I'd met a flock of swans, I wouldn't have had a way of telling the individual birds apart; regardless, I knew immediately that this was the helper who had walked beside Vivian until the end of her life.

He bent his neck toward me as if nodding.

Why are you here?

The bird did not reply. Every space lived in his black eyes, of this world and of all others.

"Did Vivian send you?" I asked aloud, although I knew the thought to be absurd. A soul-animal detaches themself from their human in the moment of death, and Vivian was nowhere any longer, at least in no place where I could have reached her. The living do not have a way to the Sea of Souls, although a few stories are told of great healers who have visited it and returned.

In calm bird-steps the swan started walking toward the sick man's room.

I followed.

The swan strutted into the room. I stopped at the doorway. Quinn had lain down again. His breath wheezed and his eyes were closed. The swan swooped onto the metal tabletop and sat down. He turned his yellow-orange beak toward the man, then back to me.

Something in the vicinity of my heart twitched, as if the suffocating weight of the sickness had shifted a little.

I took a couple of steps toward the bed. Quinn did not react. Slowly, with caution, I extended my hand and took his. Quinn started violently. The shadow of the sickness flooded into me like poison-dark water. I recognized the ghost pain that my body received, the reflection of his symptoms. The ache behind my eyes burst into a tall flame. I felt a droplet of sweat trickle along my hairline, and I was so cold I wanted to curl up into a small knot on the floor in the corner of the room.

"I told you to get out," the man croaked.

"Would you let me try again?" I asked. I was barely able to push the words out.

"You just want my money," he said. "You're one of those frauds. I've seen the likes of you in the past. Get out, before—"

I didn't get to learn what he was going to threaten me with, or how he intended to realize the threat, because just then a savage coughing fit interrupted him. The swan flew from the tabletop into my lap, folded his legs and sat down. A feather sticking out of his plumage tickled my wrist. I took a deep breath and focused on thinking through the pain.

"I'll do it for free," I said.

Quinn continued to cough. His face was red, and his eyes had watered. When the cough eventually eased, he lay quietly, with his eyes closed. His hands gripped the edge of the blanket. The swan gave a light nudge to my arm.

"What have you got to lose?" I asked.

Quinn's breath wheezed and hissed. After a long while he nodded slowly.

The swan seized my hand with his beak and placed it on the man's forehead. A bright pain flashed behind my left eye. The man twitched as if in a fit of convulsions. I used all my skill to wrap the sickness in white, softening light. Still, the reflection of the disease reached everywhere in my body. I placed my other hand on the soft feathers of the swan's back.

The swan closed his eyes.

I closed my eyes.

I sat on the swan's back, and the sky folded and the path rose to the stars. Beyond the space and tree trunk and the otherworld plain grew a forest where the swan carried me.

Sunlight filtered onto the path and onto the greenness of the twigs in patterns that followed the shapes of leaves and wind. Here the pain and cold eased; I felt almost well. The swan landed in a clearing. A small distance away I saw Quinn sitting under a tree. I headed toward him. A tangy scent of resin rose from the thick, red-toned trunk of the spruce, and a blue sky flickered between the dark green branches.

Quinn turned to look when he heard my footsteps, the far-wandered part of his soul: that which I'd come to bring back to the circle of the world.

I saw right away that my task was impossible.

The soul was veiled by a dark web marking the disease that had spread through the body; it loomed in dense knots and tight strands under the skin. It followed his movements, reaching in all directions and filling the spaces it had not yet entirely claimed.

I could offer the soul my hand and lead it back, but the body it had left behind would not be able to hold it for long. It was already crumbling and letting go of life.

You do not need to be cautious when speaking to souls. They are much more durable than the body, of a substance more persistent than anything else in the entire universe. They are not blinded or disciplined by the limits of the material world, and therefore they see the truth, they know and understand from half a word.

"You won't need to wait long," I told the soul. "The part of yourself you left behind is already crossing the border. After, you may return whole to the original home, the Sea of Souls. I will not take you to the material world again. That would be nothing but torture. Your time is nearly complete."

The soul looked at me, and its eyes were not empty, but full.

"Thank you," it said. "Thank you."

I bowed at the soul, because while they need no protection, they must be respected. Each of them is the only one of its kind.

The swan bowed his head.

The soul nodded at me and remained seated under the tree.

I turned toward the clearing where the swan had brought me. Yet the bird did not follow. His wings opened; he swooped farther into the forest and sat on a branch gazing at me.

I followed.

When I made it to the foot of the tree, the swan took flight again. For a moment I thought I had lost him entirely. Then I saw something shift farther away between the pines. The white shape of the bird was like mist among the dark boles. My movements dissolved into the whispers and rustlings of the woods, as I walked behind the swan. In the green of the damp meadow, small flowers shone with open corollas, hundreds of dim-white stars in the dusk of the forest. I'd walked such a route before.

Eventually the swan landed on top of a tall boulder at a clearing, his legs glowing orange against the gray map of lichen. I remained standing at the foot of the boulder and looked around; I recognized the place.

A short distance away lay a pond. Its dark surface reflected the trees and a few stars in the pale sky, and a smell of pine needles and resin drifted in the air. A light wind rustled the treetops above as I watched an ant carry a weathered, yellow-brown twig across roots.

A simple gate rose in the middle of the clearing. The trunks of two snow-pale silver birches twined together, and the green of their leaves glowed deeper than the other colors in the landscape.

I had passed through that gate many, many times.

Sol, there are places where healers can go, but they must not. Yet sometimes they don't do what they know is best. Sometimes they will stray from the path and put themselves and their soul-animals in danger, even though their teacher has advised them otherwise.

Where do you go, Lumi? When you disappear from me? That's what you asked, Sol, after Fuxi. *Why don't you want to be with me anymore?*

And I answered: *That's exactly what I want*. It was not a lie.

That's what I wanted, more than anything. To be with you, Sol. But you had disappeared from me too.

Sol, there is a place where memories live. I don't mean it metaphorically. It really exists. On the lynx's back I have passed through the snow-pale and glowing green gate again and again, in order to go there. I found the place almost by coincidence. I was still Vivian's apprentice, when I went to heal an elderly woman whose gaze was blank and who could only remember things that had happened to her long ago in her childhood, who didn't recognize her spouse or children. When I sought the part of her soul that had been ripped away in other worlds, that is where it had escaped: beyond the gate, among its memories.

It would not come with me and return to the living. That's how I understood that when a part of the soul travels this far, it no longer has a way back.

But I also found my own memories in this place. Everything I'd given up when I left Earth. Each moment I'd spent with Vivian. And later, each moment with you.

It's hard to explain what it's like there. It's not the same thing as reliving your memories. But it's close enough. When I step into the living room of your childhood home beyond the gate and meet you there for the first time, when you pour me quince wine, I may step into my own skin, but not completely: a part of me is always left out, perhaps that which we call free will. I can only act the way I acted then, say the same things I said. I can live everything again, but nothing ever changes, and it is a blessing, and it is a curse.

I can leave Earth again, and again I can learn things from Vivian I could never imagine I'd learn, and I can love you time and again.

I can lie on the floor again weeping my homesickness when Vivian does not see, and again I can fall into pieces when I hear about her death, and time and again I must fear I've lost you.

I can walk the streets of Fuxi again, those where no one will ever walk now, and breathe in the scent of the park and sense the humidity of the waterfall on my face, and pick up the purring Major Tom into my arms. And I can walk again, look at the sky and the leaves of the trees and the green and yellow stripes of the fields on the walls of the world, search for a sign of the beginning destruction, search to no avail for the moment when it could all have been prevented, stopped.

I can return from beyond the gate and know I will never find that moment. Even if I did, if I could see something I didn't see then, I'd only be able to do what I did then, and nothing would change.

Sol, do you understand now why I went back there, and why I sometimes didn't wish to return?

At the time, after Fuxi, you were more there than you were here. There I could be with you, the way we were at the beginning. When nothing had yet been torn apart. But each time I went there, it was more difficult to come back. Each time we walk in memories again, they grow a little stronger, and we grow a little weaker. The way beyond the gate is dangerous, and it is easy to get lost there. It is full of creatures that can attack and wound us. Those wounds are not always visible, but they still make us weaker.

The lynx was full of scars when I lost her.

Vivian warned me.

Sol, now you know.

At Quinn's sick bed, worlds away from Quinn's sick bed, two narrow silver birches arched before me in a clearing and intertwined to form a gate.

A rustle, somewhere, as if the claws of a leaping animal sank into tree bark.

I turned my gaze toward the sound. I saw nothing but tree trunks and forking branches, pale green leaves and dark green needles and shadows moving in the wind that dappled the surface of the pond.

I heard another rustle, closer this time. I saw movement between the trees across the pond. Someone was watching me from behind the boles.

I stepped to the edge of the pond and squatted near the water. I whispered the lynx's name.

It was completely silent. The wind stopped. The surface of the pond calmed down, smooth as a mirror.

I repeated the name.

Nothing moved in the forest.

I whispered the lynx's name for a third time. Claws drew grooves in the bark, a speckle-furred weight dropped among the twigs and needles.

The lynx stared at me from the opposite side of the pond. A long, puckered scar ran along her side, and around it only part of the coat had grown back. I took a cautious step toward the lynx. The fur on her back rose up; she started and crouched and backed down slowly. I saw her limping one front leg.

"I'm so sorry," I said. "I've treated you wrong."

The lynx stopped between the trees. Its gaze was still fixed on me.

"You don't belong to me," I said. "I had no right to ask you to take me to places that no one should go. You were my responsibility. I betrayed your trust. Can you ever forgive me?"

Tree branches bent; wind waded through their leaves. The lynx turned her ears, but didn't move toward me, nor farther away. Wide wings opened, folded the air. I turned to look. The swan had landed before the gate. His wings remained open for a moment, wide as the sky, blocked the opening between the two trees. When he folded his wings, I saw nothing but emptiness beyond the gate.

I understood what the swan wanted me to do.

"Will it bring back what I've lost?" I asked quietly.

The swan tilted his head. In his black eyes I only saw the reflection of my question, not an answer.

Other worlds will take the shape our minds give them. If you wish to cross a river, you must imagine a crossing. If you wish to open a path, you must think of it as open.

I walked to the gate. The swan stepped aside. This was something I had to do alone.

Beyond the gate memories called to me. I heard them like music, I tasted them like fresh bread or chocolate melting on my tongue, or the first sip of hot tea. I only needed to step through the gate, alone, and walk into my memories, and stay there. Every moment I wanted to keep forever was there. My body would wither in Quinn's room, but he'd no longer know, nor would anyone else: least of all myself. I'd walk with you in the woods of Fuxi and rest in your arms, Sol, and I could be on Earth with my parents whenever I wanted to, only in the moments I chose.

I'd never have to leave another home again.

It would only take a few footsteps.

I rooted my feet to the ground as if I was a tree myself, I allowed the spirit-world life hidden from light to flow into me. I summoned a song I hadn't sung before but realized I knew as soon as the first notes arrived. The song found shape on my tongue in the language I'd carried with me since I was born. Each of its words was unexpected, yet the only possible one. The song grew into shimmering strands that flowed through me, pushed into the ground along the roots of my feet and reached for the roots of the birches. They burst from my fingertips like sprouting branches, sealed into buds and spread into leaves, reached for the birch-branches with their narrow tips. I was a tree made of light that bent and rose higher, and the birch gate heard my song.

I sensed the light flowing under the skin of the birches like blood running through veins. Their interwoven branches grew in length and twisted into many bends, new and ever new branches pushed from the trunks that twined more closely together, grew wider and nearer each other. The thin branches wove a web between the trees that got denser and denser, shattered the emptiness beyond the gate into ever-smaller shards, until the very last holes were completely blocked.

The song withered on my tongue. Silence fell. The light escaped from the birches, and it escaped from me. I collapsed onto the ground.

If you wish to close a path, you must think of it as closed.

I stared at the snow-pale birch trunks standing before me. There was no opening between them, but a wall, grown from living branches, thick, persistent and impenetrable. I'd never walk through it again.

All strength had left my limbs. I felt something nudge my shoulder gently. When I turned, I saw the swan's face next to my own. He tilted his head toward the pond.

Across the pond the lynx got to her feet. She blinked her golden eyes directly at me. Her tail twitched. Her body tensed. The muscles trembled under the fur coat. She leaped straight onto the tree from which she had dropped down, climbed up the trunk and disappeared from sight among the pine needles.

I watched her go, and tears streamed down my face.

The swan placed his head on my lap.

"Will you take me back?" I asked.

The swan raised his head and settled before me, and he was large as the sky, but small enough that I could mount him and wrap my arms around his long neck. My fingers sank into his white plumage. I saw a path open between the trees in the woods; we turned toward the border of this world.

Just then the sky darkened, as if caught in the web of a sudden thunderstorm. From somewhere far away a tremor rose that was at first so soft I didn't even notice it. Gradually it grew into a low growl, seized the leaves and needles of the trees, rattled them, shook the trunks, until I feared the surrounding forest would fall down and bury us here, at the heart of another world, from where we'd never have a way back.

The swan spread his wings and the ground fell away from beneath us. I saw how at a distance something enormous began to erupt, spitting mist into the landscape. But that only lasted a brief moment, and then silence spread in the green vaults again.

The bird accelerated his pace, and I felt the movements of his muscles as the wings folded the air.

· •●• ·

My trance dissipated. I opened my eyes. My hands were still holding the drum, on its head my fingers drew the path back. Mr. Quinn lay on the bed, his eyes open, and watched my face attentively. Before I had a chance to say anything, he spoke.

"What happened?"

When I didn't respond immediately, he continued, "I felt a tremor of sorts, like an earthquake. It transferred from your hands to me."

He seemed much calmer now. I remembered quick mood swings were one of the side effects of Fog use.

"I cannot explain it," I replied. "But I saw the stage of your illness."

"It's too late, isn't it?"

"I'm sorry," I said.

Quinn gazed past me, through the wall, through the mountains of junk into moondust. His breath rustled. Eventually he gave a slow nod.

"It's no surprise." He went quiet. Then, "Would you keep me company?" His voice had worn so thin it was nearly gone. "I don't think this will take long. Tell me something that will pass the remaining time."

"What would you like to hear?"

"Tell me about where I'm going."

"I don't know how," I said. "The road is different for everyone."

Quinn tried to laugh. It turned into a painful cough.

"It doesn't matter," he said. "I don't believe in the afterlife. I just want to hear what you think it would be like, if it did exist." He paused and coughed again. "That," he pointed at the torn-open bag clamped to the table, "is the last of Fog I have left. It will be enough for two doses at most. Go to that set of drawers and open the top one." He lifted a tired finger to point at a drawer set, on which various worn-through layers of paint were visible.

I took a few steps and opened the drawer. Banknotes placed under weights in neat bundles lay in it. They were old, but valid. There were notes of low and high value among them. I made a quick estimate based on what I saw: enough cash for me to live on for a month, at least, probably also to buy a return ticket to Nüwa.

"Take everything you find," Quinn said. "Spend some on getting me a burial of some sort. Doesn't matter if you get a gravestone. There's no one left who will miss me. You can keep the rest, on the condition that you stay and tell me stories, until I can no longer hear your words."

What else could I have done, Sol?

I watched as Quinn mixed the rest of Fog with a small amount of water, heated it up with a soldering iron in the metal cup and stirred the liquid with a spoon. He lifted the cup to his lips, blew into it and drank.

It wasn't long until the influence of Fog settled over him like a blurring film. Through it I saw his form, but couldn't discern individual traits.

"Talk to me," Quinn said.

His body sagged in the bed as Fog spread to cover the pain that had been holding him alert. Breath sought a way in his disease-blocked body.

"Beyond the Milky Way there is a stream," I began, "that is made of wine."

A mist had fallen into Quinn's eyes, but behind it his irises were ice blue. He interrupted me.

"A bit more effort, now," he mumbled. "I hate clichés."

"I thought you didn't believe in what I'm telling you."

The corners of his mouth pulled into a smile, and for a moment I could see how he had looked before, before loneliness and junk and concrete floors, before the illness that had eaten his body, before Fog. He had been beautiful.

"I don't," he said. "But tell me in such a way that for a little while I can imagine I believe it. That'll be enough."

I nodded slowly.

"Would you like me to hold your hand?"

The man shook his head.

"The stream is made of wine," I said, "but its bottom is broken glass, and everyone must walk across it with bleeding feet, because the opposite shore is far away, and there is no other way."

The man lowered his chin into a slow nod and his eyes fell closed.

I told him of souls that were freed from the chains of the body once they had crossed the stream, and that flew in the shape of a bird beyond the stars. I told him of the Sea of Souls, above which the sky is as bright as that of Earth on the brightest summer day, and of the wondrous trees of the islands that never died but always grew again, and of the coral forests of the deep sea where souls drifted out of time. I spoke of the music that began when you longed for it, and quieted when the soul needed silence. I spoke, and the words flowed from me, and I myself could no longer catch them, but they fell by their own weight, counting the moments shorter, like grains of sand dropping in an hourglass.

Quinn's head had fallen into a slanted position. I could no longer hear his breathing. The gramophone had finished playing the record, and the needle circled the disc in silence.

I notified the local Moon burial unit about the death. I had not lost patients often, but this wasn't the first time. As I waited for the undertaker to arrive, I watched the dead body resting on the bed. A little bit of blood had trickled from the mouth. I only saw an empty shell. He was no longer here. I didn't know where he was, but this was simply something he had discarded: a skin shed, dust scattering in the wind, if there had been wind on the Moon. He looked as light as a faded leaf.

I felt at peace, for he was free now.

At the doorway of the room the swan watched me.

"Thank you," I said.

The swan tilted his head, only slightly, like Vivian used to do. As if to say, *No need to thank me.* Or perhaps, *You did it yourself. I only reminded you of what you already knew.*

The swan spread his wings and took flight, vanishing as if the walls or ceilings or anything that might forestall him did not exist.

I know I will never see him again.

Sol, after I returned to the hotel I slept for hours. Then I wrote. And now I am exhausted again. I must sleep.

You know where to find me. If you still wish to find me.

A series of violent earthquakes in the Pacific

Al-Jazeera Earth, Al-Jazeera Mars

24.5.2168 / Updated 08.33 UTC

Three violent earthquakes have been detected north of Fiji in the Pacific. The strength of the first earthquake was 7.9, and its epicenter was located at a depth of about 15 km. One hour later two more quakes, 7.7 and 6.9 Richters respectively, struck the bottom of the ocean.

No one is known to have been hurt in the quakes, and according to local authorities, they did not cause significant material damage. A tsunami warning has nevertheless been given in the region, and the residents of the coastal areas of Fiji, Vanuatu and New Caledonia have been instructed to evacuate.

Fiji and Vanuatu suffered great damage in the tsunami of 2140. Since then, the possibility of earthquakes has been taken into account even more carefully in the structures of the cities. The older building stock of the islands is particularly vulnerable to earthquakes, because large parts of it have been elevated several times due to sea level rises.

Earthquakes are relatively common in the area.

Origin of earthquakes in the Pacific unclear
Reuters Earth-Moon, Reuters Cylinder Zone
25.5.2168 / Updated 13.51 UTC

More measurement data has been received relating to the earthquakes observed in the Pacific yesterday and today. The International Seismological Center announced that the natural movements of tectonic plates are unlikely to explain the data. According to them, it is highly unlikely that so many powerful earthquakes could take place in the Pacific within such a short time. Three earthquakes were measured yesterday within less than two hours, and four more were observed today approximately five hundred kilometers north of yesterday's epicenter.

More uncertainty was added to the origin of the quakes by the information published by the Oceanographic Research Unit of New Zealand, according to which very high concentrations of spores of a previously unknown fungal species have been measured in the coastal areas. It is believed that the spores were carried by ocean currents from near the epicenters of the earthquakes. The concentrations are so significant that they can be seen in the quality analyses used to monitor the acidity, salinity, radiation levels and microplastic concentrations of sea water.

No state in the area has announced nuclear tests. Australia, New Zealand, Japan and United Korea are committed to the Soul Treaty aimed at complete disarmament. The independent science organization OEMP (Oceanic Ecosystems Mapping Panel) released a statement today, according to which only human activity could have caused such a series of earthquakes and the release of the fungal spores into the sea.

The OEMP spokesperson did not want to comment on the speculation about a potential biological weapon behind the events in the Pacific.

Tensions grow in the Pacific
UPI, YONHAP Galactic
26.5.2168 / Updated 00.04 UTC

The United Nations, the Cylinder Cities Community and Mars Security Council have called for an emergency meeting. Tensions have been mounting in the Pacific since a series of violent earthquakes shook the bottom of the ocean two days ago. To date, approximately twenty earthquakes have been measured in different parts of the Pacific. Additionally, very high concentrations of the spores from an unknown fungal species have been found near the epicenters of the quakes. The international scientific community has for the most part sided with the view that the reason for the earthquakes was not natural, and that the spore cloud spread in the Pacific is connected with the quakes.

The spores are being studied, but no consensus has been reached yet about their origin or impact. The international team of scientists emphasizes that there is no reason to believe the spores or fungal species pose a danger to humans. Nevertheless, speculation about the origin of the earthquakes and spores has been running rampant. An anonymous source from the United States Defense Ministry commented in a widely publicized interview that "we are almost certainly dealing with a biological weapon that may have originated outside Earth."

The USA, China and Russia have sent warships to the areas where the earthquakes took place. The emergency summit of peacekeeping organizations is being held early tomorrow in Tokyo.

27.5.2168

Hotel Tsukuyomi

Sinus Medii, the Moon

Sol,

I switched the news screen on three quarters of an hour ago.

They say some kind of a biological weapon has exploded on Earth. They say the entire Earth is under threat. They say all traffic leaving Earth has been placed under a strict quarantine, so the biohazard would not spread to any colonies.

They say the same message has been delivered to all channels and to each government: *Earth wakes and stones will speak, and darkness recedes over waters.*

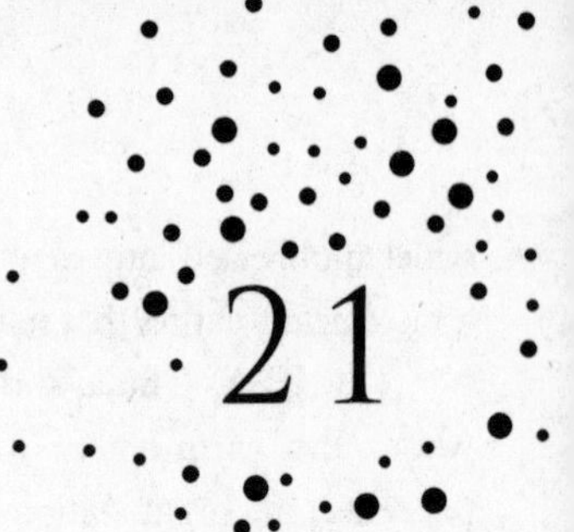

21

Terrorist organization claims biological attack on Earth

Xinhua Earth, AFP Venus, RIA Novosti Solar

27.5.2168 / Updated 05.20 CST

The relatively unknown terrorist organization known as the Stoneturners has claimed a biological attack on Earth. Speculation over a strike began when strong earthquakes were detected in the Pacific Ocean earlier this week. The organization has sent a press release to large news agencies, as well as governments on Earth and in the colonies, in which it announced it was behind the attack. The earthquakes were caused by powerful explosions that released billions of fungal spores into the oceanic ecosystems.

According to the organization, the strike is "intended to liberate Earth from the terrorist regime of Mars without bloodshed, using methods aimed at breaking human dictatorship and creating a new golden era of nature."

The strike is the largest known biological terror attack in history.

Some environmental organizations and experts have rushed to emphasize that to date, the spores have not been found to cause harm to humans on Earth. According to these organizations and researchers, calling the biomatter released in the seas a weapon should be carefully considered.

The UN, Mars Security Council, several states outside it and the Cylinder Cities Community have unanimously condemned the strike. All transport connections from Earth to the colonies have been halted for quarantine reasons.

This news item is subject to updates.

1.6.2168
Hotel Tsukuyomi
Sinus Medii, the Moon

Sol,
Earth has disappeared from sight again behind the bare Moon horizon, and it has risen up again. The scent of tea lingers. People come and go. You do not, and nor do I.

They are now talking about decades, a quarantine of dozens of years. For decades, they say, no one can leave Earth or arrive there from the colonies. I will not be able to travel home and embrace my parents within their remaining years, to look at the blue sky and sunlight with them: their lives will quietly trickle away, and I will not be there.

For the planet, a few decades is an insect in the wind blowing past, a fallen leaf disappearing beyond the bend in the stream. In human years, it is everything. It is *never again*.

I spoke to my parents today. They wept. I wept. I thought of the phone on the Moon humming with silence, of the voices it could not transmit to my ears. I thought of the Voynich Lights, the messages of strange lives and deaths that we don't know how to read. I thought of you, Sol.

Did you leave Earth before the traffic connections were halted?

Or are you too decades away from me, as far away in a hundred years as you are now, and in a million, forever where I cannot return?

Your mother sent me a message to check if I was all right. Ilsa, too: I had not expected that. I asked if they had heard from you, but I have not had a response yet.

One miracle has happened, such as I could not have dared to predict. Regardless of the risk, some colonies have opened their spaceports to the vessels that had already left Earth before the quarantine was declared and that would have found it impossible to return due to lack of oxygen or food. The passengers will of course be placed under quarantine for months, until they can be certain they have not carried anything with them that might destroy their crops. I have asked myself why these measures could not be extended to all ships from Earth.

And the greatest miracle of all: a few spaceports have opened their doors to the ships of smugglers also, which previously would have been left to drift in the abyss of space as ghost ships, of which captains and other space-farers would tell stories if their paths ever crossed. Those ports will not be able to accommodate all the ships, but they are receiving as many as they can. When the umbilical cord to the womb planet has been cut, every life is precious.

Are you on one of those ships, in a port where I may yet find you, Sol? It is a short way to the Moon. Wouldn't you have made it here by now?

I will wait for you in the tearoom from which I can see Earth as a perfect drop of water against the dark. I will wait until you come, or until you don't.

2.6.2168
Hotel Tsukuyomi
Sinus Medii, the Moon

Sol,
This happens one morning after sleep, under the ruptured skies:

I think of the snow-white gate that no longer exists, and everything that remains bright behind the wall that has grown to take its place, but fades in my mind, as memories must. I think of the life into which I must fit like a strange piece of clothing: in which I need to know how to be more than a ghost in past rooms. In which I cannot return to what was, but must build a new world from what is now.

Grief is an animal you can never quite tame.

I hear a low screech from the corner of the room.

I lift my head and wipe my eyes. The lynx sits in the corner, her golden eyes are open and alert. I discern a long scar along her side. She cracks her mouth open and screeches again.

"You're free," I say. "You only belong to yourself."

The lynx's head bends, as if to nod.

"If you come to me again," I say, "from now on I'll serve you."

The animal gets to her feet and walks to me. I can see her front paw will never be the same: its posture is permanently altered. The bone has broken and regrown slanted, and she limps at every step. She settles before me, her large paws against the floor, and lays her head in my lap. Softly I place my hand on her neck and stroke.

"I'll only go where you want to take me. Not the other way around. That's how it should always have been."

The lynx raises her head and stares at me. She blinks once, twice. The lost light of Earth glows in her eyes, filtered through green leaves. A low purring rises from her guts. Gently, she nips at the side of my hand lying in my lap, then licks my thumb.

"Is there someplace you want to take me now?"

The lynx pushes herself up, closer, and butts my temple. I place my hands on her cheeks and press my forehead against hers. Her coat is thick and coarse, her whiskers long and translucent. I breathe in as the animal breathes in. I breathe out as she breathes out. The song begins to rise from me unsummoned, of its own volition, like water surging to find its bed after a dam has been holding it for too long.

There is a path, and there is a forest, and there is an animal's fur coat under my hands. But something is unlike before, because when I let my hands rest on the speckled fur of the lynx, sensations flow into me

the scent of a mole in a root-filled passage the rustle of the movements of an owl in a treetop nest a pine cone under the sole an ache in the wounded paw the warmth of the fur that covers the skin in the mud of the pond the glimmer of fish-sides the dance of each grain of sand in the sunrays filtering through the water

and I pull my hand away.

"What happened?" I ask.

The lynx stares at me. Her golden eyes see everything.

With caution I place my hand on her neck again.

It is as if I sink into the lynx, she into me. I can still feel my human skin and my limited senses, but intertwined with them I feel the tension in the animal's muscles and the unfamiliar

familiar

paths of movement, the bunches of smells the strands of which guide me in several directions, and the bright clear colors outline shapes, lights, shadows, the same yet entirely different from the ones I'm used to seeing with my human eyes.

I understand

the lynx understands

that the boundary between us has blurred and grown thinner. We have moved closer to each other, and the senses of the soul-animal are available to me unlike ever before. We have both paid for this, but received something in exchange for what we lost.

One day she might teach you something I cannot tell you about, because everyone must discover it by themselves, Vivian had said about the lynx.

I feel our hearts finding the same beat. I feel how my skin is my own skin and at the same time a rippling animal skin.

Take me where you will.

The lynx begins to move. I feel the stiffness of the damaged paw, but we dive into space regardless, and it is wider than ever, for my eyes are new.

Ruptures open around us, light catches into a tangle and unravels into strands, between them the darkness of worlds and worlds in crevices in which I see everything,

everything.

I have saved moments in me over the years, making them into a story: our story, Sol. I have a memory of the moment in which you bend toward me for the first time and touch me like one touches a beloved. If I compared it with the moment that actually took place in time, they would no longer equal each other. Perhaps the posture of your fingers would be different; perhaps the word I said was two or three instead, or perhaps we only spoke silence. Perhaps light fell differently, and a shadow grew between us that I knew nothing about, or a whiff of dead leaves and soil blended with the scent of the fruit of the flowering quince. But however those images, the bright experiences preserved by my mind, differ from reality, the story I have told myself is built upon them.

Sol, as I look at those images, they split and multiply, shatter into ghosts interlaced with each other. Even the things I know did not happen become true. I look at the time and space, and everything happens at once, each story we might have lived or left unlived.

· •●• ·

On Vivian's advice, you invite me to heal your mother, and when I step into the room, something within you shifts, and you already sway toward me.

You invite me to heal your mother, and when I step into the room, something within you may shift, but you ignore it. If you sway at all, you sway away from me.

· •●• ·

Your mother heals, albeit slowly. You shake my hand and thank me, you may think of the passing chance to make better acquaintance, or you may not. I never stay for long. You never come to my door in the middle of the night. You never touch me like one touches a beloved.

Your mother heals, but slowly. You ask me to stay. We touch each other like lovers. Yet when it is time to go, we go our separate ways and part our lives before we have a chance to weave them together.

• • ● • •

When it is time to go, we decide to weave our lives together. There is a Fuxi where the fungal disease never arrives, where trees still grow. There is a park and a balcony and cold quince wine. There is your hand on my skin. There is a home we do not need to leave, and a future that no one takes away.

We decide to weave our lives together. There is a Fuxi that the fungal disease destroys. There is your hand on my skin. There is a future that is taken away from us. There is the moment I walk through the security gate at the spaceport and don't look back. There is a world in which I board a vessel that will take me to Earth or Europa, and I never see you again.

There is a future that is taken away from us, but I return to you from the spaceport, and the bond doesn't break. There is Nüwa, Fuxi's twin, and a light almost like Earth sunlight, green leaves and another balcony. We always come home. In the Moonday House, we are never far from each other.

• • ● • •

Then you disappear, Sol.

• • ● • •

Worlds and time and stories grow into thin ghosts overlapping and interlacing each other, our shared past is two separate ones, and many, invisible or only partially visible. What has been is different, and all pasts and futures happen at once in endless worlds.

In each world we lose each other, and find each other, and lose each other again.

I sit on the edge of each universe and watch as they all unravel and gather again into ever-different skeins, and in each one you escape from me. In the rooms of the Moonday House rifts open in the floors, the walls tremble and in the staircase I hear shards hit the stone slabs, when something precious and fragile shatters into pieces out of sight.

Darknesses clang shut, the ruptures close, everything vanishes from my view except for a blue water drop in the blackness,

everything.

Earth grows fast as the lynx and I approach it across space. The lynx sharpens her eyes, cuts with her gaze through the clouds and the air, shows us both what is happening in the atmosphere and the oceans. The animal's eyesight lives within my eyes, and I live under her skin; she lends me her senses and the strength of her muscles, and I don't want to return to my own skin again.

The change strikes me as a light storm, an explosion that cannot be reversed and forced back into its shell.

The oceans sizzle and foam, the air above them twists and wriggles and sparkles. Thousands of stars open and close as we dive ever closer, ever deeper, into the green fist of the water that grabs us. We grow smaller smaller smaller

until everything is bigger than us, cells and atoms and the dark matter in between. Everything is clear and bright, and I see it.

The spores thicken into swarms around the seagrass, they grow a layer of fungus deep in the mud on the grassroots, nourishing the grass.

And the grasses open, they sigh, for the first time in a hundred years they breathe as they are meant to breathe. The fungi rejoice as the grasses feed them, and the cells of the grasses divide, multiply, they grow grow grow

until their stalks dance a joyous dance in the waves, rushing over stone and sand, bubbling into shallows and coasts they embroider the seabed into meadows, growing a green veil everywhere like tree leaves in the first sun of spring. They surge into places they have not yet seen, and fill the oceans with life that is not for humans to own or rule or stop. And the oceans open their maws, absorbing carbon from the atmosphere, enclosing it in their new green forests that will shape it into oxygen.

The goddess Inanna has returned from the land of the dead and is walking the paths of the planet, and in her footsteps Earth sighs and lives again.

In the skin of the lynx I gasp and breathe in what I see.

The world I know may have come to an end, but for this life the world has only just begun.

• • ● • •

Following Inanna's footsteps: at the origins of cosmic bioterrorism

Excerpt from a reportage

Al-Jazeera Mars / Enisa Karim

Published 17.6.2168

The narrow flight of metal stairs leads deep underground. Unexpectedly, a comfortable and light room with worn rugs covering the floor opens at the bottom. A figure wearing a blue coverall gets up from a chair; they have covered their face with a dark mask. The pattern of the mask is designed to confuse face recognition technology, and they will not remove it despite the fact that we have agreed on a photography ban in advance. The inhabitant of the room introduces themself and reaches out a gloved hand. They wish to be known only by the name Tamm. It is not their real name.

"Tea?" Tamm asks. I thank them for the offer, and Tamm pours me a steaming cup of chamomile infusion from a thermos standing on the table.

"I knew nothing about it," Tamm says and stirs their tea. "Most members didn't."

Tamm is referring to the biological attack named the Inanna strike that the organization the Stoneturners carried out on Earth two weeks prior to our meeting. Tamm has belonged to the Stoneturners for years. They have agreed to the interview, because they want to clarify to the world that their aim is peaceful environmental protection. "We have all been labeled as terrorists because of a few extremists, although our cause is good."

The name of the Stoneturners entered interplanetary awareness overnight, when the organization claimed the Inanna strike in the Pacific. In connection to this, they also claimed the unknown fungal disease that spread on Fuxi in 2164, causing the complete evacuation of the cylinder city and the permanent closure of the colony. The Stoneturners announced that they had implanted the fungal disease on Fuxi on purpose in order to show what would happen if the Inanna fungus were allowed to spread outside of Earth.

Inanna is a so-called design bioweapon: it is based on the fungal symbiont isolated from the rare frost lichen (*Physconia glacialis*) found on Earth. The characteristics of the fungus have been genetically modified in a Martian laboratory. Implanted in the seas on Earth, Inanna is capable of forming a symbiosis with several different species of seagrass, and will boost the growth of seagrasses by several thousandfold by increasing the oxygen-producing capabilities and immunity of the plant. Releasing calcium carbonates that reduce the acidification of oceans is also among its characteristics. The ability of the seagrass to bind carbon dioxide from the atmosphere grows the carbon sink capacity of the oceans and will have a cooling impact on the overheated climate of Earth in the long run.

However, there are no seas or salt-water plants on Mars or in the colonies with which the fungus could form a symbiotic relationship. Without a symbiont, it begins to behave like a parasite, and causes a plant disease named moonrust that is extremely destructive to crops. Since the food production in the colonies is entirely dependent on farming, all traffic between Earth and the colonies has been frozen for quarantine reasons after the Inanna strike.

It is not known at the time of writing this when the traffic connections can be reopened. Even the most optimistic estimates speak of months; the most pessimistic, decades.

Tamm's opinion on the situation is clear.

"I don't approve of the attack," they say. "But I understand to an extent the thinking that triggered it."

Is Tamm able to cast more detailed light on that thinking?

"For too long humans have thought about themselves as separate from nature, above it. Exploitation of natural resources is seen as a right that doesn't entail responsibilities. That's why Earth is the way it is today. Only a complete reversal of thinking can bring a change."

I remark that the explanation sounds idealistic, but abstract. Tamm gets agitated.

"Humans have claimed the right to destroy other species, steal their living spaces and tarnish the landscape everywhere. On what grounds are human lives more valuable than those of any other living beings?"

What about the lives that were destroyed as the consequence of the biological attack? I ask. The vast damage that the explosions of the spore capsules caused to the seabed? What about the thousands of people who were between Earth and the colonies when the strike took place, and who were separated from their families and homes, possibly for the rest of their lives? What about the nine hundred migrants who lost their lives in the ships of human traffickers, when so many of the spaceports in the colonies were closed?

Tamm takes a sip of their tea.

"Like I said, I don't approve. I support nonviolent action," they say. "But soft measures don't always generate results. The Stoneturners have striven for decades to increase awareness of environmental issues and questions of power that go with them. Yet most of the time it has felt like screaming into a void. The way that Mars treats Earth has not gotten any better. I can see why someone would take the measures one step further, even if I wouldn't do so myself."

I ask Tamm if they knew any of the extremist core group members of the Stoneturners, who are considered the key persons when it comes to the strike.

"I met Sol Uriarte a few times," they respond. "I didn't know them well. Smart cookie, brain the size of a planet. Min-soo Jung was an acquaintance. I went to listen to Andrew Johansson's lectures a couple of times, but I never talked with him."

Was there anything about their behavior indicative of their radicalization?

Tamm is quiet for a long moment.

"No," they say eventually. "They had their own clique, but there were others within the organization too. There's always cliques."

Andrew Johansson and Min-soo Jung are waiting for trial on Earth. Sol Uriarte vanished some weeks before the Inanna strike. They are still being sought. Three other persons are also wanted as suspected of taking part in the strike.

Sender: Lumi Salo
Recipient: Enisa Karim
Date: 19.6.2168 03.50 MST
Security: Special encryption (password required)

Hi Enisa,
I had hoped to be able to write in order to invite you and your family to the dinner I have promised to prepare for you. However, things have happened that I could not see coming. I must ask you for one more favor.

I have opened a safe-deposit box at the bank of Sinus Medii and left some writings from the past months in there for storage. If I disappear without a trace, I hope you will go and get them from the safe-deposit box and read them. You can form your own idea of what happened based on them, and use them whichever way you like.

I am not even certain why I am asking for this. Perhaps it is a need to ascertain that someone knows the true story behind the false stories that will be told of Sol and me. Perhaps I am just self-centered and cannot stand the idea that nothing will prove I was here after I am gone.

The instructions for opening the safe-deposit box are attached.

I am grateful for everything you have done for me. You have been a friend in the space where we are all alone. Who knows, perhaps a day will come when we sit down at the same table and eat food I have cooked for you, and you will tell me how you would have made it differently. We will know each way is good, and we will smile at that together.

I raise a cup of spice-scented tea for absent friends and for worlds that could be.
In friendship, always,
Lumi

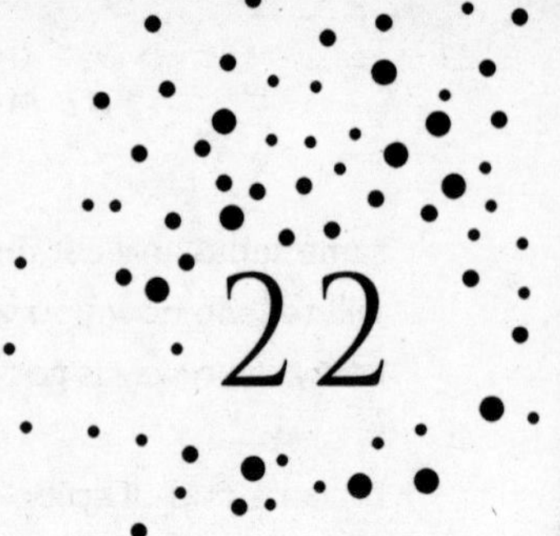

22

Undated letter on paper

Lumi,

In case we do not meet again, I will tell you things I want you to know. Not in order to buy your forgiveness. I simply want to give you an opportunity to draw your own conclusions based on the facts.

I must begin with the frost lichen.

You told me about it years ago. Do you remember?

We lay side by side in my old room in Harmonia. The bedsheets smelled of us. My skin smelled of you. I had returned from a work trip only a few hours prior. I was tired, but not so tired I did not want to touch you.

We talked about the Moonday House. We had only just begun to build it. You said frost lichen grew on its walls. I had never heard of it. You told me about the medicinal plant that healers used. As I listened, my mind was already making deductions about its attributes. Apparently the lichen purified air and water by binding carbon dioxide. Additionally, it seemed to have antiseptic, antibacterial and hallucinogenic properties.

I remember your fingers that moved on my skin. I remember how my breathing flowed faster. I remember how I asked if you had any frost lichen with you.

Your reply was a disappointment, because I would have liked to start studying it immediately. The quarantine rules forbade bringing *Physconia glacialis* to Mars.

Lumi, I did not tell you then, but I acquired some frost lichen in the first instance through my own channels.

Now I must go further back in time: to the Stoneturners and Project Earth.

You may already know I joined the Stoneturners as a student. Earth had always interested me, and I couldn't stand the arrogant way Mars treated the first home of humanity. I wanted to do something. I wanted to change something. The Stoneturners offered somewhere to belong. It was all rather harmless at the time. In hindsight, it was also endearingly naïve. We thought we were engaging in intellectual discourse about power relations. In reality we were simply polishing our own pompous egos and did not even understand it. During my last university year three people joined the Stoneturners whose ideas were more radical and motives more ambitious: Min-soo, Andy and Ariel. I was drawn to them.

After one long evening we were sitting at Min-soo's place having an afterparty, when Andy said: "Have you ever wondered what will come after the Anthropocene?"

I had not. Not even at the level of a thought experiment. I said so. "Why not?" he asked. I asked: "Why would I have?"

Andy began to talk about how humans launched the first nuclear explosives into the world a couple of hundred years ago. They left a mark on the planet for millions of years. Humans started a new geological epoch. Why couldn't they also finish it and replace it with something new? What if human traces could be erased in some manner? Make another world, where nature dictates the direction? Create a new epoch, the Biocene?

I remember asking Andy how something like that could ever be possible. Yet the idea had already begun to take root in me. Some biological element that could be implanted in the seas and soil. That would purify what humans had polluted. Liberate what they – we – had oppressed. "Exactly!" Andy said, eyes glinting with excitement. "Liberate."

Bioliberator.

The idea blew my mind. It changed my reality into another in an instant. It gave me the direction I had been lacking.

Only much later did I understand that for Andy, bioliberator was simply a prettier word for something else.

• • ● • •

Project Earth did not begin as a cover operation for the Stoneturners. It became one little by little.

I wish I could claim that my upward career as a researcher was purely my own doing, a sum of my ambitions and interests. But I am aware I would have met many more obstacles without the networks of my parents. They opened doors for me that would otherwise have remained closed. In order to relieve my discomfort, I told myself a story about how the goal of my work justified benefiting from this privilege. It would benefit so many others too. The entire humankind.

The idea of a bioliberator restoring Earth to nature would not leave me alone. I began to dedicate an ever-larger part of my work to it. Project Earth, when my research group got funding for it, offered a sanctioned, officially approved framework for my goal. The project was dedicated to restoring the ecosystems of Earth's oceans in the long run. Its challenges were enormous, but the reward was even greater: a politically, economically and ecologically free planet, purified of its past.

I decided early on to focus on the potential of algae and fungi. A still largely unknown universe opened in them that could hold anything within. When I was a child, my father told me cleansing the oceans of Earth would require a miracle. After his disappearance this thought took root in me. I had decided to perform a miracle. Within my field of research I considered it possible. I merely had to find the exact right algae or fungus, harness its relevant properties to utilitarian use.

For years I experimented. You must remember the cultures I grew on the balcony and in my office. Sometimes I – to your great annoyance – kept them in the kitchen, or under our bed. I swear I never brought anything outside the isolated laboratory conditions that could have caused real harm! My home experiments were entirely without danger, but necessary. They speeded up my work at the laboratory.

For years I came up against a wall. Sometimes it would meet me at the first bend in the road. At other times, the experiments went smoothly for months. Yet every time there was eventually an obstacle that confirmed the algae or fungal growth I was studying was unable to accomplish what I wished it would. All conditions were never met. Either it did not survive in Earth-like conditions long enough, or it caused too much damage to some organisms while feeding others. One experiment emitted toxic gas as a side product. Another culture modified through biotechnology was otherwise perfect, but impossible to transport to Earth or manufacture there.

Then you told me about the frost lichen.

The very first experiments seemed promising. My hypotheses about the biochemical attributes of *Physconia glacialis* were confirmed. Additionally, I noticed that it accelerated the regrowth of some organisms. The real breakthrough happened when I thought to separate the symbiotic components of the lichen, the algae and the fungus of which the growth consisted. I did not expect them to survive without each other. I thought each would wither and die. Yet this did not happen.

The fungal symbiont of the frost lichen had all the properties I had been searching for. It was the missing component that completed the bioliberator and made it functional.

At the time, I had yet to understand – or find the will to understand – that a radical group had formed inside the Stoneturners. Their goals were far more extreme than the ones I had imagined I had chosen to strive for. Without my knowledge, they stole the prototype of the biolliberator from the laboratory in order to try to do an experiment I could not have accepted under any circumstances.

They chose Fuxi. It was an enclosed small colony that could be evacuated and isolated, if the consequences of the experiment were disastrous.

They also chose it for another reason.

Because they wanted to. Because they could.

Lumi, the unknown fungal disease that destroyed the farming areas and signified the death of Fuxi originated in my laboratory.

I didn't know it then. I should have known to suspect it. But I was blinded by my own ambition. I only saw the beauty I had made. Dividing cells, water molecules around them. The new life of the seagrass meadows and the growing carbon sink of the oceans were in my eyes the miracle Earth had been waiting for, over more than a century.

After Fuxi was evacuated, Project Earth lost its research funding. I was furious. I was depressed. Lumi, when I disappeared after Fuxi, I went to talk with the Stoneturners. I learned then that they were behind the fungal disease. I was ready to turn my back to them. I was scared of what else they might do. But my frustration was endless. I was ready to seize anything that meant more than a decade of work had not been lost.

They offered me a chance to continue the project under a covert operation on Nüwa. I should have refused.

I said yes.

The new project was named Inanna.

Eventually last year I was certain I had achieved what I had been aiming for in my research.

Only the last phase remained unrealized: testing the bioliberator in Earth conditions. In the laboratory experiments we had attempted to take all possible scenarios into account. Nevertheless, Earth conditions could not be replicated perfectly on Mars. I spoke with the core group of the Stoneturners about how we could conduct the experiment I considered necessary to using the bioliberator. During those conversations I began to understand they were guided by a different philosophy. They were willing to implant the bioliberator in the oceans of Earth without testing it first, regardless of the risks.

I once asked you how far you would be ready to go, if the end result would also achieve good things. What would weigh the most on the scale?

If you had posed the same question to me, at the time I would have had no answer for you. Now I have.

For over ten years, I managed to convince myself that I had considered the ethics of the bioliberator from all sides. Every time I had concluded that using it was justified.

When the moment of action was at hand, I realized I was no longer certain about my choices.

The risks were enormous. If the spores of the bioliberator spread outside Earth, to Mars and other colonies, their food economy might collapse altogether. The attack would almost certainly mean that Earth would be isolated from the colonies for the foreseeable future. Yet there were risks on Earth too. If the bioliberator did not work as planned, if there was any factor we had failed to take into account – the end result might be catastrophic. Instead of triggering a carbon sink renewal process in the oceans that would lead to recovery of ecosystems, Inanna might make them even sicker. We would be endangering what life the planet could still support.

When I shared this worry with the core group of the Stoneturners, I understood they did not care.

It was all the same to them how many casualties the bioattack would claim on Earth or in the colonies. They said the only thing that mattered was liberating nature from the power of humans. But I heard another message behind those words. First and foremost, they wished to manifest their own power.

Cutting Earth's ties to the colonies: their argument was freedom, liberation. But we are all humans. We share our original home. We share the space we have claimed since. All we have built, we have built together, and all we have destroyed, we have destroyed together. Together we have made grief and sorrow, and together we have made happiness where it exists.

What will be left of us, if we separate humanity into camps rejecting each other?

I could no longer take the bioliberator away from the Stoneturners. I had helped develop and build it. I had placed it in their hands. I stole the research materials from Elysium with them. I escaped to a secret base in the desert of Mars with them. I traveled to Earth with them.

Yet on each step I asked myself: can I prevent this from within the organization, without their knowledge? Should I prevent this? If I did not succeed, at least I would have tried. If I did succeed, I would most probably get caught. I could guess how the others would take my betrayal.

Do you understand now why I could not tell you, Lumi?

Would it make a difference if I said I tried to change direction at the last moment?

As I write this, you will already see the end result. A failure, or a success: it depends on whence the light falls. The dark side of the Moon only looks dark from Earth. I know that because of what I have done, you will never be able to return home, not to the one Earth was for you. Is. But as I look at the life growing along seabeds and giving new lungs to the entire planet, I am unable to feel only grief over how things are.

I saw you at the club in Londons. Yes, it was me. I could not help but come. But I could not speak to you. I was afraid someone from the Stoneturners would see us together. I was afraid of putting you in danger. I hid among the trees in the dark park, silent and still. I watched you. You looked weary and beautiful, and I wanted to touch you.

I sent you the ticket to the Moon. I froze our shared account so you would leave Earth before the travel ban would inevitably become effective. I could not think of another way to make you depart. I myself will attempt to board one of the last Moon vessels. I obtained several false identities on Mars last year for a situation like this. They were saved on a memory chip. I kept the chip in the wooden box I asked you to bring to Datong. I meant to wait for you in the hotel room, but the Stoneturners made a surprise departure to Elysium. I had to take the box (you should use safe codes that are harder to guess!) and go with them so as not to raise suspicion. None of this matters now. I have destroyed the chip. I just thought you might want to know what I needed the wooden box for.

I know where to find you on the Moon, if I make it. Wait for me there, Lumi. Wait a week, wait a month. Wait as long as you can. I may have to take a detour.

Wait, if you still want to.

In the Moonday House I see you in the garden, under the quince. The red flowers rise around you like a halo. When I reach my hand out to you, you do the same. You are always where I wish to be: in the shared space of our thoughts.

Sol

Biocene; Anthrobiocene
***Encyclopedia of Geology*. Harmonia:**
Harmonia University Press, 125 MC.

> The *Biocene* refers to the geological epoch that follows and partially overlaps with the *Anthropocene*. The term was first proposed by geologist Karina Kiselyova in 91 MC. The term has not been officially approved, and is under review in the scientific community. According to

the general definition, the Biocene refers to an epoch that is characterized by a significant shift in human activity toward building infrastructures on the terms of nature and ecosystems.

Those opposing the concept regard discussion of a new epoch as misleading, as these changes were created by human activity and therefore belong under the umbrella of the Anthropocene. Those in favor of the concept of the Biocene argue that the vast scale of the shift and its long-term consequences justify the use of the new term. Nobel Prize winning biologist Áirá Guttorm has proposed the term *Anthrobiocene* to describe the passage of time, a sub-epoch or transition period of the Anthropocene that can be considered to be a part of the Biocene. According to Guttorm, the Anthrobiocene is characterized first and foremost by three traits: (1) the complete disruption of physical connections between Earth and space colonies for several decades, and the developments following from this on different celestial bodies; (2) the fundamental shift on Earth in relating to natural resources and their exploitation; and (3) the slow recovery of Earth ecosystems as a direct consequence of the aforementioned.

The Anthrobiocene is generally considered to have begun with the bioattack the organization the Stoneturners committed on Earth in the year 68 MC. The traces from the attack are still visible in the layers of the soil.

Some have suggested that the date of the attack should be remembered as Inanna Day, but to date only two city states have approved the proposal. In some regions Inanna Day is celebrated as an Earth liberation festival. Yet others treat it as a day of mourning.

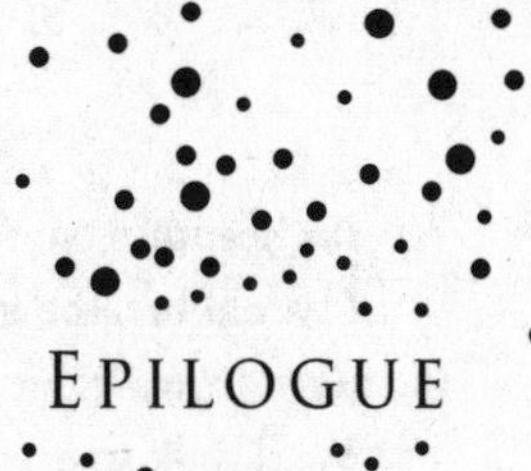

Epilogue

Undated

Sol,

I have sat by this window, by this table and this notebook and this steaming cup of tea time and again, watching the blue circle of Earth rise on the bare horizon.

I have time to think, to remember.

There is a place on Earth where light grows slanted between the pines in early autumn, and the trees reach out their thin fingers against the sky. Among the rowans that are turning yellow and the maples that carry dark speckles on their leaves rises a tall boulder, its green cover of moss oozing water after rain. Early in the morning, when frost rests on the ground and the traffic is still quiet, it is possible to imagine that the wide, gray-surfaced roads framing the woods are not there at all.

I always thought I'd take you there one day, Sol.

It would be September, a cold but sunny day. We'd rise before dawn, sleep still in our eyes. With hot tea warming our insides we'd cross the highway in the hazy chill and bare brightness of the first morning light. We'd take to the narrow path among the brown tree trunks, and our hands would reach out to each other across the path running along the forest floor. Dry pine needles would crunch under our boots.

This is a path I still see in my dreams, I'd say to you. I walked it so many times as a child. I remember that tree stump on your right, and this ant hill. Under that rowan I once found a bird's egg, tiny and light blue, but I left it there.

It's beautiful, you'd say. Why didn't you bring me here sooner?

I would breathe in the air and smell the decomposing leaves and the fungi growing out of sight, and last night's rain.

We'd walk an even narrower path into the thicket, and in its heart we'd stop at the foot of the tall boulder.

It looks like a stairway, you'd say, and point at a few notches formed by nature on the side of the boulder.

I know. I used to imagine I could climb all the way to the sky along it. Once I reached the top, it would grow a new step before me, and yet another, until I was on the Moon or Mars, or even wherever the Voynich Lights come from.

Can we climb on top of it? you'd ask.

I'd climb to the lowest step. I'd turn around to look at you. I'd extend my hand to you, and you'd take it.

We'd sit on top of the boulder, watching the trees bend in wind, and shadows would change our faces, and light. A bird would take wing from the branches. We'd be silent and together, and the day would pass by. We'd watch the sun go down and the sky glow orange and pink, and slowly ever-deeper blue stripes would paint it dark.

When small bright speckles would surface in the blackness, I'd think, *Each door is open to us, and all boundaries are as imaginary as the paths we draw between stars.*

I'd say this to you. We'd both believe it.

• • ● • •

The chair is hard under me; the side of the teacup has grown lukewarm. Earth shines on the horizon, and it has never looked this beautiful and remote before.

Against the space I see a reflection in the window glass, a distant and translucent figure that walks across the floor, stops and seeks something. Looks the other way.

I push my chair back and get up.

The figure stands on the opposite side of the room. A void spreads between us. Before they turn their face toward me there is a moment, as long as the universe, when I don't know if it is you, Sol, or someone else, unknown to me.

Acknowledgements

I would like to thank everyone who helped this novel see the light of day and encouraged me along the way, especially the following people and organizations:

Arts Promotion Centre Finland, Otavan Kirjasäätiö Foundation, WSOY:n Kirjallisuussäätiö Foundation, the Union of Finnish Writers and the Finnish Cultural Foundation for supporting the writing of this book through grants. These enabled me to focus on writing full time, a professional dream come true. Also the Väinö Tanner Foundation and Ventspils International Writers' & Translators' House, Latvia, for granting me residencies.

The Common Room Writers – Howard Bowman, Patricia Debney, Nancy Wilson Fulton, Nancy Gaffield, Janet Montefiore, Jeremy Scott. I miss our meetings, conversations and crazy Winnebago plans, and am grateful for the friendship and peer support during my years in the UK.

My Finnish writing group – Päivi Haanpää and Marika Riikonen, who are the best book godmothers any novel might wish to have.

My sharp-sighted editors who understood what this book was about and helped me make it so much better – Jussi Tiihonen at Teos Publishing in Finland and Cat Camacho at Titan Books. Also everyone else at Teos and Titan Books: *The Moonday Letters* could not have found a better home.

My agent Elina Ahlbäck, her entire team, and Rhea Lyons at HG Literary. I'm so grateful for your tireless work and faith in this book.

My Finnish family, who have always nourished my love of books, reading and writing.

My sensitivity reader Cornelia Prior for their insightful comments.

I would also like to thank Janet Montefiore for providing a wonderful English translation of the excerpt from Eino Leino's poem "The Sun's Farewell" (*Auringon hyvästijättö*) and giving me permission to use it here. The Kalevala meter, in which the Finnish original is written, is notoriously ill-suited to English, and Jan's expert skill rescued me from having to share my own rather clunky attempt.

Many thanks to Alan Watson for the concept of the Biocene, which he first proposed and we discussed at the Seeds of a Good Anthropocene workshop in Stockholm in June 2017. I am grateful to Alan for allowing me to borrow the concept, which I have here slightly adapted to fit the purposes of this novel.

More thanks than I can ever put in words are also due to Mari Paavola. Among all the things I am grateful for, I would like to specifically mention my gratitude for permission to take a look at the archives of the fictional songwriter Damien Black of the equally fictional band The Workshop Sound, and allowing me to quote one of their songs as part of my (likewise fictional) future.

Finally, all my gratitude to José Casal Gimenez for enduring love and support, regardless of what surprises life might throw at us. There have been many, yet here we still are.

About the Author

Emmi Itäranta's writing has been compared to that of Ursula K. Le Guin, and her first novel, *Memory of Water*, has been translated into 21 languages and was also nominated for the Philip K. Dick Award, the Arthur C. Clarke Award recognizing the best science fiction novel published in the UK in 2014, and the Golden Tentacle award. In addition, Itäranta has been included on the Honor List of the James Tiptree, Jr. Award. She tweets @emmi_elina